BSIDIAN

OBSIDIAN

Book II of the Book of Bera Trilogy

SUZIE WILDE

unbound

First published in 2019

Unbound
6th Floor Mutual House, 70 Conduit Street, London W1S 2GF
www.unbound.com
All rights reserved

Text design by PDQ

A CIP record for this book is available from the British Library

ISBN 978-1-78352-641-3 (paperback)
ISBN 978-1-78352-643-7 (ebook)

Printed in Great Britain by Clays Ltd, Elcograf S.p.A.

To my life support team:
Richard, Maud, Teddy and Raine

'I have no doubt that Providence guided us, not only across those snow fields, but across the storm-white sea… I know that during that long and racking march of thirty-six hours over the unnamed mountains and glaciers of South Georgia it seemed to me often that we were four, not three…'

— Ernest Shackleton

PROLOGUE

Hands are close to her face; the rust of blood. There is no pain like this. The known world convulses and a dark tunnel presses her in an agony of spasms. She is suffocating. The earth tilts; shifts. There is only a woman's face preventing her passing through the gateway to Hel. She can already smell it, close. Brymstone and blood. The woman's hands. Not safe at all.

'Breathe,' says the woman.

'Can't...'

'Yes, you can. Come on. For me.'

That voice. That's something to hold on to. But who? No time to remember. There is something dark here, something wrong. Life blurs as the ground rocks. This new, bad pain makes her pant, turns her inside out. Lights flash; a sequence of sparks that mark the places where the earth's crust is tearing apart, that feel like the start of a megrim.

'I'm dying!'

Her death throes ripple out over the land, under the sea and sky, making ruin the—

A scream tears her head wide.

'Push!'

Bones crack. Her hips yawn wide as the Skraken's jaw. The echoes are making the mountains ring, quickening in her body that is the earth. Far beneath her, fire rages, cracking the ice cap on the tallest and blowing a cloud of ash up, up towards the pitiless stars. Now liquid fire swarms downwards, coiling like a serpent; white-hot metal. A terrible beauty...

'Push, Bera!'

1

'Like a blacksmith pouring…'

'Shush, sweetheart, here's the head! Gently now.'

Bera pushes out in a long, gaping wail. She is all mouth, like Hel herself. Lightning flickers, light, dark; death, life. Liquid fire, travelling fast. Past or future? Bad now but—

'Worse is to come.' Poison. Blackness. 'I must protect them.'

Gently does it. Her skern is swaddling her tight as a shroud. His lips are fire.

'I'm dying!'

The earth thrashes, whipping the floor like a serpent's tail. It sends the woman – is it Sigrid? – staggering, swearing. That's real enough. Then a flaming gush, a rush, and the world dissolves in a choking billow of ash, with flying sparks and blazing blocks of red-hot stone spewing up into the air before raining blackly down. The red sun is hidden and a curtain of fire spans the whole horizon and up beyond sight, making the dark weave of time crackle with terrible knowledge.

This is their future.

'We will all die.'

Her skern is cleaving to her, as they had been in the womb: twin souls floating in space and time before the agony of birthing. Ash is falling, swirling like squid ink in buttermilk, coating grass and leaves. Everything turning black and sticky, withering, and starving cattle will become dry bones for the wind to whistle into oblivion.

'Are we dead already?'

No, dear one. Look!

In the corner of her eye is a small skern.

Sleep now. Your baby girl is here, safe and sound.

1

Dusk is a strange time: a blankness when light is removed but nothing takes its place. It is an absence, a robbing of the senses of what they use to navigate through the world. Sight is dimmed and smell betrays. Bera planted her feet on the earth, trying to get a sense of it but it was like iron; she was welded to the soil by ice. Here she stood in an empty landscape, made untrustworthy by a vision. It had no history. No ancestors. No answers. And dusk came early here.

Bera forced herself to walk into the ruins of an earlier homestead, facing her fear. Perhaps they should have mended these huts and stayed here over winter but the stones held a creeping sadness, like the slow breath of the coned mountain that dominated the valley. She was changed – by the land and by the baby. Her thoughts were brittle, her skill at scrying gone. Her own body had betrayed her.

'Was I right to bring them to Ice Island?'

No answer from her skern. Bera longed for the reassurance of his voice, absent in this unreadable land. Was the baby inside her keeping him away? She dared not think he had gone for good.

Back home, their dreaming mountains, carved by the gods, were eternal. Here, the tallest peaks were tricksters, vanishing in a moment and seeming to be closer when they returned. Everything shifted: the very ground she stood on was trembling like an anxious deer and the fires in her vision were always before her eyes. The birthing, mixed with the land's terrible upheaval, were ahead. She feared she would not be strong enough when the time came.

There was a sharp pain and then dull aches rolled around her hips. Bera put her hands over the swell of the baby. The pains came and went as mysteriously as the earth's trembling. Perhaps the child wanted to be born in the next instant, although sometimes she was so quiet that Bera feared she was dead. She refused to ask Sigrid what the pains might be. She didn't need her skern to tell her she was afraid of the answer. She feared for her baby's life – but at the same time feared the birth of another Valla, perhaps with greater powers than her mother. Was this why the vision frightened her so much?

Time to get home, if that was what the makeshift buildings could be called, as patched and ragged as a pedlar's clothes. Was that one, now?

A figure stood on a rise above the ruins, a darker greyness in the gloom. Watching her.

She was a Valla, like her mother and grandmother and all the long line of Vallas through the ages, like beads on the necklace that was their emblem and gift. But the next, about to be born, was already stealing Bera's courage.

She ran for home.

Dellingr had started to roof the new covered way, so she slipped round the other way to avoid him, running past the back of the new byre and latrine. When she came round the corner, puffing, he was there, sorting stones.

'You should be resting,' he said, without looking up.

'When did you last work like a smith?'

'When I last had iron.'

'You have tools to sharpen.'

She was goading him into – what? Once she would have liked watching his tidy strength and respected a smith's old magic. Together they were strong. But that was before. Without iron, he was less the man.

As she was less the Valla. She thought about the lone figure watching her.

'Have you seen anyone?' she asked.

'Other settlers? Up past the forge there's only the big farmstead. I've only seen the smoke, mind. Other smoke trails sometimes.'

'There are too many hollows,' Bera said. 'Places are hidden. I like knowing what's around us. How do we know who might be watching us?'

'We don't, not being in the open, down here.' He spat on his hands and rubbed them to get the dust off.

'Someone was up there today, above the ruins.'

'Pedlar, maybe? They'll come with the melt. I said we should have built a longhouse in the ruins. Better protection.'

Bera started to talk about marshland but he held up a hand.

'You said all that to the others, with winter coming too fast to waste time arguing. Now it's just you and me and we understand the old ways. Folk have lost faith in you, Bera, but I'm listening. Tell me what you really think.'

He meant feel, not think, and her body felt the sadness of the ruins.

'Wasn't it your grandfather who said that stones can soak up things?'

He nodded. 'Smiths' lore: "Stone soaks up Happening to warn the Future." He always said that and I believe him.'

'That's it – and that is what is there. Something bad happened – and I was warned. I didn't want to put our folk in danger.'

Dellingr touched a stone with his foot. 'Trouble is, these are the same stones. Have you brought the danger here with them?'

Her visit to the ruins had not provided an answer.

Pains woke her. They echoed deep in her hips, like waves rolling round a sea cave. She pulled up her shift and watched the waves rolling over her belly as the baby moved. Sigrid came into the billet to sweep, so Bera stayed hunched over to collect her outer clothes and managed to escape without showing she was hurting.

'I need clean air,' she called out.

Sigrid gave her loud, put-upon sniff that declared Bera was avoiding chores.

Every day when she first went outside on Ice Island its energy came as a shock. There was something in the air here that made the tiny hairs on her neck thrill, especially in the early morning.

Beyond the yard, two lads were passing with nets.

'Going fishing?' she asked.

'You coming?'

She shook her head. Too much pain to go fishing. 'Heggi might, if you wait.'

They didn't stop. Bera wondered why her son found it hard to make friends with other boys. A small bundle of blond fur came rampaging into the yard, tumbled over, saw Bera and scampered across to seize the laces of her boot and tug. She laughed and swept the puppy up for a kiss. They studied each other. The pup's bright blue eyes were full of mischief and filled her own head with its carefree joy. The pains were gone.

'You're like thistledown.' Bera pushed her nose into the fluff of fur. 'Who's a sweet baby poppet?'

The pup seized her plait in needle-sharp teeth, not like thistledown at all, and pulled it across Bera's eyes.

'You've got your hands full there,' said a woman unhelpfully.

She freed herself in time to see the woman's flickering sneer. It was the farmer's wife, Drifa, with her two cronies.

'You'll be due any day now, the size of you,' one of the women said.

Drifa nodded. 'You know what they say, "One out, one in." I wonder which of us will die when the bairn's born?'

Bera was angry. 'The fishwives never took pleasure in it, Drifa!'

They jabbed the midden pigs with sticks to make them squeal, and went off laughing. Their pleasure in cruelty sickened Bera.

Heggi strolled out of the byre. 'She's teething.'

'I feel that. Ouch! She's your pup, Heggi, do something.'

He scuffed at the straw. 'Sigrid says it's too much work, what with all the building.'

'I didn't mean fetch Sigrid.'

The small creature clasped her face with tiny claws and licked her.

Heggi took her. 'Sigrid told me not to let her near my face.'

'The pup's hardly weaned. She smells like… warm hay and honey.'

'Toasted flatbread and milk.'

6

'Skyr and biscuit.'

He gently put the puppy down and she tucked her bottom in and hurled herself round the yard, leaping up to bite anything that dangled. One piece of tarred rope was a prize and she made off with it, then flumped down to triumphantly chew it. One ear always stood up, while the other, with darker fur, stayed flopped over one eye.

'Her ears are too big for her,' Heggi said, smiling fondly.

'She'll grow into them,' Bera said. 'I think she's the spit of her father. Where is Rakki?'

He waved vaguely towards the forge huts. 'Farmer's wife is cross.'

'Drifa?' Perhaps that was why she made the pigs suffer.

'She says it's given her too much work when we're all trying to settle and too much to be done and most of it by her and if there were thralls it would all be better.' He mocked Drifa's sneering voice, making Bera laugh.

Sigrid thought Drifa had bedded a farmer to make sure she could get a passage on Hefnir's boat. Farmer had blood-lines all over his cheeks and nose and deserved her. Bera winced with a sudden pain.

'Is that the baby?' Heggi whispered.

He was frightened Bera would die, like her mother. Like his mother, too. They both had reason to be afraid, and she kissed away his frown.

'Does Drifa know…'

'It was Rakki? She ought to. The other pups all look like the farm bitch. I told her it was most probably a dog from the big farmstead.'

'Drifa won't like being reminded there's a farm bigger than theirs.'

'That's why I said it.'

'Drifa could count their toes and come after us for the brood debt.'

'Paws don't prove they're Rakki's pups. The farmer might have a puffin hound too.'

'They might not have puffin hounds on Ice Island.'

He shrugged. 'They soon will, if Rakki keeps this up. He's gone off again.'

7

They laughed and went back inside, with the pup chasing them.

Bera poured some skyr. 'Have you been up there then? The big farm?' She tried to sound breezy.

The pup lunged for the drink and Heggi pushed his beaker away.

'Too much snow up there. There's a frozen lake near it and I was skating once and met a man on a horse.'

'Had you seen him before?' Bera was careful not to let her dart of fear make the man sound exciting.

Heggi waved his hand. 'He most probably lives up there. I've seen him in the distance. He waves and smiles and he's got a lovely horse and wears a funny big hat. I fell over laughing.'

It would be good to have a friendly neighbour, with spring coming. Perhaps one who could help if the Serpent King's vow to hunt them down became real.

'Was the horse in the hat?' she teased.

Heggi grinned. Bera loved him so much that her jaw ached from wanting to bite him.

He stroked his pup's ears. 'I'm going to call her Tikki.'

'That's a good name.'

'I'm good at naming. I chose Rakki.'

'Some of the boys have gone fishing. Are you going?'

He studied his skyr. 'I told them where to go. They'll have to crack the ice. It's where we go skating, up past the forge.' He blushed.

'With Ginna?' Dellingr's daughter.

He blanked the question somehow, like his father always used to.

'This man in the funny hat... You don't go on other people's land?'

'Water belongs to no one, you always say.'

Her father was the one for sayings. She hoped Heggi would pay more attention to them than she ever did.

There were none of Hefnir's ancestors to pour venom into her ears as she passed the threshold but Sigrid made up for it. She turned her back on Bera and clanked pails and rattled spoons, smarting about something, that was clear. Bera followed her into the pantry, rootled about in one of the barrels and came up with two wizened apples.

'Want one?'

When Sigrid made no move she cut the black bits from the less wrinkled of the two and ate the pulp, meady with age, and threw the core outside for the midden pigs.

'Is it the pup?' she asked. 'Heggi says you don't like her.'

Sigrid gave her a look and then got back to work, brewing the complaint. Bera sat on the long worktop, swung her legs and waited to hear what she had done wrong. A few folk passed through, everyone busy. A woman put down her toddler with his toy and went over to the rough loom they had made of scavenged wood and stones from the beach. She was one of Sigrid's small band who had boarded the *Raven* to get stores ashore. They would have starved without quick, brave Sigrid and these women. Her dear friend. She was in her usual layers of wool and fur, as small and round as a felt ball.

Bera went over to hug her but a rancid smell made her gag.

'What have you got under there, Sigrid? A dead fox?'

'It's winter, isn't it?'

'I smelled spring coming, before your stink.' Bera pinched her nostrils.

'There's draughts all over. I've had a cough, or didn't you notice that either?'

'And I have no plants to help – as you well know. I put a medicine stick in your bed roll. So what's the smell?'

'Grease.'

'Where?'

'All over my chest. Asa says her mother swore by it.'

'It's a wonder her mother managed to get herself with Asa if she smelled like you.'

'Well.'

There was a silence. Bera pulled the last shrivelled apple from her apron pocket and held it out to Sigrid, who made a face.

'Come on, Sigrid, why are you in a huff?' she coaxed.

Sigrid bristled. 'I'm not to be told anything anymore, am I? Wait till you're at death's door and then come running!'

'If you were ever here and not up with Asa!' Bera took some deep breaths. 'Sorry.'

Sigrid screwed up her eyes. 'Is that you pretending to be kind?'

'It's me trying to find out what you're blaming me for. Though, of course, I forgot; I'm to blame for everything!'

'Off you go gallivanting as always and then work yourself up the minute you get back from those ruins. I won't go near them. Don't think I didn't hear you tossing and turning all night. You should be resting.'

'If one more person tells me to rest I shall hit them! You are as bad as Dellingr.'

'It was him that said.'

'What?' Bera shouted.

'Heggi told Ginna and she told her father. These pains of yours. Why didn't you tell me?'

Bera was trying to ignore them. 'They come and go.'

'Why worry poor Heggi with them?'

'I didn't tell him. He noticed a few times, that's all.'

'How long have you been having them then?'

'Hel's teeth, Sigrid! I get a tummy ache and you all panic. Look at me. I'm perfectly well now I can get outside and breathe some fresh air instead of the stink in here. Women have had babies time out of mind.'

'No one knows more about babies than me.'

'You only ever had one!' Bera stopped.

It was as though the dead Bjorn stood in the room between them.

Sigrid's lips were white. She threw her cloth onto the bench and made for the door. A toddler rolled away and she kicked his toy after him, then slammed the door behind her. He started an ear-piercing wail, which brought his mother, who clicked her tongue at Bera. She wanted to hide but in a way it was her fault, so Bera apologised to the woman, then went to find Sigrid.

She was sitting with her apron over her face on one of the large stones. Bera sat beside her.

'I'm sorry, Sigrid.'

The apron stayed up.

'It's just that no one makes me as cross as you.'

Sigrid snorted. 'That's your idea of an apology, is it?'

'I shouldn't have said any of that.'

Sigrid uncovered her face. 'We've both lost what we loved the best. We have to get on with it now.'

'I'm trying to! And I try to stay calm for the sake of the baby when all I see is my father standing there and the foul Serpent King swinging his axe and—'

'Don't say it!'

Bera did not want to see it, either. 'All of us must work together to make a success of this.'

'We each have our own skills, Bera. You're our leader, no doubt about it, whatever folk might say. More than that, you've learned your mother's knack of scrying and suchlike to tell what's in store for us.'

Sigrid did not know that the knack had gone and Bera would not tell her, or frighten her about what she had seen in the vision.

'Vallas keep Drorghers away, so you rule over death. But I'm good with life.' Sigrid crossed her arms over her bundled chest. 'Once there were a fair number of women of childbearing age, back home. I was at all the birthings. Folk trusted me.'

'Well, the baby will be coming soon.' She hated the fear in her voice.

Sigrid's face softened. She took Bera's hand and peace was restored.

Later, Bera swept out the stalls and took the foul straw outside to the bonfire. The driftwood was nearly ash and she was glad that no Drorghers had been seen. Back home, folk stayed in the hall through winternights to keep warm and ration food. But above all, it was to be safe from the band of Drorghers, come to take their living kin and steal their skerns. A Valla had to keep the fires that held them at bay alight, or face them if they went out. Burning corpses stopped them becoming Drorghers. With only driftwood, a pyre was beyond hope – so how did Ice Islanders keep the dead from walking?

The sweepings caught light at once, their crackle loud in the still air, and smoke rose straight up like a beacon. Bera felt again that everyone in these parts knew they were here but she had no sense of where they fitted into the landscape, or if they were welcome. Were there others, apart from the sad few they sometimes saw scavenging on the beach?

She hurried back and found Dellingr in the doorway. Bera squeezed past him into the byre, so that he could stand straighter. Further away.

'Is there a problem?' she asked.

'No more than usual.' He rubbed his hands together to shake off the grey dust of stonework, studying them as he spoke. 'I need metal, Bera. Iron. It's what I know. You can trust to the honesty of it. This work with stone… it's unyielding. It stays itself, no matter how sharp I hone the chisel. You can heat metal into a river of light and bend it to your will.'

Bera understood. 'You've forgotten who you are.'

'So have you.' He met her eye. 'I've forgotten hope. The loss of our boy… I'm not blaming you, Bera, but Asa… she can't get over it. She says no one could have stopped the bairn going overboard but I know in her heart she blames both of us.'

Bera pictured Asa turning, her face, the empty shawl… She put a hand on her stomach, then quickly let it drop.

'She hates me having a baby.'

'Thing is, it's getting worse.'

A boy came into the byre, picked up an axe and went out again. Dellingr went on. 'Now she's started on Heggi.'

'He should stay away. What's she saying?'

'Telling him he hobbled me. That he was old enough to look after himself.'

'Any one of us could have gone overboard.'

'We all know that, but still…'

'So what else?'

'Well, she's told Ginna the boy's unlucky, that—' He tightened the leather belt of his apron. 'Anyway, best get on.'

'What were you going to say? That she mustn't make a bond with Heggi? Is that it?'

He nodded. 'Because of his bad blood.'

'I feel the same about Ginna,' she said, to hurt.

He stooped and stepped out into the yard. She followed and spoke to his back.

'I didn't mean you.'

Too late.

2

A few days later, the first soft breeze of spring came at last. They were able to get out further and forage. The women kicked their boots off so that they could feel the earth coming alive. A low humming began in the soles of Bera's feet that spread up her calves, thighs, stomach and chest; caressing the baby so that she felt at peace with the new life inside her. Her scalp tingled with the sense of belonging; a feeling she could see on the faces of the other women as they looked up at the mountains. If only Asa and Drifa had been there to complete the circle. There was no place for outsiders, with so few of them. They quickly pulled on their boots before their feet froze.

Sigrid placed a hand carefully on the swell of the baby.

'He's kicking hard,' she announced. 'He'll be a strong, fine lad!'

Bera wished her baby was a boy. 'I'm going fishing.'

'Not out at sea?'

The pain of boat-loss hit, as it always did when she wasn't braced.

Sigrid quickly took her hand. 'Sorry. I'll come too. I have to keep an eye on you.'

Bera went to the byre to collect their tackle and found Rakki, tied to a rail.

'Come on, lad. Let's get some fish.'

The tussock grass was bleached and flattened by the snow that now only remained in ditches and hollows. Rakki bounded on, out of sight. The women climbed the gentle slope slowly. They heard the rush of meltwater long before they reached the river, broken by the shrill, lonely call of an oystercatcher. The chill air made Bera's fingertips white, so she put on her mittens. They would get cold enough later.

They turned onto a narrow path and the noise grew louder. Ahead was a white tumble of water, cascading over rocks and boulders. Some gnarled and stunted birch trees clung to the mossy sides, with rainbow webs in their hair. It was as if the land was opening its tight fist to reveal treasures in its palm.

Bera found hope in this and in spring awakening as it always had at home. Perhaps her vision was of a past event; one that had caused the ruins?

Sigrid stopped. 'What?'

Bera pointed at the snow. There was a line of footprints in it. 'Someone's ahead of us.'

'Heggi or Ginna, most likely.' Sigrid pulled another shawl over her head. 'Come on, I'm shrammed standing here.'

Bera whistled but Rakki did not appear.

'Perhaps he's found Heggi.'

There was a strange scratching inside her head, like thoughts trying to form, or a snatch of memory... They walked on. The footprints were a trail to be trusted, not feared. Then a memory came.

'Those prints remind me of my mother.'

'Alfdis trod in enough snow.'

'Once, when I was really small, one spring, we were out feeding the animals and there was a snowstorm, those swan-feather flakes, big and choking.'

'They lay quick, all right.'

'And deep. Home was a long way back.'

'When was this? Alfdis would never have taken you out like that, not when you were small, she'd have known—'

'I couldn't keep up and fell over, crying. Mama came back and told me to put my feet into the snow she had trodden down. She took small steps so that I could reach the next one. I've only realised that now, seeing those prints.'

'Well, that's what we all do if a child's got too big to carry.'

Bera felt a flicker of anger. 'Mama led me the whole way home. I felt safe. I knew where I was going.'

Sigrid scrubbed at her forehead. 'Jump down my throat all you like but what's your point?'

'Can't you see? That's what I need, Sigrid. I need my mother to walk in front of me and show me where to put my feet.'

Sigrid walked on. 'You do get some daft ideas. But if it's about babies, you can ask me anything.'

'That's not what I meant.'

It was wrong of her to blame Sigrid for not understanding the loneliness of being a Valla. Blame, again. Perhaps they all needed something to blame when things were hard. Harder still for her, with no skern to talk to.

They got down to the serious business of baiting hooks and choosing the right place to throw the lines. Bera cast her line into a dark pool. She listened to the trickle of small streams that could be heard above the deep, distant torrent of the falls. She saw a flash of silver and the line twitched. She played the fish, liking the dart and chase; the lure and catch. Then the skill of landing the fish, which gasped and threshed. It was nearly as good as sea fishing, but without a boat. Soon her basket was full of char, trout and a couple of good-sized salmon.

'I wish I had your knack,' said Sigrid.

Bera looked in her friend's basket. 'This river's teeming with fish and you've only got two.'

'I was thinking.'

'Thinking about stealing some of mine, I expect,' said Bera.

Sigrid cuffed her, laughing.

The scratching in her head began again; not a memory, more like a creature coming to life. Something to do with Rakki...

'I'm going to find that wretched dog.'

'The wretched dog you'd give your life for,' Sigrid said.

Bera lost the long, slow sound of the river in the chill air. She made her breath coil in different shapes and studied the criss-cross of animal tracks in the frost-pocket snow. Wide, puffin-hunter paws. He was close. She carried on, ignoring a grumbling pain, like a bad stitch. Then Rakki charged at her, pink tongue steaming. The dog's mind was jumbled with excitement. Hunting. Bera felt it too, like scrying within an animal's mind. The scratching was a connection starting to be made. It was a new skill. Was it because she wasn't listening to boat-song now? Whatever it was, she knew Rakki wanted her to follow him.

'What have you found, boy?'

He led her to a burrow. Small trails of ice-smoke whispered into the air from the sleeping creatures beneath. Rakki stood with one paw raised, savouring the scents. Then Bera thought about the time she had gathered poison plants near a river in a still twilight: plants that were supposed to kill her enemy, and how close they had come to killing Heggi instead.

Rakki looked at her, then back at the burrow. He was full of bloodlust.

Bera closed her mind to it. The sensation was troubling – and she refused to kill anything sleeping. She had tried that too, once, knowing it was wrong.

'No, Rakki. Come, let's find Sigrid.'

When they got back, she was packing up their tackle.

'All right, don't say it. I've only caught one since you left.'

Sigrid rubbed her hands on her coarse apron and put her mittens on. One of the trout flipped out of the basket and Bera threw it back in before Rakki pounced. She picked up the heavy basket.

'Well, there's all the summer ahead,' said Sigrid. 'Come on, that's too much for you. We'll take a handle each.'

They set off. The basket was lurching as Sigrid trudged along on her short, sturdy legs. She was getting slow, older than Alfdis would have been, but never complained, even though all the ones she loved best were dead.

'We're all half-starved, that's the trouble,' Bera said.

'Things will get better when we can get some crops planted.'

The trouble was, they both knew it would be worse. This was the dangerous time, when all their stores were gone and there was a long wait for crops to grow. That was if the weather stayed fair – and who knew if it would here? Or if there was worse than weather to worry about.

After a while, they stopped to change hands. Bera looked inland, at the tallest mountain, and the flames of her vision turned her sight red. They would be lucky if they had the chance to live long enough to worry about Drorghers. The trickle of smoke coming from its peak was a warning of danger coming, not past.

The season of driftwood was upon them, so the settlers went down to the shore to see what the winter storms had brought. The sky was further away here on Ice Island, and blueness so remote was harder to predict. At home, Bera could test the weather as a slice between sea and mountain, to see the clouds squeezed and the sun closer. She did not look at the closest mountain and its white smoke, which the others thought was a cloud, that lazed its way upwards into the blue air. She had no boat to take advantage of the seething life out on the whale roads. The deep loss was like their song: low, lamenting and long.

Bera had to cheer her folk, for she had brought them to this. She worked alongside Sigrid and they sang, urging the sea beasts to spit useful trappings ashore. When they cleared the largest mats of weed and began sifting, they found bones, flagons and even some strange empty barrels, useful for pickling. They were building their future together, like the old days. How her father would have enjoyed seeing it. Ottar would have been at the heart of it and she kept the thought each time it came, and it came often, because it was his due that she should hurt so much; it was part of love.

After a while, the weight of her baby was too much and Bera sank down onto a stone.

'I reckon any day now,' said Sigrid.

'There's weeks to go yet.'

Bera watched some other folk along the shore. They were busy, with better pickings from the look of it but she was glad it kept them apart. Seen closer now, they were small and dark-haired, not as thin as her folk.

'I think they settled here long before us,' she said.

'They're from the huts, them with that smoke we've seen.' Sigrid threw a bundle of driftwood into the cart. 'Wonder if they mind us being here?'

'They would have chased us off the beach.'

'I meant, settling here at all.' Sigrid's voice was tight. 'That Drifa reckons there are secret watchers.'

Bera thought about the slight figure near the ruins. Did they have different kinds of Drorgher here? She wished her scalp would prickle in warning, like it used to. Perhaps this was something else the baby had taken for herself.

'Don't let Drifa scare you, Sigrid. She enjoys it too much.'

Bera started sifting. She must stop letting her child frighten her, like Drifa. She took some deeper breaths and heard, distinctly, a summons. Not words, but a warbling whistle.

'Did you hear that?'

'What?' Sigrid carried on working.

'You know those footprints? I think they were a sign, and this is another.' It was calling from the steep slope beside their bay. Something waiting. 'I'm going up there.'

'Oh, you and your signs.' Sigrid wagged a shark tooth at her. 'It's awful high. You mind the pains don't start again.'

As soon as Bera began climbing she realised Sigrid was right. It was slow going and the dragging pains began. She could have walked into Hel's trap and her vision of land and body cleaving apart felt very close. But then her heart skipped. Her skern was lounging against a rock.

He wagged a long finger at her. *You shouldn't risk it, just to see me.*

'Nothing of the kind. You came to see me.'

He tried to hide a smirk behind a thin shoulder but they were both brimful with the joy of his return. They clasped and were whole, their breaths joined. It was a comfort to simply be with her skern and she knew he had not been far.

'Was I deaf to you all this time?'

Probably. I'm hoarse with shouting.

A ewe gave her a yellow, incurious look then lowered her head to forage for grass. Perhaps she was carrying babies too. Twins, bringing luck.

Bera began scrambling to the top. The cliffs were dotted with crevices and a puffin stood guard in each one, their bills bright orange to attract a mate. The Ice-Rimmed Sea pulsed greyly far beneath and Bera scanned the skyline where home might be. It was impossible even to see where sky met water; a colourless murk of low cloud smudged both. There was no going back in any case: home and Seabost felt like failures and would be the haunt of Drorghers.

Why come right up here? You can't see any better.

'I can turn my face towards home and smell it.'

He drew a circle with a glum foot. *Home?*

She wished there was a rune stone on the clifftop that would restore her. Bera shut her eyes and pictured tracing her fingers over the carved runes, as she once had in Seabost. ALU, words of power written by her Valla ancestors, to make everything... more. One day she would raise a stone here and show her daughter. Seeing her skern meant her powers were restored. Perhaps he also had answers.

'There's something not right about that place.' She nodded at the ruins below them. 'You told me nothing about it when we landed here. No warning.'

That's all in the past, ducky, can't help. But there's something you could try...

'I'll try anything. Folk are muttering.'

Make a bond with the land, like when you and I clench. Let the stones speak.

'I'm afraid of what they might say.'

You've lost courage because of... that. He squeamishly gestured at her belly.

A sharp gripe.

Ow, I felt that.

Bera held her stomach. 'Sigrid is cross that I didn't tell her about these pains.'

Sigrid can't see what's under her own nose. He tapped his own to look mysterious.

She would not satisfy him by asking what his riddle meant when there were real worries.

Far beyond the headland, a thrusting spike of granite pointed skywards. The settlers named it the Stoat, because it looked like one in its winter coat, made up of thousands of white seabirds and their waste. The water churned around its base as they dived, feeding in the fury of breeding. The sky swayed with billows of birds, shadows against the grey clouds. Beneath them, puffs of smoke from breaching whales and rhythmic black arcs of hunting dolphins striped the silver with sudden speed. The sea sang. Bera banged her forehead with her fist, then felt ridiculous. As if that could beat away the loss.

It's the sort of thing your friend Egill would do.

'She stole my boat.'

Your husband's boat. Strictly speaking.

Bera closed her eyes. Trails of spume and surf blazed through her eyelids; sea paths she would never travel again.

Why hurt yourself?

She turned her back on him and set off down the slope. Sheep were grazing on another long incline that projected up into the sky, where the low sun met its upper slope like an immense orange yolk. Bera remembered their arrival, when a strange funnelling cloud had bewitched her and golden runes lit the sky with promise. She tried to hold on to the strength it had given her then but all she could feel was the ache of loss.

A cold nose pushed into her hand. The simple power of a dog to give comfort. Bera smiled and bent down to ruffle the fur on Rakki's neck. He was a happy dog.

'You leave those puffins alone till they've bred.'

Rakki's grin told Bera she was too late.

'Where's Heggi? Did you run off again, bad dog?'

Her boy was up in the top meadow with their farmer. Sunlight was a ring of gold around his head. Bera smiled. He would be checking the animals. Like she would, herself. And then a bad memory came to life. A black horse and rider were approaching them. She screwed up her eyes to try to see if the man was tattooed. Surely her instinct for danger would warn her if it was someone as evil as the Serpent King. Had he found them at last? What would he do to get revenge? With no clear warning, Bera suddenly feared everything.

She shouted to Heggi but the wind whipped his name out to sea and she was too big to run.

Unknown.

Her skern was right. The rider was a slight figure in a strange, wide-brimmed hat. Was it the rider in the funny hat Heggi had told her about? What was his business? Bera set off in their direction, rubbing the stitch in her side. The dog stayed close, his mind a wrinkle of worry about her.

'I'm all right, Rakki. It's this trole of a baby.' She touched her beads.

Harsh.

'She stopped me hearing you.'

By the time she reached Heggi the farmer and rider were long gone.

Heggi's lips were blue. 'My f-f-fingers are going to s-s-s-snap like icicles.'

Bera took his hands and blew on the fingertips.

'You've been at the smoked cheese,' she said. 'Who was that rider?'

'I've given Ginna a gift.'

Heggi's face, so unlike his father's, was so generous and open that she allowed him to evade the question, as he so often did. He clearly had no fear of the pedlar and she would find out more eventually. She was more troubled that he was growing close to Asa's daughter.

'There's little enough food left—'

'I gave her Tikki.'

Bera was shocked. 'You love that puppy!'

He looked puzzled. 'Course. But Ginna wants a dog like Rakki. I won't give him away, ever, but she can have his puppy.'

Her scalp tingled.

The ground tilted and shuddered and Heggi bobbed about in front of her like a puppet. She was over-bending her knees to keep upright, as though she were on a boat, but the baby put her off balance. She staggered and fell against Heggi and then heavily onto her knees, then hands, so that she did not fall onto her stomach. The pains griped until the earth became still. One of her knees was cut and blood smudged her leggings.

Heggi was laughing wildly and stumbling around her, pretending to be drunk.

'Look, Bera. I'm being like Ottar and Egill.'

'Stop that and help me up.'

'The farmer's going to show me something special later.' Heggi took her arm. 'To cheer me up about Tikki. It's to do with the season and I'm to help. Will you come and see?'

'That's not like Farmer. Anyway, I've seen what his ram is doing.'

Heggi's cheeks flushed. 'It's not about tupping!' He kicked a stone.

The cramps returned. She worried that the fishwives were right: one out, one in. Her mother died straight after having her brother and Bera had worried since she was six that she would too.

'It's not exactly Farmer who's going to do it. Come with me and you'll find out.'

Bera let the ache roll round her hip bones. 'I'll be going nowhere like this.'

'Ginna says it's dangerous if the pains make the baby come early.'

'What does she—' Bera stopped. 'I will not die,' she promised and walked off as straight as she could.

3

Heggi told her to meet him later in a bay near the landfall beach, then refused to tell her anything else about the surprise. There was no sight of the sea from the longhouse but Bera always knew the sea state, and the tide would be full mid-afternoon.

She saw him head in the direction of the forge and hoped Asa would not see him with Ginna.

On her way back to the homestead some needles of ice rain fell. Folk scattered as hailstones swept down the valley and Bera managed to get indoors before they hit. The rattle on stone was harder than on wood, like an attack. The weather came in sudden onslaughts here, so when the sun came out it fooled no one. Sure enough, after one squall came another.

Bera declared they should eat. Afterwards, women stayed in the hall mending and altering clothes and the men began making hurdles out of the wood-finds. All of them making do to survive. Bera wished she still had thralls to do the unpleasant chores but then felt ashamed. Being in charge of Hefnir's household in Seabost had made her soft.

She went up to one of the men. 'Are you only making hurdles?'

'Aye. This driftwood is too hard to work or too soft to last, so hurdles it is.'

Bera checked the wood heap but none of the spars were big enough to make proper drying racks. Not like the huge racks at home. The memory snatched her breath away. She was there, surrounded by the shrunken corpses of stockfish at sunset, when the dead are remembered, trying to tell Sigrid her son had died – and failing.

Stop looking back. These spars should be a warning.

'Of loss? I know all about loss.'

She went into the byre. The other animals were outside all day now but Bera kept Dotta inside for safety. The calf looked up as soon as she ducked under the low sill of her stall and came to greet her. Bera wrapped her arms round the creature's neck, letting the familiar smell take her back to childhood, when she would find comfort in the warmth of a kindly beast after her mother died.

'You lost your mama too,' she muttered.

She has forgotten her mother.

'Cows can grieve, like us. My new skill is knowing what animals think. I can feel their minds, like the difference between wool and linen. Or clearer with Rakki.'

But she can't remember grief, as you can.

Dotta gave a low moan and shifted over to her hay. Bera scried the small calf's mind, like running her fingers over runes, but met only smoothness. Her skern was right. Bera envied her silken calm, unwrinkled by grief. The calf listlessly tugged at the food, then let it fall. That was odd. Her mind was numb, not smooth. There were some bright green, fleshy plants in the bale. Bera pulled them out in case they were upsetting her stomach. This was her fault for being overprotective.

'You can go out and graze, sweet one,' Bera said.

She put a halter on Dotta and led her outside. The calf blinked at the bright sun and was promptly sick. It seemed to help; she frisked on her spindly legs and slipped on the stones. Bera calmed her, picked up some buckets and they set off towards the pasture. Dotta pulled to greet the others and Bera let her go.

The day was clear and sharp now, with a brisk wind. Perfect for going sea fishing. To escape, if there was any boat.

You keep looking back.

'No. I keep missing what should have been my future.'

Make the most of what you have now.

'What if I don't like it?'

Then no one else will. You must regain your fight. Lead them.

'Dellingr says folk have lost faith in me.'

Make them trust you again.

The smell of salt air was stronger. Time to go to the bay. On the way, Bera said some words that should have brought a boat safely home. That would seal her leadership. But she stood on a bluff looking down on empty black sand. A shore without a boat was like a body without a leg. It looked wrong – and threw her balance.

Heggi came out from behind a line of rocks. He was slowly walking along the shallows instead of splashing with Rakki. Occasionally he would look behind him, or stand gazing at the sun's path across the wrinkled sea. Grief had struck him, she was sure, and Bera's heart ached for him. He bent to choose some pebbles. Skimming stones was what she had taught him, the day they stopped fighting each other. He threw one, making it skip over the water, but let the others fall from his hand and walked on. Would any of them recover from their losses?

She lost sight of him behind another ridge of black rocks, so she went down, wanting to comfort him, and found a place where it was low enough for a childing woman to scramble over.

Heggi was talking to the man in the wide-brimmed hat; it was the rider from earlier. They were both looking out to sea while a horse was grazing at some seaweed. Off its back, the man looked smaller. What did he want with her boy?

'This is my land, as far as those rocks.' The man pointed at the Stoat.

Bera went on the attack. 'Your land? Yet I don't know who you are.'

The man turned. His wide hat had bits sticking out all round the brim, as if goats had been eating it.

'Keeps flies and dust off my face,' he explained.

Her face always gave her away.

He took it off and the wind whipped a black wing of hair into his mouth.

'Come here, Heggi, and help me look for driftwood,' Bera said.

'I did yesterday.'

Heggi must have seen the flash of her eyes and mumbled something.

The man held his long hair off his face. 'My name is Faelan. I own the big farm, the waterfall, lake and ruins.'

'Can anyone own ruins?'

'It might be said that you do, now you have taken some of the stones.'

'We used them to make a homestead.'

'That's what I mean.' He waved a leather mitten. 'I watched you trying to build a longhouse before winter struck.'

'Why not come and help then, as is the custom!'

'I wouldn't use those stones. I thought you would most likely die.'

'Like the first folk? Or did you kill them?'

The man nodded at Heggi. 'Ask him.'

Heggi's cheeks were red. 'You spoil everything, Bera!'

'What are you talking about?' Bera asked. 'Spoil what?'

Rakki came flying across the sand. He flung himself at her face as she sidestepped. He was very wet and sandy and when he shook himself she was drenched.

'Take him away, Heggi. Why is he most loving when he's soaked?'

Heggi looked hurt on his dog's behalf. 'He wants to share his happiness. It's what dogs do.'

'Dogs can't help but share their joy, you're right,' said Faelan. 'Whilst men hug happiness to themselves.'

Bera said, 'If men notice happiness at all, it's only afterwards.' And then worried she might be exactly the same.

Rakki went over to share some more happiness with Faelan. Bera knew Heggi would approve of his easy way with the dog. The pleasure this gave puzzled her.

'He's a tough-looking dog,' said Faelan. 'I liked him the moment I set eyes on him.'

'I know,' said Heggi. 'He's the best puffin hunter too. Once he—'

'—caught thirty-three puffins in a single night,' said Bera.

'Forty-six,' Faelan said, smiling.

How many times had the two met? Was he the reason Heggi told her to meet here?

Heggi said, 'Folk back home treat dogs like they're just a field

27

tool or worse. They kill them if they can't work. Me and Bera aren't like that, we – oh, I can't explain.'

Faelan said, 'When you lie down in the snow, exhausted, your dog will lie beside you.'

'And you won't die.'

'Or if you die, you go together,' said Bera.

Faelan's smile reached his eyes.

'Have you been caught in a blizzard?' Heggi asked him.

'Once.' Faelan put his hat on Heggi's head. 'He's set on you watching this surprise,' he said to Bera.

'I'm not much of a watcher,' she said. 'I'm too busy doing.'

'I'd ask you to join us but it's no place for a woman so big with child.'

How dare he!

'Please, Bera!' Heggi's voice was high again; a child. She pictured his loneliness on the shore.

'The days are short. Will there be time?'

Heggi laughed and threw Faelan's hat in the air. 'She's coming! Wait till you see, Bera!'

'I haven't said I'm coming.'

Rakki seized the hat and capered round them, wanting to be chased. Bera couldn't help laughing and Heggi and the man Faelan joined in. He must laugh a lot because his face crinkled into laughter lines that were there already. Then he stopped and looked at her properly, and his eyes were the violet-blue of speedwell.

Heggi tugged her hand. 'You will watch, won't you, Mama?'

'Always Mama when you want something.'

'His name means Wolf. Faelan. I'd like a name like Wolf.'

Bera said, 'Bjorn and I liked being called Bear. All right, I'll watch this surprise of yours.'

'Do you promise?'

'Have I ever broken a promise?'

'Good. Because Rakki can't come and you'll need to make sure he doesn't.' He told Rakki to stay, then marched off, with the same set of his shoulders as his father going hunting. 'Show her where to watch, Faelan,' he called back.

Bera slipped a cord round the dog's neck while Faelan retrieved his hat, brushed off the sand and placed it carefully on his head. She began to walk towards his horse and he fell into step with her.

'I thought you'd be in a hurry to go,' she said.

'It's a chance to speak to you at last.'

'So speak.' Her heart was thumping in her chest.

'I want to offer work. Whatever you need.'

Bera stopped. 'Why would you do that all of a sudden?'

His eyes told her it was because of her. Or perhaps that was what she wanted.

'You bring new life to Ice Island,' he said without looking down. 'I'm sorry I spoke out of turn by referring to it. And you also reminded me of the old customs.'

'Not old to us.' She walked on.

'Fallen out of use, then, here. Customs of hospitality and so forth towards new settlers. Folk did used to help out but then things got so bad – that is, too many came and cut down trees – and there was the big eruption. Then we had pedlars and others looking to steal and move on. I think that's when the custom stopped here. I couldn't speak for the whole of the island.'

'Is it so big, then?'

'A man might walk it in a lifetime if he lived long enough. It's vast – and dangerous. There are eruptions and tremors.' He glanced up at the mountain.

Her vision. Yet Faelan had made her feel that she had brought something to Ice Island when she felt stripped of Valla powers by this inscrutable place. Perhaps that was what old customs were: a bedrock of safety in a mutable world. She suddenly understood Dellingr's reliance on iron. On what he knew: iron and fire.

'Have I worried you?' he asked.

Rakki tugged her forward. 'Stop it, dog. I don't like everyone knowing where our homestead is and how we live. I can't get a fix on what you folk do, how you all live, or where.'

'I'll show you a map one day.'

'Like a sea chart?'

'Yes, with mountains instead of islands.'

Bera liked the way they kept in step. Men usually went their separate ways and she was shorter than most, making it hard to keep up. This felt right, like having a twin.

'What does that mean, eruption?' she asked.

'See your high mountain there, smoking like a chimney? And that cloud behind? That's hiding a bigger one that went up in flames and then a river—'

'Of quicksilver poured down, burning stone and flesh and metal as it came, flowing out to the frozen sea, which hissed and steamed.'

He gave his wide blue stare. 'I was told you have the sight. The mountain is called the Gateway to Hel. There was a monstrous din, but almost no one was alive to hear it.'

She thought then of Egill's father.

'Now there's talk of settlers trying to come back and for sure that means you can't be helping everyone.'

Bera was used to men who could blank questions or give single-word replies. One in particular.

'You talk a lot.'

'You should hear my mother. In fact, you really should. It was her that said you have the sight. My mother says she needs you. I will help you, so will you help me?'

'I don't know how to get to your farm.'

Faelan took a stone and drew on the black sand. First, he made three long lines.

'That's the three parcels of land that are my farmstead. Where they meet, here, is the forge.'

'Old magic.'

'That's right. That piece is an old settler's. He died a while back, leaving it to me and my mother.'

Bera looked at his face, thinking his mother was probably beautiful.

'So this is our coast, here. You'll know there's no wide river to bring a boat in, so all these' – he drew short lines like tiny fjords – 'are what's around us, apart from the beaches where you go to scavenge and another that's too far to walk, over here.'

'Beyond the ruins?'

'That's it. There's a stream that comes out of the lake by my farmstead.'

'Where Heggi went to skate.'

'That's the one.' He drew a wiggly line going to a circle, past the ruins and out to sea. 'Then there's this.' He scribbled above the longhouse.

'What's that?'

'The waterfall above us.'

Bera had seen the distant whiteness.

'So now you know.'

Faelan looked at her as if he saw the person she wanted to be. She wanted to hold his gaze but that was dangerous with no husband or father to protect her, so she studied the drawing.

'Is that where Heggi's surprise is?' Bera asked.

'Where you're to watch. I'd better get going.'

'You've forgotten the Stoat!' Bera pointed out to sea.

He laughed. 'Two stoats, in fact.' But instead of drawing them in, he scuffed the map out with his foot. 'Tide doesn't come this high.'

They started up the bluff. Bera's knee was hurting and she let Faelan help her over some rocks. His hand was hot and leathery, like a dog's paw, and fitted her own.

Faelan whistled and called, 'Miska!'

His small horse looked up and trotted across the sand.

'She's so pretty,' Bera said. 'Hello, Miska.'

'I bred her.'

'He's all talk.' Dellingr stepped out from behind a rock. His expression was more guarded than his words.

'You should be at the forge, not watching me.'

'I can't work at my ancient craft because I'm having to build like a ruffian. We've no food left, and if we get some, you don't know how to keep it safe. We're starving, Bera.'

'I sent some grain over earlier,' Faelan said. 'And there's swan and goose and all the river fish coming. Then harvest, and at Blood Month I will give you meat, to save your breeding sow and the weaners.'

Dellingr stared at him. 'And why would you be so generous?'

Faelan was nowhere near the smith's height but he stood his ground. 'Settlers must pull together if any are to survive.'

'You're no settler,' growled Dellingr. 'More of a runtish thrall.'

Faelan spread his weight evenly over his feet, ready to fight.

Bera stood between them. 'Thank you, Faelan. I shall tell Sigrid to bake some new bread. We need it.'

'Then she'll have to use goose grease and spit,' Dellingr said. 'He's lying. Soon there'll only be cow shit and frog spawn.'

'Next winter, you might be glad to eat it,' said Faelan. He swung up onto Miska's back. 'Come and visit, Bera. Any time you like.'

As she watched him go, Bera wondered how his mother knew that a woman she had never met had the Sight. What had she agreed to help him with? She needed to be careful; get herself back in control.

Away on Heggi's steep cliff stood the lone figure she had seen before, as grey and still as a rune stone. Both of them, the figure and Bera, looking at Faelan. Then the Watcher was gone.

Dellingr spat. 'I doubt he even has a mother.' He must not have seen it.

'What are you doing here?' she asked.

'They hadn't the sense to look at smashed wood. Might be boat wreckage. Might be a few nails in there.' His fists were clenched.

Bera wanted to respect him but his pride was in tatters. He was spoiling for a fight but it was driven by fear. Was he right to be suspicious of Faelan? She could judge that better once she had met his mother.

Dellingr was looking east, towards Seabost. His home.

'I'm sorry we quarrel.'

She took his hand. 'So am I, Dellingr. We're both so tired; all of us are tired.'

He was waiting for something, but what? He let her hand go and set off for the beach.

It was easy to see the tallest cliff, but quite a way beyond the homestead to reach it. The sun was beginning to set. Bera was longing to rest but a promise was not to be broken, so she kept on.

Rakki stayed close. His mind prickled with possible dangers, just like a Valla's would, and Bera felt he was guarding her. She was part of his pack and she was glad, not minding being the weak one for now because there was no rivalry with her dear dog. When she started up the grassy slope her bruised knee grumbled and the new grass was so slippery that she began to think it held some grudge against her. She stopped to catch her breath long before she reached the top and was grateful for her skern's warmth.

There was a shout. Heggi was waving from a clifftop, opposite where she stood. He pointed downwards and then disappeared. Was this the surprise? Rakki forgot himself and charged to the edge. Bera scrambled after him, then held the scruff of his neck to keep him safe.

The cliffs here were the colour of a petrel's wing. On the other side of the inlet, Heggi was slithering down steep, rough steps and onto a sort of quay, covered in eelgrass. He slipped, legs and arms flailing, then slid to an undignified stop. Bera was worried at first but then laughed and waved. He did not look up.

She had not managed to explore this far but they had missed nothing useful: the narrow cleft between high cliffs might capture sea-ridden timber but it would be impossible to gather it without a boat. Now she could see the second black pillar that Faelan had drawn, standing guard over the approach to the harbour. The Stoat looked more like a humpback trole from here. Round the headland came a small boat, bravely bobbing in the short chop.

A good surprise!

Dearest Heggi. It filled her with joy and hope – quickly followed by pain.

'Is he feeling the same? Remembering?'

The *Raven* and her father, who built it, linked forever in grief. So many memories: the first small boat he made her, the work boat... Bjorn.

Face your fear.

'I always do.'

The small craft was carrying several bundles as well as Faelan and a slim youth who reminded Bera of Egill. Bera had sailed bigger boats single-handed, so this one would be easy, once the baby was born. She could go fishing! It would return her to herself again and then everything else would follow. Others would see her restored. With her skill, she would give Faelan fish the size of his horse and then she would owe him nothing.

Boats don't solve every problem.

'They do for me.'

Faelan's black hair looked even more like a raven's wing in the breeze but as soon as the boat entered the channel everything calmed. He steered right up to the ledge for Heggi to leap aboard. Her boy had not lost his boat sense and he jumped into the middle and quickly sat down to keep the small craft from pitching. Faelan let the boat drift back, then turned for the open sea and they were lost from view. Envy burned the back of her throat. They were out there on the water while here she was, fat and useless with the baby inside her, like a beached whale.

Stop that.

Bera was afraid to stand at such a height, so she got on all fours and crawled to the edge the other side. The drop was even greater. The soil trembled and a clump of earth fell over the cliff, which was so sheer that the grass looked as if it had been chopped away with an axe. Below her, drifts of birds lazily circled. Far beneath the birds, waves wrinkled and whispered and Bera was lost in giddy emptiness. She saw herself falling, like a child's toy, smacking into rocks and against the metalled waves, smashed into gobbets of flesh that would be swarmed over by all the teeming life in sea and air. Terrible. But all the grief and worry would be gone in an instant, instead of waiting for the baby to kill her. Bera got to her feet, swaying, staring at the white smash of waves beneath her, coming closer, the hiss and suck of blood in her neck…

Rakki gave a small whimper as fear rumbled through his body.

Feel the rumble and the tumble

And the boat-song in your blood

Bera sank down onto her knees, weeping. Rakki nuzzled her hand and soothing him helped her too.

The small boat appeared, riding the swell, and when the tiny dot that was Heggi waved, she waved back. It was important that he knew she had kept her word. Faelan steered to a place directly below her. She dared not stand up again, so she lay down on her side, shuffled forward with legs wide for anchorage and then carefully peered over the edge.

Heggi was holding them off the cliff while the youth took the helm. Faelan gathered a bunch of lines, which he passed to the boys, then picked up one of the bundles, slung it around his neck and quickly tied it on. He sprang ashore and the youth let the boat stand off the cliff. Bera craned further out. Faelan had started up one of the ropes and was climbing a stack, legs splayed. How could he keep his balance with the bundle round his neck? Were his legs strong enough to keep climbing? The bundle shifted sideways and Bera felt sick. He managed to get it back and carried on. There was something odd about it, as if wool stuffing was coming out of a hood. What was he was doing?

When Faelan eventually got near a ledge he swung for a while in the gusty breeze. A gull gave a small mew. Then another, and it was not the cry of a gull. Bera screwed up her eyes to see better. Faelan took one hand off the rope, swung the bundle over his head and onto a patch of grass. It was a tiny lamb! The small creature staggered and fell. Bera cried out. Surely it would slither straight off the sloped ledge; a man would certainly have fallen to his death.

She crawled back from the edge, shuddering.

It's what they do here, with the lambs. To keep them safe.

'Safe? On a ledge?'

Her skern shuddered. *Imagine what must be out there if they think a ledge is safer.*

A sharp pain stabbed deep inside, liquid fire swarming downwards, coiling like a serpent; white-hot metal. She had known it was wrong to do so much, Sigrid would be angry, but her promise… Rakki lay as if a trole's hand had flattened him and the earth growled.

It's an earth tremor. Her skern held her tight. *The boat will be safe.*

'Faelan will fall!'

The juddering land made Bera tumble.

Wait for it to pass.

Her scalp prickled with fire. Poor Rakki was whimpering but she could not reach him. They had to endure. She pictured Faelan, swinging into that terrible space and crashing down onto the boat! Heggi might drown, dashed against those rocks. On the high headland was the distant grey shape of the Watcher.

It's slowing.

Bera could hardly think straight. Was the figure linked to Faelan... or the earth trembles? There were some grunts and Faelan swung himself over the clifftop.

'That was a close one,' he said. 'Glad the boat stood off and I got the wee lamb in place. Are you all right?'

'Of course.' She was also relieved, but pain kept her on her knees.

He smiled. 'You soon learn how to stand sturdy here. Lambs keep to their ledge even in gales when the grass is as slippery as seaweed. They trust their legs.'

'Is that a lesson for me, Faelan?' She meant it to be breezy but it sounded surly. Or worse.

'I meant you should trust me.' His voice was soft. 'You can, always.'

Bera let him help her to her feet. Her skirts were clinging wet from the grass and she pulled them away from her legs, at a disadvantage.

'What about the boat?'

'I'll shimmy back down the rope.' He looked at his hand, which was red. 'Turn around. Let me look at your skirts.'

'No!' She suddenly knew the wetness was blood and was appalled that he should have it on his hands.

Rakki headed down the slope, tearing away homewards. Bera smelled it on the air this time.

'It's going to be worse this time!' she said. 'Look after Heggi.'

'I'm not leaving you.'

There was a sound like thunder – but from the ground, not the air. They both staggered. This was no ordinary tremor.

'It's what I saw, Faelan! Hel vomits fire and—'

An iron claw scored a red line of pain in her womb and she doubled over.

36

'What is it?' he asked.

'Bad… pain. Mixed up with what's happening to the earth.'

'Perhaps it's punishment.'

'What for?'

He looked at her, as if there had been something guilty in the short time they had met. Bera had no time to wonder. Scorching pain drove through her as the ground shook them off. She fell and ended up further down the slope.

'Bera!' Faelan staggered towards her, his voice ragged. 'Is it the baby?'

'Too soon.' Her sight was full of flame. 'Need… Sigrid.'

Gigantic waves rolled unhindered over the Ice-Rimmed Sea until they exploded against the land in a storm of spray. Bera stood at the bow of the *Raven* as it rose up onto the crest of a frothing breaker, surfing towards a black, black beach at furious speed. Joy and terror. Roaring, crashing, echoes, men's shouts and screeching birds.

Bera woke to the sharp rustiness of fresh blood. Alone, apart from her frightened skern, who cleaved to her until Sigrid arrived with a bucket.

4

Like the barnacled back of a humpback whale, the foothill reared out of a sea of grey ice. The glacier was unchanged. It drove its way, outside time, towards an ancient sea. The sooty ash that lined the folds and creases was from a much earlier eruption. Yet, for Bera, everything was changed. She was a mother and, like Valla, it was another loaded but empty name, with no one to show her what being one meant. That was inside. Outside, the world had shifted to reveal how precariously they lived on its thin crust. She recognised the smell of Hel's belch and in the distance, a thick plume of grey smoke gave a warning.

She was lucky to be alive after the past weeks.

She had woken to Sigrid worrying at her hands. She was brisk with Bera, with the roughness of true worry. She said Bera had lost a lot of blood; she was angry that Bera had not taken care of herself properly, that she had so nearly lost her life this time. It was not the only thing she had lost, but they didn't speak of it, not then.

During the birthing, Bera had seen the same vision – of what? The island's past? Future? The earth had split but was this good or bad? The deathly pain seemed to bring forth new life but that was confused with her own daughter's arrival. The baby did not bring the joy that Sigrid showed and everyone expected. Her only gifts to her mother were fear and death. Near-death. Bera remembered her sight growing dim until, at the sharp pinprick of life, she felt her ancestors pushing her back into the world.

It was a relief to be alive at first and she made a silent offering that she would never give in to wrong feelings for Faelan, as long as she could stop her vision of ruin coming true. Then wondered what had put such ideas into her head.

The trouble was, it was all tied to the baby. She made her weaker as a woman. The feeding and lack of sleep; the worry that something was constantly demanded of her but she had no idea what; the way her plans scattered like leaves on the wind. The tearing at the birth had left her sore, so she was waiting for her tender flesh to knit back together and only time and nature could achieve that. The bad birthing had skewed nature for good. The land was troubled. Waves of sickness ebbed and flowed with its swaying. The smell of brymstone. All linked: the baby and the earth's upheaval. Draining her Valla powers too. How could she not blame her daughter?

As the days grew longer Bera was strong enough to go outside on Sigrid's arm. The border of sky and earth was changed where the snow had shifted.

'Aye. We were lucky,' said Sigrid, nodding. 'The snow-drop went down the other side, towards the east, so Faelan said.'

She owed Faelan a huge debt and it troubled her.

'Did he visit?'

'Once. His mother's too poorly to leave for long, but she gave him some potion for you.' Sigrid sniffed. 'The thing I was using was doing the trick but Heggi and Ginna were crying, and Dellingr said to try it, he was that worried about you, and he hates Faelan, so I thought I ought to.'

Sigrid's chopped reasoning and the warmth of the sun on her back made Bera smile.

'Something worked anyway.'

Her strength was returning but she vowed to watch the signs more closely. Her body and the earth's crust were somehow linked and, although there was calm for the moment, her vision at the birth had not yet been fulfilled.

'I keep smelling brymstone.'

Sigrid nodded. 'I burned it at the birthing and afterwards, for blood-cleansing.'

'That's your old fishwives, is it?'

Sigrid was silent and Bera was ashamed of mocking her friend's care.

'If only I could sleep,' she said. 'The baby never stops crying.'

'You can, then. I have her in the day, so you can rest,' Sigrid said.

'It's you who looks ill, Sigrid. You have for days.'

'Don't start that. Babies go through stages and you need to be rested, so come back inside.'

Screams greeted them. Bera wanted to run away but went to the crib. The baby's face was puce with outrage. Her tiny fists and feet punched the air and her cries became even more ear-splitting until Bera picked her up and prepared to feed her again. She gave some token sobs then latched on, only pausing once or twice to hiccup. Her eyes, like tiny black stones, fixed on Bera's. Surely mothers felt some surge of love then? This child had the power to bend her to her will, like a thrall. She had sucked all the life from— Bera stopped herself. It was her own baby girl. Her eyes closed and the wonder of so quickly soothing her child struck like a miracle. It made her tearful.

'I do love you,' Bera whispered.

Perhaps Faelan's mother could be like a grandmother and make everything better. Bera decided to visit with the baby, as soon as she could get up there.

'Can you take her, Sigrid?' she asked. 'I want to check the animals.'

'You won't forge a bond,' Sigrid warned.

'Bonds can be broken.' That sounded like Ottar. 'I have a duty to provide for folk.'

'Your first duty is to provide for your baby.'

'Babies die. Ask Asa when you're next up there.'

Sigrid took in a sharp breath.

Bera touched her arm. 'I'm sorry. It sounded worse than I meant.'

'It always does with you. You blurt. I wish you and Asa were friends, like you were after Hefnir left.'

'We were never friends. And she's the one who's being hostile.'

'She's still grieving. It's not something any of us can shrug off but there's work to do and—'

'Oh, her and her grief! Do you think I feel nothing? You're always saying it's loss that makes you strong. We've all lost something we love, Sigrid, but she carries on as if it's only her! And the thing is, I don't know whose side you're on. How can I trust you when you go up there every whipstitch telling her who knows what? You never could keep a still tongue in your head.'

One side of Sigrid's face flushed red, as if Bera had actually slapped her. Full of shame, Bera wanted to be out of there; to run away from being this sort of person and not the gentle mother she had loved. Who Sigrid had loved too, before Alfdis betrayed her. That was the reverse side of being a Valla; with power came passion. There was a darkness in Bera that she vowed to fight.

'We need to talk about what happened,' she said. 'I need the whole truth, Sigrid, and then move on.'

Sigrid nodded and once the baby was settled again, they sat together on a bench.

'Was there a twin?' Bera asked.

The relief of her knowing poured out of Sigrid. 'Kind of a twin. It came away first, up on the slope. Not like your baby girl but a wizened, misshapen... You should never have gone up there. If Faelan hadn't acted fast, you could have... Anyway, folk are saying it's a bad omen, the dead twin being in the womb and the earth trembles and the like. Farmer's wife, that Drifa, started saying a lamb was born with two heads at the same time, but Heggi says she's lying.'

'They have a right to be afraid, though I think the twin is another sign, not a cause.'

'When did you know there was a twin?'

'I didn't, before. I had a glimpse of a skern and its child on the passage over. They must have hidden... the other.'

'It was a poor, shrivelled thing, all its life sucked out by—'

'Don't say it!' There was a limit to what Bera could bear to hear – and she needed no more reasons to blame her living child.

You fear her.

Sigrid patted her hand. 'Then count your blessings. She came early but you've a bonny daughter.'

'What did Faelan do?' Despite the shame, she had to know.

'He got his horse and rode like the wind to get me.'

'Dear Miska. What then?'

'He got you up on the mare's back while I dealt with the stillbirth and held you tight, then when I got home Dellingr was there, not Faelan, and he never left your side till the real birthing started.'

Bera thought there must have been anger between the two men.

'Then what, Sigrid? What were you using to heal me? Before Faelan's potion?'

'I never stopped.' Sigrid looked shifty. 'It was that old narwhale tusk that you used on Heggi.'

'Some good remains in it then, for all its bad start.'

'Except I've used it all now, on you.'

If the tusk was gone, what could she use to heal?

After a week of rest, when Sigrid took the baby out into the sun, Bera could count her blessings. She had a healthy daughter and Farmer said the soil was warm enough to plant seeds. Bera wanted to see how far she could walk, so she went out to the fields. Besides, it was nearly time to feed the baby. The tie that bound them was invisible but stronger than anything. She marvelled at it.

You also fear it.

There was no smoke coming from the mountain. Sigrid was tilling with the other fieldworkers, with the baby in a sling. Bera wished she was one of them, swapping tales, warm with honest work. Would they let her belong, even if she were strong enough? Drifa would give that odd smile and not let her join in. How much fatter than the others she was. She and Farmer must have been keeping food back for themselves. She would have to put a stop to it.

A horse came up out of a dip. Not Faelan's Miska. This horse rolled like a barrel, lumbering over the rocks and stones of the burns that striped the pasture. The lumpen man on its back had ropes and bags tied round him and bulging sacks tied to the saddle. A commonplace, fat pedlar, so Farmer could deal with him, or Sigrid.

Not everyone fat is commonplace. Ask Sigrid.

'Is this a riddle about Sigrid?'

Better out than in. He raised a playful eyebrow.

42

Bera gave him a look.

She picked a new blade of coarse grass, stretched it between her thumbs and blew. A couple of fieldwomen looked round. She blew again, louder, and the grass broke with a reedy squawk that made her laugh.

You're a baby yourself. Her skern stroked the nape of her neck. *It's good to see you smile again, sweetheart.*

A vivid memory of eruption mixed with the agony of birthing; violent and confused.

'I keep trying to work out what part of it was real.'

Real?

'Is it the start or the end? When I lost the twin the earth rumble got worse, and in the birthing there was a snow-drop but there's no smoke now and the air is changed.'

This is a strange land. Signs are muddled. That's why I stay close to you these days, just in case.

'I need to feel hopeful for the future.'

Why is Sigrid so plump these days?

'She has always been plump.'

Your baby needs you. He pointed to the front of her tunic.

'I hate all this! I'm like a cow!'

Bera stomped off towards Sigrid, pulling a shawl over the wet rings.

More like a bull on the rampage.

This was Hefnir's fault, all of it. It was mixed with the loss of her father's boat – *Raven* – that he had stolen from her, leaving her with a baby and a body that was sore and strange.

Faelan's mother knew Bera had the sight. Perhaps she had other answers too.

Bera pulled another fur over her shoulders, making sure she didn't smother her swaddled baby. As the ground rose, the mounds of snow grew denser, until by the time she reached thorn trees her feet had lost all feeling. Winter's grip was strong, up here. She stamped her feet and made smoke rings of icy breath in the air. The baby cooed at them and Bera snuggled into the fur to kiss her.

Trying to love her?

'You know nothing of a mother's love.'

You really think being a good mother will help?

Their distant homestead looked like flotsam on the beach. There was their sentinel, the Stoat, but from here the line of rocks that protected the beach from storm seas merged into the beginnings of the ruins.

Heggi had told her how to find the place where he skated by following a line of blackthorn trees. They were bending away from the wind like old crones with kindling on their backs. He had marked a path through them with the H rune. Bera found it and when she looked up Dellingr was coming through a clearing. His face was ruddy – either from the cold, or because he was as embarrassed as she was, thinking about what he must have seen. What only a husband should know.

He held up his bundle of thin branches. 'Kindling.'

'Not enough for a forge fire,' Bera said. He was so far out of touch with the old magic it made her tearful. 'I'm sorry if there was trouble with Asa, when... when I lost the twin.'

He turned away, then quickly back. 'How's the bairn faring? And you?'

'We are both well now.'

She pictured him carrying her into the billet, staying with her, unflinching, until he knew she was safe. A good man. He had defied his wife by staying near Bera but it was hard not to in their tight-knit community. Besides, embarrassed or not, there was nothing improper in her feelings for him.

Bera stamped her frozen feet. 'It's so cold up here.'

'This is no winter chill. I've been walking all about the edge of the three pieces of his land and there's something not right.'

Fear clutched her stomach. 'What have you seen? Not Drorghers?'

'There's a powerful sense of something, on the boundaries.'

Bera breathed deeply and let it trail thinly back through her nose a few times. 'There's no evil about here.'

'We're not at a field edge.' Dellingr came closer. 'Are your powers back, then? Like they were at home?' Full of hope.

'They never left me,' she lied.

He looked at her sadly for a moment, then walked away.

'Your kindling!' she called after him but he carried on.

Bera propped the thin bundle against a thorn tree, thinking she might take it to the forge on the way back as a peace offering. She kept feeling he disapproved of her; that she was letting him down; him, and all the other folk she had promised to lead. Could she face Faelan's mother now she had lost her Sight?

The baby began to cry. Bera set off again, to get her daughter to sleep, but kept losing her footing. Stubbornness made her carry on instead of going home, and at last she saw distant smoke. She felt excited at the prospect of being in a proper, warm homestead and perhaps Faelan would be there. She could at least be honest with herself about it. There was a new stirring inside her, perhaps as simple as wanting to make his blue eyes crinkle with laughter. Where was the harm in that?

Breaking your oath to Fate, for one thing.

'Did I make one?'

By being born.

Bera felt the weight of her baby, a Valla who was also now bound to Fate.

When she got close to the frozen lake, she could see she had come the wrong way to the farmstead, which was on the other side. There was marshland between her and strange, round huts that looked carved out of the soil. A few sheep grazed on the slopes that she realised after a while were roofs. Did they graze everywhere? Farmworkers must live up on this vast, high plain, with grazing as far as the waterfall. She began to edge round the marsh. Her hat was making her head hot and prickly, so she took it off, had a good scratch and hoped it was not lice. When had she last combed it? Too much time looking after the baby to look after herself properly.

Bera stepped to the left and dread stopped her. It was as solid as hitting a wall of stone, and terrifying. Her breath died in her throat. She had to get her baby away but could only move slowly on legs turned to stone. It did not feel like a Drorgher, except for the freezing terror.

When she finally saw Dellingr's kindling she knew she was free. Was this what he meant about a field edge? Did Faelan know about it? Then something was crashing through the scrub, but it was too late to hide. Rakki burst out and ran to her, followed by Heggi, red-faced and panting.

She let out a long breath. 'I am so glad it's you.'

'Asa told me to fetch you!'

'Must be important if Asa sent you.'

'It's Sigrid.'

'What's happened?'

'She's been stung by a spider.'

'Surely Asa can—'

'It was huge, she says. Come on, Bera!'

Heggi tugged at her and Rakki charged ahead. Bera was too out of breath to speak, until they stopped above the forge.

'Is Sigrid at the huts?'

'No, Asa came to the longhouse, soon as you left,' Heggi said.

'So they're at the longhouse?'

'Asa was scared of the spider, so she…'

'So she left Sigrid alone!' Bera was furious and went faster, hoping she would be in time.

Bera gave the baby to Heggi and told him to stay well clear. Groans were coming from the latrine, where she found Sigrid on all fours, with her clothes up round her neck.

Bera stayed in the doorway, in case the spider was inside.

'Sigrid! Does it hurt?' she called out. 'How many times did the spider bite you?'

Sigrid turned and sat, clutching her stomach. Sweat ran down her face and she began to pant.

'I'm coming back with a remedy.'

Bera rushed to the pantry and looked round, distraught. What remedy? There were no potions left and she had no idea what to use against spider-bite. No narwhale horn as a cure-all.

Her skern was resting his elbows on the table. *Told you.*

'Help me.'

Too late for a remedy, that's for sure.

A long scream made her run back to the latrine. Sigrid's clothes were rumpled, and she was rocking like a madwoman. Then she looked up and smiled. Not mad at all. Sigrid was rocking a purple, bloody baby. Suddenly it became all mouth and lungs. And was very clearly a boy.

'Get some hot water,' Sigrid said, triumphant.

Bera was hurt. 'Why didn't you tell me?'

'I didn't know!'

'What do you mean, you didn't know? You're always boasting you know everything about birthing!'

'I do. Like podding a pea, no thanks to you.'

She should have foreseen it. 'I would have helped if you'd told me.'

'My courses were all over the place with fret and I was that ill on the passage and half-starved here. Grief. This poor fatherless mite...' Sigrid, who had withstood every loss, started to sob.

'Come on, Sigrid. You're always so strong. Let's get you cleaned up.'

Bera understood the wild and mixed feelings. She helped Sigrid onto the bench and comforted her old friend, as a mother not a Valla. She wept with Sigrid in relief and love but also because she wanted to be young and free, riding the waves. Everything was making Bera feel old, as if life was rushing past her, all her choices gone.

5

Another birth, another celebration – there were songs – even with no mead or feast meats. Bera said they would have proper naming ceremonies when there was something to harvest. In fact, she was delaying because she had no idea what to call her child and was hoping the Vallas might give her some inspiration. Sigrid, on the other hand, wanted to pay tribute to her boy's father and had several possible names, which she hugged to herself.

Faelan gave them more seeds, saying they were from plants that were grown on the island, collected at the right time, so would fare better than the ones they had brought from Seabost. His kindness made her doubt that whatever evil bordered his land could be anything to do with him. And so work went on, in good heart as folk believed they could survive the next winter. Men drilled the soil, followed by women strewing the seeds. Afterwards, children kept birds away – when they remembered. It began to feel like home and Bera liked folk saying she had brought them to a good place. She hoped it was true. It was encouraging that no smoke had reappeared from the mountain, so perhaps the safe delivery of her child had stilled the land's unrest. She wanted to believe it – and when she heard the whispers about 'monster' she hoped the twin's death would seal it.

A few days later, they were in the home field and Bera was working alongside Sigrid, their babies swaddled in slings on their backs. The seed was in a deep pocket at the front of their aprons and they each took a handful to strew; left, then right.

'I think Dellingr is watching over me,' Bera said, 'since the baby. I hope Asa knows it's not my fault.'

Sigrid gave her a look. 'She knows what he's doing.'

Bera flushed. 'There has never been—'

'I don't mean that.' Sigrid sniffed. 'You always like to take comfort from him, Bera, the old magic and that. Have you thought that maybe that's what he's doing with you? He's precious little else left him. Asa knows he needs that.'

So you should be kind.

They worked on. Left, then right.

'I like everything being simple,' Bera said. 'Work, feed, sleep. No claims on me, no worries about the future because I can't see the future.'

'Well I can and it's coming fast, on a horse,' Sigrid said, and pointed.

It was Faelan. He circled them shouting, 'Stranding! Stranding! It's a big one!'

Bera raised her hands to get him to stop. 'What's happening?'

'Get all your folk to help, Bera! It's a right whale! On the strand, the beach. The days of hunger are over!'

'There's no whale down there.'

'Another place. I can take you and Heggi in the boat, if you like.'

Bera grinned. 'I'm coming.'

The settlers collected what tools they had and joined Faelan's folk, who had carts full of proper kit, to be shown the way. Sigrid said nothing would get her on a boat and was glad to be left in charge of the babies. Asa stayed with her and Dellingr declared he was needed to look after both women. He did not meet Bera's eye. Ginna defied both parents, took her father's cart and set off with the other settlers. Bera had to admire her, and told Heggi so.

'You're in a good mood cos you're going on an old boat,' he said.

She cuffed him, laughing, and they made their way to the narrow cleft where Faelan waited. Rakki leaped aboard. Bera ignored Faelan's hand, stepped down into the boat and took an oar.

'You might want to rest,' he said. 'Rowing's hard on the stomach.'

'I've rowed bigger boats than this, alone,' she said, though she hadn't had a baby then.

Heggi slid in beside her and took the other oar. 'Faelan calls this boat a vole.'

'A yole,' said Faelan.

'Faelan can swim and everything.'

'We all can here,' said Faelan. 'There's a hot spring nearby. I'll show you.'

Bera liked that he deflected admiration. She gave Heggi the stroke and they backed up, then turned. The water thrummed under the hull and she felt it in her skin, with another skin pressed against her. She was held by a swimmer beneath her and she let go, drifting, even though it was not her husband but Faelan. With a guilty start, Bera stopped her too-vivid dream and concentrated on rowing. It struck her how in tune she and Heggi were. He really was growing. Then she simply let the smells of the sea and the song of a boat, even one as ill-found as this, welcome her home. The time of being landlocked was over.

Rakki leaped ashore, barking, scaring off the gulls and carrion birds that flew up in a billow. Demented by new smells, he darted and lunged at the whale's head. Bera left the dog's mind to its frenzy and walked to the other end, where a whale calf was trapped at the point of birth. She touched her beads. There would be no other baby, for her. She would make sure of it.

'Look for some driftwood,' she said to Heggi. 'And take Rakki with you.'

'There's usually some over there,' shouted Faelan.

Heggi saluted and vanished over a line of black rock.

'Let's unload the tools.'

'Wait,' said Bera. She placed a hand on the whale, feeling a huge sadness. 'I'm going to do what I should have done a long time ago to a narwhale.'

Faelan came and stood at the whale's head, which pleased her. His respect freed her to behave like a Valla and Bera began to sing as she moved right up to the whale's unblinking eye. Its amber glaze was like one of her beads. She sensed a similar ancient wisdom even in death, like the old lore of iron; deep magic.

Amber, next to the black, keeping you from its harm.

'I thought my skills were gone but the deep magic is rousing some new power within me.'

Then softly blow on it to make it catch light, sweetheart.

Faelan touched her hand. 'Thank you, Bera. We have forgotten to be grateful on Ice Island.'

They fetched his tools from the boat.

'We hardly ever saw a beached whale where I grew up,' Bera said.

'These ropes are made from walrus hide,' said Faelan.

She tugged it and smiled. 'My father always used them on his best boats.'

'This jerkin is walrus skin too,' he said. 'It's weighty, but the sharp flensing knives could cut your chest open.'

He pulled out shoes with nails driven through the soles and then some large hooks.

'What are these for?' Bera tried to pick one up and dropped it.

'Careful! That'll take your foot off. It's a flensing hook.'

'It's so heavy! What is flensing?'

'Stripping the flesh off,' he said.

Some children arrived, running ahead of folk with carts. Faelan said they would come from all over for the first stranded whale. There weren't that many but it was still more children than Bera had seen for a long time. It made her feel unnatural to have just vowed never to have more.

'Monster! Monster!' yelled the boys.

She flinched and Faelan was quickly at her side.

'Ignore them,' he said gently.

'You know what they say about... the twin?'

He nodded. 'Folk always want to frighten each other. There was nothing, Bera, trust me. No monster, just a lot of blood.'

'I owe you,' she said. It didn't feel so bad this time.

More carts appeared. The faces of these older folk were weather-beaten and stern. A few men were on sturdy horses.

'Are they settlers, like us?'

'Long time ago,' Faelan said. 'There won't be any trouble now plenty's coming. This stranding's early but just out there is a crossing of the whale roads, where they meet and mate. Sometimes we get nine, ten or more in the breeding season.'

He left her to beckon carts up above the tideline. No thrall would ride a horse, so were they on a level with Faelan, who also rode? Bera tried to work out the grades of standing here. How would her folk look with no horses at all? How could she be a leader without being able to ride? Perhaps she could learn, if Faelan taught her.

Bera felt how that first lesson would be, with his lithe body behind her, making sure she was safe. And she would be, because she would bond with the mare. She would feel Miska's mind as one with hers so they could ride faster and faster and it would be like sailing on land.

Her skern tickled her ear. *You've no idea, have you?*

'I'll find out.'

Bera checked the mountaintop.

No smoke, so stop looking. You make me nervous.

Faelan joined in the joshing and laughter while folk got ready. Bera wanted to make sure the fellowship lasted and mark out her role, so she called them over to the whale.

'Let's stand shoulder to shoulder as one to work for the good of us all. And so we can reckon the length of our whale.'

They were just enough, with all the children, to range its length with linked arms.

Faelan reckoned it as forty ells. 'Good idea of Bera's. Now, let's get to work.'

It was all new to Bera but for them it was a practised skill. Men coiled ropes precisely then threw them over the body. Faelan told her that these would anchor the whole carcass so that they could safely work and then turn it over once one side was processed.

'Heggi's too close, look at him!'

'They haven't started cutting yet.'

'I don't want him near them.'

Bera could not describe the revulsion she felt at Heggi being close to blood. Was it the horror of him seeing Thorvald, his guardian, cut down? Or was it the worry that he might turn out like the man who had done it? His own father. Perhaps Heggi would feel stirrings here, like she had, from the whale; except his would be blood speaking to blood.

'I'm going over there now,' said Faelan. 'I'll keep him out of danger.'

If only it was that easy.

Three of the team used ropes to haul themselves up onto the whale's back, wearing the special nailed shoes for purchase. Two of them clung on with one hand and cut slits along the length of the body while another climbed on top of the whale to cut there. It was perilous work. She was glad Heggi was safely on the ground, setting up winches with Faelan. Men pulled off two huge strips of blubber, which crackled like dry kindling in a fire. The smell was intense. Each long strip was torn with the large flensing hooks and cut into blocks. The carcass was rolled over and a third and fourth strip of blubber was pulled off. Women cut the large blocks into pieces that were taken up to the carts. Bera grabbed Heggi and they helped stack the blubber, keeping busy all day, cutting, dragging, stowing, sluicing, piling.

When the sun was lower, Heggi came over to her cart.

'Do we need more driftwood?' he asked.

'Yes. We won't finish before night.'

'There's quite a lot in the next bay. Can I take one of the bigger carts to fetch it?'

Bera had a suspicion, confirmed when she saw his face. He would start a careless whistle next.

'I know you, boykin, and don't think I haven't seen you fussing around those horses.'

'I bet I could ride if I wanted, like Faelan!'

'He's been riding his whole life.'

'Miska likes me.'

'You'd go too fast and break your neck, even on Miska. Take one of the push-carts.'

Heggi walked over to where Ginna was deep in blubber. Bera supposed he wanted to show off his riding skills to her.

'Leave Ginna to do her own work,' she called after him. 'Rakki's eating the blubber, look. Take him with you!'

She caught the eye of a woman, who smiled. 'He's at that age,' she said. 'Are we rendering the oil at Faelan's farm, as usual?'

Bera was flustered. 'I'm not his kin – I mean, I'm his neighbour. Let's finish loading the carts, then I shall ask.'

By the time they stopped, Faelan was working the new flank. The whale-men were swapping shoes with his team. They were as bonded by death as any war fleet; bathed in dark red blood, dried black on their faces. The smell was thick and they crawled with flies. The resting team staggered over to the flagons and poured Faelan's thin ale down their throats.

So it went on: turn and cut, winch and drag, flense and chop until, at last, the whale was unpeeled. Bera looked west, to where the sun was an orange ball amongst purple clouds. When Faelan finished his shift she suggested they walk together to the shallows. They sank down onto the shingle, washed their sticky hands and scooped water onto their faces. Bera dried hers with a cloth.

'We won't be able to work much longer,' he said.

He used her cloth on his own face. She liked how clean it was, without a beard to catch the dirt.

Bera looked out to the darkening sea. 'When I was young, folk used to say they could walk across the Ice-Rimmed Sea on the backs of fish.'

'Not so many round the shore here, ever since...'

'Since I lost the twin. They sense that the world is out of kilter.'

'It's been worse in the past,' he said. 'And will be again.'

She nodded. 'I don't think it's yet – but I have to find the remedy.'

'Ask my mother,' he said. 'Whatever it is, I'll help you.'

'I already owe you too much.'

'Is that what frets you?' He touched her like the quickening air. 'Or have you foreseen a death?'

'I can't scry here.' Bera was surprised by her confession. It mattered that Faelan should know she trusted him. 'Please don't tell anyone. I need my skern, my twin spirit, to warn me.'

'A Fetch, we call it. It's the likeness of the person who is going to die.'

Bera thought about that. 'Our skerns don't look like us. Sometimes they look like who we might have been, though.'

'Our Fetches often appear in the distance. Then come closer.'

Like the Watcher!

Faelan went on, 'They sometimes bring a message ahead of the death.'

So far the Watcher showed no sign of trying to speak to her. Was the message for someone else, or was she entirely wrong? It was a test of her old skills to find out.

'Can you touch a Fetch?' she asked.

'My mother says that back in Iraland more than one fisherwoman has lived with the man they think is their husband, only to find the real man was at the bottom of the sea all the time.'

Bera shuddered. Hefnir was a man in the shape of a husband, who turned out to be without human kindness. He was flesh, though, and Heggi had his blood.

'Our folk's skerns silently rejoin them at the end. Only Vallas like me can talk to our skerns our whole lives. The trouble is, he uses words I don't know, or riddles.' Bera shook her skirts to get the sand out. It was one thing to share a secret but not to sound muddled or weak. 'I think my powers are coming back. We're always right in the end, my skern and I.'

'Is he here, now?'

'Not so you could see him. But if there's any danger my scalp would prickle.'

She wanted to warn him about the evil on his farmstead edge but a loud graunching noise startled her. The huge jaw was being winched up into the sky. There was a cheer. Faelan took her hand and they ran back in time to see it being carefully lowered to finally thump down onto the ground, where it lay beside the whale calf, part-butchered to provide their meal.

'Sad,' said Faelan.

'Do you mean that?'

He raised a black eyebrow in a way that made her stomach flip.

'I never say what I don't mean.'

Faelan praised the weary men, who kept sawing until others wrenched off the lower jaw from the upper. He sent the carts away to unload at his farm, ready to return the next day. Every last scrap of the body would eventually be used.

By the time the sun sank into the sea they were bone-weary.

'Look!' Bera said.

There was a flicker of yellow in the thickening light, over by the ridge of rocks. Heggi had built a fire. They rallied enough to stumble over to its warmth and clap his back and cheer. Bera was glad they saw his worth. He was smiling like a hero, nothing like his father. Perhaps they had reached the bottom that winter, and now everything would get better.

Inland, in the thickening light, a reddish light glowed at the mountain's peak. Bera told herself it was the last rays of the setting sun.

'So you render the whale oil?' Bera asked Faelan. 'A woman said you usually did.'

'It's one of the ties that binds,' he said. 'Food and light. Settlers who work together stay together.'

'We'll be staying together on the beach tonight,' Bera said.

A flash of awkwardness passed between them and Bera took herself off quickly. Folk were stripping and wading into water that was as cold as an ice-shark bite to wash off as much blood as they could before they froze. She joined Heggi and Rakki, who were splashing each other, and then Faelan followed and everything was all right again. They all raced about, laughing and play-fighting, adults and children, then rubbed themselves down with their cloaks and bundled themselves back into stiff clothing. Spirits restored, they set up a proper camp.

They ate well, with plenty of Faelan's ale. Bera saw how he managed the crowd and was liked.

'Are there beach-boggelmen here?' Heggi asked.

Bera made her eyes go wide, showing all the whites and staring at him, unsmiling. Heggi laughed at first but when she got up and lumbered towards him he ran backwards and fell over.

'Stop it, Bera!'

She opened her mouth in a snarl, flung herself on top of him and tickled him until he wept and laughed so much he was crying.

'Get her off me, Faelan!' he shouted.

Faelan and Ginna came and tickled him instead, until they all fell over, laughing. Happiness. And then guilt overcame her and Bera went off alone to fetch some blankets. Surely no mother should forget her child was with another, even Sigrid. Ottar always used to say the greater the joy, the worse the pain.

So you never feel happy without being braced for sadness.

'I worry the land will have its revenge.'

When she got back she made up for it by mothering Heggi, making a rough bedroll for him and kissing his forehead. He got his dog where he wanted him and shut his eyes.

Then rolled back. 'We've got meat now...'

'And?'

'I could have my coming-of-age, couldn't I?'

Bera guessed why it was important to him and kissed the top of his caffled hair, not wanting him to grow up yet, and not with Ginna. She went a short way off, wriggled on the shingle to make a hollow, put down a rug and lay on her back with the blankets right up to her chin. She looked for the stars that she once sailed by and smiled. Then a heart-shaped pattern became the outline of her mother's face and grief came in a buffet.

6

Bera started awake as the first bird began to sing. For a moment she thought she was in the longhouse but the pain in her back reminded her she was on pebbles. There was a sudden squabble of gulls and cawing.

'*Crowman hears us, standing at the threshold of understanding,*' croaked some voices. '*Crowman hears us, standing at the threshold.*'

Crowman? Thresholds were important, she knew that much. Crows were the cleverest of the birds, so perhaps it was them speaking. Her skills really were increasing.

Heggi was fast asleep, his blankets a tangle. She slid out of her bedroll to straighten them, gave Rakki some water and then went to see what the others were doing.

Faelan had cut away all the baleen and was sleeping where he had dropped, tools in his hand. She gently roused him and led him over to her place. He was too tired to resist.

'Lie there, it's still warm,' she said. 'The rest of us can get to work now.'

'It's the lemmers soon. I'll just...' He was asleep again at once.

Bera covered him as she had Heggi, and nearly as tenderly.

The carts had returned. After a steadying drink, the men set to work. The remaining meat was flensed with sharper hooks than the blubber, with the carcass being rolled in the same way as before. It was long, hard work for them and the support team, who were taking the blocks of flesh to the carts. When Faelan woke he took charge again. Loading, taking to his farmstead, returning, loading throughout the whole long day. Bera was one of them, glad to follow and not be the one with all the worry. She liked the rhythm of it, like hoisting a sail, or rowing.

'The lemming!' shouted Faelan.

The sun was low in the sky again when the lemmers cut out and sawed up the best bones and collected the useful inner organs. Bera insisted they should leave behind the pile of guts as an offering. They washed their tools and then themselves before trudging back with all the tackle to the carts, piled with riches that would make life easier in the long dark of winternights.

Bera was the last to leave. The immense coils of grey gut were swarming blue-black with flies. It made her think of the Serpent King's coiling tattoos. She touched her necklace. The black bead was hot, more than neck heat. She, too, stood at a threshold.

There was a long, shrill screech and a sea eagle landed on the guts. Good omens, eagles, and she thanked him.

A week later the tallest mountain's cloud lifted and revealed itself as a billow of grey smoke. Now everyone worried. Sigrid urged Bera to tell folk about her vision but then saw that it would only stoke the gossip, so promised to keep her mouth shut. Drifa, however, reminded them of the lamb with two heads.

'Crops will fail, all right,' said one of her cronies.

'It wasn't the only monster, was it?' said Drifa, watching Bera to see if she flinched.

She gritted her teeth, handed the baby to Sigrid and took herself off to the river.

Heggi followed. 'Aren't you feeding her anymore?'

'I need to think,' she told him and bent to pick a buttercup. 'Alone.'

He whistled for his dog and they ran off.

Your milk will dry up.

'That's the idea.'

She heard splashes and her heart leaped. When Bera turned round, Faelan jumped off his horse and came straight to her. His white face told her he too had seen the smoke.

'What is it?' she whispered.

He swallowed hard and Bera knew.

'It's starting, isn't it? The eruption. What can we do?'

'My mother says only you can save us.'

'How can I? It's too huge.'

'She says you made the quaking start again, Bera, only this time it will be worse, like it was before the settlings. She says the ash clouds killed folk as far as Iraland. It's why the Others started looking for new lands.'

'Then they came to the wrong place.'

'They went all over. Now you must help us, Bera.'

He didn't need to remind her of her promise, or that he had helped them all, but kept his blue eyes wide, open to scrying. He was trying to show he trusted her but her instinct told Bera that even if it was possible, it was too dangerous to delve into a man's mind.

'Tell me who you really are and what happened at the ruins.'

He rubbed his chin. 'I was brought here by the Others, in a way.'

Bera was suspicious. 'What "others"? You don't look like any of us.'

'The Others came to build a community and pray.' He picked up some soil and rubbed it between his fingers. 'Our folk are the Westermen, as some call them. They were here an age before you Northmen. Look at this soil: rich and black and fertile.'

'So what happened to them?'

'The pool wept.' The memory coursed through him. 'A boy was in the top pasture and he saw the lake weep white tears that ran down the valley and killed them all while they slept.'

Bera's deep mournfulness in this place was answered. 'You were that boy, weren't you? Why were you the only one awake?'

'I was a slave – a thrall.'

'Seabost thralls were always shorn. You have long hair.'

'I'm a slave no longer.'

'Don't you get nits? Sigrid keeps saying we have nits and combs our hair with the new sharp comb until my scalp bleeds.'

'More likely midges down here. They can send you mad. I'd cut my hair if I could but it's my sixth sense.'

'What sixth sense? What do you do, with long hair?'

'I track. Animals… and folk.'

'So there are dangerous folk round here?'

'You know I would keep you safe. Those white tears were Hel's and I can't let it happen again. If you—'

She stopped his words with a finger. 'What do I have to do, and when?'

'The mountain will tell us when we must leave.'

'Leave?' Bera was aghast. 'I can't move my folk, not again!'

'Not them. You and I must go alone. That's what my mother says.'

Bera was tired of taking orders from his mother. 'I shall ask my Valla ancestors what must be done but I'm not going anywhere until I know my folk are secure.'

Bera went inside to feed the baby. Her breasts hurt and as soon as her daughter saw her she started to cry. Bera held out her arms.

'Let me have her. Sorry I'm late.'

Sigrid held on to her. 'I can cope, easy. She's more settled, both bairns feeding together.'

'It doesn't sound like it. Anyway, I need to stop feeling like this.' Bera doubled over, to show how her breasts weighed her down.

'You need to let me do it all the time, then.'

'I'll have a wash first.'

What Bera longed for was a bath, alone, with no demands. She pictured being in the bath hut at Seabost, in a tub of blood-hot water, with soothing herbs and flowers and a thrall to soap her. Then hot stones and birch switches, clean of body and smooth of mind. Now she had to make do with a quick splash of face and hands from a bucket before going to her screaming child. As she suckled, the pain subsided. Then it struck Bera that her fears were well-founded: her daughter truly was taking all her Valla powers away to use for herself. She tried to find softness in the child's face but her determined frown and the set of her jaw was too like her father's. Bera looked instead at the fluffy down on the top of her head and stroked it until, finally, the baby's lips grew slack and she dozed.

Waves of tiredness crashed over Bera.

A boat was standing up on end, boarded like a hut, with a small door.

'*Crowman is here, waiting for you.*'

The crow voices, again.

'Here, give her to me.' Sigrid swept up the baby. 'Who's Sigrid's pretty baby girl, den?'

Bera took her back. 'I was feeding her!'

'You weren't; you were fast asleep.'

The dream had to be important. Perhaps the Crowman could explain and heal any link between the birth and the earth's spasm.

Sigrid began singing a lullaby to her baby boy and she was glowing, full of a love that Bera had never seen in her before. Her throat ached with the pain of it and yet she could not name any of her strong feelings and only knew that she had to hug her baby tight.

Bera watched the curl and uncurl of tiny fingers like some small sea creature. She gently kissed them, and then her baby's forehead that was as downy as a fawn's. A memory came to her, of her mother singing a lullaby to her, but the words had gone. Something about a raven, as she had named the boat. She had never made the connection before.

Her child had a perfect curve of cheek, as sweet as any boat hull made by her father, swept by dark lashes. This time there was no mistaking the wave of love that coursed through Bera, terrifying in its absolute and feral compulsion to protect. Her own small Valla. Was this welter of feeling usual? She properly understood how Sigrid must feel to have lost her first son, Bjorn.

Bjorn. He was the only one who had ever loved her exactly the way she was. There were times when she didn't like herself very much, but she was a different person now. Better. Kinder.

'It's these spring nights,' Sigrid said.

'What is?'

'You get crabby when you can't sleep. Always have. And you're even worse in the bright nights.'

The baby gave a small hiccup then stared at her with wide, unfocused eyes. Bera could while away years like this, gazing back.

'What are you going to name her?' Sigrid asked. 'She's the spit of her father.'

'She's not! Anyway, I want to get to know her first.'

'Birla? Birna?'

'You want it to start with B.' Bera's hand went to the bead with the rune on it. There had been enough trouble.

'Why not name her after your mother?'

Bera shook her head. She looked down again at her daughter's face, hoping for inspiration.

'Alfdis!' cooed Sigrid.

Something old and knowing peered at her from her baby's eyes. Bera gasped. How could Sigrid think of naming her after Alfdis, knowing too well how Valla power also brought an urge to possess – in every way.

'She's been on this earth before,' said Sigrid.

It was just a saying but Bera did not like it. The baby was awake and unnaturally quiet; her eyes were glazed, as if she were listening to something a long way away.

Bera said, 'You see it?'

Sigrid said, 'She's hearing something from another world,' and drew a hammer on her throat.

'Perhaps Dellingr could find a small piece of iron to protect the crib.' Bera passed her the baby. 'We need to name both our children soon, keep them safe.'

One day they would be strong, with a homestead full of light and food and everything to make life easy. Dellingr would have his iron sooner than that. She would make sure of it somehow. She had to – because smoke was pouring from the Gateway to Hel and she had to believe that Crowman, whoever he was, could stop it.

7

Bera's first duty was to protect the homestead. She liked the snugness of a covered way protecting the outbuildings, with or without Drorghers, but there were other predators. She paced the whole settlement, from byre to forge, saying words of shielding. She held her Valla necklace tight, to bind them. All the folk were gathered to watch, except Farmer and his wife.

'I have made us safe and strong,' Bera said. 'We look prosperous – and that may bring danger. Watch for raiders coming from the east.'

'Why east?' asked Ginna.

'They always do, land or sea.' So her father had always said.

Asa snorted, then took Ginna and went out with the other settlers. Dellingr said they wanted to get up to the smithy before it was fully dark.

'Ginna's got it into her head that there are ghosts up there.'

'Well, we both know there is something.'

'We can't move the smithy. It's the old magic to forge iron in fire on a hill above the meeting of roads.'

'It's the field edge that's the trouble, you said. I'll ask Faelan why.'

'I can tell you. Corpses. That's their idea of custom over here.'

'That's Drifa talk.'

'Then ask him.' Dellingr spat over one shoulder. 'And why is he being so helpful? He'll be after something.'

'Settlers are different,' Bera went on. 'It will bring bad luck, Dellingr, to fall out with our neighbour.'

Dellingr started to go. 'You mark my words. I don't like his horse-arse black hair and sneaky eyes, neighbour or not. There's bad blood in there.'

'There's no such thing as bad blood!'

He set off again. 'Then tell me you don't care about Heggi's kin.'

After supper, Bera felt Sigrid staring at her while she was feeding the baby.

She knew what it would be. 'We've talked about the smoke, Sigrid, and it won't help. There's trouble brewing and I may know what to do.'

Sigrid gave her a look. 'There's trouble with you, more like. You've a baby now and there you are, all cow-eyed over Faelan.' She held up a hand. 'Don't bother denying it. I saw the same with your mother. Bad things happen around Vallas.'

Bera was angry. 'First it was my father, now you! When will I be trusted?'

'Something else you should know,' Sigrid went on. 'Asa says Dellingr wants to move.'

'She might. But he's just explained why the smithy can't be moved.'

'Some pedlar told him there's a heap of iron up on the other parcel of land left by a settler who died and he's going up there.'

'We need him here!'

'You never sound like we do.'

'He wants a fight.'

Sigrid said, 'You click your fingers and Dellingr would jump; he'd never even ask how high.'

Had that ever been true?

Bera could not get to sleep. She looked at her daughter's lips, golden in the oil-light.

'What is your name, little one?'

The whine of a biting insect drilled close to her ear and made her feel trapped in a strange land, surrounded by folk she hardly knew anymore. If there was a boat she would have been straight on it, alone, out to sea and free. How she wished she could be like a man: to father a child and then sail off to wherever the wind took him. To Egill's Iraland, where she had begged Hefnir never to go.

Iraland, where the Serpent King was waiting. Or was he here, to look for Hefnir?

She felt a warmth at her throat. It was her skern, stroking the place where once Hefnir kissed her.

'Don't do that,' she said. 'It's irritating.'

I always irritate you.

She slapped her cheek, where she felt the insect.

You missed it.

'Will Dellingr go?'

He has to be cross with you, sweet one. It makes him think he doesn't need you.

Heggi came in, checked to see where the baby was and then carefully got in beside Bera.

'You're too big for this now, boykin.'

He was damp with sweat.

'Are you feeling well?' She kissed his hairline. He did not smell ill.

'Rakki was digging at the field edge and he found a bone. You know what he's like and I didn't want him to choke on a splinter.'

The field edge. Bera shivered. Perhaps Dellingr was right. 'What bone?'

'Oh, you know, a leg bone or something.' He waved his hand breezily. 'A bit of pig, I expect. Anyway, Ginna came out and said Dellingr wanted them to move.'

'Sigrid said—'

'But just now I had a bad dream and it all got muddled and Asa was shouting and it was Ginna's body that was buried. Oh, Mama, it was awful. Her eyes sprang open and she was this Drorgher…'

'I'm here, shh.' Bera hugged him tight to comfort herself as much as him.

'Don't ever leave me, will you?'

If she stayed, she might condemn them all to death.

'Mama?'

'I won't let Dellingr go, Heggi. Even if he did, you could still see Ginna sometimes. The old settler's land is not much further than the farmstead.'

'No – Farmer's going up there to better pasture. Ginna's going right away, Mama, for good, to some big smouldering place that the pedlar told Dellingr about.'

The pedlar seemed determined to get all the important men away. She felt there was something she had missed, through tiredness, or when her senses were dull.

'Have I seen this pedlar?'

He nodded. 'That fat rider one.'

She had to have it out with Dellingr and early next morning she set off for the forge. The fields had a blush of green where Faelan's seeds were pushing up, rapacious for the short season of sun. The land was as fertile as she had foreseen. Why should Dellingr want to leave? But Hel's Gateway was a stark reminder of what was to come, so perhaps her smith was right. It was only a question of when the earth would finally shake them off.

'Should we all go with him? Or force him to stay and go alone with Faelan? Stay or go?'

Her skern was fighting off a mist of tiny insects that danced in front of her face. Faelan said it was the midges that would drive them mad. The black flies were bad enough, compared to home. Maybe the horses brought them. Some got right into her hair, biting. Was this what prickled her scalp or was it a sign of nearing danger?

When she came to higher ground Bera stood still with her eyes closed, to let other senses sharpen. There was still no feeling that Drorghers had found them and yet her unease was growing and it was hard to remember the exact smell when one was near. Heggi's dream bothered her; she should have asked him more about finding a bone. Animal or human? It had always been hard to unpick true premonition from groundless fear – until the fear became real.

Fields of suffocating ash, the livestock dead. See?

Pearly bones and grey dust.

Bera quickly opened her eyes. Before her was the river, full of big, white-fleshed fish. Pastures getting greener. The ash was the future.

She had to find out how to stop it happening – and that might force Dellingr to stay and keep folk safe.

He was inside the forge, alone. With no fire, its heart was gone.

'I think it's time to tell me everything, Dellingr.'

He rubbed his hands, as though he still worked iron, wouldn't meet her eyes.

'We used to have Thorvald protecting us,' she went on. 'You saw his virtues when I did not. Do you think he would want you to abandon Sigrid or Heggi now? The babies?'

'Who's abandoning anyone?'

'I don't know, Dellingr. I'm waiting for you to be as honest as I thought you.'

He flinched. Bera expected him to walk away but he stayed. What would he say? That he couldn't bear her leadership? That, like Asa, he couldn't look at her without thinking about his baby son? The silence was thick with both their thoughts.

She decided to be totally honest with him. 'I thought I was dying when I had the baby.'

Dellingr looked at the doorway. 'Asa thought so too, with our first.'

Bera was impatient. 'This was different. It was as if I was the earth itself and both of us ripped apart, dying.'

'We had the tremors...'

'Come outside.'

Dellingr followed her but looked nervously at the huts.

'We are in plain view, Dellingr, Asa can hardly mind that. Look at the smoke. It's getting thicker and it's coming from the Gateway to Hel. I saw its ice cap cracking. It blew sky-high and then burning black fire streamed down towards our homestead.'

'That's one of Egill's tales.'

'Egill saw her father die here, burning in the sea like a grease taper.'

'Well, she's gone to Iraland with Hefnir.'

'That's past. What is our future here? What will you do?'

Dellingr faced her. 'I owe my family, Bera. You want the truth, so here it is, though it will hurt you. There are signs that we got this wrong. There's that' – he gestured at the smoke – 'and bones coming up and Drifa says you having that dead scrap of a twin…'

'Don't blame me for any of this, Dellingr! I will not have you fools thinking you know, when – when…'

All the grief and fear crashed into a moment of weakness. Bera buried her face in her apron and wept. Dellingr held her back and let her cry and she liked his silence, and the heavy heat of his big hand. She thought she might never stop but then she did and felt only relief.

He dropped his hand. 'You've stored that up a long time.'

'My father always said tears were a woman's way of getting what she wants. I don't want anyone being sorry for me. But, Dellingr, I feel so alone. I need my smith, with his knowledge of the old ways. You used to bring out the best in me.'

'Aye, well.' He thought about it. 'Do you know for sure this way into Hel will open?'

It's not opening for us to go in but for Hel to come out.

'I know nothing for sure,' Bera said. 'It helps to think out loud.'

'Then use me.'

Bera touched his sleeve, like an earthing. 'Hel's tears ruined the earlier homestead.'

'And soaked into the stones. I said—'

'But it is also our future. The ice cap blowing is like nothing we've ever seen, worse than the snow-drop. It might come soon but I never know when, just like the flood back home.'

'What does your skern say?'

Eruption.

'Nothing useful.'

'Some haven't forgiven you for forcing them to choose to stay or go, Bera.'

'It was Hefnir who forced them!'

'Still. Don't tell folk they may have to move.'

She met Dellingr's eyes. 'There will be nowhere to run. If there is an eruption, the sun will disappear and turn this whole island to cinders.'

There was a burst of laughter from one of the huts. Bera quickly moved away from Dellingr but it was only some youngsters who leaped over the burn and ran off into the fields. Was there ever a time when Bera had been as carefree as them? There had always been her duty of protection, with no mother to guide her in Valla power. And now no husband or father to protect her little family. Only Dellingr, inside the homestead. She briefly thought of Faelan but there was a sense that she might also protect him.

Dellingr was studying his hands. 'I was going to tell you a few days ago but you get me that worked up...'

'I never mean to trouble you,' she said.

'Oh, Bera. You'd trouble me no matter what you ever said.'

She prepared her face for being told he was leaving her.

'Anyway, it doesn't matter now,' he said. 'It's not going to happen.'

Bera followed the sound of the shouts and happy squeals. The few children were playing bully-bully. Heggi and Ginna were in the thick of it, just like she and Bjorn used to be.

Her skern draped himself round her. *He's growing up.*

'He's dead.'

Her skern's eyes were wide, like an owl's. *I meant Heggi.*

'He's playing.'

With Ginna. Heggi will be asking for a bond soon.

'His voice has hardly broken yet!'

He's twelve. Not so much younger than you were when you married his father.

'I was forced to. I was a child.'

Old enough to be a mother, sweetie.

Heggi arrived, panting. 'I went up to see Dotta and she's thriving.'

'The new grass is doing her good.' Bera picked at his tousled hair. 'These caffles! I swear you stick burrs in your hair on purpose. Keep still!'

But Heggi twisted away, laughing.

'How's my little sister?' he shouted. 'Can we have a naming feast?'

'What are you after, boykin?'

'She needs a name… and I could have my coming-of-age. Please, Bera.' He did his big eyes.

'There's not enough ale for a feast.'

'That man sold us a barrel of mead.'

'What man?'

'I keep saying about the fat rider. Before the whale came, on the fat horse.'

'What mead?' Bera asked. 'Why wasn't I told?'

'Drifa gave him some eggs for it.'

'And he took them? That's not a fair trade.' It increased her concern.

'So can I tell everyone there's a feast tonight? With mead? For my coming-of-age?'

'No.'

'The naming, then. A feast, Bera! Go on!'

Folk needed a feast but Bera was scared she would rush and name her child something irrevocable. Let Fate decide.

'Borgvald.' Sigrid was there, holding her own baby high. 'Baby Borgvald. The image of your papa.'

'I hate that name,' Heggi said, then ran off with the dog at his heels.

8

Bera put off the feast until the next day, thanks to a thunderstorm that revealed gaps in the hall that had to be plugged. Heggi made sure people knew and the promise of mead at last put a smile on everyone's face, he claimed. Sigrid went missing on the afternoon of the feast, taking both babies with her. Heggi said she was up at the forge huts with Asa. Where else? Bera thought, as she jabbed some driftwood into the fire.

'Go and get someone to help you make the floor ready for tonight.' He'd ask Ginna, of course.

Heggi whistled for Rakki and they raced out, leaving the door wide open. Smoke blew into her eyes, with something gritty that smarted. She rubbed, making both it and her mood worse. With eyes streaming, Bera crossed to the door and slammed it shut. She felt defenceless, to be alone and half-blind.

Face your fears.

'My fears are shapeless. I have no living enemy to fight.'

Blindness. Remember this.

She decided to bathe her eyes in cold water. She came into the covered way, which smelled of rotten eggs that stung her eyes. For a while the river's constant, cheery sound soothed her, until she looked across to the ruins and saw a figure. The Watcher? Her eyesight was bleary and when she looked again it had gone.

When her eyes were clear she suddenly ached to hold her baby. Asa would have to invite her in. But before she reached the hut, Sigrid came out with the babies and Asa went back indoors without a word.

Bera took her baby and wrapped a shawl round her. 'What is she accusing me of now?' she asked.

72

'Nothing. Anyway, she knows I'd stand up for you.'

'Would you?'

'What's that supposed to mean?'

'You tell me, Sigrid. I thought we would all pull together.'

'We are all pulling together.' Sigrid stopped to catch her breath.

'She doesn't, ever, and yet she's still your friend. And she's not alone.'

'We were all together through winternights.'

'Because we had to be – but now with every lengthening day the ties loosen, and there are worse challenges ahead. How can we withstand them?' Bera was too angry to speak again until they reached the covered way. 'See this, Sigrid? Built to keep us safe. Together.'

Sigrid sniffed. 'It stinks in here. It's trapping the smell.'

'It's Hel's foulness that is the problem, seeping from that mountain.'

Sigrid gagged. Bera rushed to get her baby inside the hall. Heggi and Ginna were ladling water onto the soil and stamping down on it. They were splashing it about instead of sprinkling and they slipped and fell and then shoved one another with muddy hands. If only they had blond wood to build with and spruce boughs to lay on the floor, smelling sharp and clean, banishing evil. If only her father were here to do things properly…

Life has to be lived as it is, not how you want it to be.

The baby gave a gurgle and was slightly sick on Bera's shoulder.

Sigrid passed her a cloth. 'Give her to me. I'll get them both cleaned up.' She left with a baby under each arm.

Drifa came out of the shadows. 'We've set up the mead at the back.' She gave her a strange smile. 'And I have something for the bairn.'

Bera's scalp prickled. 'There's no need.'

'You can't refuse a gift.' She pushed a small packet into Bera's hands and held it there in her strong fist.

'There's little enough yet for everyone, Drifa.'

'The old ways are best. There was always a gift at the naming.' The smile again. On, off. 'Keep it. For your daughter.'

She released her grip and stepped out of reach.

Bera unfolded the grubby waxed cloth. Inside was a small black bead, like a rat's eye; a tiny version of the one in her mother's necklace, where her free hand immediately went. Both beads throbbed like twin heartbeats.

'Where did you get this?'

The farmer's wife brushed away an invisible bead of sweat. 'This fire's hot enough.'

'Drifa. Where did you get it?'

'It was that fat rider with the mead. He said I was to make sure the bairn got it. Your girl.'

Bera's scalp prickled again. 'Why didn't he give it to me?'

The woman looked away. 'You weren't to be found. Folk are arriving, see. I'll pass round mead for the toast and send you a cup.'

'It will taint the milk!' Bera spoke to her back.

Sigrid barged past her still holding both babies. 'You're not feeding her.'

'I meant *your* milk,' Bera said, taking her daughter.

Sigrid winked. 'A drop of mead in the milk and the babes will sleep like tops.'

'Did you hear any of that? That rider gave her a bead for the baby.'

'I'm feeling that mizzy-mazey.' Sigrid belched. 'Bless me. What rider?'

'I reckon she and Farmer were going to keep it, like the mead. It's like the bead on my necklace, the same stone. Why would a pedlar give her something so precious and a barrel of mead and only take some eggs?'

'Well, what else have we got to pay him with?' Sigrid burped again. 'Let's see it.'

Bera held it out on her open hand.

'*It came from the earth and was forged in fire and air.*'

The crows' voices brought the vision back, vivid.

'*Lightning flickers, light, dark; death, life.*'

'Did you hear that?'

74

'Farmer arrived drunk.' Sigrid took the bead. 'Who'll have a pretty necklace like your mama's, den?'

She gave it to the baby, who put it straight into her mouth.

'*Burning, burning, fire, burning,*' the crows urged with wild glee.

Bera saw a blizzard of fiery fragments, blinding her, fizzing into the sea, which exploded into hissing smoke. This was more than she had seen before – and was a warning.

'Take it out, Sigrid!' Bera cried.

Sigrid held it up. 'I'll knot it on this old leather cord to keep it safe for baby… What are you going to call her?'

Bera was reeling. It was the beginning of what she had seen at the birthing. But how soon?

Sigrid carried on. 'You still haven't decided, then? Best be quick. I'm naming Borgvald tonight too. I wanted a B and a bit of his father. Borg's a good strong name, just like Sigrid's own baby boy is going to be.' She made a farting noise at his neck.

Bera could stand no more. Was she the only one who could see they might die? Sigrid's love for Borgvald felt like a betrayal of Bjorn too. She did not want to say something cruel, so Bera took her own baby, carried her over to the stool and slowly calmed as she rocked her. Perhaps motherhood brought fearfulness, like Valla skills brought passion. What name to give her? Not Alfdis. Her feelings for her dead mother were muddled. She loved her – but there was also a memory of fear, which was different from fearfulness on behalf of your child. Perhaps a Valla name would protect her baby; a link forged between one strong woman and another. Part of Alfdis, perhaps.

She became aware of being in the centre of watching folk. They were gathered – so few! – waiting, watching, for her to start the naming as soon as the baby was fed. Heggi had his arm round Ginna.

Her skern was busy measuring the length of the hall, placing one thin foot carefully in front of the other, wobbling.

Let him be a man.

'What kind of man, though?' The past pressed in on her.

Dellingr stood beside his wife. Asa made sure Bera noticed he was waiting on her: passing her cup for filling and settling her shawl; showing he was hers. Bera had no desire for a husband. It would mean forgiving Hefnir – and she earned her own respect. Her daughter began to burble with joy, beating her arms and legs so hard that Bera nearly dropped her. She raised her high to kiss her and breathed in her particular baby smell. It made her dizzy. The warm scent of her hairline was more potent than mead. Was that love?

She needed her wits about her. This wasn't only about naming; a full meeting was an important time to take charge of their future, to give them knowledge in a way they could understand. But what? There was so much she wanted to tell them but without certainty she would only frighten them. A true leader had to shoulder the worry until action was needed. This was a time to remind them they were safe here because of her and if they trusted her strength and purpose they too would be strong.

Bera steeled herself and went to stand at the hearth. Thorvald would have banged his sword for attention back in Seabost. Here, with so few of them, they were already quiet.

'My mother, Alfdis, was famed for her skills, though she is now dead.'

If folk wondered why Bera started this far back they said nothing; they were used to stories.

'Sigrid here was my mother's friend and can bear witness to her strength.'

Sigrid made the hammer sign. 'I can.'

'I am the link in the Valla chain, like a bead on my mother's necklace, and I alone predicted the dangers in Seabost when none of you would listen, and brought us here.'

There was a rumble from some men at the back of the hall, standing with the swaying farmer. Bera pressed on in case others joined in.

'We are a small but brave group of settlers who left famine, and worse, behind us.'

'How do we know?' one of the men shouted.

'Aye, we've only your word.'

The settlers shuffled and stared at her.

'Haven't I lost more than anyone here? You all witnessed what happened to my father.'

Dellingr stepped forward. 'We've all lost something and we're all tired.' He spread his hands. 'So much work and so few of us to do it. But Bera's right. We should listen to what she has to tell us.'

Bera carried on. 'I honour my father and one day I shall claim the blood debt from the Serpent King.'

There was silence.

Oh, well done. Now they're all thinking about bloodshed. Name her, quick. Make them happy.

'Now we have another Valla in the long line.' Bera lifted her high, for all to see. 'Raise your horns for the naming.'

Heggi rushed over and stood where the father should be. 'Can I say it?'

'It has to be me, to bind it.' The word 'bind' chilled the pit of Bera's stomach. But why? 'Raise your cups to my daughter, who shall be named... Valdis.'

'Valdis!' Heggi was late but his face glowed.

'Oh, that's a good one,' said Sigrid. 'Like your ma's name, Alfdis, with a bit of Valla.'

Bera recognised that Heggi had wanted his moment of importance; to be like his father at a gathering and a man for Ginna. That was what had frightened her: that somehow she and Valdis and Heggi were bound by Fate and nature to Hefnir.

Yet she was glad to see all her folk's happiness and she let them have their moment. Dellingr was right: they had worked so hard, ever since they chose to stay with her and not go with Hefnir to a land of easy wealth. It was in every line of their wasted faces. She must always be grateful to them, though she often forgot this in the daily struggle. Perhaps she could just be a mother. She could give up trying to unravel visions and persuading folk of possible disaster and striking fear in their hearts. So she decided not to think about the bad smell from the mountain and the darkening plume of smoke that was gradually clouding the sky above them. Ignored the heat coming off the black bead of her necklace. Just for this one night.

Obsidian draws out the dark in everyone.

'One night, please. No warnings, no riddles.'

Bera closed her eyes and willed her mother to unite with her daughter, Bera, and granddaughter, Valdis. The three of them, bound together against whatever this new land could throw at them.

Sigrid nudged her. 'Now do Borgvald.' She raised her cup, ready to drink.

Bera's scalp flared and she knocked the cup from her lips. 'Don't drink the mead!'

Her skern was pointing at the barrel. It was far, far too late.

A man groaned, clutched his stomach and fell to the floor. His boy fell next. They curled into tight balls of pain, shrieking.

Bera flung the baby at Sigrid. 'Have you drunk any of it?'

'I had one sip, that's all.'

'Get the babies home safe. I must see to the others.'

She ran through the hall, where more people were writhing on the muddy ground. To her horror, she saw that one of them was Dellingr. She faltered, caught Asa's eye and ran on.

Where was Heggi? Please, Mama, let him be safe. He sauntered in from the latrine as she reached the door.

Bera grabbed his wrist. 'Were you sick?'

'No – what's going on?'

She tugged him outside. 'Poison.'

'Is Ginna—'

'Grab that basket.'

They dashed through the tunnel and out into the meadow, lit by the moon.

'Where are we going?'

'The river.'

When they got there, Heggi rounded on her. 'Tell me what you're doing!'

'That plant with the broad leaves that got into Dotta's feed? I saw it growing here the other day.'

'The one that made her sick? That was ages ago. How can you remember?'

'It's what I do.'

'Why do you want that one?'

'Stop asking questions, Heggi, and help me look for it! It's thick and fleshy... Oh, Mama, where is it? There was a whole clump, only a week or so ago...'

She scoured the area, Heggi following listlessly.

'I never saw it and they all look the same in this light anyway,' he said.

Bera pounced. 'There! I need to make them sick.'

'I thought they were sick,' Heggi muttered but he began to help.

It was the wrong phase of the moon to collect a purging remedy but needs must. She would use her Valla power to give the plants some strength.

'I'll mash them here.' She stripped the leaves and pounded them between two stones. 'That will have to do. Come on!'

They ran.

The hall rang with sharp cries of pain and women's screams. Those who hadn't drunk the mead watched in distress as their kin threshed in agony. The stench of poison vomit burned Bera's nostrils so she pulled a baby cloth out of her pocket and tied it over her nose and mouth. She mixed the plant mash with water to make it go further and said some words of power.

Heggi brought Ginna to her.

'What can I do?' she said straightaway.

'Good girl.' Bera gave her a handful of dripping mash. 'Roll a small ball, like this, push it into their mouths and make them swallow. They won't want to, so stop them breathing till they do.'

A look passed between boy and girl. Bera was beginning to like Dellingr's daughter.

She gave her the last clean piece of linen. 'Tie this on. These fumes are poisonous.'

Heggi slapped a hand over his mouth. 'What about me?'

'There are some more drying in the dairy. Bring some bowls and spoons back with you, then dose anyone you like except Farmer; I'll treat him and Dellingr too. We cannot lose them.'

'I'll look after my father,' said Ginna fiercely.

Bera saw her love. 'Then go straight to him now.'

Farmer's lips were blue and slack. Bera pushed some remedy into his mouth, glad that her hands were not covered in cuts and scratches that would let in poison. Finally, he swallowed.

Heggi returned, with a straining-cloth draped over his whole head, tied with a leather thong.

'Can you breathe?' asked Bera.

'A bit.' He held out a bowl to receive the green mess. 'Ugh! Is this what you gave me that time?'

Guilt stabbed her. 'I gathered extra special plants for you, at the right time.'

Farmer reared up and sick flew out in a green stream, just missing Bera.

'Go and tend others, Heggi.' Bera grabbed a passing woman. 'Get anyone who's well to sluice the floor.'

Drifa fell beside her husband, retching. They would both be dead already if they had been secretly drinking it. Bera felt some guilt – and they did keep the settlers fed, so she dosed Farmer again and forced some remedy through his wife's chattering teeth. Drifa cursed her and lay back, moaning.

Bera moved on. She liked the baker, who was the first to show her any respect when she married Hefnir. He was kneeling beside his dough boy, weeping.

'Silly sod snatched my cup of mead and downed it,' he said. 'I had my fist balled ready to thump him when he doubled up screaming, right before my eyes, and now the poor little bastard's dead.'

Bera felt a fluttery pulse in the lad's neck. 'Still alive. How are you?'

'I've felt better but I sicked my guts up and I reckon that saved me.'

She dosed the lad, asking all Vallas to watch over the dying.

'Shift him to the back of the hall where it's clean,' she told the baker, 'and then move the others.'

'All the others?'

'The living. We'll shift the dead afterwards.'

*

Gradually the smell changed to everyday sickness. Bera went outside and gulped in clean air. The plant was working but would it get the unknown poison out of their systems? Folk might be too weak, too thin, after the winter. How many would die? Why was the mead poisoned and who did it? Was it an accident, or was the pedlar sent by the Serpent King? He had come to kill in person in Seabost. She would have to think about it later because she had to go back to tend the dying. The drag in her breasts told her it was time for Valdis to be fed but Sigrid could carry on feeding both babies.

She found Heggi. 'We must keep watch and keep asking the ancestors to save them. How is Dellingr?'

'He's saying he's strong enough to get driftwood,' he said.

'Driftwood?'

'To burn the dead.'

'It won't get hot enough.'

Bera was too tired to fight off Drorghers and if they took her baby... If any bloated corpse came near Valdis, she would rip its head off.

Folk all stayed in the hall, as if it were winter. The men were the worst hit but they all pulled through, even the baker's lad, although he was too weak to stand. Those who died were all women: the two cronies, thin as rails before they got sick, and sturdy Drifa with her midden-dog smile, the hoarder of food and bringer of bad luck. Bera feared she would make a greedy Drorgher and all three had strange, wide sneers. They lifted their bed pallets, taking care not to touch the bodies, and carried them into the empty byre. Bera sent others to scour the beaches for timber. She told a frail youth to keep tapers alight around the bodies.

When the exhausted beachcombers returned they said they had gone as far as the narrow harbour but, as Bera feared, there was no pyre wood. Even Dellingr collapsed from tiredness. There could be no pyre. The bodies would have to be buried soon, but how could they dig deeply when they were so weak? What should she do to prevent them becoming Drorghers after their violent and sudden deaths? Soon they would all rise out of their graves to seek revenge –

and the living's skerns. Or did they make a new kind of dread, like at the edge of Faelan's land? If only he was here to guide her.

Bera was struggling. A Valla should keep vigil but she knew she would fall asleep next to the sickly guard who was already snoring beside the bodies. She asked the women to take turn and turnabout alongside her. Only Asa refused.

During one watch, Bera had an idea.

At dawn she told Dellingr, 'We'll use the earth tremors.'

They carted the bodies, feet first, to the nearest rift. It was a rushed job. They tipped the cart, piling the corpses into a cleft, then shovelled earth over them. Bera said words to take them to their rest but the bodies were earth-bound; they were not cinders rising into the air and up to their ancestors. Here they would rot in a shallow grave. She said every prayer to stop them leaving it and finding the way home. Drifa's death grin kept coming into her mind.

All the while, away in the distance, the cloud over Hel's Gateway grew thicker, but only Bera looked at it.

Valdis had managed to sit upright in her cot, according to Sigrid.

She dandled the baby on her knee and declared it was miraculously early. 'My little baba Disa is such a clever girlie.'

'Don't call her Disa.'

'And she'll be as clever a Valla as her nana was.'

'Sigrid, stop jigging her about, she'll be sick. Poor Borgvald. You shouldn't say how clever she is in front of him.'

'He's asleep. I know why you're snappy.'

'All right, I wish I'd seen her sitting up. If she did.'

'I'm telling you. She was just there, sat up, looking at me. All the time you were away.'

'Am I supposed to feel guilty for burying our dead?'

Sigrid began to feed Valdis and jealousy scorched through Bera. She told herself that it was necessary so she took herself off to search for some plants to finally dry up her milk. Her duty was to leave all those she loved – and in truth a part of her craved the freedom – but she could hardly see for crying.

9

Days were noticeably longer. Folk went about their tasks, ignoring or unheeding of the dark threat of grey, billowing cloud that pulsed behind them. There was work to be done: cows needed milking more often; sheep got into more scrapes. Without his wife, Farmer needed help, and tending the animals made Bera feel like herself.

A week or so after the burial, Bera went up to milk the goats. They were not in their shelter, so she searched and found they had escaped onto Faelan's land. She was sure Fate was taking her to Faelan. She walked on, following the sound of the torrent. Bera loved being alone and close to a waterfall. There was a ghostly moon-skern, making a rainbow of every shade of green. The torrent plunged into the dark lake with a roar that was the nearest Bera could get to boat-song. A sea eagle flew in towards the mountains, just as it had the day they arrived here. She had been full of hope then, thinking that her husband would be a true partner and help build a thriving community.

No use thinking about that.

Bera moved into a quieter space and called the goats to her. She knew all their names and was pleased that they came running when they heard her voice. She hoped someone else would hear her too. One of them was limping but it was only hobbled by long strands of dry grass and bramble, which she quickly removed. She began the headcount and saw the Watcher. This time, it came slowly towards her and Bera could see it was a woman: slight and light-footed, definitely not one of the dead women's Drorghers. Yet her scalp prickled.

'Was it her footprints in the snow?'

I don't know but I'm afraid too. She has no skern.

Bera started downhill, trying not to run to the shelter, with the goats nimbly overtaking her. The Watcher did not follow. When they got there she caught her breath, fetched a stool and began milking. The task slowly emptied her mind, like watching waves. Then a bird chittered an alarm and a man deliberately stepped into her line of sight. Faelan.

'How are you?' he asked.

'Fine, no thanks to you. And I suppose you tracked me here.' She bit her lip.

That's you all over. Being nasty when you'd rather be kissed.

'I've had my own troubles, I'm afraid,' he said.

'Poison?'

'The Fetch is the image of my mother.'

'The Watcher. I saw her too, just now. Did she speak to you?'

'No need. It's clear my mother is beyond any remedy.'

Bera got back to milking to hide her hot face, and for a while there was only the rhythmic spurt of milk into the pail. She had missed his voice, its accent. She looked up and he was still there, looking up towards the waterfall. He caught her studying him and she quickly looked away, working on until she came to the last doe. She tucked her head against her warm flank and when she had finished the doe sprinted off to join the others, with an indignant bleat.

Now there was nowhere to hide. Bera stood up and stretched, feeling his mother's illness like another weight.

'I've a terrible thirst,' he said. 'Could you spare some of that milk?'

Bera scooped her horn beaker into the pail and handed it to him. Her hands were trembling. What was the matter with her? Faelan drank it in one open-throated swallow, like an animal. She watched his throat moving; the line of dark stubble that was more attractive than a beard.

She picked up the pail, ready to run away from these feelings.

'Wait! That wasn't why I came.' He was at her side.

Bera kept still, hoping her heart would stop racing.

He took off his hat, ran a hand through his long black hair

84

and touched something at his neck. The gesture reminded Bera of how she would touch her beads but whatever it was lay hidden underneath his tunic.

'I have something to show you,' he said, coming closer still.

They heard barking outside and Heggi appeared, grinning.

'Guess what! Ginna's – Oh, hello, Faelan.'

'Am I to have no peace?' Bera said. 'I am holding a meeting in here and it's like a bear hunt!'

Heggi gaped at her outburst and Rakki looked from him to Bera, his brow wrinkled.

'We're upsetting Rakki. Now, take these pails down to the dairy.'

'I'm not going there, Ginna's—'

'Do this first, please. And don't spill the milk – or let the dog drink any!'

He marched off, his spine stiff. Rakki ran after him.

Bera sighed. 'Heggi's a good boy really.'

'He's on the threshold, isn't he?' Faelan said.

Dangerous places, thresholds.

'His voice warbles all over the place but he's still a child in many ways.'

'He can nearly reach the smith's daughter on tiptoes for a kiss.'

Bera laughed.

'Is he your only son?'

'Heggi is my stepson. His birth mother was taken and killed by pirates.'

'That's a terrible burden. Bad enough to lose your mother, but like that, and so young!' His eyes filled with tears.

He was so pale that she could see the blue veins at his temple. She pictured kissing it; what his skin would smell like…

'It's about the black bead,' he said.

'Do you know the pedlar who brought it? With the mead? I think he was sent by the Serpent King to poison us all.'

Poison comes in many forms.

'The bead has… properties.'

Bera frowned. 'My baby is wearing hers now. It's just like this.' She pulled out her necklace and showed him her own bead.

He nodded and opened his shirt to reveal what lay against dark curls of hair. Bera started with shock, as though something dangerous had entered the room. On the leather thong was a sort of cross, with an S shape curved around it, carved from black stone.

'A serpent!'

He hid it from view. 'A holy serpent.'

'It's made from the same black stone, though?'

He nodded. 'Obsidian. You must make it your servant, not your master.'

I can tell you how.

'It's next to amber on your string,' he went on, 'and on the cross on mine. It was my mother's.'

Her skern looked sulky and vanished.

'Is she still alive?'

'Barely. Tell me about this Serpent King. Is he a sea-rider with black tattoos all over his face?'

'And a full dragon body.'

'With black grooves on his teeth?'

'And a forked tongue. You know him, don't you?'

'He shouldn't call himself that. The serpent is holy.' He touched his cross. 'Your man is evil.'

'He's not my man but he is Heggi's uncle. His birth mother was the Serpent King's sister and that's his burden, worse than losing her. And, as I said, I think he sent the poison, whatever it was.'

'Wolfsbane, from Iraland, most like, but I'd need to see the bodies to be sure.'

'Well, we've buried them.'

'That's the other thing I must show you.'

Faelan gestured for Bera to leave the hut first, as if from the finest longhouse. It felt good to be respected and held in awe, like being mistress of thralls, but she was wise enough to recognise that being revered came with its own danger, so she politely waited for him outside. Miska came to greet her and Bera kissed her soft muzzle.

'Want to ride her?' Faelan asked.

'How far are we going?'

'The field edge.'

Where corpses were buried. Yet she trusted him now.

'I will if you lead her,' Bera said.

He swung her up onto the horse's back and Bera instantly felt special. He took the reins and they walked on. Miska was smooth and steady, like sitting on a bench in the sun. Bera let the feeling soak into her. Too soon they were there and Faelan lifted her down. They walked round to the back of some scrub.

'Look.'

It was the rift where they had buried the women. The open grave was empty! Bera gasped.

This is a different place.

Her skern was right: of course this wasn't the same rift.

Faelan took her arm. 'All right?'

'I thought this was a grave.'

'It is,' he said. 'This was firm ground once, on a boundary. An earth slip uprooted parts of the bodies.'

'And the bones are a warning for the living,' Bera said. 'Dellingr has seen them.'

'It's not these you have to worry about. I'm here to help you keep your fellows in the ground.'

Bera moved away from him. 'To stop them becoming Drorghers?'

'The Walking Dead? We have other names for them. Come on.'

They scrambled over twisted roots and rocks to get closer. There were a few curded bones sticking out of the soil.

'Are these the Others you talked about?'

'We buried six.'

He made for a pile of stones. He gestured for Bera to help remove them and then told her to step away.

'What for?'

'I want to prepare you. We put him in the ground like this, deep, and I've laid him out again so you can see it done right. I'm sorry. You won't like it.'

'Do you think this is the first body I've seen? I'm a Valla.' She hid her crossed fingers. She only knew the newly dead, before the body was burned. What would a long-buried body look like?

Faelan lifted off some branches of brushwood and Bera stepped forward.

For a long while she could say nothing at all, while she made sense of what she was seeing. In its earthy pit the pearly bones of a man gleamed with no marks of battle. The skeleton was complete – except that its head lay between the long bones of its thighs. Its obscene mouth was kept open with a round lump of granite.

'Was he… beheaded?'

'We cut the heads off all the bodies as soon as we found them.'

'So they don't walk.'

'That's it. We laid the rest face down in the grave but he was the chief and strongest, so that big stone in his mouth is so he can't chew his way out of the winding sheet and prey on the living.'

'Thank you,' Bera said. 'I know what to do now.'

'Then do it soon. Tomorrow will be the ninth day. That's when they rise.'

10

The sun was dipping as Miska brushed through pink grasses and clattered over agate rocks. There was a special waiting silence as day slowly turned into night with little change in the light, as if the ancestors made nature hold its breath to try and pick out a difference. Like scrying light.

They were both riding this time and Bera had her arms round Faelan's waist. She felt the heat coming through his clothes and thought about the elven skin underneath. Unearthly – and both of them on a deadly task. She wanted to be safe, a normal settler, but those days were gone.

'Will it be too late?' she asked.

'We'll get there before dark,' he said.

He kicked his horse and Miska steadily picked a way across the river. The gathering shadows suggested forms and strange night calls began to whisper warnings. What did she really know of Faelan? Had the Watcher come to warn her about him? No, that was nonsense. Yet how did Faelan know about the bead and poison? Was the Watcher the one to trust? Or Faelan? Bera took her arms away from the man in front. She had only seen good in him by day, when he had substance, flesh and blood. Here, in the long, grey twilight, his outline was indistinct, as if he were a creature that drank darkness in order to find its shape.

He half-turned. 'Why did you let go?'

'I'm stretching my back.'

'It's an uneven ride if you're not used to horses.'

'Where are we? I ought to know the way to the forge. Are we lost?'

'Trust me, Bera.' His voice was smooth. 'It's a shortcut.'

They rode on.

'Why do you bury your dead at boundaries?' she asked.

'Twilight's not the time to be talking about it. Let's just say we have ghost fences here.'

'What do ghost fences keep out?'

Faelan said, 'Put your arms round me and hold tight. The next bit is downhill and a bit rough.'

'This land is different, even in the dark. Especially then. Black and white,' she muttered into his back.

Bera thought of corpses being buried at the margins; Rakki digging up bones. Boundaries were thresholds, after all. Then they were there. A smudge of smoke was coming from the forge huts and Bera wanted to wipe out the past anger; not just with Dellingr but all of his family. She even pitied Asa in this moment. Then they moved on. It was their future she must safeguard.

Bera asked Dellingr and his bellows-boy to bring shovels and join them. Dellingr did not look at Faelan.

'I'll leave Miska here,' said Faelan. 'Horses are as scared of the undead as we are.'

'Best keep her near the anvil then,' Dellingr said, smoothing her flank.

Faelan tied her loosely. Miska pushed at the smith's arms for more. Bera had forgotten how good Dellingr was with horses and she liked seeing it again. Then they set off.

It was the long hours of twilight, when the living world fell silent to hear the whispers of the dead. Well before they reached the ravine they heard it. Above the sound of trickling water was a ghastly whining and cracking; grunts, groans and wails. It was too much for the boy. He threw down his shovel and ran.

'He'll be safe enough in the smithy,' said Dellingr. His lips were set in a grim line. 'The tools will protect him, if he has the wit to go in there.'

'Did you put any iron in the grave?' asked Faelan.

'There is none to spare,' Bera cut in. 'I don't know what we shall find there but this must be done, and quickly, before dark.'

Around them, light was thickening, pressing them on to the place they did not want to be. There were no birds here, flying to their roosts, no sound other than the long hiss of evil ahead. The shame of the lack of ritual hit Bera hard. She had been right to feel it was dangerous.

She held her beads when they stood looking at the grave pit.

'If they have not already risen our first danger is poison, which will be seeping through their skin,' she said. 'The smell was bad then; it will be worse now.'

'It's only hours from the ninth day,' Faelan said. 'Best be quick.'

They tied cloths over their faces and put on mittens. Bera was glad to feel her skern move swiftly to the bare skin of her neck.

'These shrubs are still in place,' said Dellingr. 'They're still in there.'

'But restless. Listen.' Faelan stuck a shovel into the ground.

'They're not far down,' said Bera.

Dellingr began to dig and the other two joined him. The noises stopped. Were the women holding their breath, pretending to be dead?

Don't stop now!

Bera's shovel connected with something that softly gave way and she fell backwards, retching, as some putrid fumes escaped. The men carried on, until a jutting shoulder made them stop.

'The winding sheet is gone,' she said.

They brushed away the remaining earth with bushy twigs, to expose all three corpses. Their bodies glowed faintly in the gloom, like the sunless sea creatures Bera had seen once in a vision.

'We're only just in time,' Faelan said.

Two were fatter than they had been in life but recognisable, apart from dark red stains on one side of their face. Drifa was closer to the surface and it was her bloated corpse that Bera had struck. Her mouth was gaping, as though she might batten on Bera and swallow her down whole.

'Now what?' Dellingr asked Bera.

Faelan said, 'We take her head off.'

Dellingr pushed him aside. 'These are our folk.'

He stood right over the corpse, raised his shovel and brought it down hard on the woman's neck. Then again. Her head rolled to one side, as though turning away in shame.

Faelan raised his eyebrows at Bera. Would she like him to take over? She shook her head. Dellingr was right: it was her Valla duty too, and she had not done enough before. She steeled herself.

The woman's head was as heavy as a flensing hook and Bera was clumsy in mittens.

'Steady,' Faelan said.

She managed to right the head and then carefully placed it between the thighs. Faelan passed her a large stone and as she jammed it between the teeth Drifa's grim smile flickered on, off. The men gasped.

'Take the heads off the others,' she said, 'then put them face down.'

They buried all three deep, while Bera said some fast words of peace. As soon as their grim work was done they headed back towards the forge without speaking. Dellingr stopped Bera while Faelan mounted his mare and went on towards his farmstead.

'That was no sight for a woman,' Dellingr said, spitting the words at Faelan's back.

'A Valla presides over Life and Death,' Bera said, then softened. 'I had to make myself do it. I feel sick.'

Dellingr touched her arm. 'Will it work? It's filthy, not like bright flames.'

'Faelan showed me other bodies, the ones you found, and they were dry bones, weren't they?'

He conceded her point. 'What other threat is coming, though? And when?'

'I need time to plan.'

'I hope there is time.' He took the shovels and turned for the forge huts.

She could not tell Dellingr she was planning to leave. He would insist she should stay with the folk she had brought here. And he would be right.

Or will he go himself, as he planned? Her skern looked at one long hand, then the other, and shrugged.

The western sky was gashed with blood-red light and there was a second sun in the north, rising from a distant black cone. Bera felt muddled and unclean, blighted by the stinking rush of foul gas. So she took the path towards Faelan's land, up to the waterfall, to see the way forward.

Going liminal, are we? Good scheme.

'If that doesn't work, I'll visit his mother.'

Near the falls, Bera stopped. She tried to get a sense of the spirit of the mountain to see if the land itself might give her a direction. Nothing. She had no language here. All the years of gradual learning were made useless.

Stop thinking about the sea and listen.

As grindingly slow as a glacier, she got it: something inscrutable and ungovernable; not tied to this place but somewhere darker and older. An unseeing blackness that lived forever both under and inside the known world. If she sensed it, so would it be sensing her.

It doesn't care, you know. You're a midge to it. But you feel it, don't you?

'So whatever I decide doesn't matter?'

It matters to you. So try standing behind the waterfall, like you want to.

She had to scramble over some polished rocks to get there. The crashing plunge of water made her ears ring and she had the sensation of falling, so she crouched and felt her way through the soaking mist. The air was an intense version of what she always felt on Ice Island and every hair on her head tingled. She put a hand to it to make sure it wasn't rising upwards. And then the falls became one solid sheet of water making the world beyond as glaucous as looking through her glass fire stone. For the first time since giving birth to Valdis, she felt a separate person again. Like being far out to sea, she felt alive.

Bera shut her eyes and the roar of the water was the deep howl of a wolf. It was a summons. She was inside…

… A hut, slatted with blue light that came through loose boards.

There was something beyond; a lumpen shape that crouched in the shadows. It started upright and came towards her, striped with light and moving strangely. Bera saw, then couldn't see, what was coming.

'He's purblind and humpbacked, like a whale,' said someone.

The way the humpback moved his head reminded her of Blind Agnar. The figure was questing about, sniffing, and then held out a hand.

'So you have come.' His voice was as cracked as his shape. 'My name is Crowman.'

Bera shivered. She was soaked by the fine spray – but cleansed. She went through to the other side. The wolf howled again and she followed its call by the moon's path to a still pool far beyond the falls, which were only a distant throb. The full moon shone on its dark surface. She waited for the wolf to come.

A man stepped from behind one of the white rocks, naked.

Faelan. Wolf by name.

Bera could not look away from his skin. It was mother-of-pearl, like the glistening surface of a butchered bone. He carefully lowered himself into a shock of silver and gasped as he ducked under. The water was glassy, beyond clear, and every hair on his body glowed in quicksilver precision. He looked like a water elf of unearthly beauty and Bera saw herself tearing off her clothes and jumping in. It was so real that it took her breath away. Then he surged upwards in a shower of savage crystal, shrieking.

He clambered out, slapping himself with his hands to get warm. Then turned and saw her.

Bera ran, as if the elves were chasing, but then her speed restored to her the joy and freedom of childhood. She ran faster – until she tripped and sprawled, spread-eagled on the springy grass. She was already drenched by the waterfall, so she rolled amongst clover, heartsease and thyme, smelling their crushed scent, more potent by moonlight.

Faelan had not followed her. The Valla part of her wished he had; to have taken her there, bodies ice to ice, in one swift possession.

When Bera looked up, the Watcher was there – and so she met Faelan's mother at last.

She was as beautiful as Bera had supposed but her pearly flesh glowed in a way that made Faelan's white skin obviously natural – and living.

'Can you speak?' Bera asked.

Her cracked lips parted slightly. 'I am come to fetch her home.'

Bera refused to be afraid. She crossed the short distance between them and took her hand. She expected it to be corpse-cold but instead it was soft with illness and burned like a hot stone. It reminded Bera of her own mother dying. She let go.

You're pushing back the memory. One day you will have to face it.

'Do you become the person you've come to fetch?' she asked.

'A copy, with a message for you.'

Although the Fetch's eyes were dark hollows, there was a shrewdness that was like Faelan's. She, too, had long hair, as black and glossy as obsidian. Bera was sorry that she had not grown to know her and work beside her. She was being given a glimpse of another life, one she might have had, that could only be scried and not lived. Bera wished she could comfort the woman in her dying.

It's a comfort to her to know you are with her Fetch.

'So is her skern with her?'

They are from Iraland. They don't have them there anymore.

'What happened to them?'

He shuddered and unclasped, leaving her in pain, with a puzzle.

The Fetch gave a rattling sigh. 'It's close. So now your skern has gone, listen.'

Bera thought it reasonable that one twin spirit could see another. 'I'm listening.'

'The wolfsbane that poisoned your folk came from Iraland. It's grown at the farmstead, as is its remedy, but did not come from there.' Her eyes flickered. 'Faelan knew nothing until I told him. Trust him. Get to… Abbotry. Obsidian.'

The Fetch's face was screwed up with pain.

'Don't speak if—'

'Brid,' she said, surprised, and then lay on the ground.

'I will look after Faelan,' Bera said, hoping it would get through to his mother's dying body. 'I wish you had your skern with you.'

Her own skern returned. *Don't think of sending me.*

'If you comforted her Fetch, would that work?'

No idea but let's try.

He cradled its head. In that moment the body that had seemed already empty lost something impossible to describe, as if it had been waiting. Whatever the Fetch had been, it was no longer there.

Bera said, 'That was kind. But will Faelan's mother have to face the darkness alone? Can her Fetch go with her?'

It is her choice.

'What do you mean?'

I felt it when I clasped her. A Fetch is a thing: something they send away, to do a task. He shivered. *It becomes whatever folk believe.*

The thought was like falling off a big wave. 'I could never send you away.'

You know you must go with Faelan soon, don't you?

'Alone?'

You always have me.

Faelan arrived, as she knew he would.

'She doesn't need anyone now,' he said. 'She wanted to see you, to tell you something important.'

Bera nodded. 'I'm sorry you have lost her but all loss also brings freedom.'

He looked away. 'What if I don't want to be free?'

'I long for it,' said Bera. 'But my duty lies in taking care of my folk – and you. Her Fetch told me I have to journey and I think you know where.'

'We will be partners in this, Bera. My mother said you would understand when we get there – but I know where we have to go.'

'Take me to her, Faelan. I'll do the Valla's last service for the dead.'

When Bera went into the billet to begin her vigil the woman lay cold as ice, her nose a hard ridge on sunken cheeks. She prepared her for burial, turning the body so that she could wash her. Bera plaited her black hair and there, on the nape of the neck, was a tattoo of Faelan's obsidian cross, with its serpent coils. A sudden vision of an axe cutting through the sign made Bera snatch up the woven cloth and wind it round the corpse, tight.

She called Faelan in. 'Do you have wood enough for a pyre?'

He shook his head. 'It must be burial.'

'You can't behead your own mother!'

Faelan agreed. 'We will dig her grave in the mire. It's not frozen now so will be easy work – and she will be held by water and unable to cross it to land.'

Bera hoped he was right.

11

After the burial Bera wanted to go home directly and alone.

'I need time with my baby and to not think about death or loss, or the future.'

Faelan insisted they had to set off at once. 'Look at the mountain. It's thicker again today.'

'The Fetch gave me a message, something like Abbotry.'

He nodded. 'You're needed at Smolderby first and I've been told to take you.'

Bera supposed his mother had told him more, perhaps even about Crowman. She liked feeling Fate was binding their futures.

Faelan carried on. 'It's a long journey, so I'll bring two horses.'

'Can't we go in your boat?'

'The yole's not seaworthy. I've a better boat in Smolderby and we'll do the final stage in that.'

Bera's spirits rose still further. 'You can show me the way and how to ride a horse.'

'I'll bring a quiet mare but if you slow us down you can ride behind me like you did before.'

Hel could take her before she would make a whole journey as a passenger.

Careful. We're making very free with Hel these days.

'You vanish sometimes,' said Faelan. 'Your face looks empty. Is it what Vallas do?'

'You'll get used to it,' Bera said.

While they were collecting the tackle from the byre, an idea came to her.

'Do your folk pay the vigilant and gravedigger?'

'Maybe someone rich, back in Iraland… I don't know.'

'Would you pay a Valla who performed these duties?'

He grinned. 'Just say what you're after.'

'All right, I want iron.'

He raised an eyebrow in the way she liked.

'It's for Dellingr,' she explained.

'There's plenty here, old tools, ploughs. I'll get my lads to take some to the forge.'

'He mustn't know it's yours. His pride's hurt enough – and besides, I'm trying to keep him at the homestead.'

'So if they scatter it in a rift near the ghost fence he'll think it's a present from the mountain.'

'Someone told Dellingr the old settler left a heap of iron on his land. He'll think it's that.' Bera crossed her fingers again.

Wrong can come out of kindness.

'And nothing for yourself?' Faelan asked.

She thought about it while they rounded up the horses.

'Of course! Wolfsbane! I'll take some remedy plants with me.'

He led the way to the medicine garden and pointed to wolfsbane, as his mother had told him. Bera saw the neighbouring remedy and picked a bunch, wrapped it in a rhubarb leaf and then pushed it deep into her inner apron.

Before they left, Faelan set his farmhands to work the field nearest the forge.

'That will give them time to plant some iron for your smith,' he told Bera.

She hoped it would make it right but was distracted enough to obediently get up behind Faelan. The other horse was on a long lead beside them. Then the reality of leaving hit her. Valdis, her baby!

'I could have her in a sling on my horse, couldn't I?'

'You'll find it hard enough riding for the first time, even on that beauty. This is no journey for a baby. Your friend Sigrid is her wet nurse, isn't she? She'll be grand.'

'It's not the feeding, it's…' How to explain that yearning ache to a young man? She didn't understand it herself.

99

And then there was Sigrid. All the way back to the homestead, Bera planned how she might break the news to her. She pictured her heartbroken, saying she had lost a son and two husbands and could not be parted from Bera. Perhaps it was as well to be leaving Valdis with her. It was Fate that had made Bera stop feeding her child. She was determined to be kind to Sigrid, patient and loving. She persuaded Faelan to leave the horses in the ruins, so that she could break the news of her going gently.

When they arrived at the longhouse Sigrid brandished both babies, announcing for Faelan's benefit how folk kept saying she was as battle-hardened as a Valkyrie to be able to feed them both at once.

'Good,' said Bera crisply. 'Then you won't mind keeping it up. Faelan and I are setting off again now.'

She took her baby and held her tight, nuzzling at her neck that smelled of toasting flatbread. Valdis had her black bead tied on her wrist and it hit Bera's face.

'Not that scrutty boat again!' Sigrid said. 'You're needed here, Bera, taking charge. Where were you last night? Dellingr's gone all peculiar again.'

Faelan interrupted. 'Keeping vigil with my mother, Sigrid.'

Sigrid sniffed. 'Oh, well, I'm sorry for your loss.'

Bera said, 'Sigrid. We have to go. It's a long way, to…'

'Smolderby,' Faelan said.

'Sounds very nice.' Sigrid rubbed the end of her nose vigorously.

Bera shared her view, secretly. 'Never mind that. I'm going as a Valla, because they need me.'

'They? What about me?' Sigrid bristled. 'I'm to be left with all the work as usual and not even a lazy thrall to help!' She hitched the red-faced Borgvald, who looked as indignant as his mother, high on her back. 'And what about Disa?'

'Don't call her Disa.'

'I'll call her what I like when you're off skedaddling as usual.'

'I want her to come but you can't take a baby to some smoke-filled place!'

'Don't go then.' Sigrid glared. 'What if I won't do it?'

Both babies began to howl. Bera rocked Valdis distractedly.

'I told you about the visions I had during the birth. And then there were real earth rumbles and now look at Hel's Gateway!'

'It's a cloud, been there for weeks.'

'But it will get worse.' Bera pictured the humpback. 'There's someone I have to meet so that I can avert the disaster I foresaw.'

'Stop being pompous. You and your predictions.'

'And the dam? See what happens when I get ignored! Who got you all here safely?'

'You didn't warn me I was about to lose my husband, did you? Or my son.'

The truth hurt.

'How dare you, Sigrid! You, as well? The other folk have said it all my life, but you? Don't you think I relive those deaths – and others – every day?'

'You've been all smiles lately.' Sigrid gave Faelan a hard stare. 'Why's he going with you, anyway?'

'Faelan has to show me the way.'

'You're not to go alone then. Not with him.'

'Then who could I go with? Who else can we spare?'

'Your duty is here!' Sigrid was shouting.

'Does duty always mean what *you* want, Sigrid? It's my life and hard enough being a Valla. I do whatever anyone asks of me but you'd deny me one smile from someone who's not our folk?'

'Always looking after strangers, not your own flesh and blood. Me and Asa, looking after our own and yours, so you can swan off and… look after this person's mother.'

'You were grateful enough to "this person" when he was feeding us!'

Faelan spread his hands. 'It doesn't matter, Bera. Sigrid, remember I buried my mother this morning.'

Sigrid jiggled Borgvald enough to shake his head off.

She turned on Bera. 'We know what your Valla stuff leads to, don't we?'

'That's enough, Sigrid! I am not my mother!'

Faelan coughed. 'I'll wait outside.' He did not move.

Sigrid's face was purple. 'And now you're off again.'

'Well, you don't need me here, Sigrid, do you? When you're such a wonderful mother who can suckle two babies at once; so carry on!'

Sigrid put her boy in his rocker. 'Come to me then, poppet, now your mama's milk's gone sour with anger.'

Valdis screamed louder as Sigrid took her. Bera wanted to punish Sigrid; to be the only one who could soothe her baby and have Faelan see that. Sigrid walked through the longhouse nursing the baby, who wailed and beat at her with tiny fists. She was struggling to keep hold of her.

'This isn't hunger,' Bera said to Faelan. 'My baby knows I'm leaving her. I can't do it.'

'You have to, if you want her to live.'

Valdis pounded and screamed, twisted and sobbed; drool laced down her chin. Her whole face was puce with rage. Sigrid's patience finally ran out and she held her up, red face to red face.

'Stop this, Valdis, or I'll leave you out for the wolves!'

'I'll be outside.' Faelan gave Bera a long look. 'You can say your goodbyes.'

Sigrid would not meet her eyes as she passed her Valdis.

'Don't let's part like this,' Bera said. 'The trouble is, Sigrid, that you've watched me grow up and struggle. I'm a Valla now and you have to trust me to do what's right for us all. I was selfish once but now I'm a mother. Do you think I want to leave her? But go I must.'

'Go then, and don't come whining back when it all goes wrong!'

It was like a slap. Bera gently put Valdis in her cot and left before she broke down. On the way out she kicked away a stool. She wanted to scream, run, sob. She wanted her mother.

Faelan was at the end of the covered way. Dellingr blocked his way, slapping a bundle of knives against his palm.

'I need to get outside,' said Faelan. 'The air stinks in here.'

Dellingr did not move.

Faelan sighed. 'I have no fight with you, Dellingr. Let me pass.'

The smith's voice was so deep Bera heard the throb of the words. 'There's no fresh air out there.'

The ground rumbled. Bera waited, listening out for more trouble but there was an eerie silence. She went to Faelan's side.

'There's no time for any more of this,' she said. 'Faelan and I are saying our goodbyes.'

'What goodbyes?'

'We're going to Smolderby.'

Dellingr frowned. 'Smolderby? That's where I'm going to find iron to work.'

'You said you wouldn't!' Bera cried.

The floor tilted and she grabbed a lintel. Both men fell sideways, Dellingr's knives clattering on the stone. Faelan took a hard blow to protect her. They waited. Bera was terrified that the stones would fall.

It was a short one. Dellingr rolled over and up to stand over Faelan. Bera thought he was going to kick him – but he put out a hand to help her.

'You need to tell folk what you're doing. A proper meeting, Bera, so we all decide.'

He was right, in one way.

'I'll check on Sigrid and the babies first. You gather folk together in the open, just in case.' She set off, then turned back. 'And keep away from each other. I thought you and Ottar would be a good influence on Heggi. But my father is dead and you are a stranger, Dellingr. Who will set him an example of what a good man is?'

Faelan softly pointed a finger at his own chest so that the smith could not see.

Sigrid was shocked and anxious but she and Bera had no need for words. The babies were together in one crib, asleep like puppies. When Bera started to pack, Sigrid went off to the pantry. Bera missed having her fussing about, pressing more cloaks and furs on her, so she followed.

Sigrid had her back turned, busying herself with a flatbread pole. Bera rushed across, put her arms round her waist and hugged her from behind. These days she could rest her chin on Sigrid's shoulder.

'You haven't done that for a long time.' Sigrid let her head rest against Bera's.

'You will always be a mother to me.'

Sigrid turned so that they were hugging. Her face was wet.

'Pay no attention to this. Baby-tears, that's all. Having one softens you up.'

'Oh, dearest Sigrid. Forgive me.'

'It's not about forgiving, it's about love. And you've always had mine, Bera. Always will.'

Sigrid wiped her nose on her apron and poured them both a beaker of small ale.

'Are you going to call folk together? Tell them why you're leaving?'

'Dellingr's calling them now. I don't want to scare them, though.'

'Folk have a right to be scared. They need the truth.'

The meeting was important; she hoped Faelan understood that her folk were not like his workers. But Bera needed to break the news to Heggi first. She crossed the yard, following a few women as they headed for the lower field. There was Heggi, with Faelan and Ginna. Some others were ambling towards them. So was Dellingr, coming from the direction of the ruins. Then Bera saw the big claw-hammer in his hand. So much for stopping fighting. There were shouts, finger-prodding and then Dellingr punched Faelan's face. He fell over. Heggi slapped his thighs and laughed loudly, the image of his father amongst his drunken men.

Bera began to run.

'Stop it!' she yelled. 'Stop, Dellingr!'

'Papa!' Ginna shouted.

The smith turned, Faelan seized his ankles and toppled him. Dellingr dropped the hammer. Bera kicked it away and tried to get between them. They rolled on the grass, tussling, punching, gouging. They staggered to their feet, rounded on each other, wrestled and fell again.

Ginna covered her face with her hands and Bera went over to her and Heggi. Rakki, overexcited, was making dives into the brawl. A ring of shouting settlers formed round the fighters, urging them on. Something in Bera began to enjoy being part of a happy, noisy group. It must stop.

'Look after Ginna,' Bera said to Heggi, and pushed her way through.

The two men were back on their feet. Dellingr threw punches but Faelan was nippy and ducked, circling the smith, who roared with frustrated anger. Then Dellingr closed in and they wrestled.

She was shoved aside by Heggi and Ginna.

'Papa! Stop it, please!' Ginna cried.

Her mother arrived. Asa marched straight up to the fighters.

'Dellingr!' she screamed. 'And you. Stop it, the pair of you.'

Dellingr looked up and Faelan could have landed a blow. Instead, he walked away, spat, then dusted himself down. Asa punched her husband's chest a few times.

'You fool!'

Ginna rushed to her father and clung to him. Heggi began to follow but Bera held him back.

Asa was in full stride. 'You'd better have a good reason for tearing that tunic. It's the only one you've got. Ginna, go and get your father a drink. And leave Hefnir's son alone.'

Bera was ashamed that Asa had stopped the fight and hated her for publicly shaming Heggi. 'Hefnir's son' hurt too, as it was surely intended to. It was time to take charge and she stepped into the ring.

'This was the rough justice of Seabost between two free men. It was never to the death, so now there is a line drawn underneath your differences. No blood debt to pay.'

Dellingr raised his voice. 'I'm fighting because Bera is leaving us. This black dwarf is taking her away.'

Faelan moved towards him like a lynx. Bera quickly stood in his way.

'Dellingr is to take charge. It has been a hard start here and will only get worse if I don't go now. Look at the mountain. I am going with Faelan to save this homestead that you have worked to build and when I return we will talk of new laws of sharing and ownership.'

'Fine talk!' shouted a man.

Bera was angry. 'Don't you listen? I *have* to go, to save all your skins!'

Dellingr caught her arm. 'You can't go off alone, not with him.' Something in his stricken face told Bera that even now he thought he might go with her.

Determination gave her a quick answer, though she spoke as if it had always been her intent.

'I won't be alone. My son will be my escort... and my second when Faelan and I go to the far side of Ice Island to Smolderby.'

Dellingr was waxen. He gave Bera a long look, brushed off Asa's arm and walked away. It would be obvious to everyone how he felt. She hoped they could respect him enough to lead after this.

Ginna made to follow her parents, then stopped.

'We trust you, Bera,' she said.

Bera smiled. 'I think only you do, Ginna, but I am glad.'

'Can I say goodbye now?' Heggi asked. 'Properly?'

'Make sure no one sees you. Go up to the huts with Faelan.'

'But I—'

'That's where I left the horses,' Faelan told him.

Clever Faelan, using Heggi's love of animals.

'I'll finish off here,' Bera said. 'Say goodbye to Ginna, then come to the longhouse for me.'

She wanted time to think and stayed there, rooted to the unsteady earth.

Had Thorvald been Dellingr's anchor, as he had been Hefnir's? Could the smith be trusted to look after the settlers?

Fear causes aggression.

'Use words I know.'

Who he is lies in his hands, using the old ways, like curing a child of rickets.

'If he hasn't forged, his water trough can't heal.'

It was an example.

'I think he will be more the man if I'm not here.'

And you are thinking better already.

The truth of it made her sad.

Bera went back to the hall but no one was there. She was glad that Sigrid was avoiding the pain of it. She rammed a few things for Heggi and herself into two kit bags. Sigrid probably wanted company, comforting Asa with the babies. Bera found it hard to imagine this other life of hearth and home. She had to accept that Asa had been Sigrid's friend ever since the red-spot, when she helped save her life. She touched her beads and the black stone was blazing.

She looked round the new longhouse, built with sad stones. It could never be a warm hearth, this place.

Glad to escape into the yard, Bera found Faelan, with no horses.

'They've been hobbled,' he said.

'Oh no! Not Miska!'

'It was cleverly done – small cuts in the right place, so they will heal but not soon enough to travel. We have to go on foot.'

'Who did it?'

'No one there to see.'

Dellingr had come to the fight from the ruins.

'Could Dellingr have done it out of spite?' Faelan asked.

Bera wanted to convince herself. 'No smith would ever do that to a horse, especially Dellingr. You saw how he was with Miska. He treats them gently and with respect.'

'It's me he has the problem with.'

Rakki romped into the yard and licked her hand.

'Look, here's Heggi coming now,' she said. 'If we're walking we'd better start while there's light and get some distance between us and Dellingr. I can't believe he would hurt us but I don't want him to follow.'

12

Freedom.

At first, Bera revelled in the feeling and liked the idea of having the wide expanse of new land to explore in the lengthening days. She refused to think about the horses. But then Heggi started asking questions: Had Dellingr done it and why? She said it must have been some pedlar, and when he opened his mouth again she sent him off with Rakki. Her skern tutted.

'Did Dellingr do it, then?'

Past, ducky, no idea. Whoever it was knew how to only hobble the horses.

'A smith has the skill but why would he?'

So he can keep up with you?

Bera was alarmed. 'He must protect the homestead! Anyway, he heals horses with iron, not hurts them.'

You don't want it to be him, do you?

'I relied on him like a father. Now I wonder if Ottar was the better man.'

We all have our foibles. Don't be so black and white.

As they walked, other worries crowded in. Bera felt lost and guilty about leaving her baby with Sigrid, for both their sakes. Then a thought struck her: her daughter was wearing her black bead, given by the pedlar with the poison. Leaving had been fraught and rushed and then the horses being hurt had made her forget everything else.

'Should I worry about the black bead?'

Time will tell.

'In other words, you don't know.'

What do you want to believe?

'I believe that Fate has decided Valdis and I will wear a black bead so that we are joined even though we're apart.'

He laughed. *Sweet. It doesn't bring any knowledge of her, though, does it? And it's changing, isn't it?*

'All right, it feels hotter than the others. Didn't you tell me the amber bead protects me from the black?'

Did I? It must be true.

How she envied Heggi, who cried when he left Ginna but then quickly set off, whistling. It was like giving away the puppy – one minute he loved Tikki and the next she was gone. Was he as fickle as his father? There he was with his dog now, throwing sticks for him without a care. Life was simple for him.

Whatever you feel shows on your face.

Perhaps Heggi was better at hiding his feelings. Perhaps he had to be.

Walking any distance was new to Bera, instead of going by boat, like normal folk. Her hips hurt and then her feet, so she distracted herself by asking Faelan what had caused the fight with Dellingr to spark up again.

'Something and nothing,' he said, and walked on so fast that Bera had to let him go.

They reached a rise, after which the ground dropped to a vast plain. It was their last chance to look at their homestead, so Bera called Heggi back and then she blessed all their folk left behind. It also gave her the chance to see if Dellingr was following them but there was no one in sight.

Someone had wanted them dead. Had the Serpent King come from Iraland and given the pedlar the poison? Did he want to kill her? Or did he think Hefnir had stayed with her? Rakki stood close to her legs and she knew he was trying to comfort her. They moved off and Bera was glad to have him at her heels. Sometimes she liked dogs better than people.

Don't think about the Serpent King. It gives him too much power.

'I was really thinking about Hefnir.'

You watch for signs of him in Heggi all the time. It would be a kindness to him, you know, to stop.

Heggi dawdled. 'Do you miss Valdis?'

'Sigrid will care for her and Borgvald.'

'You never answer questions. You're as bad as my father.' It made her jump. He really was growing up, perhaps better than she feared.

'I know what the fight was about,' he said.

It was his way to trade truths.

'I will miss the baby,' Bera said, 'but it helps to have you with me.'

Heggi beamed. It was the right thing to say.

'So what did start the fight?'

'Oh. Dellingr said Faelan poisoned us.'

'He knows full well who brought the mead.'

'He's been saying Faelan's mother brewed it and that's why she died, from getting wolfsbane stuff on her hands.'

'Hel's teeth!'

Bera wanted to reassure him, but did Dellingr know something she didn't? What did she really know of Faelan's mother? Was the Watcher truly her Fetch? Could she trust a man called Wolf? Had they walked into a trap?

Deal only with what is certain.

Heggi's face was pink and he wouldn't meet her eyes.

'What else did Dellingr say?'

He scuffed the earth.

'I need to know, boykin.'

'Stuff. You know… you staying away all night.'

'Burying Faelan's mother!'

'But I've heard… folk say about Vallas… and your face does go funny when you look at Faelan.'

It was Bera's turn to go pink.

'So can we go back?' Heggi whispered, though Faelan was a good way ahead.

Bera pointed at the grey cloud that filled the north sky. 'That's not a woven door-hanging, Heggi. I have to get to Smolderby and find out how to stop it. And you are my second.'

She had to look her feelings for Faelan squarely in the face.

She was watching his every graceful move and not because she suspected him.

They caught up with Faelan and Heggi started to copy him. When Faelan went behind a bush to relieve himself Heggi joined him, and then his dog strutted in and cocked a leg. Bera and Heggi laughed but Faelan was grumpy, though he tried to hide it by telling them what birds they were hearing and naming animals. Perhaps he disliked being laughed at. Bera told him she liked learning and his mood slowly improved. They stopped for some food and Rakki lay beside Faelan. Dogs were good judges of character. Bera decided she would not let Dellingr's suspicion of him outweigh her own judgement ever again.

It felt better when they set off again. They were travelling companions and Bera wanted to take in the country properly. Greater knowledge would bring better prediction and perhaps help her learn how to preserve it for her children and the rest of her folk.

Rolling dips in the landscape overflowed with thousands of blue flowers, like a deep ocean swell. Their petals shimmered, trembling in a stiffening sea breeze that whispered of loss. The tide had turned. Bera let the yearning pass. The same flowers kept with them until gloaming, when their colour turned as ashy as hot pebbles before a wave wets them.

They walked until Heggi dropped onto his knees, saying he was about to die.

Faelan lifted him up. 'Come on. We're close to camp now, safer than here.'

Their camp was a small hollow that sheep used as a rubbing place. There were clumps of wool caught on brambles and a few dried turds like cod roe. The three of them kicked the earth clear and stamped it flattish, got a small fire going, gathered some moss and laid their bedrolls on it. It was snug. They were too tired to talk over their meal and the others fell asleep quickly but Bera could not get comfortable. Her breasts were tight and she missed Valdis so much she tugged her hair roots in silent anguish. Why was she aching again? Was it punishment for being such a bad mother? Rakki licked her face and lay down again with a deep sigh.

Heggi beckoned her over and when she sat beside him he clung to her, burying his face in her lap. A simple need for a mother. Perhaps he did feel his losses keenly. He kept trying to act older but she was his comfort and strength. Bera kissed his caffled hair. She would make sure his father's bad blood would never taint him. Her own dearest boykin.

The land opened in vastness, with bleached grass the colour of the horizon and a sky that was blue forever if you did not look to the north. There, Hel's snow-topped mountain was sending the plume as high as the sky was wide. Faelan caught her frown and they shared its warning. Only Heggi was his normal, unruly self again. He ran ahead with Rakki, returning with grazed knees and a filthy face. Over the next couple of days they caught enough wild creatures for them to eat well. Faelan treated him like an equal and Heggi respected him. Perhaps he would show Heggi another way to be a man. Hadn't Faelan offered it?

Faelan was a good travelling companion. He managed to eat without making sucking, slurping noises or ending up with a chin dripping in grease. He would tell Bera things, like explaining rivers to her, and draw a map in the dirt with a stick. As the map became the journey, he did not chatter but was knowledgeable and sure of the way. They would often smile at one another about Heggi's foolery, or the dog's.

Bera liked the freedom to think her own thoughts in the rhythm of walking. Her body was accustomed to it now, and young. No more aches. It was almost as good as being on a boat. Almost. But boats and the sea were her bones and blood. If only her father were here to build one.

Feel the east wind in the rigging
And the boat-song in your blood.

The other two were watching her.

'She's thinking about Ottar,' Heggi told Faelan. 'Her father. I liked him.'

'We three are all orphans now,' said Faelan.

His look made Bera forget the loss. For once she was glad of her open face and when he smiled she watched for the crinkles at the corners of his eyes and noticed a line down his cheek. This feeling was completely new to her. Was it possible to fall in love with someone's face?

They passed through a succession of gnarled forests. The trees were twisted and spindly, with grass and blue flowers growing tall beneath their latticed canopy. Dappled sunlight mottled the wood. Bera welcomed the coolness every time they entered one and was dazzled by a white sun when they emerged.

'There should be birdsong,' Faelan said.

'Birds are the first to sense disturbance,' said Bera.

They looked up at a sky empty of birds, and then inland to what threatened every creature, if they knew it.

The last wood they entered was so knotted and dense that hardly any light got through. Rakki sniffed the air and bolted, with Heggi hard on his heels. There was a scuffle, a frenzy of barking and then a long, shrill squeal.

'I know what that is.' Bera tugged at her skirt which was snagged on thorns.

Faelan cast around then picked up a sturdy, straight stick. 'You should get your weapon ready, in case.' He took out a heavy sword.

Bera patted her own sword and they set off towards the sounds.

'Where do the wild pigs come from?' she asked.

'Brought by the first settlers, the Westermen. They left them here to breed for when they came back to settle later.'

'Why are you angry? It was a good idea, wasn't it?'

'They weren't the only things left here to breed.'

Heggi stood over a striped, tawny piglet, its throat already cut. Rakki was lapping its blood.

'We braved others and everything!' he said.

'What others?' Bera asked, airily.

Heggi busied himself whittling one end of Faelan's stick, while he did the other end with three quick slashes.

Faelan ran the sharpened stick through its body. 'The mother will come, for sure, so best get away.'

He gestured to Heggi and together they lifted it onto their shoulders. Heggi struggled for balance but then they set off, heading for a gap. Rakki's mind crackled with excitement and fear. He stayed beside Bera, who quickly whispered her sorrow and thanks.

Outside the canopy, the wide sky began to oppress her with its sheer size. It was a deep-blue lid, shutting her in with Hel.

Her skern held a buttercup under his chin.

'What are you doing?'

Seeing if I like butter.

'Ridiculous.' But he had made her smile.

She hurried to catch up with the others, who had got ahead despite the weight they carried. As soon as he saw Bera, Heggi stopped and rubbed his shoulder.

'This stick digs into me,' he said. 'It hurts.'

'Am I to kiss it better?'

Heggi gave her a look but when they set off he started complaining again.

'Can't we stop for a bit? This is really heavy.'

Faelan kept going. 'We need to get well clear of the wild pigs.'

'But I'm smaller than you so I've got all the weight!'

Without a word, Bera lifted the pole from his shoulders and carried it. She and Faelan were so similar in height that it was almost level. Heggi joyfully frisked away, tiredness gone.

They walked over a black plain full of sharp, crumbling rocks that Faelan called brymstones. They looked worm-eaten and dusty. Large, round, striped stones marked their path, also spewed from the cone-shaped mountains that loomed much closer now. Bera could see them striding away into the north, linked like the beads of her necklace, and had a vision of eruptions that had happened right here. Darkness swept like a shadow over the land as an ash cloud fell, settling on the dry, white bones of animals. It was an age ago.

Here now, a speedwell-blue lake reflected the quiet mountains in stillness. The colour of Faelan's eyes. Sudden rain shattered its surface, falling in grey slants that made the mountains vanish. Just as quickly, it swept out to sea, leaving the soft sound of water in the air. Faelan said it was coming from invisible streamlets. Bera listened to its song for the rest of the day and forgot the weight of the pig.

They came to a lonely hovel, which Faelan called a croft.

'I stay overnight here whenever I travel to Smolderby.'

An old woman was outside combing some wool and she waved when she saw them. When they reached her she slapped Faelan on the back and gestured at the piglet excitedly, opening her mouth to show Bera she had no teeth to eat meat.

Bera promised her a stew. 'If you have any vegetables I'll make it with the offal and mash it for you.'

The crofter nodded and beckoned her into a dark, cool stone store, which held plenty of preserved root crops. Faelan butchered the small boar outside, letting Bera and Heggi rest. When he finished, he joined Heggi while Bera went through to the fire. There was a delicious smell of roasting meat from the haunch roasting on the spit. Bera dribbled as she made the stew and was glad she did not have to speak.

Much later, the suckling pig lived up to its promise. It had died for them to live; that was the way of things. Though, as Bera pointed out, it didn't need to be so delicious. The old woman slurped slowly through two bowlfuls of stew. Hard to eat quietly when you had no teeth. No one said much, as if the crone's dumbness had struck them all.

Tiredness really hit after the meal and they were all yawning, even the dog. Heggi placed his bedroll on the same side of the fire as Faelan, purposely crossing over to the male side. In truth, he was on the threshold, back and forth, like his warbling voice. Bera hoped that when he settled it would be Faelan's type of manhood.

Long after their breathing was deep, Bera was wide awake. She longed for rest but it hurt to lie in any of her favourite positions and she was wracked with all the worries she'd pushed away during the walk. The old crofter must have been watching, for she gently touched Bera's back, to let her know she was there. Her warm eyes spoke of understanding and she rolled a thick sheepskin, hugged it, and then pushed it at Bera. She took the sheepskin into her bedroll and thanked the woman, moved by her everyday kindness. The crone gave her some dried lavender, which Bera put under her head, and she curled round the sheepskin and fell into a deep sleep.

Next morning she woke feeling better than she had since having the baby. She pulled Heggi by the scruff to the river and Faelan kept hold of him to make him submit to washing. Rakki knew it was a game and splashed round them dementedly and then the boy and his dog ran about the field, full of the madness of icy water. While Faelan mended their shoes with more fish skins, the old crofter took Bera's hand and led her to a greyish green plant growing outside the pantry door. She tapped her head, frowning then smiling, and Bera was sure the plant was to relieve worry. They picked some of its rough, dry leaves, took them inside and the woman mashed a beakerful in hot water. She had the same skill with plants as Bera and she drank it down, hoping it would work quickly. She wondered what she could do to repay the crofter and went outside to bring in some logs, as a start. Then she had an idea.

Faelan was parcelling the meat.

'Time to leave,' he said. 'We need to round up Heggi.'

'I want to thank the old woman first,' Bera said.

'Don't be too long.'

'I'll come out as soon as I'm done.'

Bera went back inside, banked up the fire and filled a bowl with hot water from the pot. She placed a stool by the hearth and gestured for the old woman to sit on it. There was a drying cloth on the table, which Bera soaked in the warm water. She unlaced the woman's tattered tunic and then she began to bathe her back. It was what a daughter would do.

'Has anyone ever cared for you?' she asked.

The woman patted her hand but it was no answer. She reached down by the side of the fire and handed Bera a small salve pot. She took the lid off: it was a sweet-smelling balm. Bera rubbed it into the woman's back, easing her work-knotted shoulders, then helped her dress.

'Hurry up, Bera!' Heggi shouted from outside.

The woman got up, kissed Bera's cheek and pushed the salve pot into her hands. Bera's apron became a medicine chest, with two remedies and the salve. They left quickly and Bera told them what she had done. Faelan was pleased.

'It's lonely for her,' Bera said.

'My mother used to share herb lore with her, and plants. It's not so far, by horse. I'll make sure she doesn't starve.'

Another reason for Bera to like him. As they walked on and the homesteads increased, she began to get the scope of people living here. There were a few crofts but most folk had bigger homesteads, full of crops and animals. The folk from Seabost were a tiny few of the many settlers that had come to Ice Island, both now and in the past. They were all linked. It gave her a sense of the connectedness of everything and she discovered that mattered to her. It was a reason to leave her baby behind and made her even more determined to safeguard their future.

The land changed into a green wilderness and silver-maned horses galloped away like spilled mercury. Meadows were molten gold with buttercups but there was no sign of any livestock.

Heggi asked, 'Why aren't there cows and things?'

'Buttercups are poisonous,' Faelan said.

'I know that,' he said and thwacked them with a stick.

The next fields billowed amethyst with giant wild pea plants. Close to, they were like bobbled brands, tapered and spike-leaved.

Heggi pointed at her necklace. 'All the colours of your beads.'

A mossy valley came next, pressed on and shaded by green mountains so high that Bera's neck hurt to look up at the peaks. A tremor of energy in the bubbling springs that came surging up through the ground filled her with wildness. She grabbed Heggi and they flung themselves down on the mossy grass and rolled and rolled, laughing, tickling each other, while Rakki frisked about. Faelan watched them, laughing, then called them for some food. Bera gave Rakki some cheese and hugged and kissed him. Life was good – no matter what lay in front of them.

The air became heavier. Bera's cheeks were wet and her dress clung to her. It was cooling at first, then cold, and she took her sea cloak out of her pack and pulled it round her. They heard the distant thunder of a waterfall. After a while they saw its rainbow mist and then the white spindrift of the highest falls Bera had ever seen. She gaped at its plummet, deafened. It made the world bigger than she could ever imagine, and the sky higher. How could she save anything in such a place? Heggi's eyes were as wide as his mouth but his shout was lost beneath the boom. Faelan nodded, to show he understood their awe.

Bera refused to move on until she had reckoned this place. It made her feel like an ant – but there was some gift it had to give her. She stubbornly stood, while the others mouthed words, and then she lost sense of them and let the falls speak.

When she was ready, she joined them, but all she could tell them was that they must be determined and brave. Water needed no words; its purity and force had swept away doubt. She was ready to face whoever had summoned her. Understanding would come later: Vallas ruled Fate.

They walked for the rest of the day, made solemn by the waterfall; even Rakki, who gravely led the way. The ground was going slowly uphill and at the far end of the valley they came to a steep drop. Bera gasped. Another world spread out before them: scores of farmsteads leading towards the smoking mass of a mighty settlement.

'Smolderby,' said Faelan, though it was obvious.

'Where's the bay?' asked Heggi.

A sea fog was lying low over the water. A sudden breeze swelled in and it lifted like a veil. Hanging for an instant in the blue distance were three long dragonboats.

13

'Another day and we're there,' Faelan said.

'Is it called Smolderby because the sea's on fire?' asked Heggi.

'It's not fire,' Bera said, certain that it soon would be.

She glanced to the north at the glimmering redness, and away before Heggi noticed.

Faelan winked. He knew she was trying not to frighten the boy. 'It's not smoke,' he said. 'It's steam rising into the air.'

Heggi let out a fart of scorn. 'So the sea is a kind of stew?'

'It's where hot water meets cold,' Faelan said. 'There are hot water springs all over Ice Island, even under the sea.'

Not only hot water. Bera's scalp prickled. 'At the birthing...' she began.

Faelan waited for her to finish but her throat ached with tears she would not surrender to.

'I miss Valdis too,' said Heggi, surprising her.

He gave her a fierce hug, then ran ahead with his dog.

'I was trying not to speak of the vision,' she said.

Faelan rubbed his chin where a beard was starting. 'We're nearly there and I'm wondering why you have not asked me who it is you're going to meet.'

'That's because I already know,' said Bera, sure it was the humpback, Crowman. 'But do you?'

Faelan picked up his bag. 'Of course. But I was told that if you knew, you wouldn't come.'

Her stomach lurched. 'Those dragonboats – I'm not meeting sea-riders, am I?'

His look made her apologise at once. He would not be taking

her to the Serpent King and yet… he was vile enough to have some power over Faelan, with his serpent cross.

Black clouds bunched like a fist while they were exposed in the middle of the open plain. Gusts made wild wind-horses prance and skite, their manes and tails streaming, and then became a constant air song, whistling shrilly through spiny trees and in grasses. Faelan's hat blew away.

'That storm's coming fast,' Bera said. 'It's a bad place for it to find us.'

'That's why I have a hood. I've been here before.' Faelan pulled the greased wool down to his eyebrows.

She glared at his covered head and then pulled a blanket from her bedroll and got Heggi to hold two of the corners, making a rough booth over them both. Rain hit. The wind shrieked like the ancestors in Seabost and was as vicious. A violent blast made Heggi stagger and he lost one end. The sodden blanket flogged them until Bera managed to grab it again. The two of them clung together. Her hair was soaked and stung her eyes, so she kept them closed with her back to the weather but it managed to drench her.

They waited for the cloudburst to pass and then made a run for shelter through driving rain. It was an old sheep hut that rattled and sighed, buffeted by wave after wave of squalls, but better than their sodden blanket, which Bera and Heggi stretched out between them and twisted from both ends to wring the water out.

Faelan shouted, 'When the wind eases we'll make for Smolderby.'

Bera nodded. A night in wet clothes and no fire would be deadly.

The settlement was a distant smudge through misty rain when they set off. It was hard to walk in clothes that weighed like lead. The air grew chill as winter. A few wild horses stood bunched, enduring the biting gusts that drilled through to Bera's wet skin. There was no shelter in sight. It was as if the island was trying to shake her off.

Heggi refused to get under the blanket. 'I want to keep moving.'

'It will be worse very soon,' Bera said.

Faelan joined them this time, with Rakki sheltering between their legs. They all huddled together in a ripe fug of wet wool and dog. A downdraught of icy air blasted them, followed by hailstones that dropped straight down from the sky. The blanket wasn't thick enough and Bera's scalp was battered. When she tried to bunch it up she took the full force of hail and sleet in the face, blinding her, so she quickly burrowed underneath again as best she could, trying to hold on with freezing fingers.

The wind rose a notch or two and small twisters formed across the steely water of the bay. Rising white shapes like wraiths, spiralling in a dance of death, began to move closer. They were coming to get her and carry her out to sea over the long waves; out, out, to the deeps beyond the whale roads. A secret part of her welcomed them in. But she was a mother! She must refuse its promise and run. Bera pulled away into the open and hit a wall of air. She staggered, desperate to escape the wraiths. The others grabbed and anchored her but the wind was a ghastly scream and none of them could move further. Heggi's mouth was forming words in the shriek and whine of spiteful gusts and the drumming beat of ice stones big as toads on hard earth. She shouted and her spit hit his face. Bera couldn't breathe, couldn't stand upright; they were all bent against the wind, being pushed backwards. Faelan tried to take Heggi but she clasped him tight against her body. He meant to help – but she would never entrust him to someone else, as she had on the passage from Seabost.

Lightning.

She saw their little group as if from above: a knot of sheer misery on the open plain. More lightning, Thor's hammer striking the ground in savage spikes.

Thunder.

Then rain; rain that should be kinder than hail but coming sideways in sheets that snatched at her skirts and lashed her legs like whips. Bera planted her feet, knees slightly bent, bearing down to stay grounded, as she had on the *Raven*. She kept her arms round Heggi's head and he held tight, lurching in the squalls that were punishing, savage, vicious and personal. Faelan was too slight to keep them steady. Out here, alone, they were certain to be charred by a thunderbolt.

You're the Valla.

Bera found the locked self inside her that she had once packed away on the sea passage. The self who had shattered a Drorgher like stamping on ice by unleashing her strong will. She drew up her own strength into her eyes and then hurled it at the elements.

The wind dropped and she was giddy in the silence. The high, dark clouds scudded out to sea, taking the thunder with them.

'You're hurting my hand,' said Heggi.

That night the mountain began to melt. Bera woke to a sense of dread and looked inland, where the dull redness had turned into a funeral pyre of the gods. It was still so far away from them that she could feel no heat but Hel was flexing her muscles in warning. The smoke that poured from the cone was a writhing black serpent against the flames that reached up to swallow the stars.

'Has the worst begun?' Faelan whispered.

He was so close that she felt his breath.

'My obsidian bead is linked to it somehow.'

'What is it doing?'

She turned so that he could feel its heat and his face was above hers, lit by distant flame.

'Will we live, Bera?'

She was unable to speak, for many reasons.

He looked unbearably sad. 'First light, we'll set off again. I would have liked a longer time with you.'

Bera looked away. In that moment she realised that she had been trying to make him love her. It wasn't planned; she was unused to approving looks from any man and mistook that craving for love. He would be a friend for as long as they lived, but nothing more.

Now Bera knew what a city looked like. It was surrounded by farmsteads and then row after row of homesteads with smallholdings, markets, wash houses, hot tubs and tradesmen. It was like kicking an ants' nest. Folk scurried busily, pouring round them, intent on their own affairs, chattering. Besides the constant smell of sulfur there were other layers: fresh bread and dung; herbs and sweat; tanned leather, hot metal and blood. There were at least three forges and Bera felt a pang for preventing Dellingr from coming. She'd had no idea it was like this, though. Such plenty.

Faelan was heading for the bay at city speed. First they passed through a smart area where jewellers worked in fine gold and silver. Then there was cheaper jewellery in lead or copper before they hit the wynds, which pinched folk to move tighter and faster. Bera's breaths were short and shallow against the stench. She kept tight hold of Heggi's hand. A heap of leather offcuts marked where boots were made and repaired, with hanging straps, sheaths and scabbards. Next door was a maker of punches, awls and creasers, then a bone-carver showing skates and tools; decorated combs, brooches and pins; rings, gaming pieces and every size of needle and spindle. A woman was spinning yarns of every hue. The distant hum became a loud buzzing. Outside a baker's shop was a small child pulling a piece of string taut. It had small bones along it and the noise probably kept flies away.

It all terrified Rakki, who pressed himself so close that she kept tripping over him. Heggi slowed, gawping at a woman with her dress round her ears, squatting in a corner to relieve herself. Bera pulled him away, terrified of losing Faelan in the crowd. Here, his black hair wasn't so strange and sometimes she lost sight of him and then struggled to keep up. Sudden shouts and running feet, different bells and coarse laughter confused her. She lost sight of the sky and was thrown off her bearings. Her wet clothes chafed under her armpits and she had blisters. Bera longed to be way out at sea, with clean sharp air and the cries of seabirds, not pressed in this reeking throng that snatched away any Valla skill. Well, courage would have to be enough.

At last the smells grew sweeter as they passed cup- and bowl-makers supplying food sellers. There were also stalls packed with all kinds of plants and seeds, from green through to bright red. Bera could not name any by sight except possibly dill.

Then the tang of salt and a gull scream welcomed them to

the bay, with a row of ramshackle shanties at the tideline. Faelan gestured towards a newer wooden hut that reminded Bera of her first home. He opened the door and went straight in. They hurried to follow. Bera searched the gloom for the Crowman but it was too dark. She closed her eyes to get them accustomed, then opened them again. Blue-slatted light showed no one else was in there. The smells of pitched wood, fish oil and old rope brought back a yearning for her father and the boats he built. She wished she had her time with Ottar again.

'We're to wait here,' said Faelan.

'Can I go and explore?' asked Heggi.

When Crowman came, Bera needed to speak frankly. 'Just this shore and don't let Rakki chase off. Put this bit of rope round his neck.' She took a short length off the bench and handed it to him.

Faelan warned Heggi to stay at their end of the bay. 'That's where all the trading's done, further down there, see? Where the smoke's drifting? There's tough men that side.'

'Off those dragonboats?'

'Stay where we can see you,' Bera said.

She followed them out of the sea door and walked to the end of a rickety wooden jetty. Heggi and Rakki jumped down onto the beach with a rattle of slatey shingle. They raced towards the sea, luckily in the right direction. Faelan stood beside her, watching them. She had no special sense of danger but the city had confused her. Out in the bay, billows of steam wafted in thick veils, showing and then hiding the dragonboats.

'Sea-riders?' she asked. 'Those aren't warships though.'

'Those are only the usual trading pirates, from Dyflin.'

The sea fret whispered onto the shore.

'I can't see Heggi now.'

Bera listened hard, then swept her arms about as if she could clear the mist away. Faelan caught her wrist and held it. Two people, close and secret, in a white cloud. She had the strange sensation of falling.

There was hollow barking and then the plash, plash of short oars, sounding loud in the smoky fog. A small round boat emerged, tarred black, rowed by a single person, with a silver halo of hair. Easily mistaken for a boy.

'You're right,' Bera said. 'If you'd told me who it was I wouldn't have come.'

14

'I'll fetch Heggi,' Faelan said, and left.

Egill walked along the small jetty, unsmiling, unrepentant. Dressed in finer clothes.

'Bera.'

The warmth in her voice touched the quick of Bera's need for a friend. As it always had.

'Did you send for me?' she asked.

'I hear you have a baby girl now.'

'Was it you who sent the rider with poison mead?'

'No.'

'What are you doing here, then?'

'We need you.'

They circled round each other. Bera struggled to recognise the frightened, half-mad creature she had last seen in this strong, assured boy. Except she knew for certain that there was a girl's body underneath. There were so many times in the past that Bera had wanted to throttle Egill and yet there was an innocence about her that made friendship possible. She had a shared understanding of Bera's aloneness that made her leaving Bera to go off with Hefnir an even worse betrayal; yet somehow it was possible to forgive. Her fluid magic had the same effect on everyone. As for trust, though… surely none could exist after that.

Bera wanted to prick her calmness. 'How many of your new friends know you're a girl?'

'Still black and white, Bera? I can be whatever I choose – though I suppose at some point they'll start wondering why I'm not growing a beard.'

'That's not all they'll wonder about, unless you've changed. Like who your real friends are.'

'Is it a sin to want to be happy, Bera? In the land I love?'

'You're not in Iraland now, are you?'

'I came back for you.'

'What makes me doubt that?'

'I'm here, aren't I? Not Iraland, with its holy waters and proper, decent folk. Prayers, plainsong.'

'Come inside.' Egill drew something from under her tunic, touched her forehead and lips with it and pushed it away again. Bera tugged it out. This cross was made of black wood: the vertical bar longer than the one across and writhing round both, the serpent.

'The serpent again!' Bera was angry. 'What are you doing with this and not a Thor hammer, Egill? What secret faith do you belong to? The Serpent King's?'

Egill was trampling on her trust in Faelan, whose serpent cross was so similar.

'You understand things of power, Bera. This is mine.'

'This is no Valla necklace! You understand nothing, as ever! Even I didn't, until recently.'

'Tell me then.'

Bera only knew the black and amber beads balanced each other somehow but that sounded slight. The suffocating city was muffling any new skill she had too. She did not want to tell Egill, who was certain to deliver some warning and somehow weaken it further.

The door flew open and Heggi burst in.

'I'm starving!'

Egill laughed. 'You haven't changed, I see.'

Faelan explained they had to eat at a tavern and after the promise of meat, Heggi allowed him to grip his hand as he led them through a different, rougher part of town. Egill brought up the rear, so Bera couldn't get lost. It managed to be even more crowded and putrid than the wynds. Egill told her they were passing the place where graves were dug and leather tanned by the same men. The reek was almost visible and Bera squeezed her nose and breathed through her mouth. Then they were in narrow twittens where hard-faced women herded animals with skitters towards their slaughter. There was the rust of butchered flesh and runnels of blood, dung heaps picked over by mired pigs and dusty chickens, and gutters full of everything that seeped away from the rotting glut of life. Even when they were clear of the shambles and she let go of her nose, the air was foul with the breath of pinched folk bartering, shouting. The din! But there was no joy or laughter, no song of fellowship, no sense of belonging. This stale, drab bustle would turn to panic and violence when the eruption started. It was getting closer. Bera felt the beating of Hel's heart of flame. And the rats were running. She felt like a rat herself: their little party, scuttling through twittens before the slow drunks in doorways could swing at them. Rakki was scared of the bristling cats that arched and spat at him.

Then they were gone. No Faelan, no Heggi, no dog.

A hand clasped her ankle and Bera fell, knocking her breath away as she was pulled into a passageway. Filthy hands were all over her, scrabbling at her brooches and rings, in her hair. A hand smelling of fish and something earthier covered her mouth. Bera gagged. She kicked out and tried to shout but the person clasped her face so tightly that she could hardly breathe. Fingers slid up her thigh and she tasted the hot bile of outrage, as she had once before. She fought hard but this time there were too many of them. Her disgust vanished and Bera bit hard, tasting blood. Someone yanked her hair and pulled her head away. She kicked and elbowed herself free; leaped to her feet and got her sword out.

She was in a dead end, shanty huts all round her, facing a tattered mob of urchins, as feral and starved as the cats. Children. Their eyes looked huge in their grimy faces, weighing up their chance of more theft. Where was Egill?

They closed in stealthily, as if they were playing bully-bully.

'Don't you dare,' Bera growled.

And then Rakki was there beside her, snarling, followed by Egill, sword raised.

Bera spat on her sword hand. 'You'd better run fast before I decide to punish you.'

The children jeered.

'ALU,' roared Bera, touching the runes on the blade.

The urchins ran to the far end of the twitten and scrambled up the wall like green crabs on a wreck. Rakki leapt at them, nipping at their heels, but they were too fast.

Bera turned on Egill. 'Where were you?'

'We're here right beside you.'

'If you'd come at them from behind…' She trailed off. Neither of them would have killed children.

'I went through that fishmonger's store, look.'

Bera checked her things. 'They've run off with my best brooches.'

She felt a sharp pang. One was a marriage gift from Hefnir, her first and last link with him. A clasped silver grooming set that had belonged to his wife, Heggi's mother. Bera was going to give it to Heggi's wife, perhaps Ginna.

Egill was speaking: '… plenty more at the Abbotry. Silver, gold, all that. Not as good as Iraland, of course.'

'Is Heggi all right?'

'They were well ahead of us. Faelan will keep him safe.' Egill sheathed her sword. 'They should be there by now.'

'Did you know I'd be trapped, Egill? How do you know Faelan?'

'Doesn't your skern have any answers?'

Bera hated the fog of suspicion and confusion. Her only workable instinct was to head seaward, no matter where she was.

'I need clean air. Let's go.'

Bera followed Rakki and they charged past hovels with new sources of grime and stench. Then they were through, close to the sea. She faced to windward and breathed deeply, letting the salt air cleanse her lungs. The dog took a scent and raced off, nose to the sand.

Egill took her hand. 'The tavern's just along here. I bet Rakki's picked up their scent.'

'Couldn't we have rowed round?'

'Faelan keeps his boat this side, where it's deeper.'

As they went down to the shore, a line of black rocks came into view. They spiked the centre of the bay, like the spine of a sea monster, coming ashore and separating it into the two beaches. You would need to be careful at high water, even if you knew they were there. If you didn't, they would rip the bottom out of any boat.

'Why does Faelan keep a boat this side?'

'Shellfish.'

Egill began scrambling over the ridge of stones that were the spine come onto land. They were rounded by sea-pounding and covered in weed, so she slipped and slithered, crashing into Bera and knocking her down. They rolled on top of each other, towards the water. Bera shrieked, shrill and beside herself after being so pent up and afraid.

'You sound like a squealer pig,' Egill joked.

Bera, suddenly furious, pushed her. Egill drew her sword and her eyes were dark.

'Put your sword away, Egill. If you sent for me, you know I must live.'

Egill sheathed her sword. She held out her hand and Bera took it. They listened to the waves washing the shore.

'Would you have used it on the urchins?' Bera asked.

Egill took time answering. 'I'm not the person I was.'

'So I see.'

'It's not always the right choice to kill.'

'Unless it's a blood debt.'

'I'm not sure a blood debt is ever the right choice.'

Bera felt heat rising from her stomach. This was the old Egill, putting on airs copied from Iraland. It was a betrayal of where she was born and a criticism.

'So you think everything I do is wrong, do you?' Bera said. 'That I'm some idiot thrall with stupid beliefs that you can just kill?'

'I think you're scared, to be honest. I keep telling you: life isn't as black and white as you see it.'

Bera strode off.

'I'm not scared,' she shouted at the darkening sky.

They entered a wide shack, like a shrunken mead hall, where blowsy women and tough-looking men traded goods in a blue haze. They traded bodies too. Bera was glad to see Heggi at a long table with Faelan, then worried about him seeing the proceedings at close quarters. The noise was making her head ring.

'Is this a tavern, then?' she shouted.

'Or alehouse. We have lots of them in Iraland, near Abbotry, cos the ale's best.'

'Egill – is there anything I could show you that Iraland hasn't done first and better?'

'No.' She meant it.

They barged their way through the jostling crowd to Heggi, who was alone now.

'Faelan's gone to get food,' he shouted.

The scrubbed table almost ran the whole length of the shack. It was full of folk, slurping, clattering, shouting, laughing. Bera's stomach knotted with unease.

Rakki gave a sharp bark, hackles up, and gave chase under the table, through everyone's feet.

She grabbed Heggi. 'Stay here. Rats are on the move.'

'I know. Other creatures are too.'

Heggi made no move to follow his dog. Perhaps he sensed danger too. There was a new threat here, not like fighting Drorghers or beasts of prey. These were mortal men, but brutal, like the Serpent King. Pirates and sea-riders, with dragon tattoos. Bera watched Egill, trying to match her friend against this new world. Was life always going to be like this? Every time Bera won a battle, she was plunged into some new world where she could not read the signs, some new person to challenge her.

First copy the new ways, then learn how to command them.

Faelan returned with two big bowls of stew. Bera hoped he would sit next to her but he went straight off again. Someone sat at the far end of their bench and Bera was forced to slide along, ending up next to a huge man who smelled of tar. His massive forearm lay on the table, one hand on his knife. His tattoos were marks like runes. She tried scrying to make out what they might mean.

'Kiss my arse,' he growled.

Her spoon dropped into her bowl and hot stew skit her.

His laugh was not for sharing. 'Kiss my arse, girlie. That's my little joke.'

He wiped his mouth with the back of his hand, leaving a wide snail trail of grease on it.

'What do the runes say?' Bera would not be cowed.

'Them signs bring good things to me.'

Egill leaned in. 'But not to you, Bera. Keep away.'

'Is he from Iraland?'

'Eat your stew and don't look at him.'

Egill's new forcefulness was troubling. Then she gave Bera a secret, shared smile and suddenly the old warmth flickered. Perhaps she was trying to put her desertion right, and on that same landfall beach Bera had vowed that things would be more open on Ice Island. She would work to make their friendship right.

Faelan returned and sat between her and the tattooed man. There was so much Bera wanted to ask him but no one talked. Secrets and lies teemed in this nest. At least the food was honest and good. She used it to tamp down her fears and sharpen her mind, so she and Heggi had second helpings. Faelan fetched them and then left.

They soon finished and Egill showed them into a small room off the main one. It had no windows but there was a thin fire, which dimly lit a lumpen figure on a chair. Faelan was on a stool next to him, his trim figure making the person look even more mangled. Old – and a humpback. Crowman.

Faelan got up. 'This is Cronan. The man who sent for you.'

'Cronan?' She had misheard the name but was reassured that otherwise her Valla powers had been correct. Then her stomach churned at the confirmation that her vision must also be real.

Heggi pulled at Bera's sleeve. 'I need to find Rakki.'

'No, I don't want—'

'We'll both look for him.' Faelan gave Heggi a shove. 'Come on, fellow. I challenge you to a stone-skimming contest.'

'I'll win, won't I, Bera?' His face was free of recent care.

'Let Rakki find you,' she said. 'Look after them, Faelan.'

'Always,' he replied quietly. It sounded like a promise of more.

Light came and went as they stepped out.

'You can trust this man,' Egill said. 'Cronan's holy.'

Bera wondered if the humpback had seen her in the same dream. If he had, it would be the first time and another sign that her returning Valla powers were to be trusted.

'I'm Bera,' she said.

'Tide's turned.' He gave an odd gesture as he stood, making his head dip further to one side.

He was as short as her because of his deformity. The knobbled curve of his spine showed through the linen tunic.

'You're wondering why no one stoned me. I live in the Abbotry. They would say that God makes them charitable. I would say that my gift is too precious to them.'

'What is your gift?' she asked.

'They forgive my appearance for the sake of my sight.'

'I thought you were blind.'

'Purblind. But I'm talking about inner vision.' The humpback pulled back his sleeve and turned his wrist over. Blue veins coursed down towards his palm, beneath a tattoo that looked like Th and S runes together. She wished it did not look so much like Faelan's cross and serpent.

'Touch.'

'I have reason to distrust folk with tattoos.'

'This is the true god, Brid. She is three women in one. A poet, a smith and a doctor. Touch it.'

'Why?'

'You either feel it… or not,' he said. 'I think you will.'

Bera hated doing it but wanted to know more. Even before she reached the mark the air crackled like frost and she had an answer.

'I have to go north.'

'Brid has revealed herself to you.' He pushed his sleeve down. 'The Abbotry lies north and west. We go to Obsidian.'

'What do you know about it?'

'I am the one who first recognised the power of the black stone. I am the one who saw the special woman with the beads.'

Bera moved closer to see him better. She decided to give the man a chance to prove his worth; after all, Agnar may have been old and blind but he brought her nothing but luck. Cronan's face was open, easily read, and not as old as she had thought.

She placed a finger on the tattoo at his wrist. 'I've seen this before.'

'Then you know that if you see it, you can trust him.' His voice was warm.

'It's the sign of our faith, so we know one another,' Egill chipped in.

Bera was tart. 'Have you got a tattoo, then?'

'Not yet, no.'

'She has to earn the mark of Brid,' Cronan said. 'As do we all.'

'I wear this.' Egill pulled out the leather thong from her neck.

'So what did you do to earn that, Egill?' Bera hated the serpent signs.

'Keep your voices down!' Cronan spoke urgently. 'Faelan will be watching outside – but folk are killed for their faith.'

'The sea-riders in there won't let anyone through.' Egill nodded towards the inner door.

Bera was genuinely unsure whose side Egill would be on. She was confused herself, if the sea-riders were enemies of the serpent faith. She felt trapped, which she detested.

'Then whisper as low as you like but you will tell me. Why have you brought me here?'

The humpback lowered himself painfully onto a chair. 'Only you can get us into the tower within the tower.'

15

'What is a tower? I want plain speaking now,' said Bera.

Cronan struggled to alter his position. He moaned softly with the pain of it but without complaint. She could be kinder to the bent person in front of her. As she tried to ease him upright, she touched his back. The small crookedness of his bones were like a broken bird she had picked up once, fallen from an eagle's beak. She moved closer, to be gentle. There was some kind of peppery sweetness on his roughly weaved clothing.

She sneezed.

'Ensense,' he said. 'It lets me see. You might say scry.'

Bera gasped, shocked at his skill but also full of hope that there was some other way of scrying.

He clicked his tongue. 'I'm no Valla. You know that.'

'Did you see me?'

Egill patiently explained. 'He saw a woman with beads. I'm here because only I knew it was you.'

'And you both know Faelan.' Bera turned to Cronan. 'Can you predict the future?'

'I render my visions and dreams.'

'Like whale oil?'

Egill snorted. 'He interprets, like you do. He's a seer, Bera. A holy man.'

Bera clung on to hope. 'So a holy man is like a Valla?

'Do not listen to Egill,' he said. 'Holy means without sin and only Brid is that.'

The others made a long cross on their bodies, as Bera had seen before. It excluded her – but their future was in her hands.

'Tell me what you saw!' She touched the man's hand. 'Please.'

'This foul air…' The man coughed, spat, then began. 'At the last ensense burning I saw the earth heaving and spewing fire, like a woman birthing, bathed in blood.'

'The same as me!'

'It was you, birthing a child of quicksilver from the earth's core.'

That slight shiver of fear. 'Valdis is flesh and blood and all the better for it.'

'Your baby can make silver,' he said.

'She makes nothing but noise,' Bera said, needing to keep her baby human.

Cronan smiled. 'Do not be afraid. I mean only that the child is a silversmith. Her grandmother is a poetess.'

'A real skald,' put in Egill.

'My mother is dead.'

'Alfdis lives on in you and in your daughter, Valdis.'

'Alfdis,' echoed other crow voices, 'and Valdis.'

'Is my mother with the crows?' she asked Cronan.

'What crows?'

She shivered. 'Voices I hear. Not my skern. These are sinister.'

Egill said, 'Brid is three women in one. A poetess, a smith and a doctor.'

'I heard it the first time.'

Cronan said, 'You are part of that.'

'I'm not Brid. I'm one woman: a Valla. A leader. A prophetess.'

'That's three. And Vallas heal, don't you?' asked Cronan.

Her skern was at her throat. *Let them believe what they like if you want to save folk. But hurry up.*

'I can heal. But I am not Brid!'

Her scalp flared and when she touched her beads the black one was too fiery to hold but it showed her an absence of light so total that she clawed at the air to pull it aside.

Egill caught her arm, 'What is it?' She had a vision of heaving blackness and Hel's breath was poison.

Bera ran to the door. 'We need to go. Now.'

'I call upon the serpent,' Egill said, raising her cross. 'Brid will protect us.'

The earth tilted. Outside, folk screamed and there was thunder.

'This is the end of the beginning,' said Cronan.

Crashes, shouts, pounding feet and cursing.

Bera staggered back to him. 'Come!'

'Run, both of you, I'll join you at the boat.'

Egill was urgent. 'I'll show you, Bera.'

Cronan clutched Bera's hand. 'Remember: you must enter the tower!'

The world slid. Egill fell to her knees and began to pray.

'Get up, Egill, and help!' Bera heaved Cronan from his chair. 'I'm not leaving you.'

The mountain had vanished behind a huge, shimmering cloud of thick ash that rained stones, which pelted down, burning. Maddened by pain and fear, folk ran in all directions, desperately seeking cover. But where? The wooden stalls and shanties were going up like pyres. Bera and Egill pulled their tunics over their heads and made a chair of their hands for Cronan. They stumbled their way down to the beach under the hail of firestones.

Faelan was at the water's edge, dragging Heggi. Rakki was not with them.

'Come on!' Bera cried. 'Nearly there!'

She took Cronan's weight again and she and Egill got him down to the shallows. Fear made them strong.

'Boat!' shouted Faelan above the rattling storm and hiss of fiery stones.

He pointed further along the shore to a narrow rowing boat and set off again, fixed on his own purpose, forgetting Heggi and offering no help to Egill and Bera. She told him to cover his head.

'Get to the boat, Heggi, and help him!'

'Rakki's gone…'

'Run!' screamed Bera.

They stumbled after him, trying to keep their heads covered and protect Cronan. It was slow.

'*Burning, burning, fire, burning,*' the crows urged with wild glee.

A blizzard of fiery fragments came down, hitting the sea, which exploded into hissing smoke. When it thinned, Bera scanned the beach. Heggi had stopped. His gaping mouth told her it was bad. Not Rakki! She followed his gaze along the shore, where Faelan was thrashing at his head and beating his shoulders.

He was on fire. Bera raced to him.

Faelan was roaring in agony, his whole cloak alight. Bera threw him to the ground and rolled him over and over in the deep sand, towards the sea. He was screaming, struggling, until a wave broke over him and he staggered into the water, pushing through desperate, wailing others, and went under. He did not come up.

'Brymstones!' screamed a man.

He barged into Bera, knocking her to the ground and trampled some children to reach the sea. She scrambled to her feet, cursing, ducked another fiery shower and desperately tried to see Faelan. It was impossible to make out anyone in the broil and she had to help the others.

Finally she caught sight of Heggi, running up and down the beach, yelling, frantic to find his dog. Egill was slumped on the shore, rocking, her new confidence melted away in the horror. Only Cronan had kept his wits and was trying to make progress. Bera headed for him, battling through screaming animals and people. A wave of frenzied people carried her with them out to sea and she went under. A man grasped her clothes, pulling her deeper, and then stood on her when she was on the seabed. She bit his leg, wrestled herself free and came up, spluttering, choking on salt water, eyes stinging, to face another pelting of burning hail. Her heavy clothes dragged her down but she was fuelled with the need to live and managed to haul herself out.

She had come up closer to Egill and ran to her.

'Get up,' she shouted. 'I can't do this alone.'

It was the old Egill, with eyes huge as moonstones.

'I c-can't…'

'Look at me. If we don't get that boat out now we will die here. I will keep you safe, Egill, but you have to move. Now.'

It was what Egill had always dreaded, coming to Ice Island, the memory of her father burned alive. Bera could see it playing out behind her eyes. How brave of her to return – but it served to show how important Bera's mission was. She had to rouse her by any means.

'We'll fry like your father if you don't shift!'

Egill was frozen with fear.

Bera slapped her. 'For Brid's sake, get up!'

It worked, though she had to drag Egill towards Cronan. All the while Bera was looking for Heggi and finally he was at the boat. He must have found Rakki. She needed to be there to help but felt hobbled and useless with Egill. And then they would have the humpback.

Cronan waved her on when they reached him. 'I'm too slow.'

'Take him, Egill.' Bera had no time to press her. 'I'll be at the boat. Hurry!'

She ducked another shower of firestones and was swept away again and again by maddened, scorched people. It was all a rush and confusion of terror but deathly slowness when she should be running.

By the time she got to the upturned boat, Heggi was gone. Mad with fear, still Bera knew she had to get the boat afloat, for all their sakes. With no one to help, she heaved under the rail, knowing it would be impossible for one person to right. She dropped it back on the sand, cursing like her father. Egill was closer. Bera ran to her and dragged her back to the boat, hoping Cronan could reach it in time.

Together she and Egill got the boat over and hauled it into the shallows. Bera kept her voice as calm as she could to keep her part of a team.

'Look, Egill, Faelan had water flagons under the boat and we must tie them to the rails. There might be food.'

Egill's eyes flicked about: sky, sea, sand, anywhere but at Bera.

'We are safe now we have the boat. Hold tight, Egill, and keep her steady. I'm going to fetch Cronan.'

Some people ran past and behind them was Heggi.

'Rakki!' His voice was hoarse with despair.

Bera yelled at him. 'Heggi! I'm here. Rakki will find us.'

She ducked as several huge brymstones hissed overhead but then Heggi was with her and they got Cronan to the boat.

He went straight to Egill. 'Look.' He pulled up his sleeve and kissed the serpent tattoo. 'Brid has protected us and we shall be saved.'

Egill touched her cross, through her tunic. 'Brid.'

After all her effort, Bera was furious that they thought it was this Brid but she needed a calm Egill to escape. They lifted Cronan into the boat, then Egill leaped aboard. Bera and Heggi pushed off into deeper water and Egill held the boat steady with an oar, without being told.

Bera linked her fingers for Heggi to step into the boat.

'I can't go without Rakki.'

She tipped him in and scrambled in afterwards. Heggi lunged for the side and the boat rocked as she seized his tunic and pushed him at Cronan to guard.

Heggi began sobbing. 'Rakki,' he moaned, 'Rakki.' He collapsed in grief.

The humpback pulled his thick cloak round him and Bera was grateful. She dare not think about the dear dog, not yet. As she went to her oar, the boat tipped. It was low in the water and the other three were bunched together.

'Stay in the middle!' Bera told them. 'We have to keep her steady!'

Huge brymstones fell thickly round them, making the sea boil with poison sulfur. Their eyes were red and streaming and Egill struggled to get an oar in place, amongst a frenzy of frightened folk. More were swarming into the sea all the time, determined, demented, ducking down beneath the waves, screaming until they drowned. The boat was almost lifted out of the water on the backs of the terrified bodies and it twisted and turned as arms tried to grab the rails. She quickly rammed the other oar into place and the boat swung away with her first strong stroke. Someone tried to seize the oar with her second but Egill pulled hard and the boat turned again. They kept mistiming their strokes until Bera counted them in.

Egill said, 'We have to keep clear of the black spine, further out.'

'Let's hope we get that far,' said Bera, though she was relieved that Egill was thinking straight.

At last they reached a patch of clearer water, too deep unless someone could swim. Now they had to protect the boat.

'Untie the bailing buckets, Heggi, and fill them with seawater,' Bera said.

He did not move.

'Heggi? These brymstones could hit us out at sea and set us alight. We've been lucky so far.'

'Brid has protected us,' said Cronan again. 'She is keeping you safe, Bera.'

'I keep us safe,' she muttered. 'Fill the bailers, Heggi.'

This time he did, slopping water as he gazed back at the shore.

The world was grey. Sky and sea were a scumble of ash and dust, with orange bursts where blocks of burning earth and rock fizzed out of the billowing cloud. The fumes burned Bera's throat and her eyes felt skinned. Her oar stopped dead in the water and she nearly fell. There was a body, floating face upwards, with singed beard and a bald, blackened head. Bera pushed off the corpse and it grabbed the oar. A swimmer! He held on with raw, burned hands. She felt revulsion and fear of this man whose rescue, her boat sense warned her, would drown them all. They would be swamped even trying to roll him aboard. Besides, he was dying.

'There's no room for you,' she said.

'What's happening?' asked Cronan.

Egill's voice was mournful. 'There's a drowning man, burned half to death like my father.'

Bera rubbed her sore eyes and looked down. His eyes bored into her, trying to communicate in that ravaged face. They were the colour of speedwells.

She could not speak for the horror and pity of it, or look away from the man who had helped them survive the barren spring; who had brought them here safely; who she had vowed to keep safe. This face she loved, destroyed.

'We cannot take you, Faelan,' she said, despairing.

Beside her, Egill gasped and from instinct Bera put out a hand to stop her leaning over.

'It's Faelan's boat!' said Egill, shocked.

'Faelan? Can we not save him?' asked Cronan.

Faelan's cracked and bloody lips tried to smile. Bera wondered what malevolent Fate made her have to deny Faelan. She would risk drowning in a heartbeat except there was a bigger duty that would save all their lives. And she was a mother twice over. Could the humpback be traded?

'Let him have my place,' said Cronan.

His goodness brought Bera to her senses. It could not be done – and must not be.

'Some things are black and white. Fate has decided.'

Egill put her oar back in the water to steady the boat.

'I think you are saying farewell, Faelan,' Bera said. 'I believe you will live. You survived once before – and I will return.'

Heggi shouted, 'Rakki's looking for me. Please keep him safe!'

Faelan took his hands off the oar and in his eyes Bera saw resolve.

'Turn the boat, Egill,' she said.

Faelan swam back into the maelstrom. It rained rock, dust, ash, stones, blocks, cinder and pumice and then Bera had to stop looking as their own luck ran out. The boat began to smoulder and they threw bucket after bucket of water over it. They were drifting towards the black rocks and Bera told Heggi to be lookout, to stop him constantly watching for Rakki. This was no time for pity or tears. She took up her oar and together she and Egill pulled hard.

The sound of screaming became a murmur. Faelan was another piece of soot on a flaming sea, with a blazing city beyond.

They were, for the moment, safe. Bera knew grief would hit and her skern was braced at her neck. There was no dog like Rakki and no future she desired without Faelan. Only short weeks ago Bera had sung with the joy of being aboard a boat, out on the sea paths. And she had Valdis, a daughter. The vision of this burning world had come at her birth. And so, Bera wept, for the cloud of filth was gathering and she finally understood that she might not be part of her baby's life.

16

Once they were clear of the black spine, it was a dull slog. They took turns to row, Bera with Cronan, who was stronger than he looked. Bera's hands had blood blisters and she had to take shorter turns than Egill, which shamed her. Once she could have rowed all day. This was an unwieldy, wallowing boat, built to go short distances and drift while Faelan fished. She pulled away from the pain of leaving him and thought about boats. She wished her father had built this one. Even the first tiny boat he made for her was nimble and kept her safe. Bera pitied the way this boat did its best, rolling in the water, trying to ride the waves, which luckily were long and flat-topped.

Heggi wiped away tears to take his turn. 'It really hurts, Mama.'

'You can't stop thinking of Rakki.' Bera carefully slid away so the boat didn't tip. 'My poor boykin. Dogs are great survivors, though, as long as they keep away from men.'

'But he'll wait and wait on the shore for me, won't he? And then someone will kill him. If he isn't burned.'

It was her worry too. The likelihood of death was something Heggi recognised and that pained Bera. They were all orphans now, Faelan had said, and she had left him to die. And Rakki too...

She counted the strokes, knowing the importance of a rhythmic task when a person was most troubled.

Egill changed places with Cronan, who flexed his shoulders. His face had new lines of pain, graven in soot.

'Count, so you keep stroke with Egill,' Bera told Heggi.

The resting pair sat in the bottom of the boat, to keep the weight low. It was wet and cold but made the boat more stable. When

Cronan gave her a brave smile, Bera shuffled over to him and gently rubbed his poor back.

'A healer indeed,' he said.

'Don't make me Brid,' she said, but carried on, for his sake.

The sun was a deep orange, loitering on a red horizon. The rest of the sky was a foul yellow-grey, like an old bruise. Seabirds wheeled overhead, aimless, not as many as there should be. Perhaps they had been knocked off course by the strange crackling of the sky. Bera realised she had not seen a whale spout or any shoals all day. Life itself was strangely altered.

No one talked of the sights they had seen. When Cronan relieved Heggi, he came and snuggled up to her.

'I'm a bit hungry,' he said.

That was a good sign. 'I have nothing for you, sweetheart. I don't think we can be going far, not in this boat. We'll all have to wait.'

'Has Cronan said where?'

'I know we're heading north and west.'

She kissed his head, which smelled of wet smoke.

'Do my hair?' he asked.

'What?'

'When you get the caffles out of my hair. I like it. You don't tug like Sigrid does.'

He needed a sign of her love, so Bera rummaged in a pocket for the lice comb. How strange that it should be there, when so much else was lost. She ran her fingers through his hair to get the worst caffles out, then began combing. Making her voice gentle, she spoke tender nonsense to him. He began to droop.

'Remember sitting in front of me on that stool Ottar made you, boykin? We all used to be there, round the fire. You and me, Ottar, Sigrid, Thorvald, your father…' Bera felt the loss. She inspected the narrow teeth in the creamy ivory. 'No nits.'

'I really, really miss Rakki.'

Bera kissed the back of his neck. 'Loss makes you strong, so Sigrid says, and she's right.' It wasn't the worst loss in his young life – and wouldn't be the last.

He thought for a bit and she felt close to him.

He twisted away. 'If you hadn't made me come with you I'd have had my coming-of-age feast and Rakki would still be alive.'

'Fate is often unkind, boykin.'

He gave her a withering look. 'I hate beaches! Bad stuff always happens on a beach. That black beach, when we landed...'

She had known this question would come one day.

'It's all right, Heggi. Go on.'

'When we got here, you know, when Papa left us?'

Bera raised her voice. 'For Iraland. With Egill.' She couldn't resist glancing to see if her barb had struck. It had.

'Did I actually choose to stay here? With you? Only I can't quite remember.'

'Can't you, really? I wanted your father to stay, Heggi. I thought he would help build our new home.'

'So did Papa go straightaway?'

'He didn't even wait to make sure we had enough to eat.'

'So did he want me to go with him?'

This was hard. How much to say? 'I wanted him to stay. We would still have a sea-going boat, the *Raven*, made by my father.'

Perhaps she could have prevented the eruption, if that day had been different.

'But you and Thorvald stopped me going.'

'It wasn't like that.'

The shock of what happened must have made the day a blank. Bera herself struggled with which parts had happened: what were fears and what had been a true vision of the future. She felt the weight of being a Valla, alone. Her anger at her husband's cowardice turned her stomach to vinegar. The Serpent King was behind it all. He knew Hefnir was making for Iraland and had sworn to make him pay the blood debt. If Heggi had gone there with his father, the Serpent would have killed him too. He was still a threat.

'I'm only asking.'

'What?'

'Don't be angry with me. I want to know, that's all.'

'I'm not angry, boykin.'

There was something more about Hefnir, besides the Serpent King. It was to do with the black bowl they found in Egill's hut. And then she remembered how Hefnir's eyes had glittered with greed. He would trade his son to get whatever it was he most wanted and that was obsidian. She had to keep Heggi safe and away from the knowledge of what kind of father he had, who would let his uncle kill him. But how could she explain any of this to him?

'I knew it might be dangerous in Iraland and I wanted to keep you with me, safe.'

'Why didn't you make Papa stay? It's all your fault!'

'Sit still, Heggi, you'll have the boat over. Nothing would have stopped your father.'

'I wanted to go with Papa and you stopped me, like you stop everything I want to do! I bet you made Rakki run away.' For a moment it looked as if he would throw himself overboard.

Bera held him tight. 'Heggi, stop! I'll explain everything when we're alone and safe.'

'You won't! You just say stuff!'

Egill had stopped rowing. She had been hidden on that black beach and then gone with Hefnir to Iraland. Did she watch him kill a man he loved in cold blood? Who did Egill care for? Herself?

Lonely cries of hidden seabirds measured the passing time but there was neither sun nor moon nor stars to guide them. They were adrift; they might perhaps be turning in circles. The air was thick with ash, which deadened the drably crawling sea and drove its creatures down to the deep. Endless wallowing finally made Bera seasick. She hung over the rail like the others and lost what little remained of the tavern stew, which slimed the back of her throat until there was nothing left and the retches burned. Sigrid would have died out here, if even the earth going up in flames could have frightened her aboard. Hot tears oddly wound their way down Bera's cheeks. She put up a hand and her face was covered in thick dust. The tear tracks must look like worm casts.

And yet… as she lay, gazing at the blank sky, her mind emptied of regret for the past and fear of the future. She let the boat-song nurse her, until her skern came to provide more worry.

Wondering why there's no sun?

'Go away.'

The cloud is poison but it's passing. For now.

'There's no wind.'

There is up there. Shouldn't you be heading north?

'I am, aren't I?'

Not on the current course, no. You're going out to sea.

'We'll come out into fresher air then.'

You can't save anyone until you get to the north lands.

'So point the right way.'

Her skern did so with a flourish.

'Ship your oar, Cronan,' Bera said. 'We're going north.'

Cronan thanked her. 'That's why we needed you, Bera.'

Egill scowled. 'Can't find true north in this filth,' she said.

'Were you thinking we could row to Iraland, Egill?' Cronan said.

Bera began to appreciate his courtesy. He resisted a fight and she liked having someone there who knew Egill; purblind but shrewd.

Egill tapped Heggi's shoulder with her foot. 'Take the oar, Heggi, my back is breaking.'

They passed as if through buttermilk and pale, phantom islands loomed at them in the mist. The only sounds were the steady plash of oars and drips as mist turned to water.

Egill said, 'These are the Westermost Isles.'

'We're back on course.' Cronan sounded unsurprised.

The mist rolled away in the stiffening breeze and Bera smelled winter on the wind.

'There's a squall coming.'

Egill patted her. 'It's good we have you aboard.'

Her fickle friend, as changeable as the wind.

Egill and Cronan shipped their oars early. They were afraid. Bera studied the skyline and saw a black strip, widening all the time. She told herself this was a summer storm and only the memory of a huge green wave heading for the *Raven* was making her catch their fear, not a premonition of disaster.

'Tie yourselves on,' she said. 'It could be spiteful in a small boat like this.'

'You think tying on will keep us aboard?' scoffed Egill.

'No, Egill. If someone goes overboard they won't be lost.'

'I'm glad Rakki isn't here now,' said Heggi.

Bera threw a line off the stern to slow them through the water. They were ready. The others huddled in the bottom of the boat: Egill and Cronan on one side and Heggi the other. She would join him before the storm hit but first said some words of protection. Beneath the vast mantle of ash travelling west, black clouds rampaged towards them, bringing their own wind. When Bera saw dark ripples swarming across the water like a horde of rats, she threw herself beside Heggi and hugged him as the gust hit, making the boat skew. Thunder rumbled. Rain came in a smudged grey sheet. The water was lifted from the sea in a spiral, dancing towards them, as Bera had seen before from the open plain.

'Waterspout!' she shouted and they held on more tightly.

There was no running this time. The twisting wraith danced over the waves, questing for its partner. Again Bera felt drawn to the dance. It was free as air, motiveless, guiltless, enough to simply be and full of twirling joy. Out here, at sea, it was easier to find her will but she battled to bend the wraith away from their small boat, which bucked and skewed as it passed. Heggi's blond hair became dark streaks over his eyes and cheeks. Bera rubbed her sleeve across her face and then his, being sure to keep her grip with the other hand. The storm had hurried the ash cloud on its way and Bera was proud of her skills – and relieved.

'We're through it,' she said.

The rain stopped, the sun came out, a full sun of early summer, and their clothes began to steam. Bera helped Heggi untie himself and saw the set of his mouth; it was a line of anguish that she needed to settle. If there was ever time.

A bee bumbled clumsily aboard, fell against his shoulder and crawled in a tight circle. A sign of persistence and hope. She carefully put a finger under its furry body and lifted it.

'Look, Heggi.'

He managed a smile. 'Can we keep it for a while?'

'I wish we had some honey to revive it. We'll let it go again when we get closer to land. You hold it.'

Heggi turned up his palm and let the bee crawl onto it, fanning its wings to dry itself. Then it settled and he gently curled his fingers to make a windbreak. Bera kissed the top of his head, then turned to windward.

Egill was looking ahead with an expression that Bera had seen once before, when she looked at the home Hefnir would not let her return to because of his greed for obsidian. It brought Bera back to the present. She screwed up her eyes to see better.

'Is that it?' asked Heggi.

It was land: glowing green, like sunlight through a new leaf.

Egill said, 'That's what Iraland looks like, first landfall.' There was a catch in her voice. 'We're safe, now.'

Safe? Bera could feel the bead burning at her throat and knew that for her, it was going to get worse.

17

Egill took up her oar and Bera would not let Cronan do more than his share, despite her sore palms. As they neared the island, she sent Heggi forward to release the bee but he kept his hands cupped. Soon he would have to let it go.

Egill leaned towards her. 'Bera... when we get to the Abbotry I want you to leave the talking to me and Cronan.'

Everything in her rebelled. 'Oh no! If I'm supposed to help then I have to make my own decisions.'

'You don't understand our religion.'

'I don't even know what the word means but if it's to do with Brid, I don't care. I know why I'm here and so must they, or why send for me?'

'You don't know who they are and they didn't—'

Cronan stopped Egill. 'I will need to persuade them that you are Brid.'

'And who are they?'

'Westermen,' he replied. 'They came from Iraland but this... stern order has held sway here for many years.'

Egill nodded. 'They won't take orders from a woman. They despise women. They won't even like having a woman in the guest quarters.'

'I am a Valla, but why do they not despise you?' Bera asked.

Egill put a finger to her lips. 'I'm a boy to them.'

Bera kept her secret. It seemed as if she was always the one who made provision for Egill's nature but argument would solve nothing. They shipped oars and drifted, with Bera making lazy strokes to keep them following the coast.

'It's gone!' Heggi was upset that his bee had deserted him.

'Come, Heggi,' said Cronan. 'I'll tell you all about giants in Iraland.'

'Are they troles?'

'No, these are no troles but flesh-and-blood men.'

Heggi was rapt and yet again Bera was grateful to Cronan.

'Who was the first giant?' Heggi asked.

'He built a walkway from Iraland so he could fight the giant on the other side.'

Bera had a vision of bundles of tall stones, like tapers in a jar, pale and shaped at the top like honeycomb. They were left from an old, old eruption. Before time.

Egill put her lips to Bera's ear. 'I've seen a giant with flame-red hair. Brid is as real to her followers.'

Bera shook her head. 'I don't understand you, Egill, leaving the old ways behind.'

'No one has ever understood me, except Ottar. Your pa used to say I was a thinker because I spent so much time alone.'

Bera was studying the strange stone buildings on the island. 'What are those skep things?'

'They call them beehives in Iraland.'

'Skeps, beehives; means the same thing.'

'They're not skeps, though, or the bees would be as big as us!' Egill laughed.

Bera was not to be won over. 'So what are they?'

'Cells. Where ermites live.'

'I know what cells are.' Bera shivered, catching Heggi's eye. He did not need any reminder of being shut in one by Hefnir. A cruel punishment for a child.

'What are ermites?' she asked.

'They live in them.'

Bera wanted to throw her overboard.

Cronan spoke so softly that they had to lean in to hear him. Clever.

'Holy men leave Iraland to go to many places. Some build towers on vast plains of sand. Here on these islands the cells are their shelters, for men who want to go off alone to fast and pray.'

'Fast means starve, only on purpose,' explained Egill, helpful at last. 'That's what the ermites do, not the Westermen. They eat off gold plates!'

'So these ermites are madmen.'

Egill looked forlorn. 'Sometimes the loneliness drives them mad.'

She would know about that – and Bera ought to take more care of her.

She took Egill's hand. 'You don't need to ever be alone again.'

Cronan was smiling at her and she felt ashamed, because she thought the purblind could see better than the sighted.

They tied up at a stone jetty. Bera's heart beat fast. Steep steps led upwards to a high grey wall. What did it hide? It looked sinister enough to be some fortress of the Serpent King. She shook herself. Cronan belonged and he was kind.

He's hiding something, though.

Egill stepped onto the landing stage, which was covered in slippery eelgrass. She got herself steady and Bera handed Cronan up to her. He began the long trudge up the steps.

'This is the harbour,' Egill boasted. 'It's what we have in Iraland.'

'Egill, it's a set of steps, like we have at our own jetty.'

Heggi piped up. 'They're Faelan's steps, not ours.'

Egill said, 'Faelan got the idea from his mother, from Iraland. Wait till you see the Abbotry!' She swung her arms about and skidded.

Heggi shouted, 'What is an Abbotry?'

Bera was thinking that the first time she heard the word was from the Fetch, come to take Faelan's mother. It spoke of Brid too. How was it all linked? Or was it a trap?

Egill got Heggi ashore and he started stamping on small crabs that were scuttling away from the intruders. Bera went next, slipped on a slimy mat of seaweed and sprawled, feeling cross at herself. Heggi laughed – and it was worth it just to see him smile again.

'Hel's teeth and buckets of blood!' She enjoyed swearing like her father. 'You put me off, Heggi!'

Heggi made a trole face at her and then showed off by bounding up the steps.

'Go right up, Heggi,' Egill said. 'There's a door at the top.'

'Don't go through it,' Bera said.

She climbed the long, steep steps with legs turned soft. By the time she reached the top she was short of breath. A long, stone wall curved away into the distance. There was no sign of her boy.

'Heggi!' she called.

Cronan was sitting near the only door, wheezing badly. The door was wooden, with a dark red serpent daubed on it. Lines trickled down from the cross, as if the serpent had truly been nailed to it and was bleeding down the wood.

The image revolted her. Serpents were surely evil, always.

'What have you brought me to, Cronan?'

He shook his head, unable to catch his breath.

'Heggi!' she shouted wildly.

'He's coming now,' said Egill. 'Watch.' She gave a sly smile as the door creaked open.

A man came through in a rich cloak of oatmeal-coloured wool, patterned all around its hem with blood-red serpents eating the tails of other serpents.

'Pleased to see me?' Hefnir said.

He waited, with the smile of a normal husband, home after summer trading. Bile rose from her stomach to the back of her throat. How dare he be here? He should be in Iraland. And yet, of course, Egill knew the Abbotry. Had she brought him? Or, worse, had Faelan known he was here? Which one of them had betrayed her by bringing her to the man she despised? Heggi was beaming, standing tall beside his father. Had Hefnir's bad blood already begun to stir?

Bera put her cold hands on her face; it was sweaty and burning. She steadied her breathing, damned if she would let Hefnir see her shock. She was a child no longer and would not be made a fool by her false-hearted husband. He had given up Seabost blue and wore stout leather boots and a sword belt embossed with gold and silver. Riches far beyond his former trading. Bera was conscious of her scorch-marked, salt-stained, smelly clothes, mended many times since he had last seen her. She wanted him to be poor and outcast and the settlers to have prospered.

She raised her eyes in challenge. His were kindly, like the first day she arrived as his new bride. For a moment she was startled into smiling back at him but then she called to mind all the deaths that lay between them, that so nearly included her own.

Heggi took his father's hand. 'Look, Bera! It's Papa! We can be a family again!'

His small face was full of hope. How could she try and keep them apart if that meant hurting Heggi? He would also hate her for doing so. She felt furious – and powerless.

'I can see that you've been successfully trading, Hefnir. Or is it only raiding now?' Bera's voice throbbed.

'I am glad you got here safely, all of you.'

'You knew we were coming?'

'I sent for you.'

'It seems everyone claims to have sent for me. But you are lying because Cronan here says I'm to meet folk who believe in Brid and live in skeps.'

'Only ermites live in them. We do rather better. You'll see.'

'We?' How pompous he was! 'I want nothing to do with you.'

'I want to stay here with Papa!' Heggi stamped his foot. A petulant child again with his father near.

'We'll all be together now,' said Hefnir. 'A family. Come and see where we'll be living.'

'None of us will be living anywhere if I don't enter the tower!'

Hefnir smiled at her. 'You have no idea what a tower is, do you?'

Cronan coughed. 'Only Bera can deliver what is inside. As you know, Hefnir.'

Bera was triumphant. 'You see? My Valla powers are stronger here, Hefnir. This black bead says so.' She held up her necklace. The bead scorched her hand and she dropped it.

'Why do you think you're here?' he asked.

'Cronan knows. He's brought me to stop the mountains erupting and killing everything on this island.'

He studied her face. 'You really believe that, don't you?'

'What do you want of me then, Hefnir?'

'I want us to be together.' He looked at Heggi, who might have been the only one there to believe him.

'Liar! You want Obsidian. I might let Hel blow her top off if it means giving it to you!'

'You? Resist saving the world? I don't think so. Come on, Heggi, we'll go on ahead.'

Heggi gave her a look. 'You spoil everything, Bera.'

Father and son went through the door.

'I promised I'd bring her!' Egill went after Hefnir, her face washed with jealous pain.

So that was it. Poor, lonely Egill. Hefnir loved no one but himself and would use anyone to get what he wanted. Bera gave a grim smile. It didn't matter who thought they had sent for her; it was the land itself that had summoned her, an age ago, when she had scried in Egill's obsidian bowl. It was the first time she had managed to scry and she could picture it clearly: swirls of blue ice, with crimson fires curling on mountaintops beyond. Over the tallest peak there was a cone-shaped cloud of immense height – and now she knew what it was – the ash cloud spilling from Hel's Gateway. This was their land of ice and its fire within.

Cronan brought her back. 'Hefnir marches to his own tune. But we need you.'

'More than we yet know. But I am not Brid.'

'Whoever you are, Bera, I believe only you can heal the earth. You have my word that I will help and Obsidian is the key.'

18

What choice did she have? The very air here was different: softer, warmer, with light, misty rain that was like a kiss. It was like another country within the new country that she was only starting to understand. It was more deceptive here, hiding behind the warning signs of this serpent belief. Bera couldn't touch the spirit of the place; nothing was personal. Any glimpses vanished like cats at the first sign of thunder. She needed to bide her time, to regain control, and then work out what she needed to do. She remembered her skern telling her she was like a midge to the immense spirit of earth and mountain, so she would start small, one step after another. She had to succeed. What happened at Smolderby was a glimpse of what Hel could unleash, destroying Ice Island.

For now, all their plans coincided and Bera trusted Cronan more than her husband and friend. So she took his arm and they followed the others inside the wall, where Egill was waiting for them.

She stopped Egill moving off. 'One thing, Egill. Are you my friend, or Hefnir's?'

'There you go again. Black or white.'

That's you biding your time, is it?

Bera let Egill go. They passed through a high door, with another painted serpent cross, then followed the line of an inner wall. Cronan trailed his fingers across the stones, as if reading them.

'You should see the tower now,' he said.

'Can't you?' she asked.

'I can only see as far as my hand.'

A grey shape seemed to rise like a giant stinkhorn as they went down a slope. The tower was built of striped, grey stone, the colour of a hooded crow. Bera was reminded of the striped stones spewed from the mountain and wondered if everything on earth began bad and then became useful. The sun came out and tiny glints made it look jewelled. Perhaps the bad could also become beautiful.

The size of everything dwarfed Bera. The high wall was meant to be daunting, like when a man loomed over her, so she stood taller and vowed to get the better of whoever had built it. Her dislike increased when she stood beside wide wooden gates. Their sheer bulk made her feel like a mouse but they also writhed with carved serpents, with no cross.

She glared at Egill. Every time she tried to trust her there was some new serpent image. Was this some terrible betrayal to bring her to the Serpent King? No, this couldn't be right – unless Hefnir wanted her to kill the Serpent King? Surely even he was not such a coward.

Egill stared with blank owl eyes. 'I thought you trusted us.'

'If the Serpent King is here I will kill him.'

'Hefnir has told the warders to look out for him.'

'Warders?'

'Guards,' Egill smiled. 'They ward off every bad thing.'

Cronan patted the wood. 'No enemy can pass through these gates. And even if he did, he couldn't reach our quarters.'

'Why?'

'You'll see.'

It took all of them to push open the gate and then it turned out that they had been heaving against the weight of heavy stones on ropes on the other side, which swung the huge gate shut afterwards. A short, muscular man had been helping and then he stood on guard again. A warder. This vigilance made Bera more afraid. What kept folk out also kept folk in. And she knew with certainty that she would be made to stay until she got into the tower – and then what? She had been so fixed on getting here, she had no idea what would happen next.

We'll cross that bridge when we come to it. Her skern tittered.

'That's what they'd be met with,' said Egill, still jaunty. 'There are many warders all around. Human and… other.'

'In case sea-riders come?'

'Whoever comes,' said Cronan. 'There are those in the world who know what we keep here.'

'In the grey tower.'

'My dreaming spire of ensense.' Cronan turned his face to it. 'That's what they're guarding.'

Bera felt her skern's sharp nail run down her spine. Almost painful.

And you think I riddle!

'You do.'

It's what it holds that's key: black on black. Only there's a big problem.

Bera's attention was drawn to someone who looked like a walking anvil. His whole body was encased in metal and his helmet made a sharp point under his chin, with only slits to see through. His body was wedging open a tall, spiked, iron gate. Egill quickly slipped her slim body into the narrow gap and was gone. The metalled man was shouting and pushing Cronan through. If the gate shut, Bera would be the wrong side of it. She ran. The warder's eyes glinted behind his iron mask as she jinked through. He clanged the gate shut at once and made a point of locking it with a heavy key, then turned and glowered at them. Cronan meekly thanked him and set off.

Bera asked Egill why he had no authority over the warder.

'They don't have thralls as such here.'

Bera wanted to see how the man could walk in his heavy metal tunic. She wished Dellingr could see the work, especially the patterning on the breastplate. It probably hurt to wear it, though, and made her appreciate Cronan even more, for keeping his good humour despite unending pain.

'At least the warder can take his metal tunic off,' she said.

Egill said, 'It's called armour.'

So many new things she had to learn – and fast. Bera listed them, playing with the words as they hurried to join Cronan who was waiting at a wide wooden bridge. Alone.

Her skern pointed at it, smirking. *Cross that bridge, see?*

The land beyond was a mossy green sward that gently rose again. No one was in sight.

'Where did Heggi go?' Bera asked.

'Hefnir was going to show him something,' Cronan said.

'I wish he wouldn't go off alone.'

'He's with his father,' said Egill.

'Take my arm again?' Cronan asked.

Bera helped him step up onto the bridge, which rattled and boomed as they began to cross. She was beginning to think he was able to do most things for himself, so perhaps he was stopping another argument.

Beneath them, for its entire span, was a steep-sided trench filled with dark water.

'You can't see this trench from the gate, at all!'

'It's called a moat,' said Egill pompously. 'I devised it.'

'Then I hope it's better than your dam or we're about to drown.'

Egill poked her, grinning, but Bera had not meant it as a joke.

Before they reached the other side, she stopped and looked down to see how deep the water was. Very deep, and black – and she could scry. At first she saw nothing, just felt the relief of the old skill coming back, like prickling blood into a limb that has gone to sleep. Then sight came and Bera was rapt. She tried to scan the tower but there was a flurry of obstruction… silver-grey pelt, of some kind. She felt a mind questing for her, somewhere close. It was one she had bluntly sensed at the waterfall. Wild. Male. His keen eyes amber and black. Locked on him now, Bera felt his thoughts as long ripples of molten gold. They met, mind to mind, open and aware – and he would kill her if she threatened him or his pack. She sent waves of trust and smiled.

'Wolves.'

'I wanted it to be a surprise,' Egill wailed.

'You sound like Heggi!'

'Hefnir's feeding him to them now!' Egill said. 'They've just had his legs and are starting on his arms.'

Heggi must be safe if Egill could joke. Bera was exuberant, feeling she was in full command of her new power. Somehow she would prevail, whatever came. She ran at Egill and pretended to push her into the water. They were naughty friends again and they tugged each other across to the inner circle where the tower stood on its grassy mound.

'Wait for me, children!' shouted Cronan.

As soon as he stepped off the bridge it lifted behind them and they were trapped. Not a bridge but another gate. Bera's laughter died.

At the base of the grey tower the pack leader lifted his head and gave a long, summoning howl. The rest joined in, gathering about him to stare at the intruders. They were a way off but could cover the ground faster than any man could run. Did they feel threatened? Had she only wanted her kinship with the leader to be true? Bera touched her amber bead that was like his eyes.

'Are they fenced in?' she asked.

'Course not,' said Egill. 'That's why the man at the gate's in armour, in case they ever manage to cross the moat.'

'Wolves swim.'

'They don't like the black water,' said Cronan. 'Besides, we keep them fed this side so why would they want to? They are the best protection for the tower.'

'How do you get in and out of the Abbotry?'

Cronan smiled. 'We seldom leave and visitors are few in the inner circle.'

'Look,' said Egill.

A sort of cart came charging over the long downhill sward and stopped with a great clang beside them.

'Climb aboard.' Egill cupped her hands so that Bera could step up onto the contraption. 'It's called a trolley.'

Bera was suspicious. 'Is this one of your designs, as well?'

The wood was strong, better than anything she had yet seen on Ice Island. There were three short, thick planks lashed together with walrus rope to make a platform on wheels. Several coils of heavy chain lay on top.

Egill leapt up easily in her trousers. 'All my devising. I call it a trolley because it moves as fast as a trole can walk.'

'We can only hope it works,' said Cronan. 'They must have finished it while we were away.'

The more boastful Egill was, the more Bera feared the outcome. 'Where did you find the wood?'

Egill waved a hand. 'It's a door.'

Travelling by door is a first.

They helped Cronan aboard. He picked up the heavy chain on one side of the trolley and Egill handed the chain on the other side to Bera, then she paid out the links until both women had a good hold. Cronan began pulling his chain in time with Egill and Bera on theirs. He couldn't walk fast or well but Bera again marvelled at the strength in his upper body. It was hard going uphill but with the strength of three they were travelling fast and nearing the tower. The trouble was, it also brought them closer to the pack of wolves who were gathered in a circle, waiting for their approach. The pack leader's brain was sharp and commanding... but what was he ordering his pack to do?

By the time they reached the steeper edge of the mound they were tiring. The lead male fixed Bera in his sight in real time, as he had done before in her scrying. Bera wanted to hold her beads but had to keep both hands on the chain and pull.

'Is this a good idea?' she asked. 'Are you sure this trolley thing works, Egill?'

'I pray it does,' Cronan said. 'We have to go beyond the tower.'

'Why?' Bera asked. 'There's only that mountain beyond.'

'Keep pulling,' said Egill.

The wolves stood stiffly erect, staring in silence. The air was full of the iron smell of blood and death.

'Help us, Mama,' whispered Bera.

There was a thud. Bera twisted in time to see something fall and arms retreating inside. A shutter closed, high up in the tower.

'That's higher than a wolf can jump,' Egill said. 'Or climb.'

'What was it?'

'Food.'

'They gather by the tower when they see movement at the bridge,' said Cronan. 'They get to eat on days when we expect... company. One way or another. We used to lose many horses.'

Even that glimpse gave Bera the sense that a whole body had

fallen. Surely it was too large and solid to be a man. The pack were already fighting over it. They were snarling and mauling the flesh, or pouncing for scraps, in the order they had won in earlier fights, Bera supposed. Other deaths. She tried to scry but the leader made his mind blank, watching her pass beneath the mound.

Bera raised her hand in a mark of respect to him.

'What did you do that for?' asked Egill.

'It was the right thing to do.'

The large male stalked off to feast. The other wolves fell back until he had carefully selected and ripped off a huge piece of flesh and then they warily returned.

'What are they eating?' Bera asked.

'Whatever is spare,' said Cronan, closing the subject.

All men could refuse knowledge when it suited.

Egill complained, 'I'm doing all the work here!'

'I'm still pulling,' said Bera and started again.

When she turned to the front, she was surprised at how far they had travelled. Her eyes followed a cliff upwards. And up and up and up as far as she could look without toppling backwards. Bera was used to longhouses and homesteads spread across the land. What confronted her was an immense ridge rising upwards, dotted with openings like puffin holes. These were big enough for a man to stand in.

'We're going inside the mountain?' She couldn't keep the awe out of her voice. 'Do you live here, Egill?'

Egill kept her head down. 'You can't see the guest bit.'

They reached the trolley stop. Egill threw a long loop of rope over a post and another warder, wearing breastplate and helmet, chained it securely.

'We are the last,' Cronan told him.

The man helped them down, then escorted them over a shorter wooden bridge.

'Does this work the same way as the other bridge?' Bera asked.

'Watch!'

Once they were on the other side of the moat, the man turned a lever and began to wind the bridge upright.

Egill tapped her chest. 'I devised the—'

Cronan coughed.

Egill drooped. 'It becomes a barred gate. It was like that when I arrived.'

Bera felt ensnared in somewhere strange; somewhere she didn't want to be at all. But her duty was clear: her task was to get into the tower and use whatever was in there to stop the earth tumult. But what was it and how to use it? And then what? And what else lay in store for her in the Abbotry?

Hefnir arrived, with the smile he always wore when he got his way, and her doubts redoubled.

Bera gazed up at a weathered face of honey-coloured stone, dotted with peepholes. It was as if the ermites who lived outside in their skeps had produced a honeycomb for the workers to live in, whose eyes were now fixed on her. She fancied she could hear them humming. There was yet another guarded door at the foot and Egill went straight inside with Cronan. Hefnir let them go ahead and then took Bera's hand.

She pulled away. 'Where's Heggi?'

'Looking for dogs – but he won't find any here. I managed to stop him snatching a wolf cub as a foster-child.'

'So he's told you we lost Rakki?'

'He's talked of little else.'

Bera nodded. She needed Hefnir's favour until she had worked out this new abode. At the moment it was completely strange and what had seemed an island was actually a bulbous tip with mountains ranged behind the one before her. There would not be any other way out than by sea, and there was only Faelan's small fishing boat tied to the jetty. But Hefnir must have arrived in a longship. Could it be the *Raven*? She must find out where it was but that meant keeping Hefnir sweet.

'You have powerful new friends,' she said. 'They must be rich to be so well guarded.'

'You haven't yet seen the strongest safeguard,' Hefnir said. 'I've already shown Heggi.'

He had hurt her and their marriage had been full of lies. His face was always reserved, even when things were happier. But they had made one hunting trip together when they shared a special bond and so she tried to put the memory into his head of the one time when he was open.

'And is Heggi safe from all threats?' she asked, holding his gaze.

'He's our son.'

She had touched on the worst thing between them and he had answered. She believed they had shared a frank moment once more and was glad, for her own and Heggi's sake. Bera took his hand and was even glad to feel its familiar warm leatheriness. But she had not forgotten what he had done, or yet forgiven, and she would use him to get into the tower and keep the island safe. So she let him lead her to a wizened hagthorn tree, which bent protectively over a spring.

'Our drinking water,' he said. 'It's a holy well.'

Bera wondered if she could scry and bent over the deep pool, then recoiled.

'What's that?'

Hefnir laughed. 'Our protection.'

In the dark water a circle of whiteness gleamed. They were small skulls with neat round holes in the crown, obviously made on purpose.

'These were children!' It horrified her.

'Children are closer to the spirits and the skull is the house of the soul.' Hefnir recited his new belief brightly. 'It's important that running water passes right through them.'

Bera turned on him. 'And Heggi? Did you bring our son here to kill him or just frighten him?'

'You know better. I showed him how every border is defended from every foe, alive or dead. In Iraland they bury a line of them.'

'To make a ghost fence. Isn't that what it's called?' She shuddered at the thought that her homestead might be divided from Faelan's land by a row of children's heads. 'I don't believe they work.'

'Then they won't, not for you,' Hefnir said. 'It's belief that makes them strong.'

'What do you believe?'

'That our son will be protected here by our faith.'

'I keep our folk safe.'

'With a woollen blanket of Valla whisperings?'

The insult made her furious. 'Or *Raven*'s sail, that brought us safely to shore? Do you challenge all the Valla customs passed down through the ages, mother to daughter?'

He sighed, as though a fool did not deserve an answer.

'Have you really taken on their beliefs, Hefnir? Or are you using them to distance Heggi from me?'

He moved away. 'We should go inside. There's much more to see.'

'I don't have time for that. I only agreed to find a way into the tower.'

With one quick step he grasped her wrist. 'Be careful, Bera. How much more sacred the water would be with a Valla head in it. A direct link to the world of spirits and all their knowledge.'

'Don't threaten me, Hefnir. You trust Valla knowledge to help you. You're pretending these Abbotry beliefs.'

'And don't you dismiss them, Bera. I need you alive. The Westermen are not like us: one man holds all the power here. He is the Abbot and he could have you killed for looking at him. I've persuaded him you are more than just a woman but even then you need to be careful.'

'And why would you persuade him, Hefnir, except to get your hands on Obsidian. Well, I won't let you have it, ever. Obsidian draws out the dark in everyone, my skern told me long ago, and I didn't even trust you with Egill's bowl.'

His face was blank. 'You know nothing about Obsidian and nothing about me anymore.'

'It turned out I never did,' Bera said.

She insisted on going to Heggi. They passed through a long, empty space, crisscrossed with shafts of grey light high above them. Their footsteps scuffed dully on bare, beaten earth, making Bera yearn for the clean smell of spruce boughs. That would never come again. They entered a wide tunnel with narrow passages leading off in other directions. It was like being in a burrow. There were movements in the shadows and glints of metal. Warders? Then there was more light and ahead was an opening where Egill and Cronan were waiting. Heggi was not with them.

Bera stopped Hefnir. 'Where is he?'

'He's in our billet,' Hefnir said.

'I thought we were going to see him.'

'We are – but Cronan wants you first.'

Bera followed him into a wide space that seemed roofless, although there was no movement of air. Their footsteps sounded hollow and she could hear the in, out of her own breath.

A loud clatter made her jump.

'Birds, birds, birds.' Egill's shrill voice echoed, making the birds many.

'*Cronan hears us, standing at the threshold of understanding.*'

Bera remembered that thresholds might bring understanding but also danger.

Cronan held out his arms. 'Come, beauties!' he called.

Nine birds, glossy black and beady, came to him and perched along his arms. Huge crows. They regarded her over savage beaks that looked like leather masks, with closed minds but insistent wills that were scratching Obsidian nine times over.

Hefnir called Egill, ducked into one of the passages and they were gone.

Bera woke as if from a trance.

'Where will you be?' she shouted. 'You be? Be? Be?'

Cronan and his birds stepped into the shadows. There was a booming blacksmith's ring of iron on iron and then silence.

Bera spoke to herself sternly. Fear must become action. It was clear that she was on her own journey – had been from the start and wanted to be – but Cronan had knowledge she needed to share and was part of it. He must be special because the crows had spoken to her all that time ago. Reluctantly she admitted to herself that she also liked him. What folk said about humpbacks was wrong. Men could have other strengths. She crossed to where he had gone and came to an oak door with a huge iron ring-latch in the shape of a serpent eating its own tail. Bera felt the prickle of tears before the memory caught up with her.

A bracelet worn by her mother. Bera must have been very small. Alfdis had told her it was a sign of eternal renewal, like the chain of Vallas, mother to daughter, but Bera had been afraid of it. This wasn't the time to do more than acknowledge the mix of grief and fear thoughts of her mother often provoked. One day she would try and find answers – and perhaps Obsidian itself could help.

She studied the door more closely. Nailed to the centre panel was the wooden serpent cross of the Westermen. This door was part Northman, part new belief. What exactly did they believe? In such a place as this, anything was possible. There was rustling behind her and Bera was terrified that a thousand serpents were slithering towards her.

She seized the iron ring with both hands and turned.

19

The latch clacked open and she put her back into pushing the heavy door wide enough to slip through. She rammed it shut behind her and turned. Smoke formed a gauzy blue layer in the still air, lit by windows too high to see. In the half-light beneath stood a high wooden throne, with Cronan's crooked figure below it, covered in the birds she had once thought were crows. Crowman. How blunt her skills had been to make such a childish mistake – but it revealed how far she had come since then.

He gestured at the empty throne. 'The Abbot is too ill to see you today.'

She moved closer. 'Then I shall miss seeing him at all. I have work to do here, Cronan, and you know it. One mountain has already blown so I think it's all happening faster than we thought. Our purpose is good, so let's make haste.'

Bera sounded braver than she felt. It reminded her of her arrival at Hefnir's hall in Seabost, feeling out of her depth, watched by hostile, unseen eyes. Here, Cronan had grown in stature. It wasn't only the birds that made him bigger: he was in his element here and confident to step out alone in the dark and even his voice was stronger. Perhaps the crows also gave him the clue to where she was even at a distance because he was looking straight at her with unnerving accuracy. All the birds fixed her with their beady eyes too, so that she was pinned. Black eyes, black beaks. The souls of murdered men, so folk said, but she did not believe it.

Or you don't want to, if Crowman keeps them. Her skern, perched on the throne, spat the name.

Cronan stroked the head of a bird. '*Corvus corax*. The most playful of the corvids.'

'Crows,' Bera said.

Cronan gave a small cough in correction. 'Ravens, Woden's birds, you might say.'

'Woden only had two.' Bera wished he would keep to his own beliefs. 'Why do you need so many?'

He smiled. 'A humpback needs more than Woden… for whatever purpose they serve.'

'They are mind and memory,' Bera said. 'I've heard the birds speak.'

Cronan nodded. 'Some say that ravens are like a Fetch, or your skern.'

'So they can help. Is Obsidian here or in the tower?'

'The black stone is in the tower within the tower.'

'Then who guards it? The one who feeds the wolves?'

'It is guarded by the same ermite, ever since we were children. We were friends – until he was chosen to enter the tower. Even if he ever wanted to leave, the wolves would not allow it.'

'How do I get in there?'

'We next take him food a week hence—'

'A week!'

Her exclamation made the birds bate. Cronan crooned at them to settle them.

'See what your impatience produces.'

He's got you bang to rights.

Bera ignored her skern. 'I'm not impatient for my own sake. I knew the eruption would happen, so I walked all the way to Smolderby with Faelan… and rowed here and put up with all this and left my baby…' Her throat was swollen.

Cronan delved into a large leather pouch that hung from his belt and pulled out some seed. He scattered it on the floor and his birds flew down and fought over it.

'You see?' He sighed. 'They get what they want but it causes disharmony. In this place, with the help of Brid, there is always harmony.'

'Are there only men here?'

'Apart from you, yes.'

And Egill, but Bera kept quiet. 'Then they cannot be like any men I know. There are always fights, deaths sometimes.'

'Jealousy. There is no jealousy without women.'

'Or skerns,' she said.

Her skern did not deny it.

Bera thought Cronan might be deliberately moving her away from what she needed to know.

Ask him about the serpent on the door.

'We didn't finish talking about what the serpent means, like the cross Egill wears, and on the door. In our world, the serpent is to be feared, not worshipped.'

'Feared and worshipped. They are not exclusive.'

Not black or white.

'Brid chooses us. That's why we bear her mark.' He gestured at his wrist; an age since he had shown her his tattoo. 'There is one who serves her who has dedicated his life to her. He brings us food, money, anything we ask of him, back from our home land.'

'Iraland?'

'There and elsewhere. We call it Wolf Island, for reasons I think you'll appreciate.' He coughed. 'He brought wolf cubs here. We live here only thanks to his beneficence.'

He must mean Faelan.

No time for remorse. 'I need to get into the tower right now and find Obsidian.'

'Do you know yet what you must do with the stone if you manage to take it?'

'It will be clear when I touch it.'

You hope.

Perhaps he heard the doubt in her voice. 'It would be wiser to find that out before you try and break in.'

'It must be now! The convulsions have already started and if Hel's Gateway has opened the rest will follow, because they are linked below the earth's crust like the beads of my necklace.'

He whistled and his nine ravens flew to his open arms.

'*Burning, burning, fire, burning,*' cried the birds.

'There is a prophesy that the world will end in a wall of fire.' Cronan's voice was bleak.

'The start of it is here,' she said.

'Only you can take the stone, Bera. A Valla. Yet I fear that the fate you bring will be the death of my friend, the Warden.'

It explained why he hurried then delayed.

'I promise that if it's possible to take the stone without hurting your friend, I will leave him alone.'

'We believe that if ever the stone leaves the tower, it will kill us all.'

Bera was puzzled. 'If I don't take it, you will die. You know this, or why else bring me?'

'It's possible to be the hand of Brid and yet fear where it will strike.'

'If I could scry, perhaps I could find out if I can safely take the stone,' Bera persuaded. 'To save your friend and you.'

Cronan considered it. 'Then I'll show you why I'm a seer, what I use.'

He led her deeper into the dark hall and Bera wondered where he would go to 'see' but she was excited at trying some new way of prediction. Perhaps it would be more certain than scrying. It was bound to be better than her skern.

Ever the ungrateful.

'Then use words I understand.'

I can see the future, not the past, and use words accordingly. You are conflicted, for example. Both excited and scared.

'Will this ensense help or destroy my Valla powers?'

Help. I think.

Cronan slipped into a crevice and Bera hurried to see what he was doing. The air smelled sweet. He took something out of a box next to a row of candles that cast a yellow light over a dim alcove in the rock. It was already smoky in the narrow recess and the sweetness overpowering.

'I shall only ask about Obsidian,' she said.

When he put the substance into a burning dish, the smoke grew denser. He beckoned her in and then slipped past her, leaving her to the cloying scent. There was hardly room for a single person inside. No proper man like Hefnir, anyway. Or Heggi, when he was fully grown, wherever their home was, glimpsed, and even now he was getting bigger, like a… like a…

Bera let herself slide down, gazing inside her mind.

Smolderby was silently burning. The shanties were gone and beyond the beach was a wall of fire. Crispy whirls of black floated on the wind that dropped down from the cold mountain. Grey ash fell like feathers. The rain of charred stones lay in heaps, cracked and steaming, with rough, grey stones covering the sand. Faelan was a wreck of a man, amongst the wreckage around him. Then he limped through the charred streets and twittens that were full of ash and smoking lumps of clinker: a city deserted by its folk.

Lightning crackled above the ragged mountain, which still stood. A dog appeared. His fur was burned all along one side and he walked slowly on three legs. Faelan sank to the ground and when Rakki reached him he held the dog tight, letting him lick his poor burned face.

'You must stop soon,' Cronan said. 'With your powers, the ensense could…'

The smoke was sweet and choking but Bera wanted to sink back down to Faelan. She could make him better and it would be as if she had never left him to die.

Someone was shaking her.

'Listen to me, Bera. It's dangerous to stray too far in the smoke,' Cronan said.

Bera breathed deeply, wanting the danger. 'I should have been kinder. Never kind.'

Cronan put a beaker to her lips but everything was burning. Then, blackness.

Bera was standing at one end of a long table lit by thick tapers. She had no memory of getting there and no idea how much time had passed. Her head hammered and her eyesight was hazy but a shock of blond hair made her heart sing. Heggi. He was sitting at the far end, talking to his father. He looked up and they ran towards each other and hugged. She was his dear mama again, even before she told him his dog was alive and being cared for by Faelan. She did not say they were both suffering.

His pinched look vanished and he raced about, telling everyone that Rakki was alive and they smiled for him, without knowing it was a dog. Some of the people round the table were as black as her bead, their faces shining with some inner joy. Bera felt as whole as having her skern tight around her shoulders and it almost made up for having no answers about her purpose. Well, she always ended up depending on herself alone. If only her head would clear.

'There's so much food, Mama. Come and see!'

'Hold my hand, boykin, I'm a little unsteady.'

'I expect it's tiredness,' Heggi said. 'I slept and slept when I got here.'

How long had she been with Cronan? She could only remember his disappointed face when she had nothing to reveal about Obsidian.

Heggi led her to his place and Bera found herself sitting next to Egill, with Hefnir opposite them. They were apart from the rest of the company, now a blur. Egill passed a shallow copper bowl along to her so that she could wash her face and hands. Bera hoped her eyes would clear and kept rinsing her face. After she had rubbed it dry with a cloth she was shocked to see so much soot on the pale linen and hid it on her lap.

The table glowed. There were silver dishes piled high with richly decorated foodstuffs she couldn't name. What Ottar would have called 'swanky' if it had been a carved prow. But there was also a whole boar's head, with jewels for eyes, as well as glossy breads, nuts and berries; steaming dishes and various pickles; bowls of honey, skyr, and dried fruits. Cheeses. Everything lit in a warm light from special thick tapers that smelled sweet as nectar.

'These are much better than our tapers,' she said. Her voice sounded distant.

Hefnir smiled. 'They're made of beeswax.'

'Candles,' said Heggi, proud of his new word.

Hefnir's eyes looked softer in the light, like flies in amber.

Bera felt warm and happy. They were a family, safe and fed. 'I want candles at home.'

There will be no home for anyone if you fail in your duty. Her skern popped a walnut into his mouth and crunched it ominously.

She was incapable of feeling his warning. Her blood flowed like honey. It was a long time since she had been in a hall like this, with its huge roasting spits at the hearth. It was impossible not to smile, for the joy of letting go of her cares and duties and forgetting loss, illness, everything, and sitting in this scented stronghold got the better of her and she gave in wantonly. She was mazed with happiness.

If others noticed, they didn't say. They were probably too busy eating. Some thralls, small and dark-haired like Faelan, brought large platters of roast meats. Bera drooled and rammed thick slices into her mouth, closed her eyes and savoured the sweet juices.

When she went to seize some more, Hefnir raised a glass cup, full of something red.

'They're not thralls,' he said. 'They like to serve.'

'What's in there?' Bera asked. It might have contained elf blood in such a place as this, but she could drink anything now.

'Wine.'

Heggi lifted his own glass. 'Do you remember, Bera, at a feast once, Papa told us all about wine?'

Hefnir said, 'Try it and see if you like it.'

Never believe a man when he's being kind. Hefnir had told her that himself. He filled her cup from a silver flagon. She lifted it to her lips and was surprised at the coldness of the glass. When she raised it, the smell was like entering a storeroom when the fruits begin to rot. Like sweet vinegar. She sipped and although her lips stung, the taste filled her mouth. It was delicious – but heady.

'I'm not sure you should be drinking it, Heggi.'

'Papa says I'm old enough.'

Hefnir toasted her. 'His is watered.' His smile was wolfish.

Bera found the tussles comforting; they were a reminder of home, of what she was trying to save. She thought of their new homestead with a pang. Her daughter was there, but she was not thinking of the new longhouse as home at all. Well, that could change. Her wine was all drunk and Hefnir refilled her glass.

She hiccupped. 'We have a baby girl, you and I.'

'What did you name her?' he asked, with no surprise or pleasure.

'I told you,' said Heggi. 'Valdis, only Sigrid and I call her Disa, like Sigrid used to call Bera's mother.'

It troubled Bera but she sent out a silent prayer to her mother to guide Faelan safely to her baby. Although the ensense had befuddled the visions, it had let her into Faelan's true feeling for Rakki and knew that having reached him, he would protect him. And so he would her baby.

Hefnir nudged Heggi. 'You should have named her after your own mother.'

He got hiccups. 'B-Bera is my m-mother.'

Bera kissed him. Then she ate so much that she thought her underskirt would rip and she loosened her belt. The faces opposite grew more blurred. There were raised voices: Heggi certainly and probably Hefnir, but she couldn't make out what they were arguing about. She patted the place beside her but it was empty. No Egill. In fact, she couldn't remember Egill being there after she had passed her the bowl. Then the room began to spin.

Voices were rumbling, loud then soft. Cronan?

'She was in the ensense too long. I couldn't lift her and had to fetch a warder.'

'The wine's gone to her head.' Hefnir. 'I'll get her to bed.'

She was lifted off the bench.

Heggi giggled like a toddler. 'You should have watered hers too, Papa!'

'Take your drink like a man,' said his father roughly.

Bera felt sick. There was not a chance she would lose all the delicious food she had eaten, so she swallowed hard.

There was Egill again, a looming grin. 'I'll look after Heggi.'

'Need… air.' Bera waved a hand and knocked over her glass. 'Crystal.' It sounded nice, so she said it again, loudly. 'Crystal.'

'Come on.' Hefnir swung her up into his arms.

He carried her along dark passages. Up, down, jiggling, then throwing her over his shoulder. She spat out something bitter and cursed like her father. She laughed and got the hiccups, which did not stop.

At last they were outside and he propped her against a wall. It was night and the air was cool. Bera felt more drunk but less sick. She slowly slid sideways to lean against Hefnir, who stayed quiet. The sun's skern, a thin waxen moon, had risen.

'Like a fingernail,' she muttered.

'The ash cloud has gone,' Hefnir said.

She shook her head. 'Cloud's higher. Making everything milky, like through muslin.'

He kissed her hard.

It took Bera completely by surprise. Hefnir's skin brought back youthful longing. It was like the first time, when they shared mead in the same kiss.

He softly kissed her neck and chest, untying her dress and gazing at her.

'You're truly beautiful now,' he said, his familiar voice thick. 'I could almost—'

She kissed him, almost biting him; taking charge in a way that she had not done before, even on the hunting trip. She was a woman, not a girl. And a Valla, with all that brought.

He pulled away. 'I don't want you saying you were drunk.'

She was, but it only took away the strangeness. Their need was simple and mutual. With relief that Valla passion was met by wifely duty, Bera relished their honeyed and natural reunion.

20

Thirst woke her. For a moment she thought she was in her billet in Seabost but when she reached out a hand, she was alone in a cold, high bed with heavy covers, not at all like her bedroll. The light was different too: there were fat, tall candles smelling of honey. It felt like the middle of the night and she lay back, feeling worse than a megrim and sleep would not return. She tried telling herself that the ensense and wine had affected her judgement; that Hefnir was a necessary tool in her getting the black stone; that he was her children's father; that he had changed. None of it was true. Ottar would have said, guilt is for the gulled. It was as human an act as drinking when you have a thirst, so why did remorse nag her? Hefnir was her husband, so the betrayal would have been if she had given in to the feelings she had when Faelan was near… She needed to get up. None of this was of any importance compared to finding Obsidian.

The morose form of her skern flickered wanly.

I wish I was better at prediction.

'I'm not thinking of replacing you with ensense,' she said. 'It has other properties that I don't care for.'

He brightened and winked. *Faelan is good with animals but you shouldn't use that as a yardstick for trust. Think of Dellingr.*

'He will be himself again,' said Bera. 'When I get home, I'll put it right.'

Hope over experience. That's you all over.

Bera swung her legs over the bed and went in search of water. She was pleased to see she was in the same room as Heggi but the other two beds were empty. She drank a ladleful of water from the stoup at the door and then saw Heggi was awake.

'Are you thirsty?'

He nodded and she brought him a ladleful, which he drank down in one.

'That ensense stuff,' he began. 'I was wondering… did you really see Rakki?'

Bera smiled. 'Of course. Scampering behind Faelan.'

Heggi's voice warbled. 'Bera…'

'Go on.'

'When I saw my father again… I thought it would be like when he used to come home from the Marsh Lands. I sort of made him different.'

Bera nodded. 'I used to think the same about Ottar but he was always the same hard father.'

'In my head I made it that he had come back for me.'

'And…?'

He just shook his head.

'Boykin, listen. What happened on the beach. The only important thing that you must understand is that Thorvald and I wanted to protect you. I would never keep you away from your father if that's where you wanted to be.'

His poor breaking voice rose to a squeak. 'I wanted us all to be together, like folk in the old days, with me and Ginna and our babies and you and Papa.'

It upset Bera too. 'I wish it—'

'No, I know it's not your fault. I asked him last night and they never went to Iraland.'

'What?'

'They came straight here, for the black stone. They've been here all the time, Bera, so why didn't they send for us?'

Bera was reeling. It explained why Egill had the time to 'devise' the trolley. They must have tried to get Obsidian and only sent for her when they failed. She wanted to curse Hefnir but Heggi was already hurt enough. He was tugging her sleeve.

'And you know who brings all the stuff from Iraland, don't you? The one they all say is a god thing?'

Of course, with his full dragon body. How blind she had been!

Why had she not seen all this? Was she so bound to the land and the earth to her that the events of these men passed her by, like midges to the mountain? Or did her mind skip to Faelan too readily? No, the Serpent King was her enemy and she resisted thinking of him as a provider. He must not have come yet from Iraland, or Hefnir would be dead. Heggi's uncle.

'What did your father say about him?'

'Nothing. He got really cross and left me alone in here.' His voice wavered. 'Like he used to shut me in that cell.'

'I promised that you would never be locked in a cell again, didn't I? And you never will be, while I breathe.'

'I wasn't exactly locked in,' Heggi said, 'but there was a warder outside.'

'I'm here now. I'll watch over you. This is a safe billet, boykin.'

Bera pulled the blankets over him and softly sang until he fell asleep again. Or had Hefnir made some pact with the Serpent King? Was she to die in his place? Surely this was proof that the Serpent sent wolfsbane. She would keep her boy from harm of any kind – even if it came from his father – and do whatever it took to stop him.

The next time she woke, Bera saw that Hefnir and Egill were asleep in the room. She was lying next to Heggi, who was dreaming, twitching like a dog. She sensed it was early morning and the candle flames were low. Her mouth was dry but otherwise she was feeling stronger. Just as well: she wanted to hurt Hefnir for being a worse man than she thought. How could he have overwintered here, after refusing to stay on Ice Island with them? Why had he not sent for his son? Telling Heggi he had not gone to Iraland was like slapping his face. Bera's pressing duty lay elsewhere and she might need them – but she would be on her guard with Hefnir and Egill, his willing puppet.

She carefully got up, stretched like a cat, and slipped out as silently, in search of Cronan. Short, dark-haired warders stood along the passageways. They wore thick leather tunics and sheathed swords at their belts. They made no move to hinder her; in fact, she wasn't sure they even noticed her as they kept their eyes fixed to the front. It must have been these men in the shadows the day before. There were shufflings in the darkness and the humming sound again; echoing footsteps in corridors leading up into the tunnels and warrens. Sometimes Bera heard a kind of chanting. Perhaps all the noises were ermites in their separate cells.

The Beehive of Brid.

Bera began to feel herded. The unblinking men were gradually closing in. She deliberately made for an unlit tunnel and at once a warder took one step to the side to block the way. Were they protecting her from something or protecting something from her? Or were they keeping the dangerous taint of a woman away from the holy men? She kept to the lit tunnel, sure that she was being led back to the serpent door. It was where she thought Cronan was likely to be. Sure enough, she ended up in front of it. She braced herself to touch it, grasped the heavy ring in both hands, turned it and entered.

The blue smoke was denser now and everywhere; there was no separate layer and no fresh air. The room had no walls, no substance. The ensense dazed her and then took swift effect. Her skull opened to messages from the ancestors. Up in the high, dizzy spaces, some shadowy forms were gazing down at her. She could almost see their features but the more she strived, the mistier they became. One had a heart-shaped brow but... no good. It was always like this when she tried to picture the whole of her mother's face.

She was glad to have her skern with her. 'That was her, wasn't it?'

One of them. Hold my hand and look, dear one. Learn.

They floated upwards together, through the scented smoke, past birds, past bats, up towards a widening patch of sky. At the top, Bera felt the sharp claw of icy air on her scalp. The softly curved spine of Ice Island lay before her, leading south towards her new home. Beads linked by fire. There would be no escape for anyone at the homestead. The black bead on her necklace was a branding iron on her skin.

'What does it have to do with the black bead?'

Obsidian is fire-made stone.

The mountains were growing flatter as Bera drifted upwards, higher than the clouds. She was far enough away to see the ancient Skraken's slow, slow growing of the Ice-Rimmed Sea and all its islands. It lay bleeding on the abyssal plain, making the beaches of Ice Island clotted black. Then it coiled, biting its monstrous tail in pain, and became, for an instant, her mother's bracelet. Pain and fear, forever linked with loss. It was writhing in agony, lashing its tail faster and faster until Bera looked through the blur to fiery liquid flowing beneath, like the white-hot metal Dellingr poured.

Brewed by Hel.

The Skraken was a solid mass of pain, surrounded by molten fluid that would burst through the thin crust and boil the sea, far beyond Ice Island, into the White Sea.

Not yet. And maybe not at all if you get this right.

'So what do I have to do?'

Hold the black stone and gaze into its heart. It will reveal truths.

It was not at all as she expected. No wonder it was kept away from others.

There was a storm of coughing.

Bera was a giddy girl, standing on solid ground before the high wooden throne. Beside it was Cronan, glistening with sleek black ravens. Humming began in the darkness, which grew louder until it made her ribcage thrum.

'Is that bees?' she asked.

'Plainsong.' Cronan's chest was rattling.

There was a harsh, rasping breath and the ravens flew up, cawing, into the deeper black. Bera wondered if bees made plainsong.

Ermites chanting.

'Not bees?'

Of course not bees. Her skern frowned. *Are you up to the job?*

'Watch me.'

The chanting sounds odd because they are all ill here, so it's phlegmy.

'What did you see?' Cronan asked her. 'Ensense is quicker next day, but often gone bad, more like a nightmare.'

'What was your nightmare?' she asked.

'My lost childhood.' His sad voice barred more questions.

Bera also needed to move on. 'I have seen what happens next.'

Cronan sighed, making Bera wonder if he was envious of her. There was fluttering far above them and the ravens spoke.

'*Three in one for the wearer of the stone.*'

'Your ravens say I am three in one because I wear the stone.' She showed him the black bead.

Cronan nodded. 'I taught them well. Ensense is fruitful for you, it seems.'

'What is ensense?' she asked.

'It gives meaning: en-senses you.'

'I meant what kind of thing is it?'

'It's a substance that is traded. One of the precious things that travel halfway round the world to be exchanged for others.'

'Like obsidian.'

'*Obsidian!*' cawed the birds in the high reaches. '*Obsidian! Obsidian!*'

A harsh breath elsewhere, followed by the sound of a bubbling chest and wheezing. Cronan turned awkwardly towards the throne. His face twisted with pain as he made a low bow. To what? The throne looked empty, apart from a pile of rich fabrics heaped on the cushions.

'The Abbot,' said Cronan.

Bera moved closer and Cronan grasped her arm.

'No one must breathe his air,' he hissed. 'Especially no woman.'

'But I—'

'Keep this distance, or risk death.'

He stayed low and shuffled backwards into the darkness. There was a cawing as the door slammed, then silence.

Now she was alone with the Abbot. He was shrunken in furs, his face pinched between a tall silk hat and high collar. How could this be a person of power? His garments rustled as he turned to look at her with hooded yellow eyes. Hostility seared Bera like a smith's flame. The Abbot was no sea-rider or Drorgher, and yet Bera wished she had a warrior with her. Thorvald. The thought of his strength and belief in her gave her courage. She pulled back her shoulders and stepped forward.

She had never seen anyone as old. It was dishonourable and disgusted her. His breathing was so laboured that it was more like a death rattle.

'This place is making you ill,' Bera said. 'You need fresh air. You all have phlegm.'

'What… are… you?' His voice was a reedy whisper.

Bera thought he kept folk back because he would crumble into dust if anyone breathed too hard.

'My name is Bera.'

'Brid?'

'I'm a Valla.'

His words came in small whistles. 'Explain… Valla,' he said.

'One family of Northwomen are Vallas, passed down mother to daughter. We can see the future. Some of my ancestors were skilled at verse, others at raising storms; some could cure the sick with potions. That's what I'm good at. And reading weather, keeping us safe at sea.' That hurt.

'Hefnir… says you control Fate.' His tiny eyes glittered. It was a test.

This would be for Hefnir's own benefit, for he believed in nothing except wealth. No lies on Ice Island. It seemed even more important in the muddle of what she had to do now she was here, so she tried to be exact.

'Folk say Vallas make Fate – but I think we ride our fate, or steer it like a longboat on a whale path.'

'You must… believe.'

How dare he tell her what she must do?

'I chose to come here, not to help you but to quieten the land. Now, thanks to ensense, I know it's even more important. What I need to do next is to hold the black stone in my hands.'

'No one… ever… may gaze upon… Obsidian!'

'Why?'

It punched the air from his chest.

Bera went on. 'Only a Valla can do this. I have to see how to stop the destruction of this island and every creature on it. Including you.'

The Abbot hissed, gasped and then began coughing: a retching, hawking, bubbling noise that made Bera feel sick. She was frightened that he would choke and she would be accused of killing him. The noises stopped. She looked round for some water but there was nothing.

Don't thump his back, whatever you do. Her skern was on the throne, swinging his long legs nonchalantly.

'Where are his wardens?'

He doesn't want them corrupted by being close to you. Better do something, ducky, and fast.

The Abbot was turning blue. The air was so thick, it made it difficult to breathe – and there was her answer. She had to get him out into fresher air. Lifting him was out of the question. The thought appalled her but she had to act now to get air into his body. Bera pulled him towards her. It was like handling a papery moth that could crumble into dust. She pushed down his collar, lifted his chin, wiped away the dribble with the back of her hand and then clasped her lips to his and blew, suppressing the feeling that she was held by a beak.

She could die for this.

Bera tried to concentrate. The Abbot must have been brought in here without being touched, so in a pause between breaths she studied the chair. Her skern tapped its wheels, so it must have been pushed into the colossal throne. She gave the Abbot another breath, uncoupled his chair and rolled it towards the entrance. She flung the oak door wide and then trundled him outside.

Cronan was talking with a warden. They both turned white when they saw her.

'Move away!' the man shouted.

Her only hope was to keep the Abbot alive. He was still not breathing for himself, so Bera pressed her mouth to his again.

The warden came closer but then stopped, looking terrified of the crumpled body on the chair.

Cronan pulled her shoulder. 'What is happening?'

'I am breathing for him,' Bera said.

He groaned. 'The Abbot's wardens are unarmed but the warders are coming.'

The sweeter air was having no effect on the Abbot and Bera blew into his mouth again while the others dithered. Footsteps were approaching from a tunnel.

She was desperate. 'Cronan, help me!'

Two armed warders walked in but stopped dead when they took in the Abbot, slumped in his chair.

'Fetch the healer!' one of them shouted.

'I am the healer,' Bera said and breathed again into the stale lungs of the dying man.

They rushed forward, swords unsheathed.

Cronan stepped forward. 'Wait! If you want the Abbot to live, let her be.'

'But she cannot touch him!'

'You see that she can,' Cronan said quietly. 'Fetch water!'

It was all too late. The wizened lips were now covered in blood-flecked spittle.

For goodness' sake, do it properly. Her skern was testy.

'I'm trying.'

Watch. First close his nose...

Bera took a deep breath, pinched the Abbot's bony nose, covered his whole mouth with her own and felt his chest rise. She made herself do it slowly and deeply six times, then bent him forward, waiting to see if he could breathe alone. There was a small trail of air and she sat him upright.

'I've done what I can,' she said to Cronan. 'He may be too old to save.'

'Live or die, there will be consequences.' His voice wavered.

The warden crossed himself. 'No woman may touch the Abbot except Brid herself.'

Armed warders ran in and surrounded Bera but she clung on to the Abbot's chair, willing him to live. If he died, she would be killed at once. If he lived, surely even he would be grateful. They were all trapped in this moment, waiting.

The Abbot gave a deep, rattling sigh. His purple eyelids stayed closed but he took a whole breath, and then another. He was breathing again, if noisily. At least everyone there could hear he was alive. It occurred to Bera that he may think she had tried to kill him, not save him. Or even if he accepted the truth, she was still a woman, who had handled him roughly. Intimately. Perhaps he was thinking up a worse punishment than death.

The Abbot slowly opened his dragon eyes.

21

'You… have… transgressed.'

His voice was the merest whisper but the crowd sighed.

Bera stood taller. It wasn't a good word, whatever it meant. The warders stepped closer with a stamp of feet. If death was coming, she would meet it proudly. But she would have failed – and who then would save all the creatures on the island? Rakki, Heggi, Valdis… poor little Dotta, Miska… Faelan.

'I saved your life.' Bera made each word weighty.

'Only Brid could save my life. Only she.'

'Are you alive? Yes. So who do you think saved you?' Bera crossed her fingers.

The Abbot's voice was torn silk. 'Take her.'

She stepped away from them. 'Cronan, tell the Abbot what you know.'

Cronan shrank back, his curved spine making him a rune of distress. 'I don't understand.'

'What did you hear in the Abbot's throne room?'

'Nothing, I—'

'What did your ravens tell you?'

Cronan at last understood. Bera hoped she was the only one to see him cross his fingers.

He tapped the tattoo on his wrist. 'The wearer of the black stone is the three-in-one.'

The others began to murmur. The Abbot stirred and such was his influence that they noticed. He took a few breaths.

Only the powerful are given time to speak, as Ottar would say.

'It – cannot – be – you,' he declared.

Bera held up her necklace to show him the black bead. Its heat reminded her she must act fast.

'If only Brid could save your life, I must be Brid,' she said.

The deep humming from the cells throbbed like the pulse in her forehead.

'Hear that?' The Abbot raised a blue-nailed finger to the sky. 'Brid will strike you down!'

'Well, she hasn't, has she? And the only possible reason is because I am Brid.'

There was a cry and running footsteps. Egill burst into the circle round the Abbot. Bera's heart sank. If it was possible to make a bad situation worse, Egill would manage it.

'Bera can heal,' Egill said. 'She makes medicine sticks and things.'

She made Bera sound like a simple crone.

'Be quiet, Egill,' she hissed. Bera turned again to the Abbot. 'I made no claim. It was Cronan himself who told me I was Brid.'

Cronan's blind, darting eyes were like a rabbit's before an eagle-strike.

'You did, Cronan. The healer, the poet and the silversmith. Remember?'

The humpback shook his head weakly. Bera hoped he would not tell the Abbot how she denied it all the time. Perhaps he wasn't sure what to say for the best.

He speaks only truth. Or so he believes.

Egill chipped in again. 'She brews potions to take coughs away.'

'It's true that I can make the right plants potent with my – Brid's – healing power.'

Cronan brightened. 'We have a medicinal garden here, tended by the ermites.'

'Then she is no better than you.' The Abbot caught his breath. 'And so must die.'

There was a scuffle and Hefnir burst through. He would gain standing by killing her. This would be his revenge for what had happened on the black beach and fulfil his bargain with the Serpent King, cancelling the blood debt. He came into the centre of the circle.

'Bera has heard voices as long as I have known her.' He looked intently at the Abbot. 'There are moments when she looks distant, listening to things the rest of us can't hear and her lips move silently in answer.'

'Or she is mad,' said the Abbot. 'And only a madwoman would dare touch me.'

'If I had not touched you, you would be dead,' Bera insisted. 'You yourself said only Brid could do that and survive.'

Hefnir murmured, 'You may not survive very long unless you convince them.'

Bera said, 'I can prove who I am. I know what is coming, and how to save you.'

'You shall speak. I demand it.' The Abbot sank back onto his cushions. 'But I need strength to hear. I shall retire to my cell now and you will talk before supper.' He closed his yellow eyes.

Bera knew he wanted all her knowledge and then he would kill her.

'Please! If you are prepared to wait you shall hear much more. Let me get into the tower and scry. I will tell you everything.'

'Never. I do not believe you are Brid, even if you wear the black stone. Where is your serpent? And unless you convince me otherwise, this is merely a stay of execution.' He raised a hand. 'And if you have passed some filthy female miasma into me, you will die instantly, no matter who you think you are.'

His warder put on leather mittens, bowed, and wheeled the chair into darkness, the crowd falling away with lowered heads as the Abbot passed.

Cronan made Bera an odd sort of bow. 'I truly believe you are she.'

Hefnir chuckled. 'Slippery as an eel, my wife. Good at getting her way. And she wants what we want, don't you, Bera?'

'Obsidian, at the start.'

'Then we must plan, together.'

Their eyes met and Bera was on a honeymoon shore with him, the rest of the world forgotten. She reminded herself that as soon as the honest pairing of their bodies was over, Hefnir had hidden the truth, as he always did. As did Egill, who had secretly watched them.

An armed warder stepped forward to hold Bera.

Hefnir waved him away. 'Where would we run to?'

It was horribly true.

The man gave a curt nod and let her go but escorted them towards their cell. In the passageways the humming and its echo was so loud that Bera thought her head would burst.

Hefnir said, 'Lauds.'

Lords? Bera could only think about Heggi. She burst into the billet and ran to him. He was completely unconcerned and all he talked about was Cronan.

'He promised to show me his ravens! They can speak and everything, like Woden's!'

Hefnir said, 'I'll get a warder to fetch him.' He looked at Bera and winked.

Bera supposed he was helping: if Heggi did not know their plan, they would not torture him to find out. What would happen to him? Could she rely on Egill to make sure they all managed to escape once she had the stone? It was hard to stay determined when the future was unclear.

Cronan spoke quietly to Bera before they left. 'If I have Heggi, they will think you will stay and not guard you so closely.'

Bera sat beside Hefnir on her bed where they could talk quietly and pretend to be on marital duty if a warder came in. Whatever was decided, she hoped he would keep his word. Which husband was he today? Which man? Success depended on him, though she groaned when he said it began with a scheme of Egill's devising.

'It's to get you through the first gate.'

She had to do it. 'So my first task is to get onto the trolley and past the wolves.'

'We will make a diversion for you.'

'It's downhill, so it will easily reach the tower. But I will need help hauling the chains to get back.'

Hefnir ran a hand over his beard. 'Once you're through this gate, Bera, that's it. There will be no coming back.'

There was a tiny version of herself in his blue eyes that looked candid, open. Like Heggi's.

'Is your skern speaking to you?'

'He says he will stay with you here, Hefnir, to make sure all goes well.'

Her skern flickered in fright. For once, she had surprised him. Both of them, in fact.

I c–c–c–can't leave you. Her skern's face lengthened with distress.

'I do need you to watch Hefnir. He wants Obsidian so much he might betray me once I have it – and take Heggi.'

But n–n–n–n–not that. I don't know what would happen to either of us.

'Saying "either of us" makes me feel sick.'

The ache in her ribs reminded Bera how even a small distance hurt; she worried her heart would rip if they were sundered.

'Stay close to me, please,' she said and felt her skern's relief.

'Time to start,' Hefnir said. 'How long do you need in the tower?'

'I have no idea. I don't know how to get into the outer tower, or what I have to do in there, or whether I'll be able to scry even if I do.' She had not meant to be so honest but all the shocks of the day had burst through her guard.

'Poor Bera.' He took her hand. 'I'll wait for you as long as I can at the *Raven* with Heggi and Egill.'

'Is she beached?'

'Too many hazards to land. We're anchored in the next bay, south of the jetty. You'll have to row to us.'

'Keep Heggi safe.'

'With my life. But, Bera—'

'What?'

'If our lives are threatened I shall leave you behind.'

'I know.'

She only hoped his desire for the stone was enough to make him wait for her at all.

22

Egill took her a secret way to the skull spring. The small globes gleamed wetly and Bera silently asked her mother to look after the children who had been sacrificed for their protection. Egill dipped her fingers in the water and made a cross on her own forehead, then repeated it on Bera's. She shivered, as though Egill had drilled a hole in her skull to let water pour through.

Egill leaned in close. 'You'll have until sext.'

'What!'

'Not what you think. It's when they eat, so our absence will be noticed. But Hefnir won't wait even that long if he thinks there's danger.'

'Just make sure Heggi is safe. On your life, Egill.'

'I'll go to him now. We'll be waiting, Bera, onboard the *Raven*.'

She took Egill's hands because they had both loved her father and his boat. It might also be the last time they ever met.

'Watch for the smoke,' Egill said, and left.

Bera carefully watched the warder at the trolley. From inside the Abbotry there came a burst of smoke, shouts, and the man left his post to go and sort out the fire, as expected. She ran to the trolley, clambered up, unlatched the chain and had to snatch her hand away as it leapt from its blocks and hurtled towards the tower.

Look at the wolves, look at the wolves, look at the wolves, chattered its wheels.

The pack heard the clanking of the trolley and grouped in a grey, bristling mass. Their leader stood between them and the tower, a lone, threatening presence. Bera could feel his guarding hard as granite and had no idea how to get past. She would not use her sword on such a creature. He was doing his duty and staying true to his nature. Besides, if she killed one wolf the others would tear her to pieces. The danger was getting closer all the time, too fast for planning, but she trusted her Valla instinct would supply the answer when the moment was upon her. The trolley slowed as it went over the top of the mound. Time to get off – and she knew what the long loop of rope was for. She flung it over a post in the sward, like catching an animal, and the trolley jerked to a stop.

Even though it had put her nearer to the tower than the wolves, she was not prepared to risk running for it. If she could even get her legs to move: the thought of being chased had rooted her. Bera touched the runes ALU on her sword and carefully stepped down.

The tower's steep walls were rougher, sparkling in the sunlight, now she was so close. Could she climb to the high window? No footholds on the snug granite blocks. Cronan's friend lived in there though, so there must be a door to get food to him and the wolves close to the trolley stop. There was no outline of one. There would be no time to find it before the pack was on her. Her scalp flamed.

Trust your new skills, dearest, and look to the leader.

The wolves were slinking forward, yellow teeth bared in their wide heads, only waiting for the signal to kill. There was nowhere for Bera to run. Now she was off the trolley they were as tall as her, with hackles raised. She could sense their lust for the hunt. Their bodies were big-boned but thin and their ribcages showed. Bera felt her palms prickle, as though the wiry pelts had brushed them. Despite their recent meal they looked hungry and this made her pity them. She knew all about hunger in the lean months. Was that dangerous?

Bera was mesmerised, knowing she should concentrate on the large male but unable to tear her eyes away from approaching death. She could smell its mix of fetid breath and old blood. Then she did the bravest thing and closed her eyes. She was able to gaze into the wolf's amber eyes, just as she had done in the scrying. She found and held her warm amber bead to strengthen the bond between them.

'I am not your foe,' she told him.

He was aware of her, she knew it from the widening circles of golden ripples in his mind. He was considering. And all the time she sensed his pack making its hunting circle around her. She fought down the urge to open her eyes. Stay strong. Stay fixed. ALU. The runes sharpened her wits and she let their shape work for her instead of putting so much of herself into every contest.

'I can free you.' Bera pictured Heggi running with Rakki along the wet sand. 'I promise that if I get out of here, you will have freedom.' She put her long journey into his mind, all the huge expanse, very glad that the Abbotry was not, after all, on an island.

The wolf was testing her. Humans lied; humans kept them imprisoned and short of prey.

'I can save you and your kind if you let me pass. If you kill me, you are doomed to die, as we all are.' She made him see the devastation in Smolderby. Brymstones, firestones, death.

All she could hear was the pounding of her blood and sense the grainy thought of the wolf. Too long! She pushed down panic; pushed away the thought of warders realising she was gone and hunting her. If the wolves didn't get her the Abbot would kill her more slowly.

Concentrate!

The smell was a thousand times stronger. A low rumble, a snarl deep in every wolf's throat made the hairs on her neck rise. She must be strong. If she broke contact with their leader now...

He howled. He was calling them to him.

The rumble continued, a fight of will over hunger. His mind sharpened, grew as ridged as the mountain chain and steep as the sea in a storm. His pack obeyed and were loping back, a threat no longer. He was clever, this wolf.

And so was she. Bera opened her eyes. One wolf covered the ground in a few long strides and sprang. She turned and sidestepped. It twisted in mid-air, fell, then seized the back of her leg. Bera was down. The speed shocked her and at first she was rabbit-still. Her leather sea boots and thick bindings had stopped its teeth going through to the bone but her leg was in an iron clamp. The wolf was dragging her further from the pack, growling a warning to keep away from its prize, keeping hold of its prey whilst keeping its own body out of danger. Even if she managed to reach her sword, it would be hard to do any real damage and it was all happening too fast.

There was a grey blur. With no warning, the pack leader barrelled into the other wolf, knocking it to the ground. He held it there, on its back, snarling ferociously. Close up, he was as big as a trole. Her attacker suddenly reared up, gnashing. They rolled, broke apart, snapped, growled, lunged and then the leader struck. With fierce strength and one shake, he broke its neck and ripped out the throat to make sure it was dead. He bared his bloodstained teeth in a snarl of victory and as a lesson.

Bera should have already made for the tower but her legs were too weak to stand. The leader looked at her. This was real: there was no meeting of minds in a Valla vision, this was a wild beast that had just killed one of its own and been hurt in a fight that she had caused. His eyes burned. All Bera had was her promise. She had vowed to save the wolves and she would. Somehow she found the strength to stand and she spoke to him softly, like Faelan would, hoping her voice would sound true.

'I swear to you now, leader to leader, as a true Valla. I have a duty here. What I am doing will keep all creatures alive: you, and your pack too, but first I will free you. I cannot return you to where you were born but when you have the whole of this island to roam, with better prey, you will form a bigger pack.'

The wolf's fury had passed but he was weighing her words.

Bera risked taking two slow steps towards the tower, holding his gaze, keeping her mind away from her wounded leg. The pack slowly gathered behind him but kept their distance. He was guarding her. She risked glancing away from him and the tower was closer than she expected. There was a deep, warning rumble coming from the leader, who was giving her one chance to live. Walking had never been so hard but she kept on, limping, easy prey, trusting the wolf, all the way to the tower.

And then she was there – but she could not see any door. Then real pain began.

*

Words of protection kept the wolves at bay for the moment. Bera ran her hands over the stone, desperate for entrance. The sting from the wolfbite scorched up into her groin and she remembered the rampaging pains of miscarriage and birthing. This pain was nothing. She was tough and too many lives depended on her to give up now. Bera went further round, patting and probing to try to feel a doorframe. She was leaving a trail of blood on the stone that the wolves must smell. Would another defy the leader? How much time would he allow her, himself? She wanted to stay hidden here, where she couldn't be seen by the pack.

You're not playing trole's footsteps. Ask me for help.

'I ask for help all the time.'

You don't mean it. You're stubborn and want to do everything for yourself.

'How else can I learn anything?'

Are we going to argue or get inside?

'Both. Look.'

A small door was opening inwards. Bera crouched low, stepped through the gap, and the door quickly fell shut behind her. The world was lit only by a long candle that made the tall, thin man holding it look like a carved ebony taper-holder, in his black robe and hood. The Warden.

'You are Cronan's friend.'

'From childhood.' He pulled down his hood and his face was the deepest black of a tarred hull. 'I thought the wolves had taken you.'

'Northmen do not grow as old as you,' Bera said. 'Your hair is white but yet you look young.'

'You fight.' His voice was also youthful. 'We spend our lives in prayer.'

'Where is the black stone?'

'It seems Northwomen are as avaricious as their men.'

Greedy. And unsubtle. The last part's right.

'I need only to see it.' Probably. Bera crossed her fingers.

'Why would anyone risk their skin to simply see a stone?'

'Because it's so important. Which is why you guard it.'

'I am put here solely to feed the wolves.' He was lying too.

He held up the candle. Its light made sense of the smell: they were surrounded by dark red carcasses. It was like being in a whale's stomach. No time to be squeamish, she had to gaze into that stone and find out how to stop the mountain exploding.

'Please. I have risked my skin for it, as you say. I must hurry.'

'What "it" do you wish to see?'

'Is there a choice?' Her heart sank. She had imagined there would be one precious black stone in the tower. 'Obsidian.'

His face showed nothing, like black stone itself. 'And if you discover it, what will you do with it?'

The trouble was, she didn't know that either. She was sure it was more important than a scrying tool, for any puddle could do that in the right circumstances.

'It is more potent than ensense,' she said.

He brought the candle right up to her face and looked deep into her eyes. The flame carried on dancing in her vision after he took it away.

'The black glass, forged in fire, has a rare beauty.' His voice was also dark and beautiful. 'Obsidian fractures in circles and sometimes flames with gold. It is the feminine to iron's masculine; a woman's curves and warmth to the man's straight chill. Yet it cuts more keenly than any metal. A knife made of obsidian can slice a hair into six.'

Man's straight iron chill was Hefnir all right and Bera liked the idea of a black, curved, womanly blade being sharper. Then she had a vision of a woman who was holding a black knife to her own throat. Heggi's mother... Had that been obsidian? And what might that mean for Heggi?

'What have you seen?' he asked her.

'That it can slit a throat with a single stroke.'

His mouth slanted. 'You have witnessed bloodshed?'

'In a vision. The woman lost her skern and became a Drorgher.'

'What is that?'

'The walking dead.'

He crossed himself. 'This is why it must be guarded. It can... summon darkness in the soul.'

Bera was dismayed. Her skern had been right in one way, but

perhaps the black stone he guarded was a knife? Was it the very knife Hefnir had spoken of long ago in Egill's hut? She always believed he had gone to look for it in Iraland, which would explain why he wanted it so much now. Did she dare steal it and risk letting him take it from her before her task was done?

What is certain is that Hefnir will leave you here if you turn up at the boat without it.

'Still, I will risk the darkness,' she told the Warden. 'I must see it.'

'"It" again? You have no idea what "it" is.'

'True. But I know I have to somehow use it. I witnessed an event, something so terrible that nothing could live on Ice Island.'

'You have seen a memory trapped in stone. There was a bad quake here, years ago. Some people are sensitive to the event.'

'I know all that.' Bera was impatient. 'I've seen the past. This is the future and I need to find out how to stop it.'

'What has that to do with me?'

Precious time was being wasted. Were the others safe? Was Egill already at the boat with Heggi? The Warden had time on his side. His only duty was to wait.

'Stop quibbling! Just show me the stone and I can work out what to do with it to save your scrawny neck!'

He gave a long sigh. 'I know who you are.'

'Hel's teeth! I shall string you up like these carcasses if this goes on!'

He raised a hand. 'I meant only that Cronan told me to let you in.'

'When did he? How?'

'By raven.'

Messengers of Woden. Of course people would use ravens too. Her heart beat wildly at the sign: the hope in the boat waiting for her because she was the *Raven*, named by Bera in a whispered promise from the ancestors.

'I must see the stone!'

'And so I let you in.' His hand became a warning. 'But Obsidian remains in here and the decision whether to show it to you is mine alone.'

'What can I say to persuade you?'

'Nothing. I have given my whole life to the stone. I came here as a child, leaving my dear friend.'

That was why his voice was so young, because it had never been raised. And there was something of Cronan's sadness there too.

'You would die for it,' she said. 'I understand duty. So please understand that my own duty is to keep folk safe.'

'And you understand nothing about our life here. Can't you see that this is exactly what we are doing? The Westermen guard the stone to keep the world safe – from itself.' Truth rang in his strong voice.

'Then I promise you that if this is what the stone tells me, I will leave it here to be guarded forever.'

'Be silent now and allow me to think.'

There was no day or night inside the tower but with every beat of her pulse, Bera feared it was already too late. She twisted her dress into a knot of care, then caught herself and let go.

He shook his head. 'No, my one duty—'

'The event wrenched my guts and the mountains are unquiet,' she said. 'It's hard to explain but my body and this land are one. I gave birth to a daughter as the tallest mountain erupted, making the sky darken and die.' Bera was desperate to explain what she didn't fully understand herself. 'I need the stone to tell me about how feeling all this changed me.' Saying it aloud made it real. The change was in her, not just in what was happening deep beneath them; so would changing herself calm the earth?

He touched his face. 'My face froze during the worst earthquake.'

'With ice?'

'No, a sympathetic tremor that felt like fire and then afterwards… well, it's hard to eat and I can never smile.'

'So you know that Hel can make the earth ruin our minds and bodies!'

He thinks Hel is a place.

The Warden moved away. 'Come, then. Hurry.'

Bera's heart skipped and she took a step. A shooting pain ran up her leg but would have to be ignored. She followed him up a flight of spiral steps that had no rope or rail and became tighter as they climbed. The stone was polished a glossy black, perhaps by hands. Or was it glass? Shadows lurched and deceived and Bera missed a step and was plunged into mid-air, or so it felt, in black nothingness. It took all her resolve to keep going up. But then there was a glimmer of light and they finally stopped climbing. Bera stood at the threshold of a room where there was enough light to see a table. She fought down disappointment. The table was a homely wooden trestle and on it was an ordinary clay bowl, upside down.

23

Bera refused to follow him into the room. 'Don't waste my time. That is not Obsidian.'

'It has its own properties. Some would say it's more valuable, differently. Come.'

'As riddling as you,' Bera said to her skern and took a step forward.

A howling ache began and she clutched her side. Her skern was gone: not unclasped but missing. Not waving from the threshold, not whispering invisibly, but completely gone, like the unclenching normal folk had at birth. She knew in that moment that he had never left her before, not in the way he was absent now. She had believed he had left her after having the baby but it was not like this torture; this was as though he had never existed. Was this agony what drove the Drorghers out of their graves? Hot tears ran down her cheeks with the pain and fear of it.

The Warden was at the table, his blank face betraying no feeling for her anguish.

'So come and read the runes.'

Perhaps it would return her skern to her. Feeling like she was drowning, Bera made it to him. He carefully picked up the bowl, its raw clay the colour of flesh. Underneath was a hen's egg with brown marks all over it. It reminded her of the stone in the mouth of the skull that Faelan had shown her.

'What's that?' she asked.

'It's to keep demons out of the curse bowl, in case any got in before the outside was painted. The egg is inscribed, like skulls found elsewhere in many lands.'

'You've never seen beyond this tower,' Bera said, feeling cruel because she was hurting so much.

'I can read.' His face was like slate. 'You can't read or write, can you?'

Keeping the bowl rim-side down, he showed her a crude figure, whose body ran all round it, drawn in blood. Bera doubled over as pain shot through her, her guts twisting like the Skraken in the deep.

He nodded. 'All savages can understand pictures.'

She made herself look again. It was a creature, bound by rope or chain. Perhaps a wolf. Fenrir himself, Hel's brother. Mama used to frighten her, saying that at the end of days all bound monsters would be freed by the host of Vallas. They would unleash Fenrir, the wolf of destruction. Did Vallas bring destruction on purpose?

'This is sometimes called a demon bowl,' he said. 'This drawing keeps demons from entering, like your skern.'

Bera found it hard to breathe. 'Please. Let him back in!'

'I can't. The bowl has its own will and you must hold it without him.'

'Give it to me then. Quickly.'

He turned it the right way up, so that Bera could see a spiral of rune-like words inside it, winding their way from the base to the rim.

'This one came from Ninava,' he said, 'or nearby. The effect is the same.'

Bera tried to grab it before her heart broke.

'Foolish. You will fail the test at the outset and never see Obsidian.'

'What test?' The lettering was meaningless without her skern.

'You must hold it. The curse written here commands the bowl to break into pieces if you are untrue. You see the power of words? God created the world by speaking the Word and you can destroy it with lies.'

'I never lie,' she lied. She dared not take it, not yet. 'I am a Valla. We make Fate by doing, not saying.'

'You can do nothing without being. God brought us into being by saying the Word: He named us.'

'What is God?' she sobbed. 'Help me!'

'Then hold the bowl.'

Bera stretched out a hand then drew it back. 'Why test me? Don't you want me to save our world? I swear I'll leave the black stone here but please, let me go to my skern and find it!'

'And stay in here forever? I'd rather Cronan and I were both dead if we cannot be alive together.'

Her guts were on fire. She wanted to smash the bowl for keeping her skern away from her but smothered the thought. ALU, she breathed, trying to find what strength she could. ALU.

She nodded.

Bera held her arms out straight, hands cupped, and the Warden placed the bowl onto them as tenderly as if it were a baby. It had blood-heat too. She felt whole again, as if her skern were clasped. She closed her eyes and tried to recall the truth of the vision she had seen, to be a true person, but only the pain in her leg was real. She could feel the throb of her broken heart against the roughness of the clay, but the bowl was lifeless.

She opened her eyes and saw his mouth twitch.

'It seems you've passed,' he said.

Bera held the unbroken bowl over the inscribed egg, which she quickly palmed before settling the bowl upside down to hide the theft. The agony worsened. She had to get outside the room, fast. She slipped the egg into her pocket and crossed the threshold. Her skern was there at once, pressed into her neck. Instant and intense, they were whole again.

'The egg doesn't keep you away,' she purred.

All the power against demons is in the bowl.

'Are you a demon?'

Apparently I am. Better concentrate now.

Tighter steps wound to the top of the tower. They were dark, oily and nearly invisible and yet the Warden of the stone went up them lightly. Years of practice. Bera dare not look down. Up here, the darkness was almost complete, pressing on the candle flame until it was guttering. Only by feeling the hard surface beneath her feet and the smoothness under her hands could she stay anchored to what was real and now.

As soon as she joined him he blew out the candle and she was engulfed in the blackest black. It was a solid presence, rather than absence, as if she had entered Obsidian itself. All she could smell was cold stone. Bera breathed into her stomach to make her voice stronger.

'Don't seek to frighten me. I've been in a dark place before, with the worst Drorgher. I won that battle.'

Had he moved past her and escaped? Her stomach rumbled, which panicked her because it meant they were near mealtime.

Listen. You can hear him breathe.

Her skern was right. She stopped breathing and heard a murmur of air from her right.

'What is he waiting for?'

Another test. I think you have to sense the stone in the dark.

'Then hurry up and tell me.'

It's beyond reach, on top of a tower of stone.

Bera wanted to show the Warden she knew this much. 'I need a chair, something to stand on.'

'You are not tall enough to see the stone and may not touch it. No one has since the first Abbot, who built the tower within the tower to… protect it.'

'Why did you bring me up here, only to fail?' She coaxed, 'Cronan wants you to let me try.'

Silence.

'If I do reach the stone, will you let me keep it?'

'No.'

She was furious. 'Do all you ermites enjoy seeing a woman plead?'

He sighed. 'You are no mere woman and I thought you might kill me if I tried to stop you. I have no experience of violence and saw how you subdued the wolf, who does.'

'I would not kill anyone in cold blood.'

Have you come up here to talk?

'I hate you!'

You love me. It's the same thing, upside down. Use that energy to get what you want.

A tiny thrill inside her knew what he meant. The Warden moved so close that she could feel his breathing, cold in and warm out, and smell the sweet, peppery ensense. Underneath, the sharp smell of fear.

'Is it me you fear... or something else?' Then Bera knew. 'You don't just guard Obsidian, do you? You fear it!'

'The first Abbot went mad. After looking into the stone, he went mad in a way that I wouldn't choose to be near.'

'I promise you this. If I feel it sending me mad I will kill myself, rather than hurt you.'

'You cannot promise.' He moved right away. 'Yet I cannot hinder you. It's the one request Cronan has made in all the years.'

So Bera quested upwards, scanning through black for the ultimate blackness of stone, and something twisted slightly in its hollow. Like an oar in its hole. Like an eye in its socket. She had moved it with sheer force of will. The Warden gasped. So he had felt it shift too.

It is also looking for you.

Now that she was close to holding it, Bera hesitated. What if the changes she felt in herself were bad? Were all Vallas destined to become darker as their bodies aged – or changed by childbirth – or was it the land that had changed her?

Go ON!

Bera knew what she had to do and the act would bring knowledge, and knowledge is power, as Ottar would say. Planting a picture in the wolf's mind was a new skill, which she could use here. The darkness helped, like closing her eyes. She touched the black bead of her necklace, a shard of Obsidian's dark light, that had guided her like a lodestone. She was ready. Bera pictured her skern lifting the stone and bringing it down to her. She held her hands out in front of her, as she had for the curse bowl, but was still surprised when almost at once the cold stone lay heavily on them. Its shape was unexpected.

'Obsidian.' Bera said. 'I hold it – but now must look at it.'

The Warden lit the candle but kept his back resolutely turned.

The stone had roundness but not depth. Not a ball but a scrying-glass.

Bera moved closer to the candle's flame and held up the glass. A small face, which she took to be her own, loomed back at her. It looked worried and thin. Nothing else. All that torment for nothing, and she felt robbed.

'There is no danger in this,' she said. 'Nor any help.'

He let out his breath in a long sigh. 'I had begun to believe in you.' He opened a shutter. 'But I am glad it has not sent you mad.'

'Wait! More light will kill any hope of scrying. Let me try again.'

He quickly closed it. 'The warders are coming out.'

Why was the bead still burning her throat? It was making it hard to think, let alone clear her mind enough to scry.

Try, dearest.

'My necklace is the link to the Vallas. Obsidian is the black bead's occult twin, like you and me.'

So look through it, not at it.

She held the glass up once more and behind her stretched a long line of all her Valla ancestors. There was some property in the glass that made her want to keep gazing at these shadows. She expected to feel deep respect but slowly something was reflected back at her that both enthralled and shocked: she understood that all their dark will was battening on the badness inside her. Who could resist looking – or looking away – once they had? What evil would prey on the world at the command of this dark army of shadows? It was why the glass was kept in blackness and why no one should look into it.

'No!' Bera dropped the black stone onto the floor.

'What are you doing?' the Warden cried.

She felt the Vallas were urging the land's devastation through her. If it was the stone that revealed the knowledge, then it should show her what upheaval was coming, even if it sent her mad. She knelt down and leaned over it so that the black bead touched the glass. It took all her courage. She might first have to face the worst stains of her nature. What if they bloomed, once seen, like squid ink in seawater? Like bad blood in Heggi.

'All right. Let me see beyond. Let me understand.'

It was immediately worse than she feared.

She was deafened by fire. Clouds of red and orange billowed and blazed like a sunset above a bubbling, boiling stream of Hel's vomit, belching and retching molten bronze and copper. Deep within were spouts of burning white, like the heart of a funeral pyre, turning bone to ash, but this heat was beyond anything; even hotter than white metal in the smith's pourings. The earth's shrieks were the shifting hip bones of birthing. Bera flinched away.

You are seeing the centre of the earth, at the birth of Obsidian.

Then bone-freezing cold and silence. She was in a black vortex, like the maelstrom, but travelling upwards, bursting through the earth's crust and rushing far, far into space and time… an exquisite trail… unknown words that described a place she had never been. Then drifting, slowly turning, afloat in a limitless sea of stars. Joy. Before her was a perfect sphere, as jewelled as one of the beads in her hands. Blue. A beautiful, fragile sea path that widened to embrace the world. Soundless and still. She cradled it in her gaze, watching coils of clouds and the flickering green waves of the North Lights. These lights had saved her from a Drorgher and the memory came with it. Her Valla ancestors were speaking, sounding like the ravens:

'*… from deepest black, through blood red, scorched by the blue flash of an exquisite trail of trillions of dying stars, we are in space and time, until we reach…*'

Her skern was impatient. *Study the next thing.*

'No! They were saying something important!'

It's an ancient echo in space, repeating until the end of time. Watch!

A burst of orange flame blazed at the top and it was the northern tip of Ice Island. Then a second and third and fourth and fifth flared in turn, like beads on a golden chain. She had predicted this much. But then, horror! The chain of fire spread over the globe, unstoppable. The fires grew in size and number, faster and faster, until the small world split into cracks of flame and the sea path burned orange and became one huge, shimmering blaze that made a sun; a burnished, golden orb encircled by glittering flame that was beautiful and terrible and then…

Nothingness.

Bera tasted iron. She had seen the last days of the known world – and some Valla part of her exulted.

The Warden said, 'I don't want to know what you saw. Your face was...' He had no words.

'I am n-not m-m-mad.' She must have bitten her lips.

This was worse than her own inner darkness. No one must ever look into the looking-glass again – but Bera knew she must. She would have to look a third time, to find out how to stop the chain of fire getting started. She was a link between a dead Valla and her living granddaughter – so she could break the whole chain, couldn't she?

First signs of madness.

The Warden put a beaker to her lips. 'Try to drink this.'

'Obsidian was made at the beginning of time and I have just seen its end.' Bera gulped down the sweet water then pushed the beaker away. 'I have to hurry. It's clear to me now. I must find the right place and... destroy it.'

Did the looking-glass tell you that? Do you know what it means?

'I only know that no one else must look in it.'

'Do you know where you have to go?' asked the Warden.

Bera got to her feet. 'Yes. The stone told me.'

You have no idea.

Bera wanted to kick her skern. 'If you hadn't interrupted the ancestors I would know!'

They're poets, they like the sound of words...

'Then I must let you. Anyone who could release the stone from its tower must be trusted.' He raised the candle.

'And as you see, I'm not mad.'

Ha!

The Warden moved past her and stood right over the stone he had spent his life guarding, keeping the candle from dripping, unable to tear his eyes away from the stone's perfect, sable sheen.

'Do you think I...'

Bera snatched it up and pushed it up under her tunic, away from his sight.

'I wish you a long and peaceful life,' she said.

He made the Brid cross and nodded. 'How will you escape?'

She had no idea. 'I am Brid, I will think of something.'

'You are not Brid.' He crossed himself again.

'All right, I'll tell you who I am. I am a true Valla, a healer of the earth, with a mother and daughter to help me, and that's a better threesome than your old Brid any day!'

She set off, fuming, and barged into a stool. Her wounded leg hurt a lot and started to bleed again.

'Thou must first heal thyself,' muttered the Warden.

Bera grabbed his candle, which was almost too thick for her hand, and started down the steps. It was easier to see but her leg was hurting badly. When she reached the first level, where the clay bowl was, she felt her skern's long nails cling tightly to her neck. Then they were past, and finally back amongst the reeking carcasses.

'Take off your boot.' The Warden went into a small cell.

Bera felt a deep pity for the man, spending his whole life in such a place. Well, there was nothing to guard now. Had she freed him by taking the stone, or made it worse? He came back with a linen cloth and made a pad. She remembered the pot of salve the old crofter had given her and took it from her apron. She daubed some on, put the pad beneath her leggings and then strapped on her boot. It would have to do.

'Time to go,' she said. 'See where the warders are.'

She followed him to the door. He carefully opened it a crack and peered out. In the narrow shaft of light there was something noble about his poor, frozen face. Bera put a hand up to it and something quickened under her fingers. The muscle had only numbed; it wasn't dead. This was new, to glimpse the future in flesh. Perhaps Obsidian also brought out the good.

'One day your face will be restored,' she said. 'Perhaps when you are free of this burden. Your friend Cronan can help, with his herbs and love, now you have nothing to stay for in here.'

He shook his head. 'The Abbot will have me killed. Either the warders will kill me now or sometimes the Abbot likes to watch transgressors die. Slowly with poison.'

Bera rummaged in her apron again and silently thanked the old crofter, hoping she was still alive.

'If it's wolfsbane, I have a remedy.' She gave him the leaves. 'They don't look much now, but being dried should double the potency.'

He thanked her. 'But keep them for yourself. Wolves and men will be out for blood… and I wanted so much to have Cronan near me when I died.'

'Let's try this,' she said. 'I'll put a knife to your throat as we go outside. You tell them I pretended to be dead from a wolf attack and surprised you. That I forced you to give up the stone and will slit your throat if they come near us.'

His eyes smiled. 'I'm supposed to slit my own throat if I fail. Still, we must go outside and face whatever fate is in store for us both.'

Bera got her knife ready. 'I feel a deeper Valla strength. We make our own fate and I must succeed.'

They went out together.

24

There were no warders to be seen – and no wolves. Bera put away her knife and went to take the man's hand. He brushed it away.

'Go well. Remember, fierce young woman, that you bear the weight of trust.'

'Believe me, it's easier than bearing the weight of mistrust.'

Then she ran. The trolley was still tied to its post, suggesting the warders had never got as far as the tower, or surely one of them would have had the sense to stop her means of escape. They must have thought she would head straight to the main gate. She tried to clamber up onto the platform but her injured leg could take no weight. The black glass dropped out from under her belt and squatted on the grass like a toad. Did it want to stay in the tower? Bera sternly picked it up and tied it into her shawl. She was determined to be its master and told it to stay there.

Bera managed to hoist herself up to sit on the trolley and then swing her legs round. She stood up to look towards the main gate. The wolves were ranged along the slope, facing a line of armoured warders, whose backs were to the moat. Of course: the trolley didn't matter because there was only one way out and she had no choice but to go there. She slipped the rope and fear struck her.

'Have they captured Heggi?' she asked her skern.

The trolley set off before he could answer, uncontrollably rattling towards the moat. His teeth chattered. She would have to wait for his answer until it stopped but until then she needed to plan, especially if Heggi was in trouble.

The bridge was still raised and Bera made the most of her chance to take in the situation. There was no sign of her son and her worry increased. Suddenly anxious her skern's silence was a kind of vanishing after their ordeal, she checked to make sure he was still there.

He winked.

The pack leader's mind was a closed, barbed fist, with no way in. Or she didn't want one. The wolves made rushes at the outer flank of armed men, who threw themselves into the water to escape. Bera could hear their cries and when she was closer she saw them tugging at their breastplates, which were dragging them down. The rest regrouped to face the pack: death behind and death before them. If they lowered the bridge to save themselves, the guards would let the wolves into the outer compound. There were some grey bodies on the ground but the smell of bloodlust was in the air.

Bera felt remorse for both sides. Had she brought ruin to everything in this isolated community? Perhaps… but without taking Obsidian it would be in ruins later, along with the rest of the world. She had seen where she must take it but what she must do then was unclear – or how it would stop the end of days.

One step at a time, step at a time, step at a time, the trolley chided her.

It clanged against its stop and Bera was at the bridgehead and close to the fight. The warders were too occupied to notice her. She had to move but just as before, a bodily threat had deadened her limbs.

Then the wolf's saw-edged joy of killing made her own blood leap. They were as one. For a moment she was leading the pack, snarling with the battle-hunger of the berserk.

This is not your fight!

With a struggle, Bera closed her mind to him.

She looked at the raised bridge but dared not lower it. There truly was only one means of escape. She jumped down on the far side of the trolley, to screen her from the fighters. The water in the moat was thick and black, like pitch. Bera took some slow breaths, hitched her dress into her apron and tightly tied her shawl high on her back. The glass fitted smoothly against her shoulderblades, as if it was suiting its own needs. She belted her sword sheath over it, to show who was in charge. Dellingr had made the sword small and light, just for her, and it was part of her. She took several more long, deep breaths. Fishermen chose not to swim so they would drown quicker. She and Bjorn had never learned.

Oh do hurry up.

'I can't swim.'

It's floating, like you did at Smolderby, only thrash your arms and legs more.

'I nearly drowned at Smolderby.'

The rough boys in Seabost could swim. If they could do it, so could she. But how? Her skern knew nothing; if she tried to float on her back Obsidian would drag her down. Rakki could swim like a fish. Bera decided to become the dog. She opened her mind, felt his joy of the chase, and jumped.

The ice-grip on her skull forced her upwards, gasping. She tried to breathe but choked and sank. The water was not as salty as the sea and tasted of poison. Her wounded leg was too weak. There were no shallows she could reach and the other side was too far. Obsidian wanted to drown her. To Hel with it! Help me, wretched dog! Full of love for Rakki, Bera kicked strongly and was breathing again. She pulled hard with her arms and managed to keep her mouth on the waterline. This gave her confidence and she paddled as furiously as Rakki, understanding it from the inside.

Why would the wolves never enter the water? Bera tried not to think about monsters. Serpents could swim. Were thousands down there, breeding, their twining bodies making the water thick? She willed the black glass to keep all dangers at bay.

That's not what it's for.

Panic seized her. Was Obsidian luring the serpents as a sign of their cult? She had lost the dog's joy. Her legs were sinking and she gulped foul water, choked and kicked, trying to keep her head up. She carried on, until it happened again.

You'll drown, carrying so much weight.

'I need to.'

Let something go.

It could only be her sword, with the powerful runes ALU engraved on it. She couldn't.

Think of Heggi – and Valdis.

'I never stop.'

No mother would die without a fight. The thought rang in her head. No mother... The sword had never been hers to keep; it belonged to a dead woman. Her mouth went underwater while she unbuckled her sword belt and let it go. Now, somehow, she had to reach the bank or her sacrifice would be in vain. Going under had reduced her fear, so she kept her face down and paddled hard. When she next took a breath the other side of the moat was close enough to see speedwells growing, which gave her a spurt. She was determined to reach them, and with a few hard strokes, she was there.

The steep sides were daunting but Bera was able to push into the mud with her good leg and haul herself out on some savagely axed rowans. Rowans that protected from evil. Finally, exhausted, she flumped down at the top. Soaked, sickened, aching, her neck ricked by the heavy glass, she grinned with triumph. Then the loss of her sword hit her – but this was no time for grief. Besides, ALU was graven inside her and she was a Valla with Obsidian: unstoppable!

You still have to reach the main gate.

There was yelling from the moat. Had she been seen? Bera rushed to the iron-barred gate, which was unguarded. The man must have run or was fighting. The key was in the heavy lock on her side. Bera wanted to believe Hefnir had left it for her. She put her back to the rails and managed to open the gate wide enough to slip through and left it open so that the wolves would be free if they reached it.

But then she faced the huge wooden door that it had taken three of them to open. How on earth would she do it alone? It was weighted her side with heavy stones to keep it shut, so she would be struggling with stone and wood.

What are you doing?

'Thinking.'

Not well enough. What does it look like?

The rocks were held in a net with blocks holding ropes to keep it in place.

'Rigging.'

It was the same notion as on a sail. Bera got out her boat-knife, kept sharp enough to cut even walrus-skin ropes. Her boat knowledge could see which was the load-bearing block and line, which was made from some sort of plant, so she easily sliced through it and the stone fell. Now she had to haul the door open. Marriage and motherhood had softened her but she was her father's daughter and a childhood of boat-work had given her underlying toughness. She set her hands on the wood and pulled. It didn't budge.

'Come on!' Bera banged her fist against the door.

She tried again but her leg was too weak to dig in for purchase. Where could she draw extra strength? Perhaps it wasn't safe to let the wolf in again but she was desperate to open her mind and let his fierce will flood into her bones and sinew.

Will is not enough.

She sank down, weeping. 'What, then?'

Call the strong to your back.

Bera thought about those with strength who had helped her in the past, and was lifted by their courage. So she summoned the dead by name – Bjorn, Ottar, Thorvald – and pictured them taking up their positions behind her. Thorvald, the tallest and heaviest, was anchor. She tied a rope to the long wooden bar and threw it back. She planted her feet, got as steady as she could and then took the strain, the three others with her, in a ghostly tug-of-war.

'Heave!'

She had them at her back. They heaved as one and the door slowly opened. And then she was through and turned, wanting to look on the faces of those who had helped her.

No one was there except her skern, who quickly pointed at her pocket. Bera put her hand in, wondering what he meant. A man, soaked and shivering, appeared at the open iron gate. He had a black knife in his hands and she would pay with her life for keeping her promise to the wolves. Then so be it. They would still be free.

Hurry! It works like ALU.

Bera's fingers touched the smooth chalkiness of a shell. The runic egg. She took it out of her pocket, held it up for the warder to see, then laid it on the grass. She willed it to keep men out but kept her knife in her hand, ready to kill if that was what it took to get away.

You can't kill an armed man.

'Then you'd better hope this does work.'

Depends if he believes it does.

The man got to the mark where the door had worn away the grass, then his eyes widened when he saw the egg and he stepped back. Two others came, teetered on the edge and stopped, their faces set in snarls of terror. What were the words in blood?

She had to leave it there and get to the boat. Bera took the path to the jetty and started down the steps. How long had she been? She had no sense of what time of day it was: the light was the colour of vomit, with sea mists and smoke. Was the worst eruption about to begin? She was tired, wounded, clumsy, and she slipped. Her foot stopped against a piece of hacked stone.

Lucky.

She stood still for a moment to catch her breath. Her heart was beating strangely, as if a mouse were trapped in her ribcage. How much blood had she lost? She pressed on. There was no sign of any boat but once she reached the landing stage, a small skiff could be seen at the far end, hidden from above. Bera pulled a long line to get it alongside, fell aboard, pushed off and then struggled to get the oars in place. She was dizzy with tiredness. Obsidian hurt her neck, so she untied the shawl. The weight seemed heavier, or perhaps all the danger had made her unaware of it, as men said of their swords in battle. She lay it on the deck and began to row. It hurt to brace her legs, her stomach ached and she was slow.

Before she reached the headland, she heard the wolves running. Their leader stood at the top of the cliff and gave a long, triumphant howl. Their minds met for an instant in mutual respect and then he turned to join his pack as they loped eastwards. Bera had given the wolves their freedom. Now she must keep them, and all creatures, alive.

It depended how long Hefnir would, or could, wait.

Bera had to ship the oars and rest. Blood was sticky on her hands from blisters and some unnoticed injury during her escape, and she was parched. Thirst was always worse than hunger. Surely Egill would have stowed some water aboard. Bera looked behind her and found a lidded pail. She dipped the bailer into it and tipped it down her throat. It was tainted by salt and yet she wanted to drain it dry.

Careful – it'll make you even more thirsty.

There was no fast cure for the wolfbite but Bera wanted to tend it just the same. Her thick sea boots and leggings had stopped the worst, so she hoped the toothmarks would heal if there was no poison in them. She dipped the ladle over the side and poured salt water over them, yelping with the pain. She did it twice more, then put more salve on and bound it up with the Warden's cloth. When she tried to put her sea boot back on, it was very tight. Her leg was swollen.

Time to row again.

The light was bruised by foulness in the upper air, cloaking the sun. Hel was yawning and the mountain's blood-red mouth gaped wide in the distance. She hugged the headland, using the granite tower as a waymark. Egill had pointed south, where the *Raven* was anchored: the closest bay to Iraland, of course.

'Is Hefnir taking me there?'

Iraland? Could be. He'll be taking Obsidian there as soon as he gets his hands on it.

'He'll want to advance himself there with a prize trading piece. That would be typical.'

Or paying off a longstanding blood debt.

'To the Serpent King? That would be a disaster! The Serpent must never look in it, or Hefnir. I hope he has no idea of its true nature.'

Do you?

'I'm learning. Hefnir has reckoned without me. I know the winds and tides here better than he does and I can predict the weather.'

Her skern raised an eyebrow.

'All right, I can't. But whatever happens, I'm taking Obsidian home.'

Home? Where did that thought come from?

'It's right, though, isn't it? I have to protect Obsidian until I take it home. The only trouble is, I don't know which home. Or whether it's the glass's or mine.'

Bera picked up the oars and doggedly rowed, hoping she could find her way into the bay. She could not remember this bit of coast when their little party arrived and supposed the *Raven* had gone further out to sea and come in past the skep islands. There were some outlying rocks off the headland that must be skirted and she used the tower and what she could see of the mountain to steer a rough course between them.

When she was clear, Bera could no longer ignore the feeling of sorrow when she thought of Home. Her sadness came from something inside, not a particular place or building. There was her childhood home, marked by loss, and then marriage to Hefnir in richer but crueller Seabost. So to the homestead on Ice Island, which she had vowed to save.

You can be honest here.

'Out of duty, then, not love. Not home.'

That's it.

It was a place to live, where she had brought them to start again in safety. It did not diminish her need to protect them; in fact the weight of duty was greater.

'I don't have a home, unless it's a boat.' There was a hole inside her that nothing so far had filled. 'So if I'm to take Obsidian home – does that mean I've already done my duty?'

The skern smiled. *You're travelling more in hope than expectation.*

She had tried to deceive herself after having the baby and perhaps her delay had made things worse. But then Bera lost sight of the tower as a sea mist enveloped her and she had to listen hard for steerage.

The rhythmic splashing of waves against rock grew faint in the smoky mist until there was stillness. She must be inside the next bay. Now where? Bera shipped oars and told Fate to reveal where she must row. This may have begun as an ordinary sea-fret but it was trapped by fumes from the earth's upheaval and smelled like rotting sea creatures. Bera turned to look towards where she thought the shore should be and gave a long, low whistle. A small breeze parted the smog enough to make her heart leap. She was proud of her instinct to find the boat she loved, which had kept them safe in the worst storm: the *Raven*. There was no mistaking the beauty of an Ottar-built ship and she was truly special once more; a skilled craftsman had restored her to a proper sleek longship, without the rushed, rehogged midsection.

It gave her strength to pull hard and when she tied up to a boarding-rope she ran her hand along the longship's timber. Just the feel of wood was special. Even wet, it was warm and alive. Not like stone. This wood was a deep amber, smooth as silk. She fancied she could see beneath the surface the exact marks of her father's work, as distinct as fingerprints. If only she had made more of him when he was alive. If only... Regret was as useless as guilt, when you could change nothing. He was dead, and one day the Serpent King would pay for it. The blood debt could wipe away guilt and regret. Instead of fearing the Serpent's arrival, Bera was determined to find him, even if it meant going to Iraland with Hefnir.

The *Raven* made her stronger. She touched the wood and iron of the hull, meaning to tame Obsidian; to make it work only for good.

She wondered why no one had appeared at the rail. They must have heard her tying up, the hulls booming, but no familiar face came and peered down at her. Where was Heggi? Or Egill? Bera grabbed one of the ropes and tried to climb but her leg would not take her full weight. She knocked furiously on the side, hating needing help and desperate to be aboard.

'Hey! Heggi!'

There was no reply, only drips as the fog turned to water on the rigging. Where was Hefnir? This boat had a small crew, too. Was everyone dead? Perhaps they were waiting for her on the shore. Bera got the oars back in place and began to row but the brymstone smog kept deceiving her. Long before she found it, her scalp flamed. Her instinct told her it was Heggi and he was in danger.

'Where?'

Her shivering skern pointed. There were shouts and the splashing of distant oars. She waited impatiently, trying to peer through the murk; then the fog rolled away and she saw a dragonboat lying further inside the bay. Sea-riders! No one was on deck, so where had the shouts come from? The smog closed in again. At first Bera was frustrated by losing her senses. But then her bond with Heggi made her inner vision strong. She pictured a rowing boat coming away from the beach, heading for the dragonboat. Bera rowed hard and fought down the terrible worry that she was going round in circles.

The smog parted and she glimpsed Heggi, who was staring at the shore, not at her.

'Help me!' he cried, and then was lost again.

'I'm here!'

The fog smothered her voice. Bera swung her head this way and that, trying to catch any break. The dim shape of the dragonboat appeared and she groaned. The small boat was nearly there and she could never outpace the oarsmen. She wanted to keep facing Heggi, so she swung her boat and shipped oars. Perhaps he could jump overboard if he could see her. But could he swim? How could she not know? A real mother would. His small face was a white slash of fear – still fixed on the shore. He was held by a sea-rider, battle-hardened, with an ugly helmet. Any disturbance might cause Heggi's death.

Boykin! She silently willed her son to look in her direction.

At last he did. He held out his arms to her but she was too far off. No matter where he was going, she would find him and she prayed he would know that. She held one hand over her heart: to keep it in her chest and so he might know how much she loved him.

The helmet also turned to see what Heggi was looking at, but gave her no more regard than a gull floating on the water. And then they were alongside their vessel and Heggi was handed up to some others waiting on deck. Her son twisted away and leaned out to look for her. Even at this distance she sensed Heggi giving his sweet, brave smile and the knowledge made stinging tears flow. No time to wipe them away and through blurred rage, she set to rowing for the beach. Where was Hefnir? Who had let Heggi go? Egill? Surely Hefnir would not let the sea-riders take his son? Did he know?

Only when she neared the shore did Bera think her husband

must be dead. There was his body, spread-eagled on the shingle. Even when the boat crackled against the pebbles Hefnir was still, his sightless eyes staring upwards. It explained why Heggi had been taken but she could feel no grief for Hefnir with their son in so much danger.

Egill met her in the shallows and quickly said, 'He's pole axed with grief. Hefnir. He had to trade for his own life.'

'He should have paid with it!' Bera spat. 'I almost mourned him.'

They quickly beached the boat beside Egill's curricle then Bera marched up to him.

Hefnir raised his head slightly. 'It's all right.'

Bera wanted to punch him. 'All right? Heggi's been taken off to a dragonboat by strangers and you say it's all right?'

'See – they're not strange,' put in Egill.

Hefnir sat up. Bera took one look at his expression and knew that what she had feared from the very beginning had come true.

'He's claimed him, hasn't he?'

'He is kin, Bera. He will care for him – and it pays the blood debt.'

'Not my father's! You didn't have the guts to collect that!'

Egill said quietly, 'See, the Serpent blames Hefnir for his sister's death.'

Bera turned on her. 'I know that, you fool! Stop interfering and leave us alone.'

Egill's face had the wiped look that came before tears.

Bera made a great effort to lower her voice. 'All I can think about is Heggi. I'm sorry I spoke roughly, Egill. You are not the enemy.'

'You're afraid, Bera.' Egill smiled through tears. 'You always shout, then, at the ones you love. Sigrid says—'

Hefnir spoke over her. 'His captain brought the message. Sea-rider. I don't know them, or their boat. The Serpent King stayed aboard, knowing I'd fight him.' He got to his feet, as if from a long sleep. 'It's over now, Bera. We can safely return to Iraland together with untold wealth.'

She wanted to slap his slack face. 'Safe because you gave away our son! You coward! You wouldn't fight the Serpent if he'd come, would you? Not without Thorvald! It was one sea-rider! How could you?'

Egill sniffed. 'The oarsman was armed too.'

Bera was fixed on Hefnir. 'He's your own flesh and blood!'

'And Heggi's mother was the Serpent's sister, remember, and he loved her. That's the only reason I let him go. He will be all right. We shall see him again soon.'

'Love? He's vile! I want Heggi out of there. Now. They'll be leaving any moment.'

'That's just it.' Hefnir's cold laugh never reached his eyes. 'They're staying at anchor until we give him Obsidian. Then he'll hand over Heggi.'

Bera fell to her knees.

Egill crouched beside her. 'Let him have the stone, Bera. It solves everything.'

Bera pushed her away. 'It solves nothing! I have to protect Obsidian… and something else; I must scry in it again. But the Serpent is the last person in the world I'd give it to!'

'He will have seen you, Bera.' Hefnir loomed over her. 'He is only waiting for Obsidian. It's only ever been your choice. You either hand him the stone and get Heggi back or leave our son with the Serpent King. He's setting sail for Iraland on the ebb.'

25

Bera was wracked. Perhaps Obsidian only made her feel more confident when doing its bidding, whilst in fact it weakened her own powers. She scrambled to her feet and set off along the beach, needing to be alone, to hear advice from her skern, her mother, Valla ancestors, even the ravens; anyone. Anyone but Egill, who immediately followed her.

'Go away.'

'Heggi will like Iraland and he will be safe with his uncle. All right, he looks bad with all those tattoos but he did love his sister, or he—' Egill stopped.

'Or he wouldn't be claiming the blood debt from Hefnir. Egill, listen to yourself! The Serpent came to kill him in Seabost and my father paid the price! You know all this!' Bera took some deep breaths. 'Heggi knows his father doesn't want him and now he'll think the same of me!'

Egill kicked the sand. 'I didn't think you wanted that old black stone as much as them.'

'Hel's teeth, Egill! I'd give it away in a heartbeat if I could be home safe and warm with my son and baby.'

Home again?

Then she remembered. 'I've left it lying at the bottom of the boat!' Her carelessness made Bera's stomach heave. 'What if it's gone?'

They headed back to the boats.

Egill said, 'You would see the theft of Obsidian.'

'If I was any good at prediction I would have killed the Serpent years ago when I had the chance.'

'I meant you would actually see it. There's only us three now.'

'Tell Hefnir I need time. If it's there, I will look into the looking-glass and decide what must be done.'

Egill touched her arm. 'I thought you knew already, dearest.'

Bera shook her off. 'I'm not your dearest. Go and hug Hefnir. He's the only thing you truly value, unless at last you've realised that all he cares about is himself.'

'As you would know, Bera.' She ran off.

What did she mean?

The dragonboat was hidden in the yellow smog. Vile trails of sulfur curled along the beach, making Bera choke, but the ebb had not yet come. Her skiff was there but no sign of Egill or Hefnir. Had Egill betrayed her and stolen Obsidian? Were they taking it to the Serpent King? Her head and heart split in two about that. But suppose Hefnir went back to Iraland with Heggi? Egill's curricle was still on the other side, so they were hiding it here.

Bera leaned over the rail, picked up her heavy shawl and breathed again. Safe.

Still your choice alone.

'Then I must face Obsidian again.'

She took it where she would be unseen, with a rocky spit at her back. She lay the glass on her lap but it was blurred by tears.

Her skern nestled against her. *Dear one.*

'I would die for Heggi. If Egill meant that all I care about is me, she's wrong.'

It's our duty, you and I, to stand alone.

'Folk never see that! I've had to do it all without my mother.'

Still angry with her for dying.

Sobs hurt Bera's raw throat. 'She never said she loved me, even when she was dying. I was only six! Nor did Ottar...'

You have the Raven, *now.*

'True – and my father put his love into her.'

Egill is thinking about her father, too. Perhaps he taught her how to build a curricle.

'Perhaps we are more like sisters. She makes me so angry.'

Yet you also understand her. You both want to escape.

'The difference is, I stay.' Her black bead was a fiery reminder. 'I do my duty.'

But, oh, it hurt. She did not want to look in the stone again and perhaps she didn't need to. She could hand it over and save Heggi, who she owed so much. Her boy had made her a better person. His belief and trust made her strong… and so the Serpent King must not have Obsidian, for it would double and redouble his blackness. Without it – who knew? Perhaps he might one day be restored to the person she had seen once in a dream, who brought the smaller Heggi a wooden horse and laughed and kissed the woman who looked so much like him then.

Bera dried her eyes, wanting to miss nothing that Obsidian would show her. It might well confirm a course she didn't want to take but there must be no mistake. Her skern hung limp at her neck. He suspected, too. She took a deep breath and looked. At once she had her answer and it was worse.

Sacrifice. The ebb would come and there would be no release for Heggi – and none for her.

As soon as Bera returned to the boats, she called the others. Hefnir launched the skiff and Egill followed in her curricle, back to the *Raven*. Hefnir looked as wretched as she felt and Bera wondered what he was thinking. He was so much smaller without Thorvald. Well, his cowardice had led them all to this point. And his lust for Obsidian.

'If I offered to give Obsidian to the Serpent King, you'd stop me, wouldn't you?'

'Believe what you like.'

'You should have killed him before handing Heggi over.'

'I told you. He wasn't on the beach.'

'You're still not answering.'

'All right, but if I had fought the sea-riders and been killed, how would that have helped you?'

'Me?'

225

'It's only ever been about you, Bera. Valla – or Brid – whichever heartless god you claim to be today. I'm your puppet, so use me as you please. You will anyway.'

'It's not me who pretends belief, Hefnir, but you, for any advantage. You probably used it to make Heggi side against me but failed. You're no puppet, you always try to escape any blame. I'm the puppet of Fate, not you.'

Bera wanted to be sick. Her words were full of horror at what Obsidian had shown of Fate. It was all she could do to tie the boat at the stern. Two crewmen appeared – they had perhaps stayed hidden before, fearing the dragonboat. They looked like ermites and were silent and nimble crew, so everything was quickly stowed, the anchor was raised and they set sail. The *Raven*'s nose twitched to windward and they took up their oars.

Hefnir was steering to pass the dragonboat's stern. Bera went to the bow, to get as close to her boy as she could. The Serpent King himself was waiting for them, veiled in fog. She had forgotten how repulsive his body was. At this distance, he looked black but Bera knew it was not the warm sheen of the Warden's natural skin but a deliberate disfigurement to make a full dragon body. She understood his purpose now: he was pouring its vile power into himself. Every portion of skin was clotted with soot and ash, pushed into cuts, to mingle with his blood as scales and teeth, spines and claws. The memory of being close to the Serpent's slit eye in his armpit brought back the foul smell.

Now he was close, watching them and smirking. He beckoned and the captain pushed Heggi into those foul dragon arms. He thought he had won and Bera was certain that if she gave him Obsidian he would not give her Heggi. His little face was pink with hope when he saw her. He waved – and broke her heart. Her hands were clasped round her throat, almost throttling herself.

Heggi's smile faded into ash.

The Serpent King's eyes widened in his tattooed face. He thumped his chest with a solid fist.

'You, Hefnir. You gutless bastard!' he roared. 'All I want is a lump of black stone and you'd rather keep that than your son.' He pointed at Bera. 'And you are worse. Call yourself woman? Your heart is cold and black as Obsidian. You can't feel love!'

He was wrong. Bera loved that boy more than life. She would carry the look on Heggi's face to her dying day and Obsidian had shown her that it must be soon.

26

Bera was so hollowed out by grief that even being aboard the *Raven* gave her no joy. She felt swept along by Fate and unable to make any decision except to go north, and even that was what Obsidian commanded. The high mountains made going by sea the only way possible but cold air dropped from them unpredictably, like a trole trying to drown them. In between, the heavy air made the sail hang limp. They finally took it down and Bera was relieved to simply row and be left alone. Beside her, Egill stayed silent. Only the two crewmen occasionally spoke to Hefnir in a strange tongue.

Hefnir. Once, she had liked to see him at the helm, competent and strong. She admired anyone who could handle a boat as he did. Now, he looked like a frail old man, deceitful, dishonourable and cowardly. It sickened her to have him with her. But far worse was the guilt that was like a bird tugging at her entrails. Even the empty, scrubbed deck hurt. The last time she had been aboard it had been packed with settlers, heading off at her promise to a new life, to avoid flood and famine. Children played: Heggi! And animals were stowed below decks: Feima. Heartache. It truly squeezed her heart.

Hefnir steered to seaward and they raised the sail, which filled. Bera became aware of her wounded leg, which she had entirely forgotten. It was throbbing. She stopped rowing and unbound the linen cloth that was stiff with blood.

Egill slid nearer. 'Let me see.'

'What do you know of wounds? That's my job.'

'But you're not caring for yourself, are you?' Egill's voice was low and tender.

Bera shrugged, not sure she deserved caring about. Never had.

Egill took her hand. 'You push folk away, Bera, do you know that? You don't let them close.'

'I have to take this Obsidian north. I didn't choose to leave Heggi…'

'I'm not talking about Heggi. I'm talking about friendship. Love.'

How could Bera explain that no one matched up, let alone Egill? The thought surprised her. Matched up to what?

'I wanted to love my husband. I tried.'

'And Faelan?'

'You know nothing!' Bera's face flamed.

Egill laughed. 'Good. Get a bit of spark back into you.'

Was this why folk forgave Egill? So often she could turn away their anger, pretending she had planned it for their own good. What did Egill really feel? Perhaps she skated on the surface of deep feeling now, so that she was not plunged into madness again.

'Help me with this, then,' Bera said.

She bit her lip as Egill stripped off the stuck linen. There were deep bruises and the toothmarks were puffy with red and purple centres. Egill dipped a bailer over the side, soaked the cloth in it, then dabbed at the wound. She was trying to be so gentle that it had no effect.

'Give it to me!' Bera seized the rag and rubbed the wounds, which hurt a lot.

'Careful! The saltwater will clean the wound.'

'I cleaned it better before.'

'That's too small for a bandage,' said Egill. 'Stop thinking you know best.'

Bera stopped. 'You sound like Sigrid.'

'Is that so bad?'

Bera considered this. It was too complicated to unravel, her relationship with Sigrid, so she changed the subject.

'What happened to Hefnir's Seabost crew?'

Egill made a face. 'They jumped ship in Smolderby. Last seen in the tavern, fighting and whoring. You've seen the types in there. They could be dead.'

'Will be for sure, if they didn't escape.' Bera moved Egill away from the eruption. 'Why is it called Wolf Island?'

'Iraland?' Egill breathed its name like a lover, turning her head by instinct to where it lay.

'They're from there as well, aren't they? Those two.' Bera tilted her chin at the crew. 'So are there lots of wolves?'

'There are. But, Bera, it's as gentle as the rain. Green sward, mists, smiling folk and the creamiest milk you'll ever taste. Soft words, too, like lambing. Say it: lambing.'

'Lambing.' Bera liked the way it made her lips kiss.

Egill put a finger to her own lips and then Bera's. 'It will all be well when we get there, you'll see. Heggi won't be harmed; he'll be waiting for you in Dyflin.'

'There's more to come here, Egill. I will never get to Iraland.'

'Not even for Heggi?'

'Only for Heggi – if I'm still alive.' Could the looking-glass lie? Heggi would be one among so many dead if she got this wrong.

Hefnir called her over to the steer-board. 'So I'm bearing north and east. You'd better be sure where we go then.' He gave her a hard look. 'Are you sure?'

'I'll tell you when we have to change course.' Bera wanted to scratch his face for being the warrior with her now but a coward before.

'I suppose you'll say your skern told you.'

She was sharp. 'I will recognise what I saw in the glass and that's where we will land. The black stone of my beads is telling me we are close.'

'How?'

'By growing warmer.'

'It's not a game for bairns!'

'The heat is a sign of its nature.'

'Is it obsidian?'

'It is. I think deep within the earth Hel is making obsidian like a smith forges metal. Every piece of it has a spark of its property, big or small.'

'Like a knife?'

'And my bead. The looking-glass has more... It's like a weapon but I can't fathom what... Perhaps the way the circles are formed.'

She was working it out aloud but saw the glint in Hefnir's eyes.

'I'm keeping it safe, Hefnir.'

'Let me see if I can fathom it. I know more about weapons.'

'And I know more about protection. Now, we should eat.'

Bera was pleased to find the barrels in their place and packed with rations. She took some cheese and smoked meat to the crew first and then Hefnir. Egill was sitting with her back to the mast, so Bera went forward to eat with her. The boat motion was like dancing and the old, familiar movement of unused muscles in her body made her feel real.

She sang under her breath, 'In the bones, in the bones...' then grief flooded in.

'What is it?' Egill asked her.

Bera was back on another boat, with another friend. The difference between youth and age, marked in pain.

'We sang it on the beach when we landed here.'

'I heard,' Egill said. 'So why are you sad?'

Bera nudged her. 'Eat.'

Egill took her ration. 'Belly timber.'

They tore into their food and afterwards Bera felt more confident.

'I don't only care for myself, you know.' She kept her eyes on the sea rim. 'If that was what you meant.'

Egill kept quiet for so long that Bera was forced to look at her. Their eyes met but still she didn't speak.

'I have a duty, Egill, as a Valla. This time it's life or death.'

'Life always is.' Egill's pale eyes showed no curiosity.

'It's loss that makes you strong.'

'So Sigrid says. So what are you weeping for?'

Egill could be so blunt about other people's grief. In any case, Bera could not tell her that this loss was in the future. She had to bear that knowledge alone.

'Is Obsidian all Hefnir wants?' asked Bera. 'Why did you not get to Iraland?'

Egill looked round then lowered her voice. 'We stayed in

Smolderby long enough for the *Raven* to be repaired and met Faelan, fishing. Then the Serpent King arrived and we headed straight for the Abbotry when we heard about Obsidian from Cronan.'

'Did you know the Serpent brought goods to the Abbotry?'

'Not then, of course not.'

Bera wanted to be sure how Faelan was involved. 'Who told Faelan to bring me?'

'We all did, in a way, like we said. But only Cronan saw him again, after we left Smolderby. Why?'

'I wondered why he brought me, knowing I would not want to see you again. As long as it wasn't the Serpent.' She did not believe Faelan even knew him.

Egill shook her head. 'I don't know what Cronan said to him but Faelan's never met the Serpent. Bera, it's Hefnir who wants the stone, not me. He knew that if he failed to steal it you would be sent for and triumph. And so you have!'

'Only I know the terrible cost of holding the black glass, Egill.'

'Hefnir said he promised to return the stone to the Venerable Prince Abbot of All Ireland. Hefnir thinks that's why the Serpent King wants it – to get there first and stop him.'

'Stop him doing what?'

'Taking power for himself as Chief Warrior.'

'Does this All Iraland person want to use it to stop eruptions?'

'They don't have them there. Not even earth trembles, hardly.'

'Then why does he want it?'

Egill shrugged. 'Who knows? To sell for weapons maybe? They are fighting the old ways all the time. They prize anything made of obsidian above rubies in the Golden City.'

'Why?'

'Possession. Just to own it. They have huge houses full of precious things that men own. Women too!'

They both considered this.

'I don't want Hefnir, you know,' Egill blurted. 'Not like you think.'

'It doesn't matter now, Egill.'

Egill took her hand. 'Hefnir was surprised you had a baby. Or is she Dellingr's?'

Bera shoved her. 'That insults us both. Hefnir knows full well that Valdis is his. That's why...'

'What?'

Bera bit her lip hard. 'That's why she looks so like him.'

Egill knows you weren't going to say that.

'Do you love her?' Egill asked.

'Of course! But I'm not as bound to her as I am to Heggi.'

'Why?'

'It's not her fault. The birthing came with fire and fury and rending pain and—' Bera would not tell Egill how the child was taking her powers for herself. 'I think new life also brings death.'

'And she looks like Hefnir,' Egill said drily.

'So, tell me how unnatural I am! How heartless and icy and whatever else the Serpent King said... that I'm cold as obsidian.'

'I never knew my mother,' said Egill. 'My father wouldn't speak of her.'

'My mother gave up after my brother died. She didn't fight.'

'It messes you up,' Egill said. 'You and me. It messes you up with no mother.'

Thanks to her, Heggi was about to lose his second.

27

The thick sea milled. A freezing mist rose to meet the warm, putrid air above and the small crew aboard the *Raven* was helpless between the two. They were nearing the Ice Rim and small bergs were randomly floating turquoises in water the colour of copper. Egill pointed out their beauty but nothing mattered to Bera anymore. The landscape revealed what she thought lay inland from the homestead: tall, ice-capped peaks with jagged black rock beneath. Here, instead of summer-green valleys, there were sharp clefts filled with ashy ice and snow: grey-blue glaciers coursing down the ages into the sea. She could feel their chill. It was north – and bitterly cold. Perhaps the sun never came here. Perhaps she was meant to freeze to death.

When Egill noticed Bera's deep shudders she went and asked Hefnir if there were furs aboard. A crewman opened a stern locker and took out greased blankets, which they put on over the furs. Egill wrapped Bera. The crew took down the listless sail and rowed, letting the boat drift in clear water.

Hefnir laughed, in his element again. 'This is like our passage over!'

So unheeding. Bera would despise him if she could find the energy.

Take charge.

'Of what? Fate has me on the rack and nothing I do will change it.'

A flat grey rock gently sank and Bera realised it was a monster ice shark.

'I'm glad there's one creature here, besides us.'

'Where are all the birds and fish?' asked Egill.

'The earth's upheaval has begun, Egill. They are far away.'

'In Iraland, I expect. It's safe there.'

It would just take longer to die, once the ash cloud covered the sun.

Do something! Be in command of preventing it. There might be another way.

Her skern was right. The looking-glass had only shown one possible outcome; there might have been others if she had waited.

Bera touched Egill's arm. 'I think we're close to where we have to be. Keep Hefnir's attention away from me.'

'That's more like it! What are you going to do?'

'I have to get the looking-glass out and I don't want him to see where it's hidden.'

'So where is it?'

'It's safer if you don't know, Egill.'

This time, Bera saw her face only briefly in the glass before diving straight through it into a squid-ink world. She gasped and had no more breath. It was hot – so was she under sea or under earth? – and so fierce that her hair fanned and crackled. Her clothes were heavy and scorched so crisp that they might catch light. Distant flames. But the sounds were the echoes of sea creatures as they swam far away to safety. Whale song, deep and dark, and the crackling high notes of faster fish.

She touched her beads and found her skern's hand. 'Where am I?'

With Hel.

'In the dark lands?'

And under the water.

'How can it be both?'

Hush, sweetheart, and watch.

His long finger pointed ahead of them to a flicker of orange. It was thicker than water but still liquid, making the cold sea boil. As they neared, a wider vent opened and burning matter spewed out.

'What is that?'

Lava. Boiling rock.

Bera was in the deep ocean with the Skraken on the abyssal plain, watching its nail rip open its belly to spill fiery blood and guts in a heap that formed new land. There would be islands born in the fiery stream, but she would not be there to see them. The answer was the same – sacrifice – and this merely showed why it must be done, and where. She had to return the black stone to Hel and the price of saving folk was a blood debt to Hel. The answer was always the same: Obsidian and Bera, linked forever in death.

Like Valla and skern.

She came up gasping, sweating from the lava and shivering with shock. Her chest was on fire. She drew draughts of the icy air that fell from the mountains deep into her lungs. How was she to find her way to the place?

It will find you.

They needed to get ashore soon but every sight of it looked a blanket of whiteness, with no beach or river inlet; only glaciers rolling with infinite slowness into the sea. No sign of fire, or anything that told her this was the place.

Bera went back to the steer-board. 'Let me helm.'

Hefnir told her to rest. 'I can find a good enough place to stop.'

'No you can't. It has to be the right place and only I will know it.'

He shrugged. 'Then find it before we freeze. But I'm steering.'

Out at sea, it all looked too much the same. Her black bead got no hotter, so when at last Bera saw a sloping beach she made Fate choose it. Hefnir let the *Raven*'s hull glide in on a wave. They rolled the boat a short way over pebbles dappled with snow and then Bera took stock. The stark terrain that rose straight up beyond the beach was white, so no wonder it had been hard to tell if it was ice edge or land.

They did not have the strength or will to make camp, so they threw down some blankets and lay in the lee of the hull, staring up at a waxen sun. There were dagger-sharp stones at her back and freezing air falling from the mountaintops that could strip flesh off bones. Bera huddled into her furs, resisting the intense hostility that seeped up through the ground. The land itself wanted to kill her.

Bera wished she was half as powerful as her mother. If Sigrid were there, she would be. Where had that thought come from? It was true, though, and the thought of never telling Sigrid how she made Bera more the Valla was another load she had to bear. It was a real weight, and Obsidian somehow made it worse. She went to touch her sword but then remembered it was gone. Dust in the air, as ashen as the clouds that were bringing dusk early. The cloud of filth was growing too big for any wind to blow away. Fear of the dark in such a place would crush them.

She would not give in to it. ALU.

Fire.

Bera announced they should fight against the night. She told Egill to take the crewmen to collect wood, while she fetched dried grasses to get it started. Hefnir started to check the boat for any damage to the hull. Egill declared she was the best mender.

'We need plenty of wood, Egill. You'll be busy.'

Some things had not changed and Bera was glad to make things ordinary for the others.

Before nightfall, Bera needed to relieve herself. She hunkered down behind some rocks and enjoyed the rush of hotness. There were brymstones around her, with glints of black glass. Bera got up and picked some up. There was no sense of mastery; these stones were inert, warm like her black bead but holding no sway over a person. Hefnir could be trusted not to become enthralled by them. She threw them away.

The sun was low, casting long purple shadows along the frost-bleached scrubland. Over near the foothills of the closest cone-shaped mountain there moved a small animal, perhaps a fox. There was something about its shape that made her think of ice bears but they were a long way from the White Sea. She gathered some more firewood and hurried back.

The flames, as ever, raised everyone's spirits. Their faces, ruddy and happy in the flickering light, were a reminder of home, hall and good cheer. The sun settled on the top of the highest peak and Bera thought this was a sign: it was a beacon that could be seen from the homestead too. She sent out thoughts to Sigrid and then Valdis. Something stirred, like Obsidian in its cradle in the tower.

I can see nothing through the ash cloud.

'No need. There is only the lonely path I must take to Hel.'

They all needed rest, so they lay down close to each other, Egill on one side of Bera and Hefnir the other.

Egill kissed her cheek. 'Sleep now, Bera dear. We'll keep you safe.'

Hefnir was silent but with malice pouring up through the soil, she took comfort where she could. Exhausted, she fell asleep at once.

Bera woke with a start and immediately felt guilty when she saw the others preparing a meal. Yet she felt completely refreshed. It was the best night's sleep she had had, possibly since her billet in Seabost. Was it because she felt protected? She pushed the thought from her. The last person she wanted to protect her was Hefnir – and no one could depend on Egill. Once she had liked the thought that Dellingr protected her and look where that had ended. Faelan, too.

There is only ever you.

After eating, Hefnir was his old assured self. 'Plenty of obsidian here. We'll spread out and look for decent weights.'

Egill's eyes flickered towards Bera. Did she know that they were here to destroy, not to find?

Bera let them go off gathering. Obsidian was with her. These black shards were only pointers, like iron filings to a lodestone. They sensed the looking-glass, though she did not understand how it had become so powerful. Some craftsman, from Iraland perhaps, had taken its latent force and fashioned it with human skill into… something so dangerous that it must be returned to Hel, along with herself to pay the blood debt for its theft.

I'm not sure about some of that.

'Does it matter? It's in the past.'

She wanted to explore alone so that the landscape could speak to her, even if the words were poison. She had to find the gateway to Hel and enter. She had abandoned her children, so must make this final sacrifice. She thought of Faelan again, desperate to be saved… She had to prove leaving him was right. Was she right to do it alone? Doubt crept in and she began to wonder why they had left her on her own.

Mirror mirror on the wall…

'What are you talking about?'

There's no point exploring when the answer's on your back. Look in the glass.

Bera never wanted to see it again. She got Obsidian from its place, fast.

This time, she was an eagle, soaring in blue sky, looking down on her own winged shadow as it raced across the land far below. She passed over Hefnir and the others and swooped over them, drunk in the joy of flight.

Stop playing and use the skills.

Her eagle eyes could see the wind as it curled round the mountain like smoke; she could hear whalesong, lower than sound; she could smell the future in the stench of sulfur. And the future became present as she hovered over a peak. It was no single point of ice but a crown around a central hollow. She peered down through the snow and ice, piercing layer after layer, crust after crust, until there was the black heart of the earth that made Obsidian. It was what she had glimpsed at the birthing and was happening again. Far below her, on the skin of Ice Island, appeared a wrinkle, which became a channel, then a crevasse that deepened and widened and screamed out the pain of a land torn into three plates that should be one. This was what had cracked open as her hip bones shifted to push out the baby, when Bera thought her whole body was being sundered. The centre of these three plates was the gateway to Hel.

Bera fell back to earth with an eagle shriek. Because she knew where she had to go and wanted it over. This was the place. She tied the glass safely onto her back and made for the high mountain.

There was a small animal grubbing around the lower slopes where snow lay in drifts. It scuffed and snuffled about, occasionally digging and pouncing. Perhaps the small creature of the night before was this ice bear cub. It surprised her to see natural life, even this far from its home, with such terror before her.

The bear cub lifted its head. Bera tried to link her mind with it as she had the wolf but there was only the numbing blankness of snow, so she approached slowly and so did the cub. Could you tame a bear if you had it from a cub? How Heggi would have loved it. She closed her mind.

The cub moved sideways.

'Don't be frightened. I'm not going to hurt you.' Though she did not sense fear in the cub's numbness.

Bera walked on, holding out her hand, as if coaxing a dog to return. The cub sniffed the air a few more times and moved sideways again.

'Come on, little one. Come to Bera.'

At last it did, padding sweetly towards her, pigeon-toed. Bera remembered that closing her eyes would link their minds.

Death rage!

Her eyes flew open and the early sun appeared between two foothills, making the distance plain. This was no cub but a fully grown ice bear, coming straight at her. Bera stood her ground and opened her arms wide, trying to look big. The bear paused some distance away, raised its nose and swayed its head in big arcs, to and fro. It was thin, which meant it was hungry. It stopped its scenting and fixed its small black eyes on her. Bera held its gaze, willing it to leave her alone, but like a Drorgher, it was intent on one thing: prey. Their eyes stayed locked as the bear moved to its left. Its wide, thick pads made no sound.

She had no sword. If only Hefnir and the others would notice her long absence and come and kill it. As long as they did kill it. A wounded animal would be out for blood. Finally it turned its head. There were others: two small cubs were stumbling across snow hillocks towards their mother. The bear looked back at the threat to her babies, and the danger increased. Bera screwed up her face, sending out a line of thought to declare who she was. One fierce mother to another. But Bera had left her baby while this one was starving rather than leave her cubs. This mother bear was too far south, searching for food. The world was already skewed.

Concentrate!

'I need to set this land right again.'

It wants you to fail. Its anger is brewing and it yearns for violence.

'A bit like a thunderstorm clearing the air?'

It's the meaning of sacrifice. In the cycle of the earth there can be no new life without the spilling of blood.

'One in, one out, in reverse. This is Valdis's time. I was right to fear her.' Bera gave a rueful smile. 'Perhaps I did the same to my mother. Let's hope Valdis proves a better Valla than I ever was, with no mother to guide her either.'

The bear bent her head to greet her cubs and they scampered about her, raising their faces to be licked. She led them to a high, snow-covered mound and lay down with her back to it. The two pure white bundles tumbled over each other to nestle into the warm blush of their mother's creamy fur. They began to feed and grew still, their only movement the absent-minded stroke of a small paw while their mother tenderly licked them clean.

Bera took a few slow paces backwards, then stopped. This bear would be a great prize. She considered how high a price an ice-bear skin would reach. Would the Serpent King accept this pelt instead of Obsidian? Of course not.

Besides, killing her would mean leaving the cubs motherless and she could never do that.

True. So she ought to retreat but her duty was to go forward. Once the bears had fed it would be dangerous to stay. But then she calmed in the growling kind of love between the bears – and lingered too long.

The bear got to her feet, nudged the cubs away, and walked off. They lazed in the small heaps of snow while their mother began making a wide circle. The ice bear would sometimes stop and paw the ground, then reckon Bera with shrewd eyes. The gathering light showed its range and Bera saw that she was in the middle of its circle. Now it was too late to run and her feeling for animals would cost her her life.

Would dying this way be enough to stop the eruptions? Her vision was clear: to take Obsidian back to Hel and pay with her life. The land was trying to stop that happening. It wanted eruption and devastation. Her skern was right in one way. It was like the old days when she enjoyed the flare of anger that would end in breaking something and leave her feeling better. Yet she had seen the birth of this island, along with Obsidian's. Both were born in violence and exulted in it. The land was using the creatures that lived on it to make her fail. Bera stood like a stone, her own mind a blank of despair.

Her skern clutched her scalp. *Think, dearest. Do something.*

'Save me.'

How? I'm as insubstantial as the morning mist.

Bera tried throwing some stones at the bear but they only made her back off for a while, then she returned to her circle; tighter now, with blacker thoughts.

'I don't die yet, do I? I thought Fate wanted me to finish this.'

Oh, dearest, you may not have the choice.

'At least I'll feed the mother bear. I'd rather die like that than at the hands of some coward.'

Like Hefnir?

'Hefnir! Get him here!'

How can I possibly do that?

'You left me in the tower.'

I have no memory but agony.

'So do I. But now you have to go further.'

Skerns c-c-can't. I won't stretch that far and Hefnir wouldn't hear me.

'It's our only chance.'

B-b-but if the bear attacks and I'm not here you'll b-b-be…

'A Drorgher.'

Vividly before her loomed the bruised and blackened face of the chief of the Drorghers from her home village. Would she become like that? No – it would be worse! Her darker Valla powers would rise in their twilight world. Hefnir was her only chance of survival. Her skern had to go, and go now.

'Don't leave me!' she cried.

The pain of unclenching was worse than before. As the invisible cord between them stretched, the agony of lengthening and thinning was beyond endurance. Bera fell down hard, and, while she could will anything, willed him to carry on.

28

Her skern was suffering as much, getting thinner and thinner, a wisp. His touch was like smoke. Egill was sitting apart, whittling. He wafted round her head, blowing her hair into her eyes but she absently tucked it behind her ears. His voice was a whisper of sea breeze. He was wracked between returning to his twin spirit and obeying her true command. Life or death. One last try.

Help us!

Egill stopped whittling and listened.

Help!

'Bera?' she called.

The skern was too anguished to speak again.

Hefnir turned. 'Is she back?'

'Thought she was.' Egill jerked her head towards the scrubland. 'I thought she wanted to be alone, to plan the next bit.'

'When did you last see her?'

Egill stood up, the truth dawning. 'Quite a while.'

Hefnir jabbed a tarred brand into the fire, setting it alight. He spoke in the language of Iraland. 'You two. Come with me.'

Egill waved her sharpened stick. 'I'm coming too.'

'What use are you?'

'I love her.'

Hefnir laughed, and set off in the wrong direction.

The skern could only mouth at Egill not to follow him.

Bera had to stay aware, though her skern was stretching away so far her guts were straight, and keep telling the bear that she was not good to eat, that she meant no harm. Neither food nor threat: both were lies. No lies on Ice Island. Worthless words of an idiot. Why not drift away, beyond pain? No! Her duty was to endure, it was all it had ever been.

She searched inside her for the vital force of the Bera she had packed away when she first thought death would be better than more grief and hardship. She had sent her out more than once to fight death.

Nothing. That Bera was gone. She was too changed, and dying.

The bear stood on her hind legs, her breath a memory of seals and fish and blood. Her final reckoning before the attack.

Bera managed to stand, swaying. Only cowards were killed on their knees.

Then – release. Bera smiled weakly. They would die as one. Her skern swept round her, cleaved. She stood before the attack, knife in hand, knowing it would be useless. The weight of Obsidian on her back told her the ice bear would kill her; that was what it wanted.

The bear charged.

She did not want to die!

Her head felt thick and blood roared. The world became a red tunnel with Bera at one end and the bear the other. With absolute clarity, almost casually, she sidestepped at the last moment. She was reacting so quickly it felt as if everything was slow, like trying to clap hands underwater.

The bear was a silent killer, wasting no energy. She made a short circle.

There was a whooping battle cry, shrill and penetrating. It was Egill, trailing something behind her over the snow. She quickly untied the rope and walked away, leaving a body behind, big enough to tempt. Egill's singing howl was keeping the bear's attention away from Bera for now but also attracted the cubs. Would the bear guard the cubs and carcass or stay fixed on her prey?

The bear looked back at Bera.

Egill ran. 'Come on then, you old bear, come and get me!' Was she brave or mad? She was dangerously close to the cubs.

Hefnir appeared with a flaming brand and behind him, the crew.

This would become a killing field, her only instinct to protect her babies. The mother bear ran at the men, swiping at a crewman with a savage paw. His jaw flew sideways and he was down. She turned, casting about with rage.

Hefnir and the remaining crewman got themselves between the bear and Bera, leaving the carcass to the cubs, who gambolled towards it, fearless. Their mother paused, her prey strung out and her cubs unprotected. Egill was still screaming like a madwoman. Hefnir held his brand high and the bear backed off, waiting. Then she roared a warning and padded swiftly to the carcass, took it in her huge jaw and dragged it away. Her cubs scampered after her, as if it were a game.

Bera's knees gave way and she collapsed on the snow, gasping. She must have been holding her breath since Egill appeared.

Hefnir threw himself down next to her. 'Will you not keep going off on your own!'

'You didn't stop me.'

'Who could stop you when you've decided something?'

Bera rolled over and faced him. 'I have to do this alone.'

Egill was there. 'No, Bera. You always think you do but you don't. Hefnir left you this time but we're not going to from now on. Are we?'

Hefnir said nothing.

'Are you, Hefnir?' Bera's voice was soft.

He had stood between her and death, which was not the act of a coward. Surely she had been wrong about her husband: she mattered to him after all. Did he love her? She needed to think so, here, at the gate of Hel.

The mountain was spewing ash higher than the stars and the mushroom pall made the day as dark as winternights. Yet Bera could think clearly and her first thought was the Serpent King. He had tried to trade Heggi but his bluff had not worked and she was sure that he would find them and kill to get Obsidian. No matter what happened to her, she had to first make sure that no one else had the chance to gaze into the glass.

They would not leave the dead crewman for animals or some Serpent outrage but the ground was too hard to bury him. There was plenty of wood here, so they risked building a pyre on the beach. They placed the crewman on top, making sure his knife was with him. He might not turn to ash but Bera hoped it was enough. He was one of the lucky ones, to die cleanly with one swipe of an ice bear's paw instead of the long starvation that would come if she did not succeed.

While they waited for it to be hot enough to burn the body, Bera called a meeting.

'We have this fire to send our crewman to his ancestors and as a sign to Fate that this is the place of a Valla's choosing.' She turned to Hefnir. 'It will also be a beacon for anyone watching, so we must start soon.'

Bera told Egill to send the other crewman as lookout on the headland. 'He must watch for the Serpent King and warn us if the dragonboat appears.'

The flames burned white against the darkening sky. There were so few of them now. The gaps between were the whispering souls of Seabost folk, left behind, and the unburied dead of her own home. Bera looked into the heart of the fire, which gave her the words to explain it.

'We have to climb that mountain. The problem and the answer lies with Hel and you must help me, Hefnir. The finest obsidian is useless without life.'

Hefnir considered her, his eyes hard slits. 'If this is some trick...'

Bera stared him out.

He shrugged. 'So tell me why it's so bad.'

'You're already breathing it, Hefnir. The air is full of poison and more will gush up and stifle anyone downwind of the fumes. The top of the mountain will blow and the rock will be fire. I've thought about what happens when ice melts: a torrent will surge down the mountainside into the sea.'

'Like the dam bursting,' muttered Egill.

'Worse. There will be such upheaval that a monstrous wave will return to drown this side of Ice Island.'

'Like the strange wave that hit us on the passage over,' said Hefnir.

Bera nodded. 'I think that was a forerunner, showing me what is to come. But there's even more: this eruption will set alight the whole chain.'

'What chain?' Hefnir kicked a stone away, for a moment like Heggi.

'I've seen the known world and there are mountains of fire under sea and over land.'

Egill understood. 'So if all the mountains send up ash clouds there will be no sun.'

Bera agreed. 'Without sunlight, nothing can grow. No crops, no animals. The ash up in the sky will form clouds of bitter rain that will burn when it falls. There will be no hiding and no relief. No one will be left alive anywhere.'

'The end of the Vallas,' said Egill. The edge in her voice surprised Bera.

She thought of Heggi. How he must despise her, and she deserved it because she had lost his trust, after trying so hard to gain it. More loss, for both of them, who had lost so much. What had begun as a promise to Faelan to stop an eruption had turned into something more: a struggle to stay true to the Valla ancestors when she had begun to doubt them. She was at a threshold, a liminal place, as her skern would have it, between the real world and the next. Present and future. Earth and fire. Old magic, like the blacksmith's art.

Her skern was still too weak to give any comfort or advice but she did not need him to tell her the earthly struggle was nearing its end.

'Hefnir. Egill. I need you both. There may be something... at the last... I need you to be there.'

Bera bound the looking-glass to her tightly, feeling it quicken as she turned her face towards the mountain. The same unanswered question: was it upholding the Vallas' will or was she Obsidian's servant?

29

Hefnir and Egill made new tarred brands and set them alight. Bera chose the path she had seen from above when she had eagle eyes. A shower of thick ash fell and made it hard to breathe. They had to huddle close and cover their heads until the worst passed. When they set off again she thought someone was following. At first she thought the other crewman had left his post but she gradually became sure the slight figure was the Fetch. But Faelan's mother was dead – so whose Fetch was this? Hers? Whenever she faced it, there was nothing there. A notion grew that her sight was failing and giving her glimpses of the past instead of what was before her.

Her sight was certainly troubled and she let Hefnir lead. He scrambled to the top of tumbled stone and rocks to give a hand up to her and Egill. It meant she could make sure he was with them and not trying to steal the glass from her back.

And so they climbed. Bera struggled with the weight of Obsidian. She considered carrying it like a baby but the thought appalled her. With each dragging step it grew heavier, until there was a black hole in her sight looking ahead, so she walked with her head half-turned to see at the sides. The Fetch was there, and though she could not see its features, she needed no warning that she was about to die. The people she did know looked as ghostly.

'Hefnir?' she called, afraid.

He came to her side but she shook her head. He would think she was going mad and try to seize the glass.

'I need some water,' she said, instead.

'One mouthful,' he said.

She only wet her lips, to save enough for the others on the way back down.

'I am walking along a ghost fence between the living and the dead.'

Hefnir took the leather flagon and passed it to Egill. She must not have spoken aloud. Perhaps this loss of sight was the first stage of madness after all.

Her skern patted her hand. *It's Obsidian, all right.*

Its effects got worse as they got higher. The world around her was becoming insubstantial and grey, whilst she could see down through the shadowy earth into the fiery caverns beneath. It was like putting a hand in front of the sun and seeing the fingers glow red with blood round the dark shadow of bone. Sometimes there were explosions and Bera jumped to avoid being skit by boiling rock but they were far below them. She sensed the others giving her worried looks and tried not to jump, but every time she misjudged her footing she was glad to have Egill beside her to stop the fall.

Then the earth slid sideways and all three of them slithered on loose stones.

'Did you feel that?' asked Egill.

Hefnir's voice rasped, 'You stupid bint, of course we did.'

They pressed onwards and it was growing even darker. The brands were nearly burned out so they had to waste time breaking off ribby branches and get them to catch light. Without tar, they would not burn as long and then they would all be blind. There seemed no way they could reach the summit before the top blew. The earth tried to throw them off and this time they could not keep their feet. Bera's fall was stopped by a boulder and she clawed her way back to Hefnir. He held her tight, dusty faces close.

'We must go on,' Bera said. 'Only I can stop this.' She did not say he would never see her again.

He softly kissed her filthy forehead. Hefnir already knew.

As they got higher, Bera saw the inside of the mountain better than the world outside. Molten metal was rising, bubbling up towards the cone. It was a race and one she had to win. Yet every blind step tired her more; a scramble over black and slippery skree.

Egill took her hand, keeping her steady. 'Let me take the black glass for a bit. It must be back-breaking.'

'It's not that big.'

Bera so wanted to let one of them carry it. It was getting hotter and heavier all the time and the bead on her necklace scorched whenever it touched her skin. She hated Obsidian and the things she had seen in it, but who could she trust to bear it? It viciously slid sideways, making her stumble. Egill grabbed her and they skidded until they hit solid rock. Broken fragments slithered away, bouncing and skimming all the way to the bottom.

'The land wants me to fail. It's trying to kill me.' Her croaked words sounded mad now she said it aloud.

'I'm always lucky,' said Egill.

Did she really believe that, after all that had happened to her? Which one of them was mad?

Hefnir called down to them. 'Get up here on this ridged part. Careful.'

Egill led her towards him and then he held out both hands to pull Bera up to him. Where he stood, the ground was crustier where there had been seepage of liquid rock many years earlier.

Lava.

'I can see inside the mountain,' she said.

'Does that help us?'

Hefnir wiped his black face with a grimy hand. Bera could not judge his expression. Even close, nothing was sharp. The flow of lava was a shimmering veil before her eyes. Somehow she had to stop the destruction and she knew that this time, she needed their understanding and possibly their advice. Had she told them already?

'I can see the firestorm that's brewing in there.'

'You keep telling us,' said Hefnir.

'How close?' asked Egill.

'A whisper away, coming soon. Listen.'

The others were shadows in the brymstone dark. They trudged on in silence. Trusting her, she hoped.

The air was thick, like poison phlegm. Bera begged any Vallas to bring a breeze to whisk it away but nothing stirred. They had gone, like all the animals. They tied linen rags over their mouths and noses and Bera felt smothered. Her eyes streamed with bitter tears that scalded her raw face. The glass was bruising her spine and she finally pulled her shawl to one side without taking out the glass. It took all her will. Then it slid to the front, making it hard to move forward. She had to hold it to stop it escaping, and without handholds she kept slipping back down the slope that was growing steeper as they wound upwards.

Hefnir held her. 'Admit that you are struggling. You said you needed us, so let me carry the stone.'

'You want it too much.'

'You can watch me.'

'I can't see well enough!' She wondered who was shouting.

Hefnir kept his voice low. 'Give it to me, Bera. Trust me.'

'I saw your face the moment Egill unwrapped the black bowl.'

'Obsidian in-thralls you,' said Egill.

'So long ago,' Hefnir said, 'and it was your bowl, Bera, not mine.'

'I had to wrench it out of your grasp.' Bera's chest ached. She coughed and a spike of pain stabbed her ribcage. She longed to rest, to give it to someone else. But never Hefnir.

'I gladly gave you the bowl, remember?' Egill took Bera's face in her gritty hands. 'I kept it all that time but gave it to you straight, and let you scry in it and all. I'm not in-thralled to anything.'

It was true that Egill had kept the black bowl wrapped in sacking. She said she was waiting for the right person to come. Bera. Or had Egill been hiding from it?

You trust her already. Hand it over.

Egill was a mystery. Not boy, not girl, not good or bad.

'Give her some water.' Hefnir's voice boomed like a shout in fog from a distant boat.

Bera felt a pouch at her lips and drank.

'Did I faint?'

Egill touched her forehead with her lips. 'Fever. You swooned right out.'

251

'I used to kiss Heggi like that, feeling his heat.' Bera looked around. 'Is he here?'

'He'll be back soon. He's scouting ahead.'

She meant Hefnir.

Egill went on, 'So if you're going to do it, be quick.'

Bera untied her burden. 'You have it for a bit then, Egill.'

'You sure?'

'I may already be dying. I can't see you, hardly.' Too hard to explain its quickening. 'Guard Obsidian, my friend.'

Egill kissed her. 'Put this rock in the shawl and Hefnir will think you still have it.'

Hefnir returned. 'Up you get. You keep saying it's coming soon, Bera, so crack on.'

'She can hardly move,' said Egill.

'Well. I've found a better path, so we'll be quicker with whatever it is you're trying to do, Bera.'

If only she could tell him. She had spent her life watching for signs and trying to make sense of them. There must be a time and a place when it was right to return the stone and sacrifice herself. But the world had shrunk, like her sight, to a pinprick of no purpose.

Cling on! What's important?

Heggi and Valdis.

Bera struggled to her feet, dazzled by the bright fury inside the mountain. She was completely blind. Egill came to her side and they began the long climb together, her huge moonstone eyes seeing for both of them.

Gradually, without the weight of Obsidian, Bera began to see their dismal world. Lightning crackled above them; a constant glimmering of wan light that made the land starker. They all trudged: Hefnir in front and Egill bringing up the rear. Desolation haunted them. The sun became a pinprick of red light and then vanished, leaving a sky that was as yellow and curdy as chestnut blight. Day was night and only wildfires kept them on their grim track. Stumps of trees were broken and black, warnings of doom past and doom to come. Cracks in the ashy crust smoked and then Bera held her breath as long as possible. Her chest felt scorched and she only prayed they would get her to Hel before they all died.

From time to time they had to stop. Even Bera, who was aware of the widening channels of lava beneath them, realised that they needed to rest if they were ever to reach the summit. On one of these stops she lay on the ground, listening to the fire song beneath, and welcomed her skern.

Hel's calling you to the place.

'It's that simple, is it?'

Simple? Look at you.

'What must I do then?'

There are no choices.

'I need to think I might live. Otherwise it's too hard. I think Egill knows, which is why—'

Hefnir spoke quietly. 'Roll over very slowly, Bera. Look. Can you see something moving? Down there, see it? A flicker of light.'

'It'll be coming up through a rift.' Egill didn't trouble to look. 'Another wildfire.'

'It's moving,' Hefnir said.

In a flash of forked lightning it was possible to make out figures.

Hefnir softly swore. 'Did you see them?'

Bera nodded. 'I can sense them. Who else could it be?'

Another white flare confirmed it: a small group was trailing them. At its head was a monster with a full dragon body. Bera's bones chilled with dread.

'I've expected him,' she said.

'The Serpent King.' Hefnir spat.

'And the small one is Heggi.'

Hefnir stayed low. 'I'm going to get a better view. See how many of them there are.'

Bera wanted to scramble down the slope, kill the Serpent and carry Heggi back to safety. She yearned for it. But even if she was successful, that meant Heggi would have to witness her death. Or worse: die with her.

With no sword, how could you kill the Serpent King? And he has crew with him.

'They would kill Heggi if I attacked anyway.'

Her only option was to keep climbing, though it broke her heart. The Serpent King must not come near Obsidian in such a place as this. What particular darkness would it coax in his dragon body? Her desperate hope that sacrifice would not be demanded was doomed – because even if she could keep Hel from Obsidian, she could only save her life and Heggi's by giving it to the Serpent.

Egill rubbed her thumb down Bera's cheek. 'Don't cry, Bera. Heggi's safe, and close.'

Her eyes were already smarting so much she didn't know she was crying.

She got to her feet. 'Best move on. I'll take the looking-glass back now.'

Egill pulled away. 'Let me help, Bera, please. I feel it's what I was born to do.'

'Perhaps you were, perhaps not. But the Serpent King is mine and I must keep Obsidian safe from him.'

She took the rock out from her shawl and Egill reluctantly slid the glass into it and Bera made sure it was secure.

Hefnir returned. 'You silly bints, trying to hide it,' he said. 'It's one stone. Once we're up there I'm going to collect hundreds, bigger than that, and I can buy the known world.'

'Only if I manage to save the world, Hefnir. And you must believe I can, or you would never have agreed to help.'

He gave a mock salute and led off, all three of them as wheezing and stiff as old folk. She wondered what he really believed. Did he manage always to forget evil, or was it deliberate lying?

'He can only think of buying the world, not saving his son,' she muttered to Egill.

'Don't misjudge your husband, Bera. You didn't see him on the beach. We all know there's only one black stone the Serpent wants and for himself, not for sale.'

Bera nodded. 'The world and its creatures will be better off dead if he ever seizes Obsidian.'

30

The final climb was the worst. The path became a gully and Bera had to claw her way upwards. Black thoughts swirled around her like bats. Her purpose remained clear but her body was failing. The wolfbite was poisoning her blood; her leg was weak and so swollen that her boot had sunk into the flesh. Her hands were bleeding and nails broken on the sharp rocks. She trusted an outcrop to take her weight, which then gave way, and only Hefnir's quick hand saved her. After that, they were sliding and scrambling back on a skree of large glassy nuggets. It was all they could do to breathe.

The darkness had thickened into a suffocating enemy that stifled speech and decision. The Fetch returned, just in the corner of her eye. Its lithe movement reminded her of Egill when they first met. She had thought the world was opening up for them all then. Now they were staggering towards death.

They reached a small level and the path disappeared. Hefnir went to look for a place to go on. Bera rested where she stood; the ground was too hot to touch. They took off their useless linen veils and wrapped them round their hands for more protection.

'Do you see the person with us?' she asked.

'Is it your Fetch?' Egill whispered.

'It must be.' Bera took off her shawl and rolled her shoulders.

The looking-glass slipped enough to make her look in it. In that moment a shaft of self-knowledge entered like an obsidian dagger. Any hard word that had ever been directed at her came flying at her like a fist. All true. Stupid, useless, clumsy; selfish, cold, heartless; she could hear them all and every failing brought death. Bera counted them on her fingers.

'What are you doing?'

'Reckoning,' Bera said. 'I deserved to lose things: boats and the sea; every home; my whole childhood.'

You didn't lose it, sweetheart, you never had one.

'I thought you didn't deal with the past.'

I don't. But who we were is always inside who we are.

'I was cold to Heggi at the start. So I'll lose him too.'

Now that is the past.

'He's here now and I left him. Does he hate me?'

Yes.

'Can't you go to him, make him understand?'

I am not, ever, going to leave you again.

'He wouldn't be able to hear you anyway,' said Egill.

Bera reeled. 'Who are you talking to?'

'Your skern.'

'How long have you heard my skern?' Shock turned to outrage. 'How dare you not tell me! It's worse than theft… it's like – like – rape!'

'It only started before the ice bear. I thought it was you calling, it sounded like you.'

It has to be in liminal places, a threshold – which can be a special time or circumstance.

'Is this a threshold?'

Oh yes, of course – but you knew that. That's why we're here.

'Did you know she could hear you?'

He went long and thin like smoke through a keyhole.

She has a certain knack. It's because she is… borderline herself.

'What does that mean?'

Egill rubbed her nose with her sleeve. 'I think it's like I told you at the start, Bera. You're so black and white. You want me to be a boy or a girl. I'm neither. Both. It's not a question of choice, I just am.'

'Tell me your real name.'

'You think you can pin me down then? Own me? Names are power.'

'So why do you use your father's name? Guilt?' She meant to hurt.

It took Egill a while to answer, as if she were working something out for herself.

'I let him die, Bera. I... wanted it to be him, not me. The moment I met you I knew it was the start of something that would make it right, so I chose his name when you asked. There's death coming, for sure, and I want it to be mine.'

Had she recognised the Fetch? 'No. Listen, Egill. I—'

Hefnir shouted, 'Stay there. I'm coming back.' He lost his footing and slid down to them. He gasped and wheezed. 'So... hot. Scalded my lungs.'

Bera rescued the flagon of water and he poured it down his throat. It spilled onto his shirt, already clinging to him with sweat.

'Careful!'

Bera offered it to Egill, who refused to drink.

'Is that the way up?' Bera asked.

Hefnir took more breaths, sounding like bellows stoking up a fire. 'Blocked. Old fall of rocks, melted then cooled, huge lumps. No way to top.'

'You two stay here,' she said. 'I'll find a way and come back.'

She knew Hel had chosen the time. This was where she had to go on, alone.

Bera went to where Hefnir had been standing when he shouted down to them. He was right: the way became a wall of rock made of sharp, metallic stones and porous boulders. She tried to go around it but large cracks poured fiery heat, driving her back. On the other side, the earth's crust fumed and heaved, a stinking morass of fire and putrid gases. Not that way either. Perhaps Obsidian would give the answer. She hauled her shawl round to the front. It was too light.

'No, no, no, no!'

The shock punched her: how could she be so stupid? Her brain must be mazed by the fumes, or she would never have lost it. Or did it choose to fall? A belching cloud choked her and she stumbled away downhill. Had she put it back after seeing all her failings? Did one of them steal it?

The mountain was roaring, exulting in its rage and ready to blow. It had won; she could not stop it now, so must get back to the others.

Bera swayed and staggered, frightened and lost. Surely she should be back at the place by now. Then, through the yellow steam that was seeping from every crack and crevice, she saw Egill's linen veil lying on the ground. She was right; this was where they had stopped. She cast about, willing Obsidian to be waiting for her there. It was not – and Hefnir and Egill were gone.

Bera sank to her knees and howled. The mountain was so loud that she could not hear herself. To have come this far, when she could have stayed at home and died with her own folk. Her baby, Valdis. Sigrid – how sorely she missed her bustling friend, full of life and strong. She, like Faelan, Dellingr, trusted her to save them.

'I need you, Mama.'

Only her skern was there. Her knees were burning yet she didn't move. She deserved to suffer. Obsidian had shown her what an angry, unforgiving, boastful fool she was. She would die here alone, a failure, while the greedy ones below were probably already fighting over it, killing each other. They could not stop the chain of events that would end in death for the whole precious blue globe hanging in space and time.

Bera got up. There was one last chance. With or without Obsidian she would enter Hel's gate. Sacrifice. But that would leave Heggi with the Serpent – with the looking-glass.

He is in danger.

She had always known it, but now the threat was real and present and there was no choice to make. The world must take its chances, for she must save her boy.

Then hurry!

Nothing was moving below her, though spurting fumes and sudden fires hid parts of her way. Bera slithered down the loose skree when she could for speed, determined to get one thing right.

At last there were voices, so she must be close. Bera fought her way through a mix of rough boulders and startling yellow-green grass. She could hear Hefnir. A scrabble of stones fell. She hid behind a huge boulder, heart pounding. Had they seen her?

'Not even biggest stone. Look!' It was the Serpent King's thick voice for sure. His forked tongue. 'Don't insult me.'

'Then take all of them,' Hefnir said. 'There's plenty here, man.'

'Obsidian is what I want, not some toy.'

Bera had to know if Heggi was still alive. She flattened herself against the rock and edged closer. The nearest to her was a crewman with tattoos. The marks were the same as the man in the tavern: Keep Away. Marks made in Iraland. The rest of the group were standing on a wide ledge. Hefnir with Egill, the Serpent King... Where was her son? She risked a quick glance out, then back. Nowhere to be seen, so Bera hoped he was the other side of the crewman.

Her skipping heart was unsteady. Breaths too short to calm. It was the air. So near the gateway to Hel. Bera shook her head to make her scalp prickle. Surely she would know if Heggi was dead?

'If the Serpent kills me, Hel will accept my sacrifice, won't she?'

We are already dying, together.

Their small life was the squabble of midges. The mountain roared again and the men's voices were lost. It was irrelevant. It was not their fight but hers.

Bera whispered, 'Keep me strong, Vallas. Let me get this right.'

If the Serpent had already killed Heggi then life was not worth living. If he was alive she would save him. All she had on her side was surprise, so she planned to seize the crewman's sword and plunge it into the Serpent King's black heart. Was he still a man, or had his dragon body made him immortal? Whatever she faced, she found her strength.

'ALU.'

Lightning crackled overhead as another cloud of ash mushroomed up into the sky. The world tilted, sharp and strong. On her side. Bera braced herself and stepped out.

The crewman was on his back, unmoving. She kept to her plan with determined fury, dragging the heavy sword to the Serpent King, who was the only one she could see. She must strike while he was down and she lunged at him. The blade missed his thigh as he painfully rolled to his feet. The poison air weakened them. Bera used the hilt like a crutch to take her weight. Her enemy turned, slow and sluggish, like being in a nightmare, then was gone. The stench was visible and made eyes deceive. And then, through the brymstone fumes, a shadow Serpent King returned with Heggi, holding a black knife at his throat. The sight of her boy alive gave Bera strength and she risked looking at Heggi to share it.

He was bloodless with terror, his lips invisible. He thought he was about to die, unprotected by parents who had traded his life for Obsidian, and she could not make him look at her. She looked round for help. Where was Hefnir? Or Egill?

She must prove her love.

Could she deny her own fate, her Valla ancestry, and condemn the rest of the world to death in order to save one boy? A willing sacrifice here might do both.

She lay down the sword. 'Let him go, Serpent. I take his place.'

The monster laughed. 'Gladly. When I have the stone.'

If the Serpent thought she had Obsidian and must kill her for it, he would have to let go of Heggi.

'Come and get it.'

His forked tongue flickered over black lips while his cold eyes judged her. Once, she had thought him stupid.

Here they stood at the highest place of the known world at the very point of its destruction. Birds had long since gone; no creature stirred and Bera pictured the three of them as graven rune stones. Why did the Serpent King not want any of the black stones that were all round him? Because Obsidian had made him desire it. Bera understood now. The glass had been fashioned to lure minds into gazing at what they needed to see. Perhaps only her mind could bear what it saw, although it had driven her half-mad. Was it even now tempting frail Egill? Or Hefnir? She had to keep the Serpent thinking she had it. Perhaps she could save her life by saying she was the only one who could use it to scry. Would it be enough to bargain with?

'No.' The Serpent King put out a hand. 'You bring to me.' His four rows of teeth leered.

She saw her mistake: he wanted her alive. He was claiming Bera as his prize, with Obsidian as his power. Still, she traded for Heggi's life.

'Let my son go first.'

He laughed again and gave Heggi a shove. 'Run to little Bera then. You can't go far, either of you.'

She opened her arms and Heggi ran to her. Fierce love.

'I'm so sorry, I'm so sorry,' she kept saying into his hair.

He did not say she was forgiven but he clung to her. How could she keep her boy safe and the Valla world too? Her mind was addled.

The Serpent King beckoned her. 'I'll have that kiss now, and then Obsidian. Together we will rule the known world.'

From behind them came a deep-throated battle cry. With raised sword, Hefnir jumped down from a ledge and thrust at the Serpent King, who had his axe ready. He swung – and chopped at air. Hefnir stumbled and turned. They were breathless and clumsy; they twisted away from each other at the last moment, staggering, their weapons weighing them down. But they rallied, brothers-in-law and sworn enemies, and came on. Bera saw bloodlust in their swollen eyes. The Serpent King was a murderer and if he killed Hefnir, he would come for them in his rage.

She pulled Heggi back towards the large rocks. Heggi collapsed as soon as they reached her hiding place.

'Will Papa…?'

'We're safe here. Safe together,' she lied.

And then the whole land slipped, taking Heggi with it.

31

Bera's eyes were so sore that she was peering through slits. She had to find Heggi. The ground was pitching like a stormy sea and whenever she tried to stand she fell again. Unlike a boat, there were no handholds here to help, so she crawled. Her throat was raw, she was parched and her tongue was stuck to the roof of her mouth. She tried to shout his name but could only croak. The heat blazed, but she willed herself on. Time unreeled backwards and the darkness was below deck in her father's boat, the *Raven*, and the small figure, hugging itself and rocking, was Egill, half-mad, down in the foul, dark bilge. Poor, frail Egill, her false friend; the ruin of all Bera's plans. Then she knew why the memory was sharp: the shock of white hair was really there, in the shadow of disaster. Perhaps, even at the last, she could take Obsidian from Egill and restore order to the world.

Bera clawed the burning soil with bloody hands and reached the small, still body, curled like a toddler, with caffled, silver-blond hair. A flare of love told her this was Heggi, her son, and she had found him.

'Boykin.' Her voice was like wind through frost-dried grass.

She would trade anything on earth to let him be alive. The heat of his forehead burned her cracked lips.

'Mama...'

'I know, my love, I know.'

She got down next to him and they held on tight, until this moment was the only thing that mattered. Bera was with her son and with every part of her body, she gave her vital force to him to keep him alive.

Then, finally, the mountain blew.

She expected them to die. Only their dog was missing and she wished they could all be together here, at the last.

They heard the rush and fall of the eruption and when the worst stopped, Bera's ears were ringing. It must have blown on the southern side, which she had seen from the Abbotry, but her instinct told her that this was not the end but a demand. Her life had been spared so that she could keep her promise to Hel to find and return Obsidian. This had never been the place. Obsidian had tricked her. This was where the earth was most brutal, where it wanted to stop her, not where the safe delivery of Obsidian was to be made with her death, like Sigrid safely delivering Valdis. New life for the world.

Something was digging into her side. Heggi had a water flask on his belt! She took it off, afraid to shake it and find it empty, but there was a dull slushing. She put it to Heggi's lips and let a trickle into his poor mouth. His whole face was filthy, with burns and blisters livid under the grime. There were more lines than a boy his age should have: too many cares. Bera supposed her own face was the same. The thought surprised her; her face had never concerned her until she had glimpsed it in Obsidian. Odd, to become aware of something when it was half-destroyed already.

Bera wet her mouth so that she could speak. 'When you fell, did you see your father…?'

Heggi shook his head, but then kept shaking it, like a horse plagued by flies.

'There, dear one. I'm sorry, boykin. I shouldn't have asked. There, sweet.'

The ground stopped shaking. Bera did not press him and he fell into a deep sleep. What should she do next? Was she right, and the Serpent King could not die? Was Obsidian lying amongst all the other black stones? Her plans kept changing, being bent – by Obsidian? – like holding a lodestone under cloth and watching pins jump.

What is lost can be found.

'Is Egill alive?'

She wants to give the stone back to the mountain.

'But that's not what we have to do, is it?'

She always tries to be special and now thinks she can be.

'How? She's in the wrong place, and anyway, I have to do it.'

She is trying to save you, Bera. The one she loves. You know this. She is giving herself in your place.

Bera closed her eyes but could not connect with her friend's skittish mind. The Fetch was hers after all. Perhaps Egill's sacrifice had worked, though she doubted it. When she opened them, Heggi was staring at her, needing comfort.

'Egill gave her life to stop the eruption,' she said. 'You don't need to go on being so afraid, my dearest one.'

He could only make a cawing sound, like a tiny crow.

'Your throat is burned. Don't speak.'

Bera cradled his head and wept. She did not hide her feelings from him or try to be strong. She was crying for her failure, for falling under Obsidian's spell when she thought she was stronger than anyone else. Obsidian had also shown her what beauty was lost, before the world had seen itself: that tiny jewelled globe in velvet blackness.

'Sad... about Papa?' he asked.

She was sorry about Hefnir. And she was afraid, terrified, that in whatever time they had left, the Serpent would come after them.

Heggi touched her face with the back of his hand. 'You have... me.'

'Then let's meet Fate bravely, on our feet.'

They helped each other up and looked for any way through. They went in circles, trudging and confused. The sun was entirely cloaked, so Bera had to take a reckoning from the natural markings on the rocks. Then she recognised three that leaned together and started downwards but it was bad enough to turn them back. Every way was blocked. Finally, she thought that a new track had opened up but they had not gone far when they saw that below them the next gully was burning with crawling, fiery metal, like a disgusting black dragon. They stumbled away from the heat, desperately looking for any way down, trying to stay calm. Bera touched her hair, thinking it was smouldering. It was hot and brittle but not yet alight.

Then they came upon a stump with an axe mark on it.

'Look,' she said, pointing at a trampled furrow through sooty undergrowth.

Heggi's eyes were huge. 'The Serpent King!'

'It's our only chance, to follow him.'

Bera led the way, with Heggi behind being snagged on thorns. So it was Bera who saw the blood first. It was startling red against the ash. She tried to block Heggi but it was too late. He was staring at it and began to shake his head again, over and over. Bera held it tight between her sore hands.

'Listen to me, Heggi. You have to be strong now.'

His teeth chattered and he would not look at her. She pushed up his chin so that he had to. Kindness would make him collapse.

'I'm damned if we go through all this and then die up here. Do you understand? Stop looking. Stop thinking. All that matters is staying alive!'

He began to cry.

Bera took him by the shoulders. 'You said I have you – so you also have me. I will never leave you again.'

His hands were fists but Heggi slowly blinked his eyes. He was agreeing to carry on.

Bera was terrified that the lava would soon be chasing them on this side of the mountain too, so she took them as far round it as she dared. Too far, and they would never get back to the *Raven*. She groaned aloud. Don't think it! Heggi was young and strong.

Not after you poisoned him. He's not breathed fully since. And now this!

Could her guilt get any worse? They followed the smears of blood, getting thicker.

'Papa's?' Heggi asked.

'It may not be a man's.' It might be a dragon's.

Her courage was failing her. With every weary step Bera tried to convince herself that the earth had vented its anger and was growing calmer. Compared to the ledge, the air was almost sweet here. But lava was flowing and the ash cloud threatened. Up in the highest point of the sky, it was like some live thing, quickening and billowing, silvery grey like a wolf. Bera looked away, wanting to believe they were saved in the future; that gale-force winds would be strong enough to blow the ash away.

It's too large and heading south and east.

Over the homestead.

Heggi kept stumbling, taking Bera with him. Their legs were too weak to stop the fall and they slithered, slipped, and stopped against boulders, waiting to catch their breath and then link arms and do it again, and again. Sometimes they simply tripped on a stubborn stone and fell where they stood. Bruised, shaken, worn out, Bera's strength finally failed and when they reached ground that levelled out a little she lay flat on her back and felt Heggi do the same beside her.

After a while she looked around them. They were on a blackened platform with mounds of smoking stones lying in rough heaps. The sight made Bera even more thirsty. She felt ice-cold glass on her blistered lips and then sweet mead to soothe her tongue. Did they even have water? Heggi's leather flask was filthy but not ripped. With flayed fingers she untied it and gave it to Heggi.

'Sip. Small sips.'

'Nearly gone,' Heggi rasped.

Bera upended it and could only wet her lips.

'Sorry, Mama,' he said.

She touched his hand.

The world was clinker, so that another few whirls of grey and black did not stand out. She had been staring at the thing without knowing. She checked to see if Heggi had noticed but he was looking up at the leaden sky. The light lifted a little and Bera looked back.

The serpents danced on the body of the man who could not be killed.

Once again Bera noted that fear would reach a peak and then the body could not become more terrified of the same thing. As she stared at the body of the Serpent King, the ceaseless rumble of lava became only a low, background booming. The shifts of the quaking earth made his tattoos appear to writhe. Or was he only pretending to be dead, sleeping with one eye open like a dragon?

A long, shrill note demanded her attention.

Bera slowly traced it to Heggi, who was staring down at what remained of his uncle. It was an unearthly sound but it made her move.

She pulled him away. 'Hide. I will call when it's safe.'

Heggi's single note became sobs and she sensed him backing away. She kept her eyes on the Serpent King. She slowly approached, ready to run if he made a move. His mouth was wide open, like Drifa's strange death snarl. His carved teeth were even blacker in the furrows . One arm was splayed and the unwinking eye stared at her from his armpit. She looked back at his corpse grin, hideous as it was, because the mess of his legs made her sick to her stomach.

Then his tongue flickered out to touch his lips. She jumped back.

'Water.' It was an order.

She shook the empty flask. 'None.'

He gave his sly smile. 'I knew you come for me at end.'

His skern passed her. It was smooth and innocent, the opposite of his foul body. They were not yet cleaved in death and Bera marvelled at the smoky gentleness that watched over such a beast as the Serpent King.

'Not skern – you,' he grunted. 'You come for blood debt.'

'You killed my father.' Her voice was flat with exhaustion. Who was her father to the Serpent, out of so many?

'My sister…' He tried to sit up but his face screwed up with pain.

'I am a Valla. I know what happened to your sister, and it was worse than you could know.' It was said in pity for them both, for his skern revealed the sweet child he had once been, who loved his older sister.

'Hefnir is bad man. Liar and coward. But he paid blood debt now.'

Bera felt dismay and shock, though reason always told her the Serpent would win. She dared to go closer, now he would never move again.

'Hefnir is dead?' She kept her voice low, for Heggi's sake.

'I kill him. Through heart with own sword.'

'Where is he?' She looked around them, in case his body was hidden.

The Serpent's gaze shifted. He was reckoning some advantage. What could he possibly want? There was no healing, not with those wounds. Only an axe could sever a leg like that.

'Did Hefnir use your axe?'

'Mountain gave it to him.'

'Where is he now?'

'Pain bad but I am strong. Long wait for blood to drain. Like reindeer.'

'And?'

He took some time to answer. 'Poison on axe. Wolfsbane. Bad death.' He turned his head, looking for something. 'Sword.'

Hefnir's sword was lying in a pool of blood. The Serpent's blood – or Hefnir's? Bera did not want to touch it.

'I am not so stupid as to hand you a sword.'

'You Valla. Fate. You make, and are there at death, like skern.' He looked straight at his own skern. 'Yes, I see it. But is not close enough.' He was panting.

You know what he's asking and goodness knows he deserves it.

She had wanted to kill him. She might have done if he had harmed Heggi. But now she could not. It wasn't to prolong his suffering; it was because this was not who she was.

'I am a healer.'

'To kill is to heal.'

'I can't.'

'I can.' Heggi stood beside her with his father's sword.

Bera rocked with horror. 'No, Heggi. Lay it down. He will die soon anyway.'

'He killed my father. He must pay the blood debt.' His flat voice was deep and hoarse.

It was the voice of the Serpent King, unmoved by the thought of killing a man. How blind she had been! The bad blood had not flowed from his father but from the other side: his mother's kin. She would brave anything to stop him becoming like his uncle.

'His death will cancel the debt. Lay down the sword, Heggi. Let your father's axe wounds be the killing blow.'

'No. I have to.'

The Serpent sneered to hurt the boy's pride. He was so easy to read. Heggi would be enraged and the Serpent would get his quick death and the pleasure of knowing his filthy blood was coming out in his nephew. Bera pleaded with Fate to help her but they were at the sharp point of ill circumstance.

'Leave him the sword, Heggi. He can kill himself.'

'He can't. He won't.'

He stood with a straight back, desperate to look older but more obviously a child. Bera doubted he could even lift the sword. She had got so much wrong with him when their lives became joined that she did not want to strip him entirely of his pride. She knew it was all madness: here they stood on a world as thin and crisp as eggshell. If the ice cap exploded, they would all die. Their only chance was to get to the boat and ride out the tidal wave. They had to get to it fast, so that meant making a decision. It was time to understand that duty came in many forms, and who that duty was owed to.

That's the girl.

'Give me the sword, Heggi, and move away. I shall avenge my husband and my father but more importantly, I will show mercy and end suffering. One day you may understand.' Her voice held command.

If he would gladly pass over the duty he would also step away from his bad blood.

Heggi slumped. He turned his back to her, though his shoulders were shaking. Bera gently took the sword, which was heavy. She wiped the hilt on her dress and dragged it over to the Serpent King.

His skern was closer.

'You are dying,' she said, relieved.

His eyes glittered, dangerous as ever. 'I die like warrior, not rat in hole. I wait for you.'

Bera knew it was true and what she did not have was time. She needed a clear reason to kill any man and found the blood debt was not enough.

'Did you send that man with poison?'

His lips curled. 'Meant for bastard Hefnir. Now – kill.'

And then she remembered the remedy, and cursed. How could she kill someone she could perhaps heal?

Too late.

'Want me to beg? Kill fast. Please, Valla.'

'Show me how.'

He slowly raised his hand and felt his neck with two fingers until he found the notch in the collarbone.

'Put point in here.'

She let the sword tip trail over his body up to the spot and then he carefully got it in place. Her breath was fast and hard and all she wanted to do was run. How had she ever vowed to kill anyone? She felt exposed and afraid. Only the thought of saving Heggi from this duty kept the sword in place. Where would she find the strength? It was surely wrong to use ALU where her purpose was so murky. It should make only good intentions more powerful. She tried to picture her father and Thorvald at her back but failed. That would also be wrong.

'Get body over sword and push down. Very hard. Strong, like Brid.'

Their eyes met and once again Bera remembered the tall youth who had given his nephew a toy horse, and let him sit on his back to make his mama laugh. Tears for this person, now destroyed, made her falter. She needed a dark kind of courage, so she called on her mother to aid her and touched her necklace, making every bead a Valla ancestor that she summoned to her back.

Time to end his pain.

Bera pressed down, holding his gaze so that he would not die at a coward's hand. His skern joined him at the last, so that their face became one smooth innocence.

Whereas hers felt stained and black. Bera left the sword in his throat and sank to her knees, thinking she would never get up. Had Obsidian triumphed and brought out the bad entirely?

She felt an arm round her shoulders and Heggi's wet face pressed against hers. 'Thank you, Mama,' he sobbed.

32

Time to get going!

'I can't, not yet.'

Bera could not bear the thought of pulling the sword out from the Serpent's throat. By rights, Heggi should have his father's sword – but how could she ask him to hold his uncle's head while she tugged?

'I should try to bury him,' she said, with no conviction.

His skern joined him so he will not be hungry yet.

'Perhaps the iron through his neck will hold him, like the beheading.' Fate had given her Faelan to show her this.

The cross will stop him rising – if he truly believes in Brid.

'Can what folk believe make itself real? I worried I might bring Drorghers to this place but is it all of us?'

His serpent body and cross look like the signs at the Abbotry.

'I'm glad it's Hefnir's sword that will stay in his throat, not mine.'

If he did become a Drorgher, there would be no prey for him anywhere, unless they could survive the earth's destruction.

Heggi tugged at her sleeve. 'Can we look for Papa now?'

Resigned to having to move, Bera wearily got up. They struggled down the stone-strewn path, helping each other over boulders. Then simply stopped. Bera slapped her cheeks to wake up and got Heggi propped up on a rock before slumping against him. The earth shifted under their feet but what would once have terrified them seemed a small disturbance. They let it pass.

'I think he was mad.' Heggi's eyes were streaming.

'Did he hurt you?'

He shook his head. 'Not like you mean. He brought me presents from all over, when I was little... when Mama was still alive.'

'I understand, boykin. He was the last link with her. The last of your mother's blood-kin.' She hoped it really was the last.

'So do you think he was mad?'

'We must try to get down to the beach. It will be safer. We must be nearly there,' she said – and feared the *Raven* was probably a heap of ash.

Heggi rubbed his eyes. 'But do you?'

Bera gave herself time to somehow soften his well-found worry. 'Maybe he had the madness of too much power.'

Heggi whispered, 'Papa says it's in my blood.'

Ancestors could all pass on bad blood. She had just killed a man after all.

Vallas exult in destruction.

'Listen to me. We can change what's in our blood for good or ill. Too much power can turn anyone bad but it's not catching, like red-spot.' She was telling both son and skern and needed to believe it was true. 'But it can be exciting. You must never stay too close to badness.'

Cleansing water. And thirst! Bera pictured standing behind the waterfall, Faelan's quicksilver body in a crystal pool that she could drink dry...

'Well, then, why did you let my uncle take me?'

'I wasn't on the beach, not even in the bay!'

'You came later.' He pulled away from her. 'I'm going to look for Papa!'

'No, Heggi, listen...' How could she ever explain?

He set off but could only move slowly, which made him curse every blockage, his parents and his own body in the gruff voice that didn't suit his size. Bera kept with him but he moved away if she came too close. It distressed her to be so apart. Had killing the Serpent made it worse, not better?

All the way back down she dreaded Heggi finding his father's body, but there was not even a sign of blood.

Beyond hope, they found the *Raven* on the beach and no dragonboat in the bay. The Serpent King's crew must have abandoned him.

'Cowards to the last,' Bera said. 'They're running back to Iraland now he's dead.'

Heggi shuddered but she was too weary to make it better. This side of the mountain was untouched by the fire-spill, as though the eruption had not happened. There was only a layer of ash on the boat. It was like going back in time, to earlier in the day, when they were all alive. Unless you looked at the sky, where flickering, formless lightning pointed at worse to come.

'If the *Raven*'s all right, Papa might be too. He might be hurting and we just went right past him!' Heggi's voice cut like a thin blade.

What could she say? It was true and she was too exhausted to know what she thought about that.

'We won't set sail until we know.'

'How will we know? If he's too hurt to move...'

'Be quiet, Heggi!'

Bera took one of the leather flagons of water from their boat and threw it to him, then drank from one herself, pouring it down her throat, not caring about the damage. Her insides burned and she collapsed onto the pebbles. It was clear her son had sided with Hefnir. She had not pictured it like this.

You wanted to be the glorious sacrifice.

'No. It was my duty. I have everything waiting for me at home.'

And you value everything?

She tried to picture what a happy family would look like: a kindly mother cooking for a grateful father, two or three smiling children and a dog quiet by the hearth.

She had no idea. 'I've been robbed of that too.'

Oh, sweetheart, you always rob yourself.

Bera was flattened under it all. She let her head loll to one side to look at Heggi. He threw a stone into the sea, making a big splash. He probably wanted to throw it at her. He saw her watching.

'You said you'd fight like a bear once. Like your name,' he cried. 'You said you'd do anything.'

How could she say, I just did; I just killed your uncle? She had not rescued him from Hefnir's cowardice and must pay the price. There were no words, with the bile-burning of regret that no amount of water could quench.

His little face was pinched, blackened and creased with worry. There was a deep line between his brows, like his father's. She had a vision of what he would look like as a man and it was not a good one. Cruel and hard; his frown constant in bitterness. And that would be because of her, not the Serpent King, who would never trouble them again. She opened her arms but he turned away. He was quite right. She must go to him… but she was so, so tired.

Bera went down to him and touched his shoulder gently.

'Go away!' He pushed her.

They fell, exhausted, but then Heggi rolled towards her and pressed into her side. He had seen more than any child should. Bera hugged him but they didn't fit and bones dug into other bones on bruised bodies. She dared not pull away. How else could she show Heggi how much she loved him? Gradually she heard his ragged breaths grow longer. Her boy had fallen into the bottomless sleep of total fatigue and with that thought she went gratefully into blackness herself.

It was dark when they next woke. Bera could not remember stoking the burial pyre but the heap of ash was still red-hot in the centre so they used the last pieces of wood to make it flare up again. Heggi hoped it would be a beacon for his father. Bera wondered how long they should wait for him. Or, really, how long to wait for Heggi to think they had waited long enough, for surely he was by now dead. She refused to ask her Valla ancestors for help but some human feeling made her want him alive.

Bending down out of the ash cloud came Faelan's burned and blackened face. No, not Faelan: it became the Fetch who was Egill. It came closer until the whole sky was dark and blistered and it whispered knowledge of other beliefs, painting the rune of Brid in gold. Bera knew she was in a dream and tried to learn what the beliefs were, but when she woke Brid was all she could recall. She still had the taste of the words but no detail. Egill had last words for

Bera, which would return if she did not chase them and send Egill to her rest.

A small pinkness in the east might have been sunrise; could have been another eruption. Bera needed to think that they had slept at the right time of day and all the upheaval and oddness was turning into some kind of order, so she chose the hope of dawn. She went to the water's edge and stared as far out to sea as the murk allowed. She was young and a mother of two. She would be a different kind of Valla. It was time to start.

'You are never there, Mama. So I won't listen anymore. Not to the ancestors, or the ravens, or crows, or whatever else lost me my son.'

There was only the washing of waves on the shore. Had she been abandoned by the Vallas? Well, the first act of motherhood was to feed her child. Bera waded further out and scried the water until she saw the fast flick of silver. Happy days with Sigrid. Her skill was still there. Bera caught their dance through the water, plunged, and swept a fish up onto the beach. Her smile cracked her lips and the rusty taste of blood whetted her appetite more. She caught another and collected some driftwood.

When she got back to the fire Heggi was awake. 'Bera?' he called out in his new, older voice.

She made a decision. She would treat him as a reliable person, not as a childish bundle of care and duty. He would be her helper and friend. Her true second. With that thought came determination.

'I'm back. We will eat and then, if your father has still not arrived, we are going to look for him.'

There was one full flagon of water left on the boat and they drank their fill, then ate well. They needed something good inside them – and possibly the smell of cooking would give Hefnir the spur to crawl, or at least shout.

Heggi looked out to sea. 'You know the homestead?' he started. 'You know Ginna…'

'I don't know if she's still alive, Heggi.'

Hope shines brightest in the darkest night of Hel, as Ottar would say.

'You could have lied,' he said. 'To make me feel better.'

'I promised never to lie to you again. Ginna may very well be waiting for her young man to return.'

'So I could have my coming-of-age feast at Brightening!'

Bera was glad to have given him this small comfort, but how strange the feast of Brightening seemed to her, in such a place and time.

Hefnir did not appear. A prickle of her scalp made Bera look round – but when she touched her head it was a burst blister. Dismayed that her instinct for danger was not restored, she became brisk.

'Fetch some more wood.'

'Papa would have come if he'd seen the fire already.'

'I'm banking up the fire, ready to clean and seal his wounds.'

Cauterising. Her skern shivered.

Heggi's jaw dropped but he hurried to do as she asked and they laid some seaweed on top to keep it hot.

'Now, Heggi. If your father can't come to us, we must go to him. If we're to search properly, we have to split up.'

'What about bears and... things?'

'No living creatures are left. You need to call so your father might hear, so that will work if there is anything else. Look and listen. Use your hunting skills.'

He began to cry. 'I wish Rakki was with me.'

She went to hug him, then remembered her resolve.

'So do I, Heggi, but he would be very frightened. It's better that he's with Faelan. Perhaps they're with Ginna and the puppy Tikki and they're all waiting for you.'

'If we ever get back.'

He was right; and Bera had the vision of Rakki bravely struggling on three legs. Even if he did get home, was life worth living without puffin hunting, for a dog? There was no comfort, only courage.

'Chin up. You are my second, Heggi, don't forget. Let's see if Hefnir could have come down another way.'

They walked along the shore until they saw the sluggish flow of lava, which tumbled over itself into the sea with a hiss of melting snow and ice. Even at this distance, the heat pushed them back and made every burn hurt more. They tried the other direction, which was devastated, and decided Hefnir could only use the same gully, filled with boulders and difficult.

'There is no other way,' Bera said.

'I expect he's probably fallen,' said Heggi, 'that's all. He'll be waiting for us up there somewhere.'

They sharpened their knives on a stone, took a stick each and then Bera sent him over to the left-hand side, while she took the right, the side nearer the lava flow. She climbed the gully, beating rocks with the stick and calling, though her scalded throat hurt badly. Once she thought she heard a reply but it was only a gust carrying Heggi's voice over to her, sounding like his father. They both called over and over. It was hopeless and Bera stopped.

A blackbird began to sing. Its lovely song in so unhappy a place was a sign and only when she felt that spark of hope did Bera realise how deep her despair had been. This was a true hope, in her heart, not her mind, and not for Hefnir but for the world. The blackbird had returned, telling the world it was there, alive, and restored Bera to her true self.

There was a sound of excited clapping. Her skern was leaning against a rock, looking as if they were on a summer's day hunt.

It just came to me. What your Valla gift is. You are knowledge, that's your part in things. Hope.

'Folk always say my knowledge brings the opposite.'

Knowledge is itself hope. He's over there.

Her skern airily circled a long finger then pointed at two tall boulders, leaning together like drunkards.

Bera had noticed them on the way down but they were hard to reach. Only the fact she knew Hefnir was there made her cut and slash through blackened stumps. When she was closer she could see where a body might have crashed through from above and then slid down. There was a trail of blood leading down into a gap between the boulders. She pushed her way closer.

Hefnir was propped against the rock, his head on his chest. She squeezed through a tight opening and went to him but he did not stir. Bera knelt and put a finger below his ear. There might have been a slight flutter – or was it her own heartbeat? His eyes were closed and his face deathly. Had her skern found him too late? She put her cheek to his lips but could feel no breath.

'Hefnir?'

Bera rested her head on his chest and listened for a heartbeat. Nothing. But Hefnir's skern was not there. Had he taken on the new belief and revoked his skern? She turned his hand and studied the blue veins that coursed over his wrist, where Cronan had his serpent tattoo. Wrong arm. She took the other, with a sense of dread. Hefnir had the same tattoo, freshly stained. It shocked and disgusted her. What had he done to earn it that Egill had not…? What had Cronan said? It was the mark of Brid. Perhaps Egill's Fetch was telling her about Brid in the dream so that she would understand Hefnir and save him. Whatever the truth, whatever he now believed, Bera was a healer. She held the unblemished wrist again and pressed. Was there a tiny movement? There… and again, there. Slow, weak, but a heartbeat.

'Come on, Hefnir!'

She took the leather flask from her belt, tipped his head back and let some water flow down his throat. He coughed and his eyes flickered. He smiled.

'Hefnir!' She had to rouse him. 'Where are you hurt?'

He tried to turn, then fell back. She pulled back his jerkin that side and gave a small cry. The wound itself was bad enough but its edges were angry welts that spread towards his chest and back. It did not look like a sword cut.

'This is poison.'

Hefnir licked his lips and she gave him more water. Waited.

'Wolfsbane. Not axe. He…'

'Don't speak that vile name.'

'Not all bad. Serpent – benefactor…'

'Shh, now. He can't hurt us anymore. You killed him.'

He closed his eyes to deny it. 'Hel… got him.'

Let him think so. 'Then you tried to reach the beach?'

'Earth shook, fell. Head.' He raised one finger.

'I do know where a head is.' Bera smiled.

His eyes smiled back.

She carefully parted his matted hair. 'There's a gash but it's your poisoned wound that worries me. I have a remedy, I think.'

The only true remedy for wolfsbane from Iraland or the Abbotry would be growing next to the plant but she hoped the dried leaves from the farmstead would help, if any were left.

'Too late. Stay.'

'I can't, Hefnir. Your son is searching for you. He needs to know you are safe.'

'I'm dying.' His eyes pleaded. Was it her he wanted or any company in death?

'I will cure you. You have to trust me. It's my duty to heal.' She got to her feet.

'Wait!' He weakly gestured her closer. 'Please.'

It took him a while to gather his strength to speak. 'Must say... sorry.'

He should say it to Heggi. His eyes clouded and his head fell back. Who told her hearing was the last sense to fail?

'You will not die.' She stayed brisk. 'I will send Heggi to watch over you and then I shall return with a remedy.' She quickly crossed her fingers. 'I'm leaving you the water, here, in your hand. Feel it? Then you'll feel better and we will get you back aboard the *Raven*.'

He did not flicker at the name.

'I will be very fast, Hefnir. Don't you dare die before I get back.'

Outside, she let her tears fall. The poison had been in his body a long time. Would he die before he had the chance to make his peace with Heggi? She prayed to every past Valla healer to give her their skill and that Faelan's plants might work. But was it only to give Hefnir time with Heggi? She couldn't say. Death was bringing her no closer to understanding what she felt about her husband.

She shouted for Heggi and heard an answer. He had to go a long way down to scramble back up and she lost sight of him but kept calling, so he would find her. When he did, she could see from the brave set of his mouth that he was braced for bad news. She quickly told him his father was alive and he burst into tears.

'He's very sick, though,' Bera said.

'Where is he?' Heggi asked, looking all round them.

'It's how we missed him. He must have crawled into that tight crevice over there for safety. You'll have to squeeze through. Stay with him, Heggi. If he falls asleep, wake him. He must not slip away into darkness. Talk to him, but don't make him answer. It tires him.'

'Where will you be?'

Hiding the fact there may not be a remedy.

'I shall do my best to save him and that means making a purge, like before.'

He nodded. 'But be as quick as you can because I might run out of things to say.'

An ordinary boy's concern. They seemed already at peace, father and son, simply in the blood-tie. Would Heggi forgive her so easily? She had to save Hefnir as the first step. She was almost too frightened to put her hand into her deep apron pocket. She found the crofter's salve, nearly all gone, and right at the bottom a few crumbling, black, dried-up leaves. Not enough.

How like the Serpent to lie, even at the last, and say it was a clean blow through the heart instead of the coward's way. He must always have planned to use wolfsbane.

Bera returned with the mashed salve, trying to sound bright. She daubed some onto the wound then tore long strips of cloth from her skirt to bind it. Hefnir did not stir throughout, and Heggi flinched for him. Then, somehow, they had to get him down to the boat. And so she and Heggi slashed and trampled a path down to the beach. For the first time in days, the air was clear and bright enough to see their way. They took the oars from the boat and lashed a small sail to them, making a rough sled to lay Hefnir on. They dragged it back, tugged and pushed Hefnir through the gap and rolled him onto it. Luckily, he was still in the deep swoon. Then they battled and barged the sled down to the beach. Hefnir was like a ghost by the time they came to a stop beside the *Raven*.

'He's dying, isn't he?' Heggi's voice was hard and tight. 'You're not to burn him.'

She remembered they had banked the fire to seal his wounds.

'I won't, Heggi. You're right, he's too poorly. We must get him aboard the *Raven*.'

'Why? Why keep moving him?'

Bera believed that Ottar's skill made the *Raven* lucky; that the vessel's seaworthiness would heal. Its iron nails would keep them from harm. Everything aboard was shipshape and orderly. It was a world she understood and, if he stayed alive long enough, so would Hefnir.

'We have to, Heggi. It's our only chance to save him – but if he dies, he would rather be on a boat, out on a sea path. As would I.'

33

'I said we have to lift him, Heggi.'

His eyes were wide. 'But it will kill him!'

How to explain? 'All right. I believe in the power of boat-song and Hefnir does too. It is his blood, as much as mine.'

Bera acknowledged for the first time their shared flesh in their baby, Valdis.

Heggi said nothing but went and stood by the boat.

She joined him. 'Do you feel *Raven*'s boat-song, Heggi? Put your hands on the hull, here. Look at Ottar's work. If you feel, you'll understand, and help me risk it.'

He nodded.

First, the horror of searing Hefnir's wound. It was best done quickly. Hefnir was already in a deep swoon, but Bera got Heggi to put a piece of wood in his father's mouth and then hold his shoulders down. She took a burning spar from the fire and held it to his cut side. They all screamed with the agony of it. The smell was stomach-turning and Heggi stumbled away, dry-retching and groaning.

Hefnir somehow stayed alive. His underlying strength must have been greater than she thought. Bera used the block and line to winch the rough sled aboard. Her guts wrenched, sharing Hefnir's pain precisely as they hauled him up. Then she and Heggi moved the rollers, one after the other, to take the boat into the shallows, pushing with their shoulders, tired to their bones. It was a long, slow job but the *Raven* was launched, with Hefnir aboard, looking deathly.

Bera thought it would be all right now, but then Heggi kicked the hull and stepped back ashore.

'I don't want all this,' he blurted. 'I can't… I miss Rakki so much. And you and he might…'

'I shall do everything I can to save your father.'

'I didn't mean that!'

Bera dare not leave the boat to drift but she reached towards Heggi.

'Leave me alone,' he shouted. 'You left me with the Serpent. Your enemy! You left me.'

This again, and again. Of course the anger was still inside and had to vent.

'Heggi, you're my own precious son.'

'No, I'm not. You're as bad as him! You just say it when you want something. Ever since you had that baby you've been different.'

'That baby is your sister.'

'She isn't! I hate her! She hates Rakki. She's not my sister! You love her and you don't love me.'

Her skern had told her to learn to love the male of the species a lifetime ago, and she did love Heggi – in a different, sweeter way, not the furious pain and longing that began with the birth. Valdis was her flesh and her bone, her sinews, guts and every indrawn breath of her, like her skern. It wasn't willed, it just was.

Valdis is no ordinary baby.

'As a Valla I hated her.'

And you fear her still.

Not simply because Valdis was the next link in the chain – Bera was going to die, anyway – but because Obsidian had revealed that the chain of Vallas could enjoy being vicious destroyers. Now her distinct feelings as a woman and a Valla were clear, but had nothing to do with her choice. If Egill's death had not stopped the eruption, Bera must die. But where was Obsidian?

'We need to talk honestly, Heggi, but this is not the time. You can see the ice cap up there, can't you? When it blows there will be no safe place, except possibly right out at sea. We have to be strong and all you need to know is that I love you.'

'I hate you.'

'I love you.'

'I don't care!'

'All right, listen. Sometimes in life you have to do your duty and put aside everything and everyone you love. You can't do what you want to do but what you have to do. It's what being a Valla means but in every life someone has a moment like this. You will. It took me an age to understand it but I was ready to die to save everyone; to save your life and all the animals and all the people who breathe. That seemed to me a better thing than sparing our feelings for a few hours or days before our world ended.'

'It hasn't ended,' he mumbled, sullen.

He kicked some pebbles and for a moment Rakki was there, chasing them. The loss was in that moment greater than all the creatures in the world.

Bera brushed it away. 'Egill may indeed have saved us. She told me she had been born for that moment and perhaps she was. Now we have to go on. I hope you can forgive me in time and until then I shall look after you as I always have done, even when it seems I've turned my back.'

Heggi gave her a look of ice-blue steel, his father's boy. 'It didn't seem anything.' He clambered aboard. 'You did turn your back and you know it.'

Bera pushed off with an oar. Heggi took up the other and they pulled out to sea in silent rhythm, like a corpse boat.

Bera left Hefnir undisturbed on his sled and covered him with his own bed roll, hoping familiar smells might soothe him. They lashed him amidships where there was the least boat movement. He was in the grey world between life and death. There was no more she could do for him until she had the right plants. Were they growing in the Abbotry, or Iraland? If the poison came from the medicine garden at the Abbotry there was just a chance that Faelan's farmstead was near enough for the remedy to work.

Heggi was rubbing his eyes with his fist and then with the ragged end of his tunic.

'You'll make them worse,' she said.

'They really hurt and I can't see very well.' He was less angry now he needed her.

'Once we're under way, you can keep them closed. There's fresh water aboard, so we'll bathe them now and that will stop them smarting so much.'

Bera bathed her eyes too, and they were less sore, but as they were making ready to leave there was a red line across her vision. Her skern had warned her about blindness right at the start. She had been blind in both eyes and mind at times. The red line suggested her sight was damaged for good but that was a worry for later. She stood at the helm, faced to windward and breathed clean air for the first time in days, it seemed. On board the *Raven*, nothing could destroy her joy.

She clapped her hands. 'Let's get cracking!'

It was exhilarating to be in charge of Ottar's boat, her lines sleek again; proper, as her father would have said. And to be completely in charge, with only Heggi as crew. The wind was fair, so they set the sail for the south and east. There was no point doing anything now except trusting to Fate. Bera felt the boat-song in her bones. In the blood. In the bones. In the heart.

When they got out into open water Heggi tugged her arm. He pointed behind them.

'Look!'

Beyond the headland the dark dragonboat of the Serpent King was cutting through the water towards them with warlike speed. The red line in her sight made it look faster.

'They must think we have the Serpent aboard!'

'Are they coming to get me?' asked Heggi.

'Why would they? It was your uncle that was bargaining. They probably think we have him, so will trade for his life and then get back to Iraland fast.' She hoped once they saw he was not aboard they would leave them alone.

'What if it is me they want, though?'

'No, Heggi. There's nothing here for them: no Serpent King. No Obsidian.'

Heggi moved away.

He is afraid and needing you to prove your love.

'But they will have me to deal with if they try to take you!' she added, too late.

He shrugged and went to sit near his father. Bera knew she would not win him over with one speech that sounded false. And, of course, they must have been lying in wait for the *Raven* for a reason. Her scalp was burned, so she had no idea if her instinct for danger was still there. Did they want the Serpent? The tattooed crewman either left him to die or didn't care and sailed without him. Surely they were only heading back to Iraland. She willed it. Both boats needed to head south but why didn't they leave more sea room? With a full crew to keep the sail trimmed and its war lines, there would be no outrunning a dragonboat.

Bera kept on the wind and concentrated on the feel of the *Raven*. The helm sang true, now the rehogging was gone, like the ring of crystal with a flick of a fingernail. Her clever father. This may have been his finest boat – and he would have known it – yet he offered to bodge something quickly to help her save their enemies.

The dragonboat was closing. She squinted her eyes and the red line in her sight showed the sea-riders were at a ramming angle. Bera followed the sun's path over the waves. There was something strange about it; instead of flickering at the surface, it seemed to glow up through the green water to meet the red line.

It's not the sun.

Nor was it a red line but a river of flame; a sea current that was the breath of a fire serpent.

'It looks like the burning that flowed down the mountain.'

That's exactly what it is. Lava.

Bera let out a throat-ripping roar of anguish. It confirmed all the stifled fears that she had tried to persuade herself were left on the shore behind her.

The chain of eruptions was only starting: the red line was one of the scorching links that went under the sea to set the world ablaze. The lead weight settled in her chest again. She had failed in every possible way. Poor Heggi. Empty words. She could not stop the sea-riders from taking him, nor save his father from dying. Suddenly that was a small thing.

'Hel wants me, doesn't she? But now I have no Obsidian to take with me.'

Her skern pointed. There was a blinding flash and Bera closed her eyes to let the redness pass. When she opened them she saw what had caused it.

Egill was at the stern of the dragonboat, angling the black glass to reflect the sun. She slowly turned to face Bera, laughing.

34

Ruin.

Egill's talk of sacrifice had come to nothing because of one man, who was on the deck of the *Raven*, dying. Egill had the black stone Hefnir craved and now she had come for him. They must have planned to escape with it together from the start. Bera could not look away from Obsidian. It sucked in light and threw it back at her with a gloaming malevolence. Even at this distance the looking-glass called to Bera, making her anger and jealousy worse, tempting her to take revenge on Hefnir for his treachery. Love? There was no love in the twilight world of Obsidian. It belonged to no one except Hel herself. Bera tugged herself away to look at her son.

'It's not going to ram us!' Heggi cried out with relief.

The dragonboat cut ahead and was moving away at speed. Nothing was worse for Heggi than being taken again in this moment.

Egill must have looked in the glass and now she could not withstand the urging to her dark nature. She had seen what she was and the knowledge had sent her mad. There would be no catching them and recovering the glass, or using it for good. Bera knew now that Obsidian wanted to be evil.

Nothing counted: the effort and pain, her baby, Heggi, Rakki, the wolves, everything gone. The earth yawned and rumbled beneath the hull. Hel had been cheated and the known world would suffer.

'I believed Egill when she said she wanted to die. To pay the blood debt to her father.'

Egill lies to herself, even before she took the glass. It doesn't mean it's not true when she says it.

'So what do I have to do now?'

I only know that there is worse to come.

'There always is.' And Bera was weary of it.

'What must I do now?'

What you always do.

Go forward.

All the teeming life of the ocean was gone. There were no seabirds in the darkening sky, no leaping backs of dolphins or play of seals. No life. Despite the breeze, the sea was strangely calm. Ahead, the dragonboat had slowed, leaving an odd, shadowy wake. Bera went to the side and looked at the flat water. The waves were not still, but like an oil-slicked sea they were too heavy to roll. The water was thick. Dirty. Going forward was like sifting through a midden. After a while there began to be long, tarry streaks in the water that gradually grew thick enough to slow the boat's speed. The dragonboat must have met the same state before them.

She called Heggi to the rail. Her voice echoed, as if they were in a room, not out at sea.

'It's like lumpy gruel, look,' she said. 'Perhaps it's a kind of mud.'

This was no sea path; the dirt was grainy and crackled beneath the hull.

'I feel sick,' Heggi said. 'It's Hel's breath again.'

He was right, and if the grinding unclenched some nails they would be just as lost as in a storm. Bera was in turmoil: the same deadlock between saving Heggi but sacrificing herself.

Heggi ran to his father. 'Papa, wake up! This is your boat, help us!'

'This is Ottar's boat,' said Bera, 'and he is dead.'

'Look, Bera!' Heggi pointed at a plume of white smoke beyond the dragonboat.

At first Bera thought it was a whale spout but then realised it was something much bigger, further out to sea.

'The Skraken!' Heggi shouted.

'It can't rise.' Or had she seen it in a vision?

The wind was urging them forward, filling the sail woven by her mother with words of power. But the sail told her it was coming from the wrong direction and she realised that they were being sucked into something, along with the other boat. Too late to turn back, even if they had the strength to row. Was Obsidian drawing them? She found her beads and held on to the amber.

Amber, that holds the black bead in check.

She prayed for the living but had no name for who she was asking for help. Doubt crept in. Egill's Fetch had appeared to Bera, so had it come to foretell Bera's death? That she could only be 'fetched' in a dream? The boat stalled. Dead in the water. Bera lurched, managed to grab the rail and looked down on the beach where she and Hefnir had their honeymoon. Prickles under her feet, the hope of love. But this was pale and porous sand, like ground brymstones.

That's exactly what it is.

Very slowly the *Raven* began to go forward, leaving a swathe of clear water through the floating layer in its wake. The air thickened with the stench. Bera looked towards the mast where Hefnir lay dead; she had been too occupied to see his skern join him. There would be time to mourn, but not now. She would not die here, at sea that was land, muddled; she had to protect Heggi. He would be alone in the world if she died. She needed to forge a proper bond with her daughter. Sigrid – and Dellingr – were right. How to do it all?

Vallas command Fate.

How often had she chanted that but never quite understood it? A Valla could also command other Vallas, to make their Fate. Bera was in her full power. She stood tall, grasping her necklace, spreading out her body and mind to fill the broadening sky.

'What are you doing?' Heggi asked in a small voice.

'Watch.'

Another spout and this time the plume was black, rising high and making a squid-ink cloud that snatched the watery sun and began to spread its blackness, frilled as an eel-mouth over all the whale roads. It was colossal, as urgent and rending as the moment of birthing. This was the vision Bera had had then but this time she was making herself as one with it. The past and future had become the present. ALU. She was an eagle, flying over the *Raven*; a figure in a seascape was become the land. When Valdis had arrived, Bera had let go. Now she used her inner core of strength to resist looking backwards in weakness and instead she willed herself to drive onward into the weave of Fate she was telling, aloud, in hope.

'Hel! You will not have me. If you want Obsidian, take it. I will never be used by it.'

The *Raven* crunched aground on shingle and stopped. They were beached, far out to sea. The sky was black and the sea molten gold, like waves painted on an obsidian bowl. Orange sparks flew past them, beautiful burning.

'Like firebirds!' cried Heggi with joy.

Like waters breaking. Another birth.

Then Heggi screamed.

A tidal wave was forming out at sea; a monstrous wall of water bulging up into the shadowed sky. The fate Bera chose had summoned the Skraken. Steam creamed off the edge of giant waves as the monster reared up from the deep like a gale. The dark mass fumed off three giant fins that poured clouds into the day, making it deepest night. The monster gave a terrible roar out of its abyss, splitting its belly wide, bones cracking apart.

Blood always calls to blood.

And black to black.

At the brink of catastrophe stood Egill.

Bera could read her friend's thoughts: Fear. Triumph. Despair. Hope. On, off, on, off, like a signalling beacon. Light, dark. All, nothing. Beneath them was a white-hot river of liquid earth. A new world. Egill was poised on the threshold between the old world and the new, always had been. Liminal. Alone amongst others, as ever, and Bera pitied her with all her heart – and was her reflection. Bera stood alone, straight as the prow, unbending in delivering the fate that Egill had brought on herself and had yearned for. Bera was pinned there by the pain of loss.

'Goodbye, my friend.'

The Skraken flexed and coiled, making a hole in the deep as it dived. The dragonboat went straight down, swallowed whole, without listing. Gone. Dropping, like a toy boat down a well. The whole ship, its crew, Egill and Obsidian taken into the heart of Hel.

'It's not finished. Tie yourself to the mast,' she told Heggi.

The *Raven* was steady while beyond them a maelstrom boiled and hissed. It was the making of new land. Bera felt that she was seeing the beginning of time; she could feel its heat on her face and smell its birthing.

'Hold on.'

A roiling wave fanned out, pushing the boat backwards through the thick water. Bera trusted her father's boat build; bow or stern first, the *Raven* would not sink. Sure enough, the longship soared through the breakers and then they were out into a clear sea path.

Now she could breathe. She untied Heggi and they looked behind them at the new island, waiting to be named. Bera knew what it would be. There was only one thing it could be.

New land brings new hope, like the birth of a child.

One day it would be studded with brave cliff-edge sheep and home to thousands of seabirds. She sensed them returning to their roosts and whales singing about homecoming on the long roads north.

Relief washed over her, an ordinary woman again. Their settlements were saved. Their old home on the Ice-Rimmed Sea. Iraland, the Marsh Lands saved too. Those other lands that Hefnir had seen, that she had not. Perhaps there were even more somewhere on the jewelled globe that no one yet knew. All of them, safe. Huge processes beneath the earth continued; plates under the earth's crust shifted but did not collide. Three of them. Deep below that, the Skraken threshed, but this time he would not devour the known world.

35

'Where is the stone?' Hefnir's thin voice.

Alive.

And his first thought was Obsidian. Bera felt anger and regret like the ringing of iron on iron, a true but tinny noise after what had gone before.

He picked feebly at the ropes that held him safe. 'Let me touch it!'

'I wouldn't, even if I could, Hefnir. Egill has Obsidian, as you planned all along. Except you're here with me – and she is with Hel.'

'No, I…' He looked at her with eyes rimmed with filth.

Bera bathed them and wet his lips and then wolfsbane took him back into the grey world.

There was something she had to do, to keep Hefnir alive, that she did not want… The knowledge refused to return but now she was certain this was what Egill's Fetch had told her. Having a Fetch at all meant Egill had revoked her skern to choose what they believed in Iraland. Bera felt her own skern's leaving and shuddered. Was that why Egill could hear Bera's skern? Had she tried to steal him, as well Obsidian? Bera would never know. Egill had talked of Brid. If keeping Hefnir alive had anything to do with Brid he was lost.

Heggi curled up next to his father like a dog and Bera told him to keep wetting his lips. Your dog will lie beside you in a storm, Faelan had said. She had coaxed, battled and woven Fate long and hard, and now she was tired. Let it unravel the future. She left thoughts of Rakki and Faelan along with her husband and son. She would use her natural weather knowledge and the boat skills given to her by her father to get them safely home.

At some point she sang:

> *The raven made twelve pairs of rope from the twists and*
> *   turns of its bowel;*
> *its claws were long and thin and sharp and made six pairs*
> *   of trowel;*
> *the beak was a black and shiny ship that cut the Ice-Rimmed*
> *   Sea;*
> *the feathers oars that tipped the waves as they flew across*
> *   at speed...*

The wind slapped her awake and she got back on course. The
raven song. That was it, her mother's lullaby that she had tried to
remember, right at the start with her baby. A savage sort of lullaby
her daughter would like, if she had anyone to sing it to her.

The grey smudge of land.

Bera should be glad, yet she kept the helm on a steady course
south, when she should be heading eastwards for home.

Off a distant headland stood the Stoat. He was her sentinel, not
a rune stone like her mother had placed to mark home. So why did
she not steer for it?

You know what Egill's Fetch said in that dream on the beach.

'She called me Brid and said only I could get Hefnir home.'

And will you?

'I don't know where his home is. Or mine.'

Only the sea path. Perhaps she could sail on and on and never
make landfall. This boat was her home. Out here, life was simple. All
you had was one decision, made by the weather. On land were people
with separate demands. Expectation and uncertainty. Conflict. Even
amongst her own folk, the settlers, there was division. Or worse.
Who would have died? She flinched from the thought of charred
bodies. And what if they were now Drorghers? The pain of loss; the
guilt.

Her baby.

The power of three.

'Meaning?'

It's a strong number.

'I know. But I'm still not Brid.'

You know now that you can be who you like. What you like.

Bera longed to be a child again, before she knew what being a Valla meant.

She thought of Sigrid, proudly nursing two babies; of Dellingr taking charge. Did they need her? Was Faelan still alive? If he was, he would be more scarred than Thorvald. Perhaps he never got out of Smolderby.

What if everyone she loved was dead? She dreaded knowledge.

Out here everything was possible: Rakki could be scampering along the sand, young and fit, chasing birds. She wanted him to be full of joy like that forever and ever and never die.

Heggi left his father and made his way to her.

'Where are we going?' he asked.

'Home.' Although, as yet, she had no idea where that would be.

'We could be home for Brightening,' he said, his little face washed with hope.

ACKNOWLEDGEMENTS

I salute Dan Kieran and Liz Garner for keeping the faith. Liz makes editing creative fun and releases the story from the tangle of Good Ideas. Iceland Writers Retreat helped turn a vague Norse setting of Ice Island into the precise magic of Iceland whilst enhancing my writing in workshops with international authors. Alistair Moffat told me about naming ancestors as ghost soldiers at warriors' backs. Reading his wonderful book *The Sea Kingdoms: The History of Celtic Britain and Ireland* reversed land and sea to explain where power lay. SCBWI has my back.

I return often to saved images on Instagram, especially sagatrail_iceland, ravenmaster1, rannvajoensen and urwarsdalkarl, but anything like #iceland #faroes #vikinglife #norsemythology #historyvikings are inspirational.

Above all, I thank my friends and family. I didn't mean you to have to do the heavy lifting again, but if Sisyphus had you holding the stone at the top, his torment would be over.

A NOTE ON THE AUTHOR

Suzie Wilde is the author of *The Book of Bera: Sea Paths*. She grew up in Portsmouth, studied English at UCL, has an MA with distinction in creative writing and taught for over ten years. Whilst living aboard a sailboat she began writing full-time. She is married for the second time, with a supporting cast of Labradors.

Website: suziewilde.co.uk
Twitter: @susiewilde
Facebook: @suziewildeauthor

Unbound is the world's first crowdfunding publisher, established in 2011.

We believe that wonderful things can happen when you clear a path for people who share a passion. That's why we've built a platform that brings together readers and authors to crowdfund books they believe in – and give fresh ideas that don't fit the traditional mould the chance they deserve.

This book is in your hands because readers made it possible. Everyone who pledged their support is listed below. Join them by visiting unbound.com and supporting a book today.

Pamela Abbott
Eric Ahnell
Sandra Armor
James Aylett
Sarah Bailey
Brigitte Baker
Lisa Baldwinson
Jason Ballinger
Katrina Barg
Mike Barnett
Fran Benson
Jonas Bergstedt
Tessa Beukelaar-van Gulik
Heather Birchenough
Tim Bouquet & Sarah Mansell
Karen Boxall
Rory Bremner
Andy Brereton
Struan Britland
Richard Brooman
Harriet Cherriman
Camilla Chester

Corrinne Cload
Catherine Coe
Charlotte Comley
Dom Conlon
Kate Cook
Alan Copsey
Robert Cox
Nancy Crosby
Lesley Dampney
Margaret Dascalopoulos
Gill Davies
Linda Davies
María De Lucas
Charles Dedman
Miranda Dickinson
John Doff
Mia Dormer
Kevin Doyle
Robert Eardley
Vicky Edwards
Abla El-Sharnouby
Shannon Elliot

David Fennell
Sue Fosbrook
Terry Fosbrook
Linda and Andrew Gebhart
Lynn Genevieve
Josephine Gibson
Julie Gilmour
Geoffrey Gudgion
Patti M Hall
Robert Hamlin
Julie Hart
Maximilian Hawker
Andrew Hawkins
Emma Hawksworth
Peter Hawksworth
Thea Hawksworth
Grace Hawksworth-Pratten
Hope Hawksworth-Pratten
Anwen Hayward
Anita Heward
Antoinette Hickey
Jeremy Hill
Shirleyann Hillier
Kim A Howard
Pamela Howard
Lizzie Hutchinson
Mike James
Samantha Jennings
Tiffin Jones
Larus Jonsson
Dave Joyce
Val Kemp
Katie Kennedy
Liz Kent
Dan Kieran
Jonathan Kim
Patrick Kincaid
Lizzie Ladbrooke
Ewan Lawrie

W Tom Lawrie
Jon Lawson
Jean Levy
Kim Locke
K. M. Lockwood
Anita Loughrey
Bridget Lubbock
Adrian Lynch
Sarah Mansell
Ferran J Marí Rivero
Jessica Martin
Joy May
Nigel May
Phil May
Tim May
Tom May
Elizabeth McCann
Susan Henderson Miles
Fiona Miller
John Mitchinson
Virginia Moffatt
Alison Morgan
Cass Morgan
Iain Morrison
Robert Mudie
Tim Mudie
Maria Mutch
Carlo Navato
John New
Captain Sean Noonan
Ken Norman
Rodney O'Connor
Mo Oakeley
Lucy Oliver
Michael Oliver
Isaac Parker
Louise Parker
Emily Perry
Marc Perry

Melanie Perry
Chris Pollard
Justin Pollard
Samantha Potter
Jenny Prager
Sara Read
Janet Ritchie
Peter Rossiter
Richard Sanderson
Arthur Schiller
Jenny Schwarz
Alethea Scott
Kate Scott
Bri Seares
Linda Sgoluppi
Ste Sharp
Sue Shattock
Victoria Kate Simkin
Sarah Simpson
Mary Smith
Susan Smith
Heather Sorrell
Glynis Spencer
Valerie Spencer
Ian Springall
Jason Stevens
Bob Stone
John Surace

Ingrid Sutherland
Jillian Tees
Lizanne Thackery
Nick Tigg
Adam Tinworth
Sarah Towle
Robin Townsend
Denise Turner
Rosie Turner
Mark Vent
David Wakefield
John Wakefield
Katherine Wakefield
Kitty Wakefield
Niamh Wakefield
Sue Wallman
Tanya Walters
Philip Ware
Laura Westmore
Maud Wilde
Suzanne Wilkins
Sarah Willett
Derek Wilson
Jacquie & John Wilson
Meryl Wingfield
Clare Wong
Matthew Wood